A Novel, A Novella and Four Stories

Andrew Lytle

A NOVEL, A NOVELLA

AND FOUR STORIES

mc dowell, obolensky

Library of Congress Catalog Card Number: 58-12577

All Rights Reserved under Pan-American and International Copyright Conventions. Published in New York by Mc-Dowell, Obolensky Inc. and in the Dominion of Canada by George J. McLeod Limited, Toronto.

First Printing

Acknowledgment is here made to the following publications, in which some of the material in this volume first appeared: *The Kenyon Review*, "Alchemy"; *The Sewanee Review*, "The Mahogany Frame" (then entitled "The Guide"); *The Southern Review*, "Jericho, Jericho, Jericho"; *The Virginia Quarterly Review*, "Mr. MacGregor."

Manufactured in the United States of America by The Haddon Craftsmen, Scranton, Pennsylvania.

Designed by Alfred Manso.

To Allen & Caroline Tate

CONTENTS

FOREWORD

Whenever a writer talks about a story or a novel he has done, he is not speaking in his true voice. That voice has already been heard in the rendition of the action, and once done the covers of the book enclose it. It is no longer the malleable thing he worked with; it is set to its form, beyond further help or damage from him. If he persists in talking about it, instead of leaving it alone to make its effect, it is generally by way of a paraphrase or an apology. It's why we tend to skip the passages on the historians and the man of destiny in *War and Peace.* Tolstoy is not then speaking as the artist he is; he is using the voice of a Russian theorizing about a segment of Russian history. This is all the more restricted in its appeal, because Tolstoy has already put the man of destiny in the book acting out concretely his theory, and thus negating it as theory, since he has brought Napoleon alive. No abstraction can stand before Prince Andrew lying under the blue sky, thinking he is dying, and looking up to see in the flesh his former idol. What he sees in this moment of truth annihilates the argumentative assertions of the essays.

It should be obvious that polemics is one discipline and fiction another. If you are going to preach, get into the pulpit; if you want to bring about political reforms, run for office; social reforms, behave yourself and mind your manners. The professions appear in a novel for technical purposes. A preacher may be needed to save a fictive, not an actual, soul, just as a bore may be put there to bore some other character; but the skilled writer will not bore you with a man of total recall any more than his preacher will save you your soul. Sometimes, though, the sense of damnation in a book may be grounds for spiritual review, as Dickens's *Bleak House* is said to have set about the reforms in the Courts of Chancery. Such is residual, however, not the essential intention of the writer towards his reader. When a novel obviously makes an appeal other than its proper aesthetic one, you may be sure it has been written with the left hand.

This intention of the writer towards his hypothetical reader involves many delicate and insoluble matters. Ideally the artist creates his reader as well as the book, establishing in his mind that perfect communion of sympathy and understanding which, unfortunately, remains ideal. There are no limits to hope, but there are limits to the artifice; and these are his main concern. Granted that an art is of greater truth than the accidental nature of human affairs which is its source, the artist should never forget how precarious are the

grounds of attention he must ask for. The most trivial inter-
ference from the actual affairs of life is always a threat. A
child falling down the stairs and screaming bloody murder
will bring a mother from the very death of Hamlet. This
very frailty puts an obligation upon the serious reader; he
should bring to a book no preconception which will prevent
him from following in all its levels the action. I am taking for
granted that the story has found its formal expression. After
distinguishing between the simple art of narrative and the
comprehensive art of fiction, Lubbock says the critical reader
becomes an artist, too. He must recreate what has been done,
a greater reward always than some sensational impression of
it. The pleasure of illusion is small beside the pleasure of
creation, and knowledge better than simple entertainment.

The lack of a critical nomenclature commonly accepted
and practiced certainly does not help reading. We hear too
often the term "prose fiction," which seems to make of it a
branch of rational discourse and not its true self, an art in
its own right, with its own laws and conventions by means
of which it enters the large field of the creative imagination
common to all the arts. In academic circles, but not always
and not only there, this lack of the proper critical tools fosters
the habit of reducing a book or story to its theme or idea,
which is to say to an abstraction. This does violence to its
singular aesthetic appeal, that illusion of an action imitating
men and women caught in some one of the human predica-
ments forever repeating themselves. The meaning in fiction
should always be received actively, in the structural rela-
tionships between the parts. Reception is crucial; the reader
must be moved affectively, so that his insight will comprise
the fullest meaning which lies before him.

There is another approach which misses the mark. It is

older than fiction, the game of discovering sources and influences, which is all very well up to a point. Too much is made of these influences, however, when they pretend to disclose the secrets of the creative act. There are only two ways to learn anything, by actual experience and imitation. If you are a writer, you partly learn by reading other writers. But the moment comes when, to quote indirectly T. S. Eliot, you steal instead of borrow; that is, you make it your own. At this moment you pass from apprenticeship to the beginning of mastery. Henry James, as we know, never listened to the end of a story. He wanted from it only what would set his own skill to working. Besides, to hear it all would have brought him up against a false sense of the history of it, false because all the facts would seem to be but could not actually be present in the report at second hand. He could not know another's mind, but he could take the risk of his own imagination. It is just this about sources and influences; the scholar can know them only in their raw condition, not how the imagination used them.

One of the influences on "Jericho, Jericho, Jericho" was *The Time of Man* by Elizabeth Maddox Roberts. I finished her book and, in the fullness of the catharsis it had given me, sat right down and in less than two minutes wrote the first page. I remember very clearly the feeling that her rhythm had set my own to going. After writing this one page, I set it aside for four years, because I was not sure whether I was beginning a novel or a story. I might have set it aside forever, if the editors of the *Southern Review* had not asked me for a story. Or in the fullness of time I might have gone back and turned it into a novel. All kinds of accidents play their part, but in the end the writer has only one subject, and he spends his life discovering how to unfold it. And when it lies all before him, he is done for.

To put such store by influences, then, is to make a basic mistake about the nature of an art; it is to reduce it to a rational act. This attitude also falsifies the thing made by confusing what is unique to it, the artist's own way of seeing and doing, with the common grounds of experience any artist of necessity must draw upon. This common ground is the repetitive involvement with himself and his fellows which is man's affliction and his delight, the archetypal experience which forever recurs within the human scene. For example, the loss of innocence or the initiation of youth into manhood is an archetypal experience. The young Spartan who did not falter, as the fox was chewing his bowels, discloses his way of undergoing what every youth suffers at a certain time of life. But the young men of differing societies will respond in various ways. Unlike Sparta we do not formally instruct our young men. What there is of it is private and accidental. This lack of ritual limited, at the very start, the archetypal conflict in "The Mahogany Frame."* The boy's initiation happens "by accident," through the ritual of hunting, itself debased; and the change in him which comes at the end in a shock of illumination is the measure of how he achieves maturity without formal guidance. The way it came out was not the way I saw it when I began it. I began with the wrong enveloping action and had to lay it aside, again curiously enough for four years. When a neighbor, Sinclair Buntin, invited me to go on a duck hunt, I accepted and returned not only with duck but how to do the story. Anything, a mood, an incident, a character, an idea, can set you going; but the end must be, not any story but the one story which will deliver the meaning. The process is the advancing discovery, always controlled,

---

* The story was originally called "The Guide." Mr. Allen Tate suggested "The Mahogany Frame," which now seems to me much better.

of the hidden meaning. Michelangelo spoke of releasing the image in the stone. Material, any material, produces a kinetic change in the psyche of the artist. The subject matter is never inert, a thing merely to be observed and used. An interaction takes place between the writer and what moves him to write. Any kind of reading which ignores this is committing a kind of aesthetic crime, by taking away from the author what is rightly his.

Fiction is an action then, and an action which tells the only story which makes of the form and subject a single whole. This is the first limitation which the writer as artist confronts. So conscious was Flaubert of this wholeness that when he was asked to take away a line in *A Simple Heart* he protested that to do so would cause the structure to fall apart. The action must have a beginning, a middle, and an end; and the end is in the beginning, as the plant is organically found in the seed. An art is a craft confronting the mystery of the imagination and an even more private impulse; so the artist warily but persistently tries to discover the proper environment for its singular growth. It becomes apparent then that there is not one action, but two: the action proper, which is the conflict, and the enveloping action, sometimes miscalled background (a borrowing from painting); miscalled because background implies a static condition. Since fiction is an action, nothing should be left inert. The two actions take place simultaneously in fiction as they do in life, just as a man must be made convincing as man before he can become an individual man. Let us say that it is his masculinity which more nearly represents the enveloping action, and his unique response to a conflict the action proper. However, this is not quite adequate. The enveloping action is that universal quality, some constant, forever true aspect of experience; the action proper its concrete showing; or the action proper may be the very obverse and so show it by contradiction or contrast.

The action has two main parts: the pictorial or panoramic summary and the scene. That's all it is, reduced to its basic structural components and controlled by a point of view. Of course, such does not describe the conscious or intuitive arrangement of these two kinds of effects, or the special attention to the use of the five senses to evoke the illusion of flesh. No matter how well you write in fiction, or what profound meaning you feel suffuses the action, unless you can imitate men and women caught in some one of the tensions we all know, you fail. And it is by means of the senses, more than anything else, that the word in fiction delivers the immediate sense of life. It is by and through them that we receive the world, know we are alive; they are the avenues, the nervous cords, which unite the physical and spiritual parts of being. They are the invisible, in a way, servile aids upon which the more crucial matters depend, and without which the archetypes would hover in the distance of ideal concepts. At this point the artist discovers a restraint as conventional as blank verse. And this is location. People do not live in a vacuum. They live somewhere. Mention of this has already been made, but too much emphasis cannot be given to the varying artificial distinctions of a culture's polity through which the archetype repeats itself. The natural man is an abstraction. He has never been seen, but what is natural to men always shows itself shaped by the manners and mores, the institutional restraints, of a given time and place. Underneath, as the impulse to action, is the degree of strength or weakness of religious vision; for without belief there would be no coherent incentive to any kind of performance, good or bad. To say this would once have been a platitude; it is no longer.

We used to have hopes, and there are occasional echoes now, of somebody writing the great American novel, as if it could be some agglomerate concretion of the American spirit. This is a naive expectation, which will become clear when it is asked, Did Tolstoy or Dostoevsky write the great Russian novel? Or even here at home, which is the great American novel, *Moby Dick* or *The Ambassadors*. They are both great and both American certainly, and yet how they differ in style and meaning, as they differ in location: New England confronted by Paris, New England confronted by the sea. From the beginning the cultural, certainly the political, stresses have in this country been local and sectional. Whatever novels we have, good or bad, will show this, no matter how disguised the sectional attitude. The very assumption that there can be a melting pot is an unrealistic belief, all the more for the pretense that it is universally American. This is not to say that the great divisions of this country do not have in common something aside from their local awareness of themselves; or even that the sectional differences can be so marked as in older cultures, let us say Normandy and Provence. But the diversity of difference goes beyond political attitudes; it is even found within the sections themselves; and certainly as the sections are changed by historic accident: New England before the War of 1812 and New England now. What there is in common we might call the diminished vision of the Christian inheritance. Liberty and freedom as we understand the words, and that understanding is growing vaguer and more confused, are secular interpretations of a more complete Christian polity now lost to us. The westward movement of Europeans, beginning with

Columbus, not only shattered the narrow physical boundaries of Christendom but, like all extension, weakened it by reducing a union composite of spiritual and temporal parts to the predominance of material ends. With us it is called pioneering, and every part of the country was involved in it; but even in this common inheritance we find distinct local differences. The New England theocratic shift of the Mormons was unlike the Southern cattleman's gradual advance from a semi-pastoral stage to an agrarian society. And there were those individuals, the hunters, who went alone or in small parties, following an even more ancient impulse. The general is always defined by the particular; so, even what we share together cannot escape expression in terms of local history and culture.

Of the South, and the South is a more complex term than is generally recognized, too much is made of ethnic complications as its distinguishing feature, although of course this can in no way be ignored. But it is the family which best describes the nature of this society. And by family I mean the total sense of it, the large "connections of kin" amplifying the individual unit. There are the geographic limits which allowed the family in this larger meaning (it was the community) to spread itself in a mild climate and over alluvial soils to give to the institution its predominance as not just one but *the* institution of Southern life. In New England, at least the coastal areas, there was always the sea to intervene, holding up a distant image and not the familiar, seasonal one such as land allows. Of course there was a seaboard in the South and farms in New England, but the county and township represented the difference. Both the sea and land are feminine images, but the sea takes only men; and so the communion between husband and wife was

interrupted and for long periods of time. Relate this sea-
faring to the theocratic oligarchies, and we discover the
cultural forms acting upon man's relation to woman, which
at one time made witches. What is a woman deprived but a
witch, especially under the discipline of a Puritan distortion
of the senses.

Man's attitude to woman is the foundation of society,
under God. In the South, because of the prevailing sense
of the family, the matriarch becomes the defining image.
The earlier insistence on purity, an ideal not always a fact,
was not chivalric romanticism but a matter of family integrity, with the very practical aim of keeping the blood
lines sure and the inheritance meaningful. Before machinery
was made which lessened the need for the whole family to
do its part on the farm, husband, wife, children, cousins,
dependents, servants all served the land and were kept by it,
according to their various demands and capacities. The parts
of the family made a whole by their diversity. Before the
automobile destroyed the country communities (the Civil
War did not) people lived fairly close together without
losing their privacy or their family distinctions. The radius
of visiting and trading and marrying was generally not more
than seven miles, but seven miles at a walk or even in a buggy
takes time. You just didn't drop in for a chat. You spent the
day at least. And the railroads did not disrupt these communities; they merely connected them. Conversation reached
a high art, and it generally talked about what most interested
itself, and this was the endless complications within the family
and what gossip or rumor hinted at in the neighbors. Every
human possibility was involved, including politics, but the
blood lines were the measure of behavior. There was never
any doubt about the argument between environment and

heredity. Environment was what heredity inherited. At a family gathering, when people were not working but celebrating, there would always be one voice more capable than another of dominating the conversation. It was a kind of bardic voice. This opened my eyes to a technical device about the point of view, what might be called the Hovering Bard. Everybody in a country community knows something about a happening; but nobody knows it all. The bard, by hovering above the action, to see it all, collects the segments. In the end, in the way he fits the parts together, the one story will finally get told.

This is not to say that the subject of Southern fiction is limited to what goes on within the family circle, or even that the family is always the enveloping action. But this larger sense of it must always be taken into account. It is the structure through which the cultural image, with its temporal and spiritual rituals, complicates the human drama, receives and modifies by its conventions the archetypal happenings which forever recur between birth and death. There are societies where the family as institution is subordinated to some abstract idea of the state. At one time such was Sparta, as now it is with Russia or the welfare state anywhere. But in the great days of Greek drama what would the dramatists have done without the House of Atreus? Or would we have had the fall of Troy, if Paris had merely run away with one of Citizen Menelaus's women? Or the classical idea of Fate, which both men and gods had to reckon with, how that would have been diminished if a tyranny, based on abstract economics, had held the total meaning of life? There would have been no Sophocles or Aeschylus; there might have been some kind of Euripides. There certainly would have been no Homer.

To repeat a platitude, we are caught between two conflicting world views which operate within and without our society, but most acutely in the South, because the South has been the losing cause. The prevailing Faustian view, to borrow from Spengler, has until recently seemed invincible. Relying entirely on the material ends as the only proper reward for action (the delusion that man can know the final secrets of matter), it defines itself as laissez faire in economics (the shift from the individual to the state does not alter this), faction in politics, social welfare in religion, relativism in history, pragmatism in philosophy. The older belief in The City of God as the end of the drama has persisted, if defensively, in the South. But it is the fractured view of this Christian drama, the loss of its inner meaning, which has confused Southern institutions and required of the family more meaning than it can sustain. Yet this very situation focuses the artist's approach to his material. If he tries to free himself from it, he can only do so by betrayal, which is not infrequent.

A.L.

The University of Florida

August 15, 1958

A STORY:

jericho, jericho, jericho

SHE OPENED HER EYES. SHE MUST HAVE BEEN ASLEEP FOR hours or months. She could not reckon; she could only feel the steady silence of time. She had been Joshua and made it swing suspended in her room. Forever she had floated above the counterpane; between the tester and the counterpane she had floated until her hand, long and bony, its speckled dried skin drawing away from the bulging blue veins, had reached and drawn her body under the covers. And now she was resting, clear-headed and quiet, her thoughts clicking like a new-greased mower. All creation could not make her lift her thumb or cross it over her finger. She looked at the bed, the bed her mother had died in, the bed her children had been born in, her marriage bed, the bed the General had drenched with his blood. Here it stood where it had stood for seventy years, square and firm on the floor, wide enough for three people to lie comfortable in, if they didn't sleep restless; but not wide enough for her nor long enough when her conscience scorched the cool wrinkles in the sheets. The two footposts, octagonal-shaped and mounted by carved pieces that looked like absurd flowers, stood up to comfort her when the world began to crumble. Her eyes followed down the posts and along the basket-quilt. She had made it before her marriage to the General, only he wasn't a general then. He was a slight, tall young man with a rolling mustache and perfume in his hair. A many a time she had seen her young love's locks dripping with scented oil, down upon his collar . . . She had cut the squares for the baskets in January, and for stuffing had used the letters of old lovers, fragments of passion cut to warm her of a winter's night. The General would have his fun. *Miss Kate, I didn't sleep well last night. I heard Sam Buchanan make love to you out of that farthest basket. If I hear him again, I mean to toss this piece of quilt in the fire.* Then he would chuckle in his round, soft voice; reach under the covers and pull her over to his side of the bed. On a cold and frosting night he would sleep with his nose against her neck. His nose was so quick to turn cold, he said, and her neck was so warm. Sometimes her hair, the loose unruly strands at the nape, would tickle his nostrils and he would wake up with a sneeze. This had been so long ago, and there had been so many years of trouble and worry. Her eyes, as apart from her as the mirror on the bureau, rested upon the half-tester, upon the enormous button that caught the rose-colored canopy and shot its folds out like the rays of the morning sun. She could not see but she could feel the heavy cluster of mahogany grapes that tumbled from the center of the headboard—out of its vines curling down the sides it tumbled. How much longer would these never-picked grapes hang above her head? How much longer would she, rather, hang to the vine of this world, she who lay beneath as dry as any raisin. Then she remembered. She looked at the blinds. They were closed.

"You, Ants, where's my stick? I'm a great mind to break it over your trifling back."

"Awake? What a nice long nap you've had," said Doctor Ed.

"The boy? Where's my grandson? Has he come?"

"I'll say he's come. What do you mean taking to your bed like this? Do you realize, beautiful lady, that this is the first time I ever saw you in bed in my whole life? I believe you've taken to bed on purpose. I don't believe you want to see me."

"Go long, boy, with your foolishness."

That's all she could say, and she blushed as she said it—she blushing at the words of a snip of a boy, whom she had diapered a hundred times and had washed as he stood before the fire in the round tin tub, his little back swayed and his little belly sticking out in front, rosy from the scrubbing he had gotten. *Mammy, what for I've got a hole in my stummick; what for, Mammy?* Now he was sitting on the edge of the bed calling her beautiful lady, an old hag like her, beautiful lady. A good-looker the girls would call him, with his bold, careless face and his hands with their fine, long fingers. Soft, how soft they were, running over her rough, skinny bones. He looked a little like his grandpa, but somehow there was something missing . . .

"Well, boy, it took you a time to come home to see me die."

"Nonsense. Cousin Edwin, I wouldn't wait on a woman who had so little faith in my healing powers."

"There an't nothing strange about dying. But I an't in such an all-fired hurry. I've got a heap to tell you about before I go."

The boy leaned over and touched her gently. "Not even death would dispute you here, on Long Gourd, Mammy."

He was trying to put her at her ease in his carefree way. It was so obvious a pretending, but she loved him for it. There was something nice in its awkwardness, the charm of the young's blundering and of their efforts to get along in the world. Their pretty arrogance, their patronizing airs, their colossal unknowing of what was to come. It was a quenching drink to a sin-thirsty old woman. Somehow his vitality had got crossed in her blood and made a dry heart leap, her blood that was almost water. Soon now she would be all water, water and dust, lying in the burying ground between the cedar—and fire. She could smell her soul burning and see it. What a fire it would make below, dripping with sin, like a rag soaked in kerosene. But she had known what she was doing. And here was Long Gourd, all its fields intact, ready to be handed on, in better shape than when she took it over. Yes, she had known what she was doing. How long, she wondered, would his spirit hold up under the trials of planting, of cultivating, and of the gathering time, year in and year out—how would he hold up before so many springs and so many autumns. The thought of him giving orders, riding over the place, or rocking on the piazza, and a great pain would pin her heart to her backbone. She wanted him by her to train—there was so much for him to know: how the creek field was cold and must be planted late, and where the orchards would best hold their fruit, and where the frosts crept soonest—that now could never be. She turned her head—who was that woman, that strange woman standing by the bed as if she owned it, as if . . .

"This is Eva, Mammy."

"Eva?"

"We are going to be married."

"I wanted to come and see—to meet Dick's grandmother . . ."

I wanted to come see her die. That's what she meant. Why didn't she finish and say it out. She had come to lick her chops and see what she would enjoy. That's what she had come for, the lying little slut. The richest acres in Long Gourd valley, so rich hit'd make yer feet greasy to walk over'm, Saul Oberly at the first tollgate had told the peddler once, and the peddler had told it to her, knowing it would please and make her trade. *Before you die.* Well, why didn't you finish it out? You might as well. You've given yourself away.

Her fierce thoughts dried up the water in her eyes, tired and resting far back in their sockets. They burned like a smothered fire stirred up by the wind as they traveled over the woman who would lie in her bed, eat with her silver, and caress her flesh and blood. The woman's body was soft enough to melt and pour about him. She could see that; and her firm, round breasts, too firm and round for any good to come from them. And her lips, full and red, her eyes bright and cunning. The heavy hair crawled about her head to tangle the poor, foolish boy in its ropes. She might have known he would do something foolish like this. He had a foolish mother. There warn't any way to avoid it. But look at her belly, small and no-count. There wasn't a muscle the size of a worm as she could see. And those hips—

And then she heard her voice: "What did you say her name was, son? Eva? Eva Callahan, I'm glad to meet you, Eva. Where'd your folks come from, Eva? I knew some Callahans who lived in the Goosepad settlement. They couldn't be any of your kin, could they?"

"Oh, no, indeed. My people . . ."

"Right clever people they were. And good farmers, too. Worked hard. Honest—that is, most of 'em. As honest as that run of people go. We always gave them a good name."

"My father and mother live in Birmingham. Have always lived there."

"Birmingham," she heard herself say with contempt. They could have lived there all their lives and still come from somewhere. I've got a mule older'n Birmingham. "What's your pa's name?"

"Her father is Mister E. L. Callahan, Mammy."

"First name not Elijah by any chance? Lige they called him."

"No. Elmore, Mammy."

"Old Mason Callahan had a son they called Lige. Somebody told me he moved to Elyton. So you think you're going to live with the boy here."

"We're to be married . . . that is, if Eva doesn't change her mind."

And she saw his arm slip possessively about the woman's waist. "Well, take care of him, young woman, or I'll come back and ha'nt you. I'll come back and claw your eyes out."

"I'll take very good care of him, Mrs. McCowan."

"I can see that." She could hear the threat in her voice, and Eva heard it.

"Young man," spoke up Doctor Edwin, "you should feel powerful set up, two such women pestering each other about you."

The boy kept an embarrassed silence.

"All of you get out now. I want to talk to him by himself. I've got a lot to say and precious little time to say it in. And he's mighty young and helpless and ignorant."

"Why, Mammy, you forget I'm a man now. Twenty-six. All teeth cut. Long trousers."

"It takes a heap more than pants to make a man. Throw open them blinds, Ants."

"Yes'm."

"You don't have to close the door so all-fired soft. Close it naturally. And you can tip about all you want to—later. I won't be hurried to the burying ground. And keep your head away from that door. What I've got to say to your new master is private."

"Listen at you, mistiss."

"You listen to me. That's all. No, wait. I had something else on my mind—what is it? Yes. How many hens has Melissy set? You don't know. Find out. A few of the old hens ought to be setting. Tell her to be careful to turn the turkey eggs every day. No, you bring them and set them under my bed. I'll make sure. We got a mighty pore hatch last year. You may go now. I'm plumb worn out, boy, worn out thinking for these people. It's that that worries a body down. But you'll know all about it in good time. Stand out there and let me look at you good. You don't let me see enough of you, and I almost forget how you look. Not really, you understand. Just a little. It's your own fault. I've got so much to trouble me that you, when you're not here, naturally slip back in my mind. But that's all over now. You are here to stay, and I'm here to go. There will always be Long Gourd, and there must always be a McCowan on it. I had hoped to have you by me for several years, but you would have your fling in town. I thought it best to clear your blood of it, but as God is hard, I can't see what you find to do in town. And now you've gone and gotten you a woman. Well, they all have to do it. But do you reckon you've picked the right one—you must forgive the frankness of an old lady who can see the bottom of her grave—I had in mind one of the Carlisle girls. The Carlisle place lies so handy to Long Gourd and would give me a landing on the river. Have you seen Anna Belle since she's grown to be a woman? I'm told there's not a better housekeeper in the valley."

"I'm sure Anna Belle is a fine girl. But Mammy, I love Eva."

"She'll wrinkle up on you, Son; and the only wrinkles land gets can be smoothed out by the harrow. And she looks sort of puny to me, Son. She's powerful small in the waist and walks about like she had worms."

"Gee, Mammy, you're not jealous are you? That waist is in style."

"You want to look for the right kind of style in a woman. Old Mrs. Penter Matchem had two daughters with just such waists, but 'twarnt natural. She would tie their corset strings to the bed posts and whip'm out with a buggy whip. The poor girls never drew a hearty breath. Just to please that old woman's vanity. She got paid in kind. It did something to Eliza's bowels and she died before she was twenty. The other one never had any children. She used to whip'm out until they cried. I never liked that woman. She thought a whip could do anything."

"Well, anyway, Eva's small waist wasn't made by any corset strings. She doesn't wear any."

"How do you know, sir?"

"Well . . . I . . . What a question for a respectable woman to ask."

"I'm not a respectable woman. No woman can be respectable and run four thousand acres of land. Well, you'll have it your own way. I suppose the safest place for a man to take his folly is to bed."

"Mammy!"

"You must be lenient with your Cousin George. He wanders about night times talking about the War. I put him off in the west wing where he won't keep people awake, but sometimes he gets in the yard and gives orders to his troops. 'I will sweep that hill, General'—and many's the time he's done it when the battle was doubtful—'I'll sweep it with my iron brooms'; then he shouts out his orders, and pretty soon the dogs commence to barking. But he's been a heap of company for me. You must see that your wife humors him. It won't be for long. He's mighty feeble."

"Eva's not my wife yet, Mammy."

"You won't be free much longer—the way she looks at you, like a hungry hound."

"I was just wondering," he said hurriedly. "I hate to talk about anything like this . . ."

"Everybody has a time to die, and I'll have no maudlin nonsense about mine."

"I was wondering about Cousin George . . . If I could get somebody to keep him. You see, it will be difficult in the winters. Eva will want to spend the winters in town . . ."

He paused, startled, before the great bulk of his grandmother rising from her pillows, and in the silence that frightened the air, his unfinished words hung suspended about them.

After a moment he asked if he should call the doctor.

It was some time before she could find words to speak.

"Get out of the room."

"Forgive me, Mammy. You must be tired."

"I'll send for you," sounded the dead voice in the still

room, "when I want to see you again. I'll send for you and —the woman."

She watched the door close quietly on his neat square back. Her head whirled and turned like a flying jennet. She lowered and steadied it on the pillows. Four thousand acres of the richest land in the valley he would sell and squander on that slut, and he didn't even know it and there was no way to warn him. This terrifying thought rushed through her mind, and she felt the bed shake with her pain, while before the footboard the specter of an old sin rose up to mock her. How she had struggled to get this land and keep it together— through the War, the Reconstruction, and the pleasanter after days. For eighty-seven years she had suffered and slept and planned and rested and had pleasure in this valley, seventy of it, almost a turning century, on this place; and now that she must leave it . . .

The things she had done to keep it together. No. The one thing . . . From the dusty stacks the musty odor drifted through the room, met the tobacco smoke over the long table piled high with records, reports. Iva Louise stood at one end, her hat clinging perilously to the heavy auburn hair, the hard blue eyes and the voice:

"You promised Pa to look after me"—she had waited for the voice to break and scream—"and you have stolen my land!"

"Now, Miss Iva Louise," the lawyer dropped his empty eyes along the floor, "you don't mean . . ."

"Yes. I do mean it."

Her own voice had restored calm to the room: "I promised your pa his land would not be squandered."

"My husband won't squander my property. You just want it for yourself."

She cut through the scream with the sharp edge of her scorn: "What about that weakling's farm in Madison? Who pays the taxes now?"

The girl had no answer to that. Desperate, she faced the lawyer: "Is there no way, sir, I can get my land from the clutches of this unnatural woman?"

The man coughed; the red rim of his eyes watered with embarrassment. "I'm afraid," he cleared his throat, "you say you can't raise the money . . . I'm afraid—"

That trapped look as the girl turned away. It had come back to her, now trapped in her bed. As a swoon spreads, she felt the desperate terror of weakness, more desperate where there has been strength. Did the girl see right? Had she stolen the land because she wanted it?

Suddenly, like the popping of a thread in a loom, the struggles of the flesh stopped, and the years backed up and covered her thoughts like the spring freshet she had seen so many times creep over the dark soil. Not in order, but as if they were stragglers trying to catch up, the events of her life passed before her sight that had never been so clear. Sweeping over the mounds of her body rising beneath the quilts came the old familiar odors—the damp, strong, penetrating smell of new-turned ground; the rank, clinging, resistless odor of green-picked feathers stuffed in a pillow by Guinea Nell, thirty-odd years ago; tobacco on the mantel, clean and sharp like smelling salts; her father's sweat, sweet like stale oil; the powerful ammonia of manure turned over in a stall; curing hay in the wind; the polecat's stink on the night air, almost pleasant, a sort of commingled scent of all the animals, man and beast; the dry smell of dust under a rug; the over-strong scent of too-sweet fruit trees blooming; the inhospitable wet ashes of a dead fire in a poor white's cabin; black

Rebecca in the kitchen; a wet hound steaming before a fire. There were other odors she could not identify, overwhelming her, making her weak, taking her body and drawing out of it a choking longing to hover over all that she must leave, the animals, the fences, the crops growing in the fields, the houses, the people in them . . .

It was early summer, and she was standing in the garden after dark—she had heard something after the small chickens. Mercy and Yellow Jane passed beyond the paling fence. Dark shadows—gay full voices. *Where you gwine, gal? I dunno. Jest a-gwine. Where you? To the frolic, do I live. Well, stay off'n yoe back tonight.* Then out of the rich, gushing laughter: *All right, you stay off'n yourn. I done caught de stumbles.* More laughter.

The face of Uncle Ike, head man in slavery days, rose up. A tall Senegalese, he was standing in the crib of the barn unmoved before the bush-whackers. *Nigger, whar is that gold hid? You better tell us, nigger. Down in the well; in the far-place. By God, you black son of a bitch, we'll roast ye alive if you air too contrary to tell. Now listen, ole nigger, Miss McCowan ain't nothen to you no more. You been set free. We'll give ye some of it, a whole sack. Come on, now*—out of the dribbling, leering mouth—*whar air it?* Ike's tall form loomed towards the shadows. In the lamp flame his forehead shone like the point, the core of night. He stood there with no word for answer. As she saw the few white beads of sweat on his forehead, she spoke.

She heard her voice reach through the dark—*I know your kind. In better days you'd slip around and set people's barns afire. You shirked the War to live off the old and weak. You don't spare me because I'm a woman. You'd shoot a woman quicker because she has the name of being frail. Well, I'm*

not frail, and my Navy Six an't frail. Ike, take their guns.
Ike moved and one of them raised his pistol arm. He dropped
it, and the acrid smoke stung her nostrils. *Now, Ike, get the
rest of their weapons. Their knives, too. One of us might turn
our backs.*

On top of the shot she heard the soft pat of her servants'
feet. White eyeballs shining through the cracks in the barn.
Then: *Caesar, Al, Zebedee, step in here and lend a hand to
Ike.* By sun the people had gathered in the yard. Uneasy,
silent, they watched her on the porch. She gave the word, and
the whips cracked. The mules strained, trotted off, skittish
and afraid, dragging the white naked bodies bouncing and
cursing over the sod: *Turn us loose. We'll not bother ye no
more, lady. You ain't no woman, you're a devil.* She turned
and went into the house. It is strange how a woman gets
hard when trouble comes a-gobbling after her people.

Worn from memory, she closed her eyes to stop the whirl,
but closing her eyes did no good. She released the lids and
did not resist. Brother Jack stood before her, handsome and
shy, but ruined from his cradle by a cleft palate, until he
came to live only in the fire of spirits. And she understood,
so clear was life, down to the smallest things. She had often
heard tell of this clarity that took a body whose time was
spending on the earth. Poor Brother Jack, the gentlest of
men, but because of his mark, made the butt and wit of the
valley. She saw him leave for school, where he was sent to
separate him from his drinking companions, to a church
school where the boys buried their liquor in the ground and
sipped it up through straws. His letters: *Dear Ma, quit offering so much advice and send me more money. You send barely
enough to keep me from stealing.* His buggy wheels scraping
the gravel, driving up as the first roosters crowed. *Katharine,*

Malcolm, I thought you might want to have a little conversation. Conversation two hours before sun! And down she would come and let him in, and the General would get up, stir the fire, and they would sit down and smoke. Jack would drink and sing, *If the Little Brown Jug was mine, I'd be drunk all the time and I'd never be sob-er a-gin*—or, *Hog drovers, hog drovers, hog drovers we air, a-courting your darter so sweet and so fair.* They would sit and smoke and drink until she got up to ring the bell.

He stayed as long as the whiskey held out, growing more violent towards the end. She watered his bottles; begged whiskey to make camphor—*Gre't God, Sis Kate, do you sell camphor? I gave you a pint this morning.* Poor Brother Jack, killed in Breckinridge's charge at Murfreesboro, cut in two by a chain shot from an enemy gun. All night long she had sat up after the message came. His body scattered about a splintered black gum tree. She had seen that night, as if she had been on the field, the parties moving over the dark field hunting the wounded and dead. Clyde Bascom had fallen near Jack with a bad hurt. They were messmates. He had to tell somebody; and somehow she was the one he must talk to. The spectral lanterns, swinging towards the dirge of pain and the monotonous cries of *Water*, caught by the river dew on the before-morning air and held suspended over the fields in its acrid quilt. There death dripped to mildew the noisy throats . . . and all the while relief parties, moving, blots of night, sullenly moving in the viscous blackness.

Her eyes widened, and she looked across the foot posts into the room. There was some mistake, some cruel blunder; for there now, tipping about the carpet, hunting in her wardrobe, under the bed, blowing down the fire to its ashes until they glowed in their dryness, stalked the burial parties. They stepped out of the ashes in twos and threes, hunting, hunting, and shaking their heads. Whom were they searching for? Jack had long been buried. They moved more rapidly; looked angry. They crowded the room until she gasped for breath. One, gaunt and haggard, jumped on the foot of her bed; rose to the ceiling; gesticulated, argued in animated silence. He leaned forward; pressed his hand upon her leg. She tried to tell him to take it off. Cold and crushing heavy, it pressed her down to the bowels of the earth. Her lips trembled, but no sound came forth. Now the hand moved up to her stomach; and the haggard eyes looked gravely at her, alert, as if they were waiting for something. Her head turned giddy. She called to Dick, to Ants, to Doctor Ed; but the words struck her teeth and fell back in her throat. She concentrated on lifting the words, and the burial parties sadly shook their heads. Always the cries struck her teeth and fell back down. She strained to hear the silence they made. At last from a great distance she thought she heard . . . *too late* . . . *too late.* How exquisite the sound, like a bell swinging without ringing. Suddenly it came to her. She was dying.

How slyly death slipped up on a body, like sleep moving over the vague boundary. How many times she had laid awake to trick the unconscious there. At last she would know . . . But she wasn't ready. She must first do something about Long Gourd. That slut must not eat it up. She would give it to the hands first. He must be brought to understand this. But the specters shook their heads. Well let them shake. She'd be damned if she would go until she was ready to go. She'd be damned all right, and she smiled at the meaning the word took on now. She gathered together all the particles of her will; the specters faded; and there about her were the anxious faces of kin and servants. Edwin had his hands under the cover feeling her legs. She made to raise her own hand to the boy. It did not go up. Her eyes wanted to roll upward and look behind her forehead, but she pinched them down and looked at her grandson.

"You want to say something, Mammy?" —she saw his lips move.

She had a plenty to say, but her tongue had somehow got glued to her lips. Truly it was now too late. Her will left her. Life withdrawing gathered like a frosty dew on her skin. The last breath blew gently past her nose. The dusty nostrils tingled. She felt a great sneeze coming. There was a roaring; the wind blew through her head once, and a great cotton field bent before it, growing and spreading, the bolls swelling as big as cotton sacks and bursting white as thunder-heads. From a distance, out of the far end of the field, under a sky so blue that it was painful-bright, voices came singing, *Joshua fit the battle of Jericho, Jericho, Jericho—Joshua fit the battle of Jericho, and the walls come a-tumbling down.*

A STORY:

the mahogany frame

THE BIG CAR ROLLED SMOOTHLY INTO THE NIGHT. THE SHARP bright smudge of the headlights slid under the darkness with mathematical exactitude. Dressed in his hunting clothes, the boy sat beside his uncle and watched the road. He sat rather stiffly. His new boots, greased by his mother, prodded the boxes of shells piled carelessly onto the floor of the car. He was not comfortable. The shells gave him no easy rest for his feet, his clothes were strange in their bulk, and he could not make up his mind how to act with his Uncle Bomar. This was to him at the moment the most serious matter in the world. He tied himself into knots thinking about it. He rather felt that the childish deference to an elder was out of place now that they were going hunting together, and not merely hunting but to the Lake for ducks. The invitation was plainly Bomar's way of accepting him as a man. Bomar did not take boys duck shooting. Quail or dove hunting, but never duck. He had begged too often not to know. The boy felt that at last he was ready for a man's pleasures and responsibilities. This thought made him all the more anxious to behave as he should. This and the way his mother had seen them off.

But how was he to behave? Nobody had told him, just as nobody had told him what it meant to put on long pants. His mother had cried, his father had asked the cost, his grandfather had spouted Latin about the *toga virilis*. And his brother Bob, all he had said was, "Keep it buttoned up, kid." "Of course I'll keep buttoned up,' he had answered with shame and petulance, thinking only of the technical handling of the clothes. He knew at once he had made a mistake, even before he saw the smirk on his brother's face. Suddenly the long months of expectation, at last realized, turned bitter under his tongue and he did not know rightly why. Vaguely and with confusion it came to him how narrow had been his understanding of what he had wanted. His wish had been little more than to masquerade in grown-up clothes. But the fact was another thing. Changing clothes had changed him. He felt the same and yet he was not the same. For days it puzzled him how this could be, then he gave it up as he grew accustomed to his new condition, but for a while longer he carried about him a feeling of unease. This made him sensitive and timid, so that he would cross over to the other side of the street rather than speak to someone he had known all his life.

The car took a curve. From the darkness a large stock barn with white doors appeared, disappeared. A board fence made a slapping noise as they passed down its narrow lane. He watched the posts go down like piles. The air sucked in, the fence was gone, and he knew they were entering poorer country.

"Tommy phoned me the big flights were coming in," Bomar said. "Had been for two days."

The boy stiffened in his seat, thinking desperately hard what reply a sportsman would make to such an important statement. The moment of his indecision dragged interminably, so that he blurted out, "You reckon they'll still be there?" His cheeks burned with shame at the over-eager, inadequate words.

"If the weather holds," Bomar replied in his slow, unexcitable voice. "It's got to be cold enough for the streams and back water to freeze over before the ducks come on to the Lake in any number. It's pretty cold. I expect they'll be there."

The boy leaned back in his seat. His uncle had answered him seriously. His question no longer seemed to him childish and ineffective. He even recovered from the humiliation of the leave-taking, his mother following them to the car, pulling his scarf about his neck, telling him not to get shot, not to take cold and to promise her, if his feet got wet, to tell the man to row him in, a few ducks is not worth pneumonia. . . . Great God, Effie, the boy's going duck shooting, not to the North Pole. He had been grateful for Bomar's words then. He was more grateful now. They had not meant regret for asking him to come along. Maybe Bomar, too, knew what it was to be hindered by the solicitude of women.

The older man reached up and turned on the car's spot. He played it about the countryside, objects in the rough fields, then set it to the center of the road. The headlights swelled to a new fullness and the car took up speed. "A spot is a good thing to have in the country," Bomar said, as if his gesture needed some explanation.

"It sure is," the boy replied.

His uncle had turned as he spoke, turned easily, almost lazily, and yet all his movements showed perfect coördination. The boy felt a slight shock of surprise. His uncle was not so old a man as he had always thought, or rather he had never thought about his age at all. He had been Uncle Bomar, his mother's younger brother, sometimes whispered about in the family, but one of the opposition nevertheless who stoor for authority, dullness, and obstacles to freedom. Except that he had never been so dull as the others. He had threatened older boys with Bomar's name and he would always let you go along to pick up doves. And Bomar had taken time to teach him how to shoot. He looked at the older man's eyes as if for the first time. They wore a look of furious haste which seemed out of keeping with his fleshy cheeks. As the boy looked more closely, it seemed to him that the fury had grown cold and the haste had set like the film over the racer's pupils as he is being led from the track, blinded to the shouting in the stands, to winning and losing, to all but the burning strain of the race and the gorged heart.

Bomar said, "You had better take that heavy coat off. You won't feel it in the morning. It gets cold as hell out on that Lake."

Hastily the boy took off the coat, for the second time thinking bitterly of his mother, whom he had allowed in his ignorance to dress him as she had once done for parties and Sunday School, as if the whole affair were no more than a fashion parade. His uncle wore his good clothes. Hunters changed for the Lake after they got there.

"How do you think you will like it, kid?"

"Oh, fine," he said hastily. "I've always wanted to go. Old Jake used to tell me about grandfather Laus going there. He said he went in a wagon and it took him two weeks to go, and he always stayed two or three weeks hunting and fishing. Jake said he was a little boy, and they took him along to gather up fat pine and keep the fires."

"It's quite a difference these days," the older man said.

"Oh, yes, sir. When will we get there?"

"Well, we could make it tonight, but I think we'll stop off and sleep at Center. There's a good hotel there. The quarters at Hornbec are pretty rugged. And the guides keep you up drinking your whiskey."

"Oh," the boy said. He kept silent a moment, then resumed eagerly. "Jake said there were all kinds of hunting, and on one trip grandfather Laus brought back a live bear."

"The old boy must have been quite a sport."

"Oh, he was. Sometimes he would sleep under the trees, by a spring or creek. Jake said when he put up with people along the way, he would copy the design of a quilt he liked and have his wife make it when he got back home."

Bomar looked curiously at the boy at his side. "You seem to know a lot about that old guy. Which one was he?"

"He's the one that hangs to the right of the mantel in the living room."

"Let's see. That's the . . ."

"He hangs in the mahogany frame."

"Yeah. He was the one that was such a rounder."

"But he reformed. Mother says he received the mantle of grace when the Methodists held their great revival and built a Church for his slaves."

"When the hell was that?"

"Oh, a long time ago. I don't know rightly."

"You might know it would be a long time. The United Daughters like'm dead."

The boy regarded his uncle with a puzzled expression. "You mean the United Daughters of the Confederacy, sir?"

"I mean all united daughters. The club don't make any difference. In union is strength. That's their battle cry. But hell, boy, you don't know what I'm talking about," Bomar said with impatience. "What I mean is the only man they'll have any truck with is a dead one. After a certain age, that is. The deader the better, if he's buried deep enough so he don't stink."

The boy nodded knowingly, although his head was awhirl. He had heard his father and his father's friends occasionally refer to women in disparaging terms. One spoke of women and preachers, he discovered, in the same tone of voice. It apparently was a thing one did to relieve certain difficult situations, but there was never a particular women, or a particular preacher, named. The reference was invariably general. And his grandfather—only with him it was religion. He never spoke impolitely of ladies, but he could fling himself into a passion about the Church, especially at the dinner table when the conversation fell off. And his grandmother gave always the same reproving speech, in the same falsely affronted manner, "Don't blaspheme before these young men, Mr. Hancock." And Mr. Hancock would reply with righteous vehemence, "The truth, Madam, cannot blaspheme." None of this banter had he taken to mean anything, but with his Uncle Bomar he felt a difference. Bomar had actual women in mind and a grievance which seemed, however mysterious, real and vaguely threatening. He could not help but be disturbed the more he thought about Bomar's remark. Did he mean his own mother? She talked a great deal about her family, living and dead. The truth heretofore hidden in things familiar confronted him: most of the people she talked about were dead.

After a while, in the silence which had fallen between the man and boy, Bomar said, "Forget it, kid." And the boy knew it was hard for him to speak, that inadvertently he had allowed talk which he considered unseemly to pass between them.

But he could not forget so easily. Considerations too disturbing to be summarily dismissed had been set loose in his head. Was it true that ladies of his mother's years thought only of the dead, or thought of them to the disfavor of the living? He was sure it could not be so with his mother. The tales she told never called to mind the dead but only the very dearest of kin who perhaps lived too far away to visit. Above all was this true of grandfather Laus, whom she set him for example. "Hold your head up and step lightly," she would say and he knew who it was she had in mind. Or, "Always be able to look any man in the eye." And again, "Think what you please but never speak loosely and you'll have nothing to take back." These admonitions he was conscious of but never in the forepart of his mind. They underlay and gave firm texture to all he found delightful in his great-grandfather's life, and he somehow knew that had they been lacking the stories which won his heart would have seemed less true. But now that he thought of things in a way he never had thought before, all which touched him dearly lay bright and clear before his vision, the beginning, the middle, and the end clarified in a burst of illumination, where the parts were the whole and the whole defined the parts. And so it came to him that from his mother he got most of the admonitions but the stories he had from his grandfather or from Jake.

The near duel with General Jackson he liked best of all, for the two friends were parted over a horse race. This seemed to him right and fitting, for only some such great occasion was proper cause to break the bonds between two "gentlemen who held each other in the highest esteem." The story as it was told, without directly accusing the General, was told to his discredit. Large sums had been placed on the race. In the last half mile the General's horse was gaining, when his grandfather Laus's horse threw his rider and crossed the finishing line several lengths ahead of his rival. Proud of himself, he turned to the stand where his master sat, and whinnied. At this point in the story his grandfather would pause dramatically. "The spectators to a man rose and cheered the gallant animal." But of course no riderless horse could win a race. Words passed, just what words he was never told, a challenge was given and taken, but the night before the morning of the duel friends intervened and the matter was disposed of to the honor of both parties. "Else," his grandfather would say, "Else," he would repeat, looking significantly about him, "the history of our nation had been played out in different fashion."

Tall, gallant, and forever young, this was the man whose image he carried, not that of the picture in the mahogany frame. That never made him think of grandfather Laus. It looked like the dead or would have so looked if the straight-glancing eyes had been closed. But they narrowed too sharply out of some great reserve, above the stiff neck and stock and the black broadcloth coat. He could never imagine the man in the picture lying under the trees, wrapped in a bear skin, with the shine of the camp fire on his face and the sound of the hobbled horses grazing in the dark. The grandfather who was hunter was the man he liked to think about. Now he was going over the same road he had taken and to the Lake where he had had such great sport with all kinds of game. The road was changed, there was no more a forest, but the Lake at least would still be wild and the guides simple, noble men.

"Wake up, kid, we're here."

He opened wide his eyes, but for a moment his senses delayed. Startled, he thought the car was drawing up before the hotel in Center under its large neon sign glowing evilly red in the darkness. Here the night before they had stepped out of the frosty air into the shabby newness of the lobby, had been shown to their room by a gray-haired elevator boy. It had seemed to him that he had scarcely closed his eyes before his uncle was shaking him awake. Behind the desk the proprietor greeted them. He was dressed in hunting clothes. His eyes were bright as a bird's and he jerked about like a mechanical toy as he cocked his head to one side and talked glibly of the shooting, but what he wanted to find out was whether they would be back that night. "Bastard," Bomar said as they turned away. It was still dark as they passed a second time under the neon sign. The car was white and glistened in the dark. The exhaust made a loud noise in the deserted street. In the distance he had heard an ash can clattering. . . .

"Well, here we are," Bomar said and got out of the car with a motion which was quick for a man his size. He called into the darkness, "Anybody seen Tommy?"

A voice answered, "He stepped up to his house. He'll be on down in a little."

"Are we really here?" The boy asked. He noticed that he had lowered his voice. His uncle had spoken right out.

"This is Hornbec. There's the Lake over there."

The boy glanced towards a rough pier, but it was all dark beyond and he could see nothing of the water. They walked up the narrow street which bordered the Lake. Lights from the windows and door of a plain two-story building glared from its porch and threw a milky shadow onto the steps. But the light did not penetrate, although he could see his uncle's face and the half-solid forms of men stirring busily around him. He was wide-awake now, with the cold wind from the Lake blowing his face, but he felt as if he were acting in a dream, where all was topsy-turvy yet all seemed natural. It was this very naturalness of things which made him feel as he did: people going about their business, talking in a normal voice, but all in the dead of night.

"Let's go in the hotel," Bomar said.

Inside it was warm and bright. Some dozen men dressed in their hunting clothes, several of them in hip boots, sat around a pot-bellied stove. It was red hot about its middle. He shivered and walked over to warm himself.

"How about a little breakfast, Nelly?" Bomar called out and walked into the long dining room.

The walls were plain and unfinished. Most of the tables were in disarray and he could see that the guests of the hotel had already eaten. Where he sat, there were crumbs on the cloth and somebody had spilled catsup. The woman Nelly came in with fried eggs shining white with grease, thick bacon, large thick biscuits, and coffee in heavy china cups. She flung her head and shoulders about as she walked. The boy thought he had never seen less sense in a face, but he could see the hunters liked her or at least that she thought the hunters liked her.

"Good old Nelly. She won't let us starve," Bomar called out with too loud a heartiness and grabbed playfully at her waist. She tossed her head and flung herself out of the way, but her wide bright eyes grew brighter.

"Quit, now-wah," she said.

The brazen stupidity in her dare that was not a dare chilled his spirits. The eggs were cold, but he ate the bacon and poured a lot of milk and sugar in his coffee and drank it. The coffee was steaming hot.

"Paul's wife may come up with him today," Bomar said to the girl.

"I hope she does."

"Do you now?"

"Why not. I ain't got nothing to hide."

"No. Nothing to hide. Nothing at all."

"That's right."

"Who did I see kissing you?"

"He was jest being jolly."

"Yeah. Jolly. Good old jolly Paul."

"That's right," she said. "Jolly and friendly. You all want lunches?"

"Sure. You want us to go hungry on that Lake?"

"I didn't know. I thought maybe you'd brought lunches with you."

Bomar turned to his nephew. "This hotel think it's got a monopoly."

"We don't care where you stay." Her head came up. A light flush at the cheek bones rushed to her eyes. For the first time the woman seemed real to the boy. His mother had told him that plain people were quick to take offense but it was her show of pride which gave her being, and he understood that it was a thing she held in common with those around her as she shared a speech which his mother called country.

"Well, will you be here tonight?" she continued.

Bomar paused. "Yeah. The kid and I'll be here."

"I jest wanted to know. I have to plan about supper."

She left the dining room, and the man and boy ate hurriedly and in silence. From the other room they heard spurts of talk. None of it flowed easily, as happens with men who are idling. It jabbed at the silence, a silence enclosing a time of waiting upon action, when the mind grows fearful lest its edge grow dull from images. The boy was trying to catch the drift of the talk. He had not heard the soft steps approaching. He heard only the words, "Now if you ain't a pretty bastard."

He stiffened and waited for the blow which Bomar in all honor must give. He waited a second. There was no stirring of the chair. He raised his eyes upon his uncle's smiling, placid features.

Bomar's lips were moving. "You ain't no handsome son-of-a-bitch yourself," they said.

"Getting in here this time of day. You drive all night?"

"Hell, no. We stopped off at Center to get a few hours sleep."

"What you think you are, a goddam tourist?"

"You got an interest in this hotel?"

"Hell, no. It's just the company you keep. When I want to sleep in a whore house, I don't want no pimp to show me my bed. That mealy-mouthed bastard dressing up like a hunter to catch the suckers like you, only I didn't know you was a sucker before. And they'll steal there, too."

"Hell, Applegate."

"Hell they don't. Last week a man from Indiana lost his purse with ninety-seven dollars in it."

"You're just afraid he'll take away your business."

"Hell. None of the guides around here will go up there. And we don't let him down here."

Bomar turned to his nephew. "Kid, shake hands with Tommy Applegate."

The boy rose and gave the small heavy-set man his hand. He was a little dazed. Bastard and son-of-a-bitch were fighting words, not friendly greetings. He didn't understand. He knew his uncle had fought for less, much less. And he well knew that no such greeting would have passed between grandfather Laus and his lean, weathered guide, when they met again at the return of the hunting season. But of course there were no professional guides in those days. The people who lived about the Lake at that time hunted or trapped for a living. They might go along with a friend out of pure courtesy, or for companionship, but he was sure they took no money for it. But it was not money either. It was the greeting which shocked and puzzled him. For a second his hand gripped the guide's hand. He felt the inert calloused flesh, and the strength within, near the bone, but there was no response to his clasp. The man was not being unfriendly; but as he drew away the boy felt he had been rebuffed. Later he remembered the eyes. They were brown, which he did not expect. And there was something else, something wrong about them. They lacked the sharpness of a hunter's eyes.

"We are about ready to shove off, kid," Bomar interrupted. "We're going to the first pocket. Tommy got you a good guide. Watch him, though, or he'll shoot up too many of your shells. And you give him this at the end of the day."

The boy looked at the money. "All of this, Uncle Bomar?"

"Yeah, I know. It's too damn much, but it's what they charge."

Outside the darkness was thinning. The Lake spread out for a way like a black floor. The boy hesitated on the edge of the porch. His clothes were slick from the cold, but the blood charged through his body. It seemed a trivial thing that he had worried at not finding the place and the people what he had expected, for the surroundings are nothing. The only thing that mattered was the shoot. Hunters passed him on the steps, all with a common purpose, the same thoughts, the same sense of excitement and expectation. He could feel it as they went by. One or two looked curiously at him. He knew he must go on or they would think him strange, but still he delayed to savor the full measure of the experience before it was played out by the act. All this stir, the time of day, the learning of the guides, the rich men who hunted, who came from places where their word was law, others who came out of some urgent need they did not rightly understand—all of them now and in his great-grandfather's day, were guided, were governed by the instincts of a bird. Bomar half turned. "Where are you?" He called sharply.

"Coming," the boy answered and hurried down the steps. He noticed that Bomar's bulky clothes spreading out over his hips enlarged them. He looked from the rear like his mother.

At the water's edge two boats were drawn close into the bank. Tommy was standing in one. Bomar was handing him his gear.

"Your gun unloaded?" Tommy asked.

"You know I wouldn't hand you any loaded gun," Bomar replied.

"Be goddamned sure. I don't want you to blow my ass off."

"Don't put it where it'll get wet."

"If it gets wet, you'll get wet. Hand me that sack of charcoal."

"Your arm's not broke. Pick it up."

"What's the matter with your back? Been riding it too hard?"

"My back's all right. This is Jack Daniel's number seven. Catch it."

"Three's my lucky number."

"Well, this will more than double your luck. Won't it, Goosetree?"

A man looked up from blowing the charcoal burner in the adjoining boat. The light from the charcoal showed a pair of flat eyes, with sharp points at their centers. Even in the steady red glow his features seemed pale. He said dryly, "He'll double your drinks."

"This is the kid, Goosetree, that's going with you," Bomar said.

The man nodded. "They'll make the noise, sonny," he said. "We'll bring in the meat."

"Hell," Tommy said with heavy scorn.

"I've got the gun will do it," Goosetree added. "And this boy looks like he can shoot."

"You may get a mud hen or two."

"I'm going to hole up at the point. We'll bring'm in."

"Bring in my ass," Tommy said.

"Now that ud be a right heavy load."

The boy no longer felt ill at ease with these people. At first he had been repelled by their obscenities. The words had struck him with all the force of their literal meaning. And in his disgust there had been fear, not so much of the men and the place, as of his own sensations. All things he had found different from his imaginings. Bomar's unintended remarks in the car had begun it. He had got in beside his uncle, never doubting that things could ever be otherwise than as they seemed. He had found that even a fact about which there could not be the slightest uncertainty, such as Bomar's eyes, was not a fact at all. Almost without attending it, so fast did it happen, one certainty after another had slipped away from him until he felt exposed in all his privacy. Now this in some way had changed. He had scarcely listened to the guide's talk. He watched them get the boats set for the shoot. What they did went quickly, but there was no haste to their movements, and their banter was spoken with as little attention to the meaning as the congregation repeating the doxology on Sunday.

Goosetree straightened up. His movement was unmistakable. There came a pause and Bomar turned hastily. "Now, kid," he said, "you got to lead these ducks."

"Like doves?"

"Yeah. Maybe further. I can't tell you exactly. You'll have to judge. But when they come flying in at you, shoot at their bills." He stepped into the boat. "All ready, me lads?"

"We been ready," Goosetree replied.

The boy sat forward in the boat, astraddle the charcoal burner. There was barely room for his legs and he had to watch to see that his boots didn't burn. They pushed off and he thought surely the ice must chew up the bottom of the boat. The going got better after a while, but every now and then the guide had to strike the ice several times before he could set the oars to water. The darkness thinned and the cold began to bite into him. It had a different quality over water. He felt weight as well as chill. He wore two wool shirts, a heavy wool coat and next to his body close-knit woolen underwear, but it went through all these garments like air through a sack in a broken window light. He got to wondering if he could stand it all day and leaned forward to rub his hands over the open mouth of the burner.

His teeth began to chatter and he drew down his chin so it wouldn't be seen. He could hear Bomar and Tommy. Their voices had the flat clear sound of coming from a distance and yet they were not far away. And then he looked up. . . . Dawn had swamped the sky. There was no light and yet he could see. He was first conscious of a wonderful ease to his eyes. Wide open, without a thread's strain, they saw every-where through the colorless haze. Never had he been able to see so clearly and so far. He thought it must be like this with animal eyes at night or whenever they hunt, to see and not know they are seeing, when the vision and prey are made one for the spring. A wonderfully fresh strength streamed through his body. All things seemed at a beginning. It was the world on the first day.

The boat struck a snag. He looked more closely about. Black slick tree trunks stuck up out of the water like the splintered piles of a pier which had rotted away. Occasionally they passed a stump that was still alive, but its stunted growth only made the desolate surroundings more forbidding. And the Lake, he saw, was forbidding. Miles upon miles of saw grass, more grass than water, and everywhere the illusion of solid ground. Slimy ooze, even quicksand, was its floor. His first elation drained away. He told himself the place was not meant for man. It was more foreign and distant to his ex-perience than the most outlandish reaches of human habita-tion. Over him came a great and terrible loneliness.

The boats entered an open pocket of frozen water. His boat began to rock and he grasped the sides.

"Give with the boat," Goosetree commanded.

"What's the matter, Mr. Goosetree?"

"Nothing's the matter. I'm breaking the ice."

"What for?"

"To throw out the blocks." Goosetree's voice made him feel the depth of his ignorance.

The ice broke up in sheets and the boat sloshed it out of the way. Into the open water the guide began to throw his decoys. He unwound the string, glanced at the water with quick precision and then threw out the painted block. In no time the false birds rode their anchors in front of the blind. Goosetree now drove the boat into the edge of the grass. He handed the boy a pole. "When I pull, you push on that," he said and stepped into the water. His hip boots sank down and he said, "All right." At each push the boat slid further into the blind. Empty shells and cigarette butts soiled the flattened tufts of grass. One cigarette, scarcely smoked, touched the water, its damp brown insides spilling and staining the paper. A smear of lipstick gashed its upper end. Instinctively the boy averted his gaze. A blot formed in the blue-gray haze, hung for a moment to the air, desperately, noiselessly fluttering its wings, turned and disappeared. Motionless, he watched the spot where it had been, feeling he could almost have touched the duck, if duck it was, for how could its wings beat so and not make a sound?

"I reckon it's hid," Goosetree said.

"No, it just melted away," the boy replied.

Goosetree's eyes came on guard. The boy said hastily. "Oh, the boat. Yes, sir, it looks hid."

"What'd you think I meant?"

"I didn't hear you well."

He felt that his guide was studying him, trying to make up his mind whether he was responsible enough to risk in the close quarters they must keep. At last Goosetree pulled himself out of the water and began to prepare the boat for action. He set the burner between them, changed the seats so that they faced each other, set his lunch beside him, his water bottle to the rear. He took bunches of grass from both sides and tied them together over the boat. Carefully he loaded his gun and set it down pointing into the grass. He loaded the boy's and handed it to him. "Point it that way," he said, "and always keep the safety on until you get up to shoot. And don't get up until I tell you."

"Where are Uncle Bomar and Tommy gone?" he asked.

The guide was dropping charcoal into the burner. "They went to the other side of the pocket." He leaned over to blow the coals. The boy noticed that his hands were black and his face sooty from handling the coal. When the fire suited him, he dropped a tomato can over the low tin chimney, then rose in the boat. He stood with his body half bent and with a short jerk of the head looked up. A shadow passed over his eyes as he flicked them across the arc of the sky.

"See anything?" the boy asked.

"They'll be in," he replied.

Then they sat in silence, leaning towards each other over the burner. Around the boat, out of the grass, the cold boiled up through a slimy mist. Now that they were settled and waiting the boy felt his body relax and his head grow dull. He was wondering how he could get up from his cramped quarters in time to shoot. He did not see the guide rise. He heard the shot and looked up, his heart fluttering, in time to see the red feet draw up under the white belly, see the inert body slanting to the Lake.

"When they hit the ice, they don't git up no more," Goose-tree said. He added, "I seen him too late to call you."

His first feeling was chagrin and resentment. A guide should give others a chance to shoot. But in his heart he knew he had been a bad hunter. Too much excitement had worn him out. He must learn how to wait, be idle and still wound up, like a spring. That was it. Like a spring.

"There they come," Goosetree hissed.

"Where?" he breathed.

"A Susie. In front of you."

Almost overhead and to the left he saw the duck. The spring in him snapped. He heard the report of his gun, saw the bird falter, fly for a hundred yards and then go down. He shot at another passing to his front, missed, shot and missed again. He tried to aim but his eyes felt frozen and wide open. His gun and Goosetree's went off together. The bird stopped short in flight and fell straight down. For the first time Goosetree smiled.

"I missed the second shot," the boy said and his voice was trembling and his throat dry.

"You didn't lead him enough. The air from your load fanned his tail."

"We both shot at the same time. Think we both got him. I expect you got him."

"It was a teal," Goosetree said, glancing swiftly around. The sky seemed to open out of his eyes.

It seemed a long time before the next ducks flew over. At last he heard, "There!" He grabbed his gun, half rose. "Git down," the guide ordered and hastily put his hands to his mouth and called, the reedy imitation of the duck's cry rasping the air. The call seemed too urgent to the boy, faster than a bird would make. The birds dipped and turned, then flew away.

"No use aiming. Whenever they see you, it's too late."

"Did they see me?"

"Hell, yes. Never get up until you're ready to shoot."

The nasal call to death and the sound of guns travelled from different parts of the Lake, gradually drifted into silence until the whole world grew as still as the painted ducks riding

their anchors in the pool of rotten ice. He and the guide
were close enough to touch. The intimacy which was not
intimacy began to close in on him. He felt that he ought to
say something. He said, "Is your son going to follow in your
footsteps, Mr. Goosetree?"

"Hell, no. There's no money in guiding. Soon's he's old
enough I'm going to send him to college."

"I would think this was a wonderful life," the boy said in
surprise, "being able to hunt or fish every day and get paid
for it."

"It gits stale, up before day freezing your balls off sloshing
around in this ice."

The guide picked up a jug of milky water and poured it
into a pan and set the pan on the open mouth of the burner.
"I'll make us some coffee," he said. "And we can eat. The
ducks won't be back until about eleven o'clock. I've noticed
that's the time they been coming in."

He measured the coffee and dumped it into the water, took
a dirty rag and carefully wiped out two cups and put them
beside him. Then he took a spoon and began to stir the
coffee and blow the coals. "No," he said, "it's hard on you.
I'm going to quit it soon. I bought me the finest summer
house ever built around this Lake. Old man Simpkins built
it, a rich lumber man from Mississippi. He spent eight
thousand dollars on it. Built it of pine and not a knot in it,
plumbing, lights, frigidaire, and good water. I heard his
widow wanted to sell and I let her know by the woman who
looks after it that I might, might mind you, try to buy it.
So old lady Simpkins called me long distance. And I asked
her what she wanted for it and she commenced telling me
how much she'd put in it. I cut her off. I said I'll give you two
thousand cash for it. She couldn't listen to any such figure,

it was giving it away. Two thousand's my offer. Take it or leave it. She hung up on me. But a week later I got a letter from her son saying his mother couldn't bear to come up here no more since her old man had went away and that they'd close the deal." Goosetree poured a cup of coffee and handed it to the boy. "I'd of give twenty-five hundred as easy as I give two thousand." He unwrapped a sandwich. "I'm going to build two cabins, put a toilet and shower in em, they's eight rooms to the house, and rent by the week or month. A man and his wife can come up and fish. They come sometime with women they claim to be their wives. There'll be money in it."

"How many'd you get?" A voice from the Lake asked.

It was Bomar and Tommy. Goosetree rose, "Aw, we got'm boys. How many'd you knock down?"

"None," Tommy said. His face was grave and averted, as though still turned from the incomprehensible workings of Fate.

"We shot twice, but they were too high," Bomar added apologetically.

Tommy began throwing out his decoys.

"Don't throw them blocks out here," Goosetree said.

Tommy rowed about, continuing to throw them out. He asked, "Don't we work together?"

"Hell. The quarters is too close."

Bomar said in his slow, soothing voice, "Goosetree, I believe you are afraid we'll outshoot you."

"Who's got the duck?"

"Well, how many did you get?"

"Three," Goosetree said, his voice less belligerent.

"I really got one, Uncle Bomar. On the nose."

"Fine, kid."

"Yes, sir, this boy's gonna knock'm," Goosetree said. The boy felt a glow of pleasure. He was beginning to think more of his guide.

Tommy masked his boat in the grass behind the others. "You want some coffee?" Goosetree asked.

"We got something better'n coffee," Tommy replied.

"Here, take a drink," Bomar said.

Tommy turned up the bottle. His Adam's apple worked like a piston as the bright brown liquid flowed down his throat. He wiped the mouth of the bottle on his sleeve and returned it casually. "Warms you better than any charcoal," he said matter-of-factly.

From where he reclined in the boat Bomar took a drink. The boy noticed it was much less than Tommy took. "How about it, Goosetree?"

"I got ulcers. Drinking too much in Arkansas," Goosetree replied. "God, but that stuff lightened you as it went down. Set your tail on fire."

"Kid?"

"No, thank you, sir." The boy knew by the way the whiskey was offered that he was supposed to refuse, but he mightily wanted to taste it. He drank his coffee instead and took a bite out of a ham sandwich. There was too much bread for the meat and he threw away the top slice.

"My daddy tole me to stay out'n Arkansas," Goosetree continued.

"Ain't nothing there," Tommy added sourly.

"I went over there to a duck-calling contest oncet. I called as purty as ever you please." Goosetree added bitterly, "They give the prize to a eleven-year-old boy."

"Ain't nothing for nobody in Arkansas," Tommy said.

The boy tried another sandwich, peanut butter and jelly

spread together on the bread. It tasted good. At least it wasn't so dry. He finished his coffee and felt better for the food.

"Tommy, where are these duck you called me about?"

Tommy looked shocked at the question and glanced over the Lake towards the woods. "They're roosting on the reserve," he said.

"Government birds, eh?" Bomar said. "Well, they'll sit on their fat asses until we starve to death."

Tommy looked even more serious. "They'll come out after a while," he said.

"That was humor, Applegate. You wouldn't recognize it, though. It bore no reference to fornication."

Bomar drank again and passed the whiskey to his guide. Tommy took it and turned it up in one motion. He swallowed like a thirsty man drinking water. "That's seven times seven," he said. "What does it make?"

"You drunk," Bomar replied.

"It'll make you holler." He opened his mouth and his voice rang lustily over the Lake.

Bomar examined his companion's face for a moment. "Applegate," he said, "if you had rings in your ears, you'd look like a damn pirate."

Tommy shouted again. "Hi-yo!"

The boy thought he did look like a pirate, anyway like a foreigner, the way his eyes didn't suit his rough, swarthy features but looked both boldly and evasively at the same time. With Mr. Goosetree it was different. He looked like a guide ought to look, although he was a little small and didn't think much of guiding, which was a disappointment the boy didn't explore but which lay uneasily in the back of his head. But Tommy at least was human and it was somehow because of his eyes. Watching the sky, they absorbed it like a blotter.

Maybe it was this which made him seem always on guard. When Mr. Goosetree looked at the sky, he skinned it.

"Hi-yo!" Tommy shouted again. As if suddenly spent by the shouting, he said, "My daddy was a Jew and my mother an Indian. Now ain't that a hell of a combination?"

He had half turned away. Bomar looked at him but said nothing. Tommy continued in a conversational tone. "He used to trade up and down this country. I reckon he made a pretty good living until he took to drinking. When I was a shirt-tail boy, he'd come in on Satday nights and run all of us out of the house. I sort of liked it in summer, like a kid will. My mother would bed us down in the leaves and moss. It didn't seem to worry her much. I reckon Indians are sort of used to the woods. There was generally plenty to eat. She made a good truck patch. She'd take the littlest one and go out in the corn when it was tosselling and sing to it. Homesick kind of a singing. As I got older, I didn't like it so much. Looked like he didn't do so well trading. He'd come in during the week drunk and beat her up. She never hollered, but if he tried to take his scantling to one of us young-uns, she'd scratch and bite him like a cat.

"I was about eleven, I guess. We still had plenty to eat, well not a plenty but enough. She always managed to keep us in victuals, but we was all ragged. It takes money to buy clothes. He wasn't doing no trading at all, except he'd take her corn and swap it for licker. Well, he come a night of the worst blizzard that ever you saw, mean drunk and dirty. He looked like he'd been laying out for a week. He commenced cussin' and stumbling around and hollered, 'Clear all these half-breeds outer here.' I said, 'Daddy, I don't aim to go out in no blizzard.' His red eyes kind of bulged at me. He picked a old table leg that was laying around and come toward me. I raised the gun. He still kept coming. I let him have it right in the belly." Tommy's voice ceased. He said after a while, "Sober, he wasn't no mean-natured kind of a man."

Without saying anything Bomar passed the whiskey over to Tommy. Nobody spoke again for a long while. Goosetree had covered himself up and gone to sleep. Bomar lay back, reclining in the boat. The day had advanced but there was no sun to relieve the cold. The frozen clouds stretched tight across the sky. After a while the boy became conscious of Bomar's soothing voice. It flowed too smoothly. It was getting confidential. He recognized the signs. Miserable from the cold and the long, trying wait, he felt the shoot would be a failure. Nobody would watch for the ducks, maybe there wouldn't be any more to come in. He felt the need to stand up. It was a little less cold up in the air. There was not a duck in the sky. He looked down and his blood danced. Three were playing in the water before a jutting strip of the grass. "Look, Tommy," he cried.

"Mud hens," Tommy said and sat back down.

Bomar had turned where he lay. His eyes were gay. "What," he asked, "would the old boy, what's his name, Menelaus, say if he knew his grandson had taken a mud hen for a duck. The pious Menelaus, our noble ancestor, unequalled in the arts of field and stream and Ovid's pupil. What would he say, kid?"

He was too surprised to say anything—Bomar wondering about grandfather Laus, too, for it was plain that he only pretended to recollect his name. . . .

"Never, oh, never, would that nonpareil, that prince among men, that cock of the walk, have mistaken a mud hen for a duck. Or so we're told. What I like, Applegate, about this

revered ancestor of mine and the kid's, was his timing. Now
I know that timing is everything, but damn if I can bring
it off. But this guy Menelaus did. When he was young, he
went the rounds. When it came time to settle down, he didn't
settle, but nobody held it against him, least of all his large
female connection. He hunted when he wanted to, he had
plenty of money, he played the races and was a family man
all at the same time. He was a genius, Applegate. And while
he stepped high, wide and handsome, his Helen stayed at
home making quilts and raising his young. That's the way to
do it, Applegate. Be fruitful and multiply. And don't forget
the quilts. He didn't. He made it a point to keep her in fresh
patterns, just in case. . . . And then when he had dropped all
the grains of corn from one jar to the other and it was time
to change'm back, he saw the light. At a camp meeting at
Walnut Grove the dove, not the kind you're thinking about,
Applegate, but the blessed, the miraculous dove, came bearing the twig of salvation." He paused. His voice had grown
harder as he spoke. "Don't take it hard, kid, you're not the
first to take a wooden nickel."

He couldn't make heads or tails of what his uncle was saying. What did a wooden nickel have to do with it? It was very
important. He could tell by Bomar's voice. Before he could
try to figure it out, Tommy interrupted.

"There was a lady here fishing once named Helen," Tommy
said. "She come here with a doctor from Chicago. They
claimed they was married, but I been rowing a long time.
These two didn't much care whether they caught anything or
not. She wasn't having much luck and I said—I wasn't thinking anything—'diddle on this side.' I meant her hook of
course, and she said, 'What? Right there?' and giggled. You
know, it was the way she giggled. And the doctor, he laughed

too. They did a sight of loose laughing." Tommy leaned over and stirred the charcoal in the burner. "When I first took up guiding people, didn't no women come here to hunt or fish."

Bomar raised his bottle, "Here's to Argive Helen and all her kin."

The boy felt the boat move. Goosetree was awake and staring at Bomar's large, well-wrapped body. "Look at him," he said, "laying over there like a fattening hog."

Far away, over near the island a lone gun shot once. It made no more noise than a popgun but the men in the two boats grew very quiet. Then all rose to their feet. Goosetree took out his watch. "Eleven twenty," he said.

The importunate duck calls, still at a distance, now buzzed like insects. More guns went off over by the reserve. The firing was scattered. Then somebody said, "Get down." The boy didn't see anything and he got panicky. "Coming over you." "Where, where?" he asked in a tight voice. And then all four of them were shooting furiously. He thought he hit one but he wasn't sure. Two of the ducks turned and flew over a blind across the channel. The hunters there shot up a lot of shells but the ducks went on their way. Goosetree called out, "You want my gun?" His voice was taunting and cheerful. "You can have my gun if you want it."

"How about that for shooting, Applegate?" Bomar asked. His voice was even and full.

"Boy, you stopped him."

"Didn't I stop him, though?"

"Did you? A mallard, too."

"Purty good shooting," Goosetree said. "But look over here in the water."

"Here's where to look," Tommy called back. "Them ducks jest killed theyselves, but we had to shoot to bring'm down."

"Hell."

"We're hitting them, ain't we?" Bomar said.

"Watch it, boys," Goosetree snapped.

Down in the boat Tommy was calling. The hunters across the channel called. The boy crouched and watched the bird, the bending wings, the red feet drawn in. . . . The duck dipped and dove toward the water. The world vanished. There was nothing but space, a streak in space. The moving bolt was all. His ears crashed, the thud against his shoulder, another crash, the red feet gashed the white breast. The dead body dropped and the world was.

"Not bad, kid."

"I think you got him, Uncle Bomar."

"Hard to say. We shot together."

The two of them, the boy and his uncle, were alone in the boat. They watched the guides row from place to place, gathering in the ducks. At last the long full day was over. Behind the island the darkness crouched. As if sensing the hunters could no longer shoot, the ducks now lighted everywhere around them. "God, God . . ." Bomar whispered. Then the guides turned their boat about. It sped toward the hunters. Quietly the water parted about the prow, quietly closed behind the rippling wake. No sign of passage marred its surface —waiting to receive the falling night.

"It's been a good shoot," Bomar said evenly. "But it's over."

The boy turned towards his uncle. What he saw made him raise his hand, as though for support. Bomar stood erect and waiting. His eyes were regarding the boy: they were the eyes in the mahogany frame.

A STORY:

mr. macgregor

"I WANTS TO SPEAK TO MISTER MACGREGOR."

Yes, sir, that's what he said. Not marster, but MISTER MacGREGOR. If I live to be a hundred, and I don't think I will, account of my kidneys, I'll never forget the feelen that come over the room when he said them two words: Mister MacGregor. The air shivered into a cold jelly; and all of us, me, ma, and pa, sort of froze in it. I remember thinken how much we favored one of them waxwork figures Sis Lou had learnt to make at Doctor Price's Female Academy. There I was, a little shaver of eight, standen by the window a-blowen my breath on it so's I could draw my name, like chillun'll do when they're kept to the house with a cold. The knock come sudden and sharp,

I remember, as I was crossen a T. My heart flopped down
in my belly and commenced to flutter around in my breakfast; then popped up to my ears and drawed all the blood
out'n my nose except a little sack that got left in the point
to swell and tingle. It's a singular thing, but the first time
that nigger's fist hit the door I knowed it was the knock
of death. I can smell death. It's a gift, I reckon, one of
them no-count gifts like good conversation that don't do
you no good no more. Once Cousin John Mebane come
to see us, and as he leaned over to pat me on the head—
he was polite and hog-friendly to everybody, chillun and
poverty-wropped kin especial—I said, Cousin John, what
makes you smell so funny? Ma all but took the hide off'n
me; but four days later they was dressen him in his shroud.
Then I didn't know what it was I'd smelled, but by this
time I'd got better acquainted with the meanen.

Ma was rollen tapers for the mantel. She stiffened a
spell like she was listenen for the North wind to rise; rolled
out a taper and laid it down. She went to the door and put
her hand square on the knob; hesitated like she knew
what was comen; then opened it. There stood Rhears. He
was the coachman. Him and his wife Della was ma's pets.
The both of'm was give to ma by her pa at the marryen;
and in a way that folks don't understand no more, they
somehow become a part of her. Ma liked horses that wanted
to run away all the time, and Rhears was the only nigger
on the place that could manage'm. He was a powerful,
dangerous feller. He'd killed the blacksmith and two free
niggers in the other county before ma brought him to
Long Gourd. His shoulders jest but stretched across the
opening, as he stood there in a respectful-arrogant sort of
way with a basket-knife in his hand.

"What do you want, Rhears?" His mistress asked.

"I want to speak to Mister MacGregor," he said.

Pa had been scratchen away at his secretary. At "Mister" the scratchen stopped. That last scratch made more noise in my ears than the guns at Shiloh. Without a word, without even looken behind him, pa stood up and reached for his gun. The secretary was close to the fireplace and had a mirror over it. He didn't waste no time, but he didn't hurry none either. He just got up, took off his specs, and laid them as careful on the secretary, just like he meant to set'm in one special place and no other place would do. He reached for the gun and turned.

Rhears warn't no common field hand. He was proud, black like the satin in widow-women's shirt-waists, and spoiled. And his feelens was bad hurt. The day before, pa had whupped Della and Rhears had had all night to fret and sull over it and think about what was be-en said in the quarters and how glad the field hands was she'd been whupped. He didn't mean to run away from his home like any blue-gum nigger. He jest come a-marchen straight to the house to settle with pa before them hot night thoughts had had time to git cooled down by the frost.

Pa turned and walked towards him. He still moved as steady and solemn. I watched the even distance each boot-heel made and calculated that two more steps would put him up to the threshold. Just to look at him you might have thought he was a-goen towards the courthouse to pay his taxes or walken down the aisle to his pew. All of a sudden he come to a stop. Ma's brown silk skirt had spread out before him. I looked up. There she was, one hand tight around the gun stock, the othern around the barrel. Her left little finger, plunged like a hornet's needle where the skin drew tight over pa's knuckles, made the blood drop on the bristly hairs along his hand; hang there; then spring to the floor. She held there the time it took three drops to bounce down and splatter. That blood put a spell on me.

A gold shiver along ma's dress made me look quick at their faces. Her hair was a shade darker than the dress she was wearen and slicked down around her ears. There wasn't no direct sun on it, but a light sorghum color slipped up and down as if it was playen on grease. The light might have come from her eyes, for they was afire. She was always fine to look at, although her face wasn't soft enough to rightly claim her beautiful. But she would have taken the breeches away from any ordinary man, I tell you. She'd rather manage folks than eat. Pa ought to have let her do a sight more of it than he did. She was happier than ever I seen her the time he went to the legislature. But he didn't take to politics somehow. He said the government rooms smelled too strong of tobacco and stale sweat. He couldn't abide the smell of tobacco. He was a mighty clean man, the cleanest I ever come across. Took a washen once a day reg'lar. When I come to think about ma, I see her a-studyen about somethen, with a wrinkle in her eyes. She didn't have to tell the servants not to bother her then. They stayed out of her way or went tippen around if their work took'm near her.

Well, pa saw he couldn't get his gun out of her grip without acting ungentlemanly. He gave her a curious look and a low bow; then turned it loose. Taken off his coat and folden it, he laid it across a chair. Ma was marbly-pale when she stepped out of the way, but she moved easy and steady.

For a long time I never could make out the meanen of

them looks, nor why ma done what she done. And she never set us right about it. She wasn't the explainen kind, and you can bet nobody never asked. I'd just as soon've asked the devil to pop his tail. It's bothered me a heap in my time, more'n it's had any right to. I reckon it's because I always think about it when I'm taperen off. That's a time when a man gits melancholy and thinks about how he come not to be president and sich-like concerns. Well, sir, when I'd run through all my mistakes and seen where if I'd a-done this instead of that how much better off I'd be today, and cuss myself for drinken up my kidneys, I'd always end up by asken myself why that woman acted like that. I've knowed a sight of women in my day, knowed'm as the Bible saints knowed'm, as well as in a social and business way; and I'm here to say, sir, they are stuffed with dynamite, the puniest of'm.

It was a question of authority, and a time when whuppen was out of the argyment. All you had to do was look at Rhears and that basket-knife sharpened thin like a dagger, a-hangen as innocent agen his pant leg, to see he didn't mean to take no whuppen. He must have felt in his Afrykin way that pa had betrayed him. Folks jest didn't whup their house servants, and Rhears was a-meanen to teach pa his manners. Niggers can think straight up to a certain point, and beyond that the steadiest of'm let their senses fly like buckshot, high to scatter. It never struck him that Della needed her whuppen. No, sir, he was jest a-standen in the door tellen pa he warn't his marster.

Now ma might have thought that pa ought, with his proper strength, to show him who his marster was. There ain't no doubt but what he had to show it in some way, or he might as well have sold all his niggers for any work he could a got out'n them. Still it was a powerful big risk to run. And it was plain she was a-meanen for him to run it.

Anyway, that was the construction the kin put on it, and it was natural they would. But it never satisfied me. I got it in my head that Rhears warn't the only person on Long Gourd who didn't claim pa his marster. Before I tell you what I mean, give me a little taste of that shuck juice— half a glass'll do, jest enough to settle the dust in my belly. I'm about to choke to death with the drought.

Aah . . . that's sweet to the taste. Now, sir. You'll excuse me if I lean over and whisper this. *That other body was ma.* I know it ain't a-goen to sound right, for she and pa had the name of be-en a mighty loven couple. But a man and woman can fight and still love. Most of'm enjoy fighten. I ain't never seen one get wore out with it. They can go on with a fight for years. Can git fat on it. When they win out, they put the man down amongst the chillun and give him a whuppen when he forgits his manners or sasses back. But if he's stout enough to put her and keep her in her place, she don't hold it agin him. She's proud to think she picked such a game one. That's how come I never married. I'm peaceful by nature. Ain't but one thing ever gits me fighten mad: that's putten salt in my whiskey. That riles me. I'll fight a elyphant then.

Well, sir, that morning Della was late. Ma had had to send for her twice, and she come in looken like the hornets stung her. She fluffed down to her sewen and went to work in a sullen way, her lip stuck out so far it looked swole. And they ain't nothen meaner-looken than a blue-black, shiney lip of a sullen nigger woman. It looks like a devil's pillow.

Directly ma said, "Della, take out that seam and do it over again."

"Take it out yourself, if it don't suit," she flounced back.

In a second pa was on his feet: "Woman, lay down that sewen and come with me."

Them was his words; and if a nigger can git pale, Della done it. She seen right away what a mistake she'd made. She fell on the floor and commenced to grab at ma's skirts. "Don't let him whup me, mistiss. Don't let him." For a while ma didn't say a word.

"Get up off that floor and come with me," said pa again.

"Mister MacGregor, what are you going to do with this girl?"

Pa never made her no answer. He walked over and lifted Della up by the arm.

"Don't you tech me; you don't dare tech me. I belongs to mistiss."

Pa shuck her till her teeth rattled; then she stopped her jumpen and goen on and stood there a-tremblen like a scared horse.

"Mister MacGregor," come ma's even tones, "you're not going to punish that girl. She's mine."

And with that pa turned and said in a hard, polite way he never used before to ma: "And so are you mine, my dear." Then he nodded to Della to go before him, and she went.

When he came back, ma was standen in the middle of the floor just where he had left her. She hadn't moved a peg. She just stood there, stiff as a poker, her head thrown up and her eyes as wide as a hawk's.

"I have whipped Della and sent her to the field for six months. If at the end of that time she has learned not to forget her manners, she may take up again her duties here. In the meantime, so you will not want, I've sent for P'niny. If you find her too old or in any way unsuitable, you may take your choice of the young girls."

He waited a breath for her answer and when it didn't come, got on his horse and went runnen over the back road down to the fields. No other words passed between them that day. At supper the meal went off in quick order. There wasn't no good old-fashioned table talk. Everybody was as polite to one another as if they was visiten. Ma sat at the foot, froze to her chair. Pa at the head like a judge expecten shooten in the court. We knew somethen was bound to blow up and bust; and I do believe if somebody had tromped on a hog bladder, we chillun'd a jumped under the table.

Next mornen it come. That bow of pa's, as he let go of the gun, was his answer to the challenge. For you might almost say pa had whupped ma by proxy. And here was Rhears, agen by proxy, to make him answer for it . . . a nigger and a slave, his mistress's gallant, a-callen her husband and his marster to account for her. I don't reckon they'd been any such mixed-up arrangement as that before that time; and I know they ain't since.

I scrouched back in the corner and watched, so scared my eyes turned loose in their sockets. If Jesus Christ had a touched me on the shoulder and said, "Come on, little boy, and git your harp," I'd a no more looked at him than if he'd a been my dog come to lick me. For pa and Rhears was a-eyen one another. This fight was to be accorden to no rules. I saw straight off it would start fist and skull and work into stomp and gouge. If pa didn't manage to git that knife away from the nigger, it would be cut and grunt as well.

Pa was the slimberer of the two, but he wouldn't a looked it away from Rhears. From neckèd heel up he was six feet—no, six feet four—and his boots raised him an ench higher. Right away he took a quick easy step forward, and both of'm tied their muscles together. Rhears tightened his fingers around the knife. I looked at pa's breeches. They fit him tight; and the meat rolled up, snapped, then quivered under the cloth. His butt give in at the sides and squeezed away its sitten-down softness. His waist drawed in and pumped the wind into his chest, a-pushen out his shoulders just as easy and slow. I don't believe you could have found a man in the whole cotton country hung together any purtier.

Pa, quick-like, sunk his hand in and around the black flesh of Rhears' neck. The knife swung backwards, but pa grabbed it with his left hand before it could do its damage. A breath, and Rhears was a-spinnen round the room. The basket-knife lay in the door as still as any of the pine floor boards. This rattled the nigger some. He had figured on gitten Mister MacGregor in the door, where he could a used the knife to advantage. Fighten in his mistress's room, a place he didn't feel at home in, rattled him some more. So before he could come to himself good, pa lambed a blow into his black jaw. It was a blow fit to down a mule, but Rhears shook his head and run in to close; changed quick; dropped low and butted. Four quick butts jambed pa agen the wall, where he saved his guts by grabben Rhears' shoulders—to hold. That kinky hunk of iron slowed down. Both men shook under the strain. The noise of destruction held up. All you could hear was a heavy, pumpen blowen, like two wind-broke horses drawen a killen load . . . then a rippen cry from Rhears' coat—and it was good broadcloth —as it split both ways from the small of his back. Both men drawed in their breaths for a long second.

Pa shifted neat and shoved hard. Rhears smashed a

sewen table top into kindlen wood before he hit the wall. That table saved his neck, or I'm as good a man as I used to be. Before he could get his bearens, pa was a-pounden his head into the hard pine floor. I looked for the brains to go a-splatteren any time, and I begun to wonder how far they would slide on the floor's smooth polish. But God never made but one thing tougher'n a nigger's head—and that's ironwood. Slowly Rhears raised up and, with a beautiful strain of muscles, got to his feet. Then him and pa went round the room. It looked like that bangen had set the nigger crazy. A stranger comen into the room would a thought he was set on breaken up ever stick of furniture, a-usen pa for his mallet. Once the two of'm come close to ma, so close the wind they made blowed her skirts; but never a peg did she move. She held as rigid as a conjure woman.

Directly the nigger begun to wear some. All that crazy spurt of energy hadn't done him no good. Gradually pa's feet touched the floor more and more; then they didn't leave it. The panten got heavier, more like bellows. A chair got in their way. They went over it. They did a sight of rollen—up to the door crowded with house servants, all a-looken like they had fell in the ash-hopper. You could follow how far they'd rolled by the sweat on the floor. It looked like a wet mop had been run by a triflen hand. Then, sir, my hairs straightened up and drawed in to hide under the scalp. Rhears had ended up on top and was a-shiften to gouge. Pa looked all wore down. I tried to holler to ma to shoot, but my throat was as parched as it is right this minute. . . . Thank you, sir. You are very generous.

Have you ever seen a long dead limb stretched between sky and droppen sun? Well, that's how still ma held on to that gun of pa's. I couldn't stand to see them black thumbs go down. As I turned my head, I heard the nigger holler. Pa had jerked up his knee and hit him in a tender spot. He fell back and grabbed himself. It must have been an accident, for pa made no move to take advantage of the break. He just lay there and let Rhears take hold of himself and git at pa's throat. I never seen such guts in nobody, nigger or white man. Bump went pa's head on the floor. Bump and agen. Ever time he lifted pa, he squeezed tighter. Ever time he come down he pushed him forward.

It had been one of them frosty December mornens, and a fire had been burnen in the chimney since first light. The front stick had been burned in two and left between it and the back stick a heap of red and blue hickory coals. They don't make no hotter fire than that. I saw right away what Rhears had in mind. Every time he bumped my father's head against the floor, he was that much nearer the hearth. Pa wriggled and jerked, but his wind was cut and the black blood ran into his eyes. Those heavy black hands growed deep in the red, greasy flesh of pa's neck.

They moved slower towards the fire, for pa had at last clamped his legs in a way to slow'm down. Then I saw him reach for his pocket. Rhears didn't see this move. His eyes was bucked on what they had in mind to do, and the heat from the hickory logs made'm swell with a dark, dry look of battle luck. After some fumblen pa finally brought out his knife. He opened it in a feeble way over the nigger's back, and let it rip and tear through his ribs. The blood first oozed; then spouted. It fell back from the knife like dirt from a turnen plow. Then pa made a jab back of the kidneys. That done for him. He grunted; turned loose and rolled over like a hunk of meat.

Staggering to his feet, pa went over and leaned agen the mantel. Directly Rhears spoke up, so low you could hardly hear him:

"Marster, if you hadn't got me, I'd a got you."

Then he shook with a chill, straightened out, and rolled back his eyes. Mister MacGregor looked at him a minute before he turned to his wife. And then no words passed his mouth. He reached out his hand and she walked over and handed him the gun. He reached over the mantel and, his arms a-tremblen, set the gun back in its rack.

"Bring me a pan of warm water, the turpentine, and the things out of my medicine chest." That was ma speaken, sharp and peremptory, to the servants in the doorway. "And take this body out of here," she added in a tone she used when the girl Sally failed to dust behind the furniture.

"Sit down in that chair, Mister MacGregor, so I can dress your wounds."

Pa done what she told him. She worked away at him with deft, quick fingers. Directly I heard her in a off-hand way, her head benden over and her hands busy wrappen:

"Colonel Winston will be through here on his way South. I think it would be best to sell him Della."

"I think that, my dear," said pa, "would be the most sensible thing to do."

A STORY:

ortiz's mass

FATHER FRANCISCO OF THE ROCK TIED THE CORDS OF THE
amice, dropped the flowing alb over his head and quickly,
with deft and accustomed fingers, fastened the girdle about
his middle. His server handed him the stole. The cords of
the girdle were brought up, looped, the maniple slipped on
his arm, and then with care he put on the rich and stiffly
embroidered chasuble. Abstractedly he looked through the
door of the hut. The altar stone was in place upon the
cypress log, the crucifix stood up, slim and pure, before
the great dirt wall of the mound. Upon the corporal the
Sacred Vessels waited. The flames of the two candles, he
noticed, twisted and curled before the morning breeze. He
should have ordered some kind of screen. He turned to his

server to bid him find something, changed his mind. The army had already gathered, the entire army. They had never shown themselves so eager for worship before. He would speak to them on the vice of curiosity. He continued to look abstractedly at his server. That Cacho was a worthless lad, slothful and he feared already marked with every sin. Assisting at Mass in spurs. Perhaps, though, there was nothing vain in this. It was only the way the boy wore them. "Cacho, take off those spurs." The acolyte looked as if he would disobey; then leaned over and reluctantly unbuckled the straps. The spurs dropped to the ground with a clink.

He must perform well this morning. The Governor had asked Mass to be said especially for this Ortiz. For twelve years the Christian had gone without hearing God's Word. Twelve years . . . the man had forgotten how long it had been. He had had to ask the time he was cast away. It was fearful to contemplate, this loss of the knowledge of time. Day following dark day, time hurrying him to death and judgment, when time would be no more, and he so deep in savage sloth as not to know or care. One had only to look to see that he had been wholly lost. There in the presidio rubbing the Governor's shoulders for greeting like any heathen until even the Governor had mistaken him for an Indian. "No, no, Ortiz, greet your lord in a civil way," the Constable had said and laughed.

It was not a thing to laugh about. There was too great levity in certain quarters of this armament. Ah, Holy Mary, ever Virgin, is it not enough that Your Son has died once so bitterly for man? Is the spirit so weak, so ready to fall into forgetfulness, that each morning He must be sacrificed afresh? Must He each day cross the brook of Kedron and climb the Mount of Olives, climb anew to his agony, to the kiss of betrayal? Must He stand by the Roman Pilate's couch as he laves his hands and hear, Crucify Him! Crucify Him! from the lips of those who when He went down into the city sang hosannas and cast palm branches at the feet of his ass? *Ah! Jerusalem! Jerusalem! Thou that stonest the prophets! How often would I have gathered ye under my wings as a hen doth her chicks, and ye would not! Ye would not!*

"Look, Father," Cacho said. "Juan Ortiz dressed in the black velvet the Governor gave him. . . . How strangely he walks."

Father Francisco raised his eyes.

Beside de Soto's brisk step Ortiz swung wide his legs and set each foot down in place after the other. He twisted his neck as though the collar choked him. He scratched himself. It was a cool morning, but sweat gathered in beads on his forehead.

"—besides he gave him his second best coat of mail, a breastplate of silver gilt and . . ."

"Peace, boy," the priest said sharply.

Ortiz paused uncertainly. The Governor was sinking to his knees and crossing himself. For an instant Ortiz watched his superior; then quickly followed him to the ground. Father Francisco sighed. At least he has not forgotten to do reverence before the altar. . . .

"Did you speak, Father?"

Perhaps after all the Church is wise to make daily the Sacrifice of Our Lord, the Sacrifice which consecrates, the Consecration which is the Sacrifice—Christ Himself offering Himself.

"It is time, Father. The Governor looks this way."

The priest nodded his head and followed the acolyte out of the hut.

In nomine Patris, et Filii, et Spiritus Sancti.

He had come to the foot of the altar.

An object came between Ortiz and the crucifix. He ran his hand over his eyes, removed it: the priest was bowing and striking his breast—through my fault, through my fault, through my most grievous fault. Standing at a distance, contrite, the concealing heart punished, bruised, and humbled; the human race fallen and driven from Paradise: four thousand years of misery, sickness, and death, four thousand years of repentance for sin and hope in the promised Redeemer.

Again that promise was about to be fulfilled. If only he could quiet his body. Spasms had seized it the moment he sank to his knees, all trembling, before the Presence on the altar. Out of the forest at his back the light which flows before the sun fell upon the silver cross and, as he watched, it ran with blood. For him it ran. He beat his breast in a frenzy of remorse and fear and hope, and then he grew very quiet, his head thrown slightly back as though transfixed suddenly by a blinding light. In that instant he felt the darkness of his purgatory slip from his eyes . . .

He was pulling towards the shore, he and González, dipping their oars in the limpid water, pulling towards the letter held up on the stick by the Indians. Surely there was no treachery. The companions they had left on the brigantine were overcautious. Obviously it was a letter left by de Narváez telling where he had gone, and to find him they had been sent out from Cuba. It was their service to look

into so plain a clue. And then some impulsion had made
him look back. The brigantine was riding at anchor and
it seemed that all on board were dead. The tiny men hung,
motionless, over the gunwales; the sails drooped; at the
water line the small craft leaned on the sea. In that moment
he knew that he and González were lost. He turned to
González to speak of his forewarning, but González was
bending over the oar. And what could he say to him? The
Indians ran down into the water and pulled them ashore.
Others came whooping from the forest. González drew his
sword. Once he heard him cry out, only once so quickly
was it done . . . on the sand the flat and naked trunk quivering
and spurting blood, the dark sponge of sand, an arm, a leg,
the hair, the very privates of his companion swinging in the
air. Cries and whoo-whoo-whoops. He shut his eyes and then
he felt a stinging at his shoulders. He was being pulled along
a path through the forest.

The priest ascended to the altar, bent over it.
Oramus te, Domine . . .

A short distance from the gulf, but deep in the forest,
the Indians halted and built a fire. All but two scouts who
went off to stand watch gathered around in silence as the
war leader stretched González' scalp on a hoop, tied it with
gut, and carefully, so as not to burn the hair, dried it
over the coals. This done, the savage took a red paint from
his pouch and painted the scalp and the hoop. His server
brought a branch of the green-leaved pine, and to this the
hair was tied. Then calling the scouts, the leader set out
again on the path. As he, Ortiz, followed in file, his eyes
would not turn away from the arms and legs of González

scattered in the hands of his captors. "He was here. He is gone—gone." He repeated the word as if by repetition he might surprise the meaning, but the words were like the sounds of a foreign tongue. He began again. "An hour ago he was alive and pulling at the oar." He tried to see him, but just as González' form was about to appear an arm or the hoop of hair swung before his eyes. Then the leader whooped and answering whoops came back through the trees. He turned cold: they had reached the Indian town.

The trees gave out at an open ground on one side of the town. As they came in view, the Indians spread out in single file, each a few yards behind the other, whooping and insulting the prisoner. They entered the yard singing the death song, raising at intervals the shrill whoo-whoo-whoop. Women and children, young warriors and old men came out to meet them. In the center of the yard stood a pole. To this his captors tied him and then carried the hair and González' members into the town. His turn would come soon, he thought, and as he began to envy the fate of his friend, the crowd gave way. An Indian of great dignity was coming towards him, at his side an old man with an owl-skin headdress and claws through his ears. Seven tattooed warriors followed close behind. Ortiz looked narrowly at the Indian but something made him avoid his face. He was crowned with eagle feathers. From his shoulders fell a skin held up by an attendant. About his ankles loops of shells tinkled as he walked. Upon his arms he wore bracelets of shell. Upon his breast hung a copper plate. And then, as he drew nearer, Ortiz saw the face. Below the feathered head, below the malevolent eyes, two holes gaped for nostrils. Through a lipless mouth teeth parted in a perpetual snarl.

Slowly the Indian approached. Like doom he bore down on the Christian. On he came to within a foot of the pole. Ortiz pressed his back to the wood but the Indian had stopped. He tried to look away but the cold red eyes sank into his and held them fast. Strands of flesh about the death-like holes trembled as the breath sucked in and out. A long time the two men confronted each other; then slowly large tears gathered under the flaming lids and rolled down the tattooed face. Suddenly the cacique threw back his head and gave a wail of despair. The cries were taken up and rose through the crowded yard. At the height of the wailing the cacique fell upon Ortiz with his hands. The long nails scratched at his eyes, tore the flesh from his face. As suddenly the cacique turned and walked away.

From where he was tied, Ortiz could see the war leader's house. In front of it, on either side of the doorway, two rows of women faced each other, singing in their soft shrill voices a solemn, moving air. They would sing for a minute and then keep perfectly silent for a long interval, when they began again. And as they sang, they gave their legs a small muscular motion without lifting their feet or bending a joint. All night they kept this up. Every two or three hours the war leader came out and danced about his war pole facing the door. Three times he went around it, against the sun, whooping and singing.

Towards dawn Ortiz fell asleep. He had scarcely closed his eyes when he was aroused. His guards were stripping him of his clothes. Half-dazed, he leaped up and kicked out about him. They struck him with a club and he came to his senses. Overhead he heard a hissing and popping noise. He looked up. A burning brand had been tied to the pole. Moccasins were being put on his feet, bear skin with the black fur turned out. At one corner of the yard women were piling brush and sticks under a low scaffold. Black on his feet; fire over his head. He had received his sentence. Black is the sign for death.

Around the corner of the yard the Indians gathered. Between him and the scaffold women were forming in two lines. He saw them go to the leader of the party who had taken him and give into his hands an herb. Suddenly he saw he was naked. He began to shiver and shame overwhelmed him. The cacique passed with his family and nobles and sat himself on a bench covered by brush. At a signal from the cacique the guards unbound Ortiz' hands. The women began to jeer and shake their sticks. At the head of a line an old woman, her thin gray hair falling over her face, danced, her long, dry paps flapping at her sides. Feebly she raised a stone hoe and shook it. A girl turned about, lifted the moss over her rear and thrust it towards him. His guards pushed him forward. He held back. They jabbed him with the ends of their clubs. Not until then did he understand what they meant him to do. He took in his breath and began to run down the lane. The sticks and hoes fell upon his back and shoulders. He dodged and struck out at faces which came too close. Behind he heard the clatter of sticks beating together. Half way through he stumbled. As he was going down, a blow across the eyes blinded him and he lay for a full half minute and took his punishment. A fat leg came down by his ear. He grabbed and bit it, jumped up and butted his way clear, caught two women off balance and rammed their heads together. Gales of laughter greeted this stratagem.

When he came to, he was tied to a wooden frame. The frame was raised in the air and two old men were putting clay on his hair. He looked at his feet and his hands. They began to throb. "I am a Saint Andrew's cross," he said. And then four men lifted him and carried him across the yard to the scaffold. He began to notice the sounds, the death whoops and shaking of rattles, but most of all he noticed the high, shrill yelps of the women. He got a whiff of smoke, a crackling persistently travelling, like a lone man running through brush. So would the last man run on the day when the graves open and give up their dead. . . . A yellow flame leapt up at his side. It was thin and without heat. Under him he felt a round spot of heat. He squirmed out of its way. The cords cut into his flesh. A hot awl bored at his ribs, melting and spreading. He raised up. It still bored. Another struck his backbone. He began to scream. His screams were drowned by the laughter of the Indians. . . .

The priest returned to the center of the altar.
Kyrie, eleison.
   Lord, have mercy upon us.
Christe, eleison.
   Christ, have mercy upon us.

Mercy, mercy, mercy. He was lying on the floor of a cabin, his dry lips moving in supplication. Soft hands were spreading a cool paste over his blisters. He closed his eyes not to see for fear it would cease, in fear that it was not true but an illusion of pain. The hands continued to soothe, and where they passed the sharp throbbing grew duller and he could feel the heat of the fever. He tried to remember what it was to suffer from fire but his senses were dull and blank. Pain cannot be heard or seen or touched or smelt.

It lacks a taste. It has no memory. Under the cool hands his mind wandered, grew drowsy.

When he awoke splinters of light fell through the cane walls. He had slept into doom and out again or was this another station in his progress? He sat up, but the motion twisted his wounds so that, leaning on his arms, he made a low moan. It was then he saw the girl. She was standing by him and words came out of her mouth, and she pointed to the couch. The skins were damp and his own odor was mixed with the stronger smell of cat. Watching the girl, he let himself carefully down on his side. She did not come nearer or move away. Her hair hung loose over her shoulders and the moss skirt hung loose about her thighs and as they looked at each other he understood it was she who had saved him from the frame. And then an old woman passed between them and gave him a cool, slimy drink out of a conch shell.

He did not count the days, but quickly, so it seemed, quickly, his body mended, although there must have been a time when the flesh under his blisters had mortified. By bending and straining his neck he could see the track of worms. How close, he thought, the worms had come to the full measure of their feast but for his luck, the unaccountable, the against-all-odds luck. Or was it luck? What had she seen in him, scratched and bleeding beyond any comeliness? Had it been pity or had it . . . The old woman, her mother, the first wife of the lipless, earless, gaping cacique, had said, moons later—when he had come to be held in some esteem—had said that it seemed to them— to them—a pity for one so young, without war honors, a boy with smooth and unpricked skin, to be burned like a fighter who has brought in much hair. And when the girl had begged his life of her father, the cacique saw only the child he loved. He forgot the dishonor the Christians had done him, forgot his mother thrown to the dogs. Her he could forget now that the hair of González had released her spirit from haunting the eaves of the lodge. Little did he, Ortiz, think that comfort would ever come from seeing the hair of his friend waving at the end of a pole. This scalp had saved his life, for once the dead are at peace the living do not recall them to mind lest memory renew their sorrow. But Ucita, though he could forget his mother, found always fresh cause to remember his shame and his grief. Dipping a shell into the great jar of water, he would see the two holes where his nose should be, the fangy teeth, the clipped ears such as adulterers have. And he would hurl the shell into the jug, raise the whoop of grief.

Ortiz would hear and flee to the woods and there he would stay until the girl, coming upon him like silence, would tell him it had passed. He might return to the town, not to the lodge but to the hut of the wind clan whom the skunk, Ucita's clan, called nephew. Then quietly one day he would sit down with the uncles of his master, dip into the same pot with him and them, first throwing a choice piece of fat into the fire to make it merry. But as the days passed and he grew strong and well, the cacique's anger returned. The Indian would not look at him or in any way recognize his presence, but once by chance Ortiz turned and saw him watching, and he knew that some evil was preparing in the cacique's mind.

But those days he was too weary for thinking or fear. The women set him to menial tasks but mostly he brought in the wood. They gave him a stone axe and thongs to tie the sticks and all day he must pass through thick woods to be torn by thorns and brush and worn away lifting and carrying. How simple one good Biscayan axe would have made his task! The sun brought sores to his shoulders and chest; the wind parched them; the heavy loads tore them afresh, made them bleed. And then he would lie down by the wood, too weak from weariness and bleeding to drag it or lift it. In those moments his comfort was the Lord Jesus who had suffered and bled for him.

One morning a man of the potato clan ran out of his house with a lighted brand and waved it over his head, lamenting and crying out; then he dipped the brand into water and watched it sink down. The cacique's wife came out of the lodge and stood by Ortiz and all the people came out and watched the Indian. "What happens, old woman?" Ortiz asked. She replied, "The spirit of his son has left its body." When he returned that night, green boughs of mourning hung all about. For four days the child's kin, at morning and evening, whooped and cried around the house where it had dwelt so that its spirit would not linger to haunt them. The morning of the fifth day the cacique spoke to Ortiz, "You will watch the bones of the dead," he said.

Stepping in their tracks, he followed the two old beloved men. At first he had been pleased at his change of occupation but now that he was on his way to watch the dead his thoughts turned sober. Instinctively he felt that his position was more precarious than at any other time since he had been condemned to burn on the frame. He had begun to understand the beloved speech but more than that, he had learned somewhat the things the Indians held taboo, especially of the dangers to the sacred fire in polluted people. He had watched the women at their time of the moon slip into the woods to stay until their uncleanness had passed, and in that time he knew how careful they were never to let the wind blow by them to others or wash in water that would flow by the town. He had seen war parties withdraw into the lodge of their leader and fast for three days, with a Knower watching the youngest to make sure they drank the white drink and kept away from their women, so that no pollution could damage the ark of war and bring disaster upon the war party. It was indeed serious to watch the dead, or he would not be so carefully escorted. Four times they had made him wash in the stream and chew green tobacco until he had retched and vomited. And the girl had slipped him a sabbia to keep him from harm. It was wrapped tight in white deer skin and tied to his flap. Very carefully she had taught him the song to sing and what to do to make him see well at night. She had tried to steal a true male sabbia, for that had many powers. It could charm a deer within range of the arrow and what could charm a deer would charm a woman. She had said this openly and frankly, coming close so that the moss about her middle teased his thighs and he reached out to take her but she shook her head. They could not have love with him as he was, a boy set down among women. So the cacique had planned, although it was known to all when she saved him from the frame that she had seen he was good and without blemishes. Perhaps soon now, if he guarded well the bones. But there were many perils— the wolves that would come stealing the breath of the bodies they loved and the ghosts of the dead who were like wolves of the air. And then she gave him some hilis hatki to chew. This would drive away the ghosts, but he must watch the old beloved men as they approached and do as they did.

And then she slipped away, for he would be called to purify himself and she must not be seen. . . .

The priest finished the Collect. He placed both hands upon the Missal and faced the east. *O Orient, splendor of light eternal, thou Sun of Justice, come and enlighten those who are sitting in darkness and in the shadow of death—* Ortiz watched his lips, moving swiftly and soundlessly, as he read the Epistle. He could not hear but through the priest's lips passed all the prophets, soundlessly to the ear but crying in the heart, out of the wilderness smelling of goats, in the streets where the stench of the market rose with the words. . . . And that one man sent from God who is not the Light but is sent to bear witness of the Light, the Light born not of blood, nor of the will, nor of the will of the flesh. . . .

The old beloved men were no longer moving. He stopped at their heels. He was not abrupt and yet his motions beside theirs seemed violent and clumsy. Their very stillness was motion, the motion of sap hidden under the bark, their walking a kind of flowing, an unobtrusive extension, an integral part, of the wilderness which enclosed them and him. Not a leaf shook as they passed, but where he went vines and thorns leaped to bind him. An overwhelming feeling of strangeness oppressed him. He would never discover the mystery of this absolute oneness between the Indians and their world. And yet to live he must do more than understand it.

They were taking hilis hatki out of their pouches. Quickly he put some into his mouth and began to chew it. He tasted the earth which still clung to the herb and his spit ran bitter, and into his nose crept an odor, sweet and faintly nauseous, a thin cool odor which stuck like glue. He chewed and watched. The old men spat out of one corner of the mouth, then out of the other. Turning slowly and with slow dignity they spat four times each way; and as they moved, the stuffed horned owls on their heads turned and bowed, turned and bowed, and their red eyes watched him as he followed the ritual, step by step. Then his mouth grew dry and silently he dropped the root at his feet. The old men had faced about and were viewing him gravely.

The oldest put two darts into his hand and pointed to the green thickets to the right; then, stepping around him, the Indians departed. Not more than a hundred paces away he saw through the trees what looked like great eagle nests, but eagles do not build in the low forked limbs. "They build in the tops of the highest and the deadest trees," he said aloud. All at once he felt an acute nostalgia for his wood-gathering, the buffets of the old women and all the contempt which had been heaped upon him since he had cried out at the frame. He looked at the darts. They were good ones, flint-pointed and balanced well. He gripped them tight and began walking towards the burial ground, and then drifting through the air he smelled the same cool sweet odor, invisible, resistant, clinging yet penetrating, surrounding him yet passing, and suddenly thick with nausea. He reached up to brush it from his face. It had saturated his hands. He leaned over and wiped them on the ground. It rose in waves from the ground. Holding his breath, he pulled moss out of the trees and stuffed it in his nose. The moss was corrupt. He tore it out, drew in his breath. His stomach heaved but he held it down and ran into the center of the burial ground. There surrounded by the rough log coffins caught haphazardly in trees or resting on frames, he slowly freed his lungs, tried the air. One short gasp and the full force of afterdeath, streaming in viscid flow from the adipose substance of the dead, tightened like a vise about his middle and threw him to the ground.

With lips clenched he thought the borders of purgatory must be like this, and hunted for those bones which were driest, for he knew that when the bones were utterly clean Ucita's people gathered them into the house with the owl on its roof, the owl with the red bead eyes. He found a tree and sat down by it, burying his face in his arms, and waited for the retching to cease. He must have dozed, for when he looked up it was dark. A slight wind was at his back and the air had blown almost clean. Across the yard he could see the glow of the expiring fire which had burned at the foot of the child's coffin. Not trusting the wind, he held his breath and brought away on a piece of bark enough live coals to make a fire of his own. This was a serious business, his fire, for in this coastal country when the sun went under, the air grew chill and damp. He had awakened shivering. He fed the coals with moss and twigs and blew them into a blaze. He broke off dead limbs, picked up what down wood he could find and soon had the flames leaping. He warmed himself on all sides. Once through the yellow swerving light he thought he saw the coffins shift and swell. He smiled at this, so much better did he feel now that he was warmed and cheered. He was even beginning to have some liking for what he had to do. He was alone, in a disagreeable place, but he was alone and that was something he had not known for months. Sleeping in the round lodge with Indians of all ages and sexes where the air was never free of smoke nor the room of smells, he had not realized how much he had missed the privacy of Christendom. Even in the woods gathering sticks he had felt eyes spying from behind every bush, and in the town the Indians went freely about and strangers would walk into a dwelling as if they were come to their own house with an "I am come." And the only reply, "Good, you are come." They would leave as suddenly. "I go now." "What, you go?"

But when the fire fell into its coals and the night settled thick and close about, to guard the dead did not seem so good a thing. He reached into his pouch and took out the sabbia and rubbed it vertically over his eyes; then horizontally. This would help him, she had said, to see the wolves and other scavengers who were now his enemies. Yet it was not the wolves but the lids of his eyes which troubled him. They grew rough and dry and his head rolled heavy as a stone. It was a long straining to keep awake. At first he had been able to follow the sharp soft snap of a twig, hear the soft pads, he thought he could hear them, as the animal trotted away. Perhaps it was a fox or a mink, or even a rat. And once he had seen shining the still eyes of a cat. Many of the grandfathers of Ucita's people are out tonight, he said softly to himself, but I shall waste no darts on them or else I shall have to pay forfeit to their kin. But the time came when he no longer heard. The time came when there was no time, only the heavy slow effort of the will to stiffen his neck and shake out the heavy fog which settled over his eyes, which blew thick and slow through his eyes, into his head, weighting it, pulling it down, down, and a down . . . down . . .

Dominus vobiscum
Et cum spiritu tuo
Oremus . . .

He sat up, his eyes all awake and his heart beating: it was broad light. Voices wailed, low and then high. He leapt to his feet and in a glance took in the coffins. They were all intact. Where the child lay, two women sat before it wailing. Their white mulberry bark mantles they had drawn over their heads. He could not see who they were. Obviously the child's mother and grandmother or two old aunts. He wondered if they had seen him lying asleep by the dead fire. If they had, they would surely report it. Perhaps their grief had saved him. His luck rather. Suddenly he remembered that malevolent look on Ucita's face and knew why he had set him to watching the dead. The cacique had foreseen the trap of the long vigil, that almost irresistible drowsiness that comes to all who watch without relief, that comes just before dawn.

Carefully he walked towards the women. They did not hear him approach. Overnight, he repeated it, overnight he had come to walk like an Indian. He moved into the sound of their voices. "Why did you leave us, Little One? Did your bow not please you, the one your uncle gave you to make war on the rats and flies?" The woman paused as though listening for an answer and the older one's wails fell into a low, an almost voiceless moan. The woman continued, "Did your playboys displease you? Perhaps you feared the gartooth's scratch? It was but to make you manly. The Dog-cacique told you he would not kill you. Had you not enough to eat? Long did I let you suck—Why did you leave us?"

Very quietly he slipped away and when he came near the town, he washed in the stream four times and then went to the sofki pot to eat, without fear of polluting the holy fire. Afterwards he lay down on a skin. He lay under a great water oak, and the hanging moss stirred the gray air over his face. He had thought to sleep all day and prepare himself for the night's vigil, but sleep he could not. To stretch at his ease without any to bother him was so great a freedom that he lay in a kind of stimulated doze, awake and yet with all the ease of sleep. The old women no longer abused him and the old men, the young warriors, saluted him respectfully and called him Ispani. He knew he was still a slave but at last he had a name. Idly he thought that to be free among Christians is to have a place, but to be free among Indians you must have a name and a name must be won. You must bring in hair or do some great feat on the hunt or pass the examinations set by the Knowers and learn to read the secrets of nature. None of these proofs did he have to his credit and yet they had given him a name. The fighter receives his after he shows the scalp. What had he, Ortiz, shown? Nothing, for to move among dangers is not enough with Indians. And then it came to him: they had given him a name because they considered him as one lost, and bravely lost.

Accept, O Holy Father, Almighty and Eternal God, this unspotted Host which I, Thine unworthy servant, offer unto Thee.

Back in the burial ground towards the close of day, his hours of rest, unrest, gone, for who is cunning enough to forfend the many ghosts that wander the caverns of the wilderness or upside down walk the roads most used by men, wandering in search of their substantial kin, crying blood for blood that they may travel west; or when their own kin fail them, take blood, any blood, to speed them on their way to the land of the Breath-Holder. This was what the Indians were thinking when they called him Ispani. Nor did they forget that he must watch in darkness when wolves see and man is blind.

—grant that by the Mystery of this water and wine . . .

He heaped wood onto his fire. This night he would not fall asleep, nor any other night. Ucita should not pay off his score with him. It would be hard at first but in time he would learn to turn night into day. He would escape. The chance would come. There was the cacique of the Mococos. He had asked for him. The two tribes were at peace but they would not always be at peace. Some fine day a boy would covet to sit with the men or he would ask a girl to lie with him and she would jeer and say she was unworthy to lie with one who has brought in so much hair. And the boy would hide where the Mococo people went to fish and get his hair. And the path would run red. Then he would get his chance. Until then he must wait and keep his watch.

We offer unto Thee, O Lord, the chalice of salvation . . .

Waiting would not be too bad. A man could be put to hard measures and still find life bearable. It would be more than bearable if he could persuade the girl to lie with him. She had made it plain that she had saved him for this very purpose. The cacique had thwarted them by setting him down among the women, but that was over. Nothing now stood in the way but his occupation. Just how that interfered he was uncertain. She probably feared to follow him into so many known and unknown dangers. Perhaps it

was taboo in a burial place. He must find out. Certainly the
odor of corruption did not make for love. But there were
other ways, there must be other ways. The days were long
and the woods deep, but how the nights would pass if she
would spend them with him, if not actually here, then close
by, near enough for him to be at hand if anything should
go amiss. There was a fine retreat near the spring, where
the moss made of the ground a bed, deep and soft and
cool . . .

He rose from before the fire lighter than a deer. Out of
the darkness she came walking towards him. Everywhere
it was dark but she walked in an even light. And then he
was beside her, close enough to touch but he did not touch
her. He called her name yet no sound came from his lips.
He reached to draw her to him but without moving she
evaded him, smiling and shaking her head. Not now, she
seemed to say. When we have passed the dangers on our
way, but not now. She took his hand and they began to
walk up the air. Strange, he thought, that one can walk the
air, and yet it is no different from a path. He could have
fled had he known. She was smiling and holding his hand.
She was smiling when they reached a broad way strewn with
stones shining of milky light. Why, this is the spirits' road,
he said and she replied, Yes, of course. Then I must be . . .
You are, she replied.

How easy it is to die in Heathendom, he thought. No
purgatory, no hell, no sins to account for. Only to travel
without tiring, without hunger or thirst, across the sky
to the land of the Breath-Holder. What is it like in that
land, he thought. Lacking breath, he had only to think to
speak and she, thinking, replied, It is a warm pleasant country where maize grows all the year and springs never dry

up. In that land the nuts drop of their own accord near the cracking stone, the bear jars overflow with grease, and on the fire pots of sofki and venison forever simmer, for in any moon the hunter may hunt knowing he shall never lack for game.

It's a good land, he said. Let us make haste.

—There are no red towns but all are white and the people dance and play ball and feast without interruption, and that place which the fighter has loved most on earth he shall find again and raise his lodge.

—Let us be off.

I have loved, O Lord, the beauty of Thy house and the place where Thy glory dwelleth.

She had scarcely ceased to speak when the broad way they were travelling ran into a body of water. As far as he could see there was nothing but water, and his heart fell within him. Not one piragua lay on its bank.

This is the first danger, she said. If a woman has sold herself to a man and then sleeps with another, even though her ears are not cropped or her nose cut off, the water will not part for her. And if a man has spilled his own blood, he must swim, if he can swim it.

I have killed no man, he replied, and looked hard at the girl. She returned his look.

Like others, she said, I have had my pleasure at the time of the busk dances, but to no man have I sold my freedom, to no man until now.

Without pausing she walked down upon the water and he followed her. Before his eyes the water parted to right and left and the path of milky stones rolled through it.

The winds blew down and stood up like mounds of dirt, and they passed through without hurt.

But I have walked in my innocence; redeem me and have mercy.

The path rose through curving hills, the ways grew rough and full of stones, and the stones made caves. In these caves and along the ledges before them he saw where tribes of snakes had raised their towns. And on the path they danced and rolled the chunghe stone. Some shook their rattles, the big bull snakes beat the drum and around the fire, coiling and uncoiling, the Highland Moccasins danced the death dance. Slowly and cautiously they raised their heads and struck the air, and out of the rocks there came a noise as of a thousand pots hissing and singing.

Let us find some other way, he said to the girl. We cannot pass here.

There is no other way, she replied and pulled baksha branches, wrapping them close about his body. These will stop their fangs, she added and took his hand and led him through the stamping ground, and as they passed the fangs struck the baksha like hail.

The priest turned to the people:
Orate, fratres . . .

They climbed to the top of a mountain, a mountain so high that, standing on its very top, they could see the underside of the sky. Below lay a plain and beyond another mountain. There our journey ends, she said, where the sky ends. Between those two peaks we leave the path, passing out under the sky to the land we seek, but first we must overcome two other dangers.

What are they?

Without replying she led the way down into the plain. As they approached, he could hear from afar the whoops of death and the noise of men fighting. At the foot the path curved about a rock so high the sun never reached its base and, as he went around it, he could smell, rising from the slimy floor, the odor of the dead.

Let us hurry on, he said and, stooping beneath an escarpment, came out of the mountain onto the plain. She was beside him. He heard her say: Take this pipe and blow the smoke, first to the north, then to the east, and to the south, lastly towards the west where we go.

But he did not hear, watching the battle as it moved from side to side across the valley's floor. From above the valley had seemed a wide plain, but now he saw it for what it was, a basin with neither inlet nor egress except by way of the mountain they had come down and the one yet to climb. Eagerly he looked towards the last barrier, but it lay hidden in mist. And as he looked, the battle spread out before him. At the same instant he saw it in part and as a whole: each Indian who behind a tree pulled his bow, each separately and all together as they crept through the grass; each insult and whoop of defiance; each axe that fell and split a skull; each knife that took its hair—and those farthest away seemed of a size with those who fought near by. In between the two parties lay the path they must travel and over it the arrows so sped that they made a flickering darkness, and so fast the air whistled one shrill never-ceasing moan. And out of this clearly he heard a bell ringing three times and a voice saying *Sanctus, Sanctus, Sanctus.*

Who are these who fight and never die? he asked.

—They are those who walk the path without pipe or tobacco. Outcasts. Hunters and fighters who have died without proper burial.

—And must they fight forever thus?

She nodded her head. —Once struck by an arrow you may never leave this plain. But take this pipe and smoke it as I have directed and we shall pass invisibly by.

Very carefully he blew the smoke to the north, to the east, the south, the west and, as the smoke rose and disappeared, the sound of fighting died away, the warriors vanished, and the path ran unblocked over the stilled grass to the forest which circled the mountain at the other end of the basin.

We may now walk without fear, she said.

Be mindful, O Lord, of thy servant, Ortiz . . .

—Be mindful of your step, Ispani, as you climb. All our dangers are past but one and that one you alone must overcome.

—What is it?

—You will see.

He did not press her further, for suddenly he began to shiver. This chill is strange, he thought, and then he saw that frost lay heavy on the ground. The forest stood out in a clear cold light, bare of leaves. Brown shrivelled clusters hung in scattered patches to the oaks. The bark was tight and gray and dead. The sun fell to the ground in broad slick strips. Tree shadows lay athwart the strips flat and black and sharply lined. Where am I, he wondered, that a glance may bring winter where all was green and pleasant?

Hurry on, she said.

Walking faster, he came out of the forest to the foot of the mountain. Ice covered the path. A frozen river winding among the blue-white slopes fell motionless into a gorge. Out of the gorge a wind blew, driving the snow, piling it in heaps, and bringing to the upper air an endless blizzard.

—So this is the danger each faces alone, with no mantle to cover us, no sticks for a fire.

—Not yet. Climb.

—Climb to our death.

The dead cannot die; climb, she said and, speeding before him, disappeared into a flurry of snow.

Wait, he called and leapt after her.

Almost losing but never quite losing her, he followed running up the frozen path. The snow blinded his eyes, his feet drew tight with pain. They burned, they throbbed, they lost all feeling. He ran clumsily like a man in heavy shoes. He ran until he came to a place swept by winds. The ground turned soft. Not ten paces away he saw the girl. Bent slightly forward, she pulled along the path. Her hair and the most of her skirt stood out behind her, streaming through the air. As he watched, she jerked forward and stopped and the hair settled about her shoulders. She motioned to him and he came up beside her. The wind fell away, the air grew mild and all about them the sides of the mountain turned yellow green, buds swelled on the trees and underfoot strange herbs were in flower.

How is this? he asked.

Big winter, little winter and the wind moon . . . all have we passed. Now we are come to the planting moon. Look before you, she said.

He looked and saw that the mountain was no longer steep but sloped gently upwards into summer. From tender shoots to the full-grown stalks fields of maize followed the slopes. In the distance thunder storms passed, twisting and shaking the fields. In the very distance there was the brown look of drought.

There are still other moons, she said. The mulberry, the blackberry, the big ripening moon, and after them the black water and the whip-poor-will. There are many moons but only the four sacred seasons. Of all things they are the last.

Then all now is simple, he said.

—You carry your darts?

He held them up.

—Then let us be on our way.

Into winter, out of it; into, out of, spring; through summer, summer's heat, summer the ripening time, out of it and into autumn. And at last they came to a place where no seasons were. Time they had left where the path began. Now they stood in No-place, the last station. All the way they had walked, through every danger but the last, out of time, out of the seasons, out of space. They saw the sun's bed, where he slept with the moon. They saw night and day.

There, she cried.

—Where?

—There.

Two stones no taller than a man enclosed a passage. On either side the sky came down. Straining his eyes, he saw at the passage end a point of light, clear and bright and of such a blue that it struck pain at the back of his head.

Now, she said.

—Now?

—Throw well your darts, or we are lost.

As she spoke, down the passage a great wind rushed.

Strike this with a dart? he shouted, but the words blew
back into his mouth . . . he was being sucked towards the
entrance, the point of light went out, he stumbled and fell
to his knees; then darkness bolted from the mouth of the
cave. It passed over him and pinned his back to the ground.
It screamed as it passed and overhead he heard a noise as
of the mainsails of a ship popping in a storm.

Up, before it dives, she cried.

Then he saw the eagle curving on the air, its wings outspread and its talons drawn up against the smooth white
breast. From the tip of each tail feather hung the hair of
a hundred scalps. The bird soared like a thing of down,
curved into a spiral, and for one long instant held itself
poised in space; then it reached down its open beak, folded
its wings and, like a ball, dropped from the sky.

He sighted along the dart, flung it. With a side sweep
the bird caught the shaft in its beak and broke it.

Too soon, the girl cried.

He waited until he saw the two small nostrils in the beak.
He raised his arm and let the last dart fly. It went straight
and upward. The eagle screamed and caught itself in its
flight.

Now run for the cave, she shouted.

—Where is it?

Here! Here!

A dull heavy thud struck and the dark fell between them.
Where? he shouted. Where? returned his voice, high and
strained, and then he felt himself standing alone in a vast
silence, then in a tight, close, too familiar place. His body
was taut, his arm raised, and his hand clasping the darts.
At his feet spread a soft red glow. Even before he looked,
he knew that he had leapt up out of a dream before the

ashes of his fire and in that instant he received the full
impact of the world. And then out of the woods beyond
the burial ground he heard a thing being dragged through
the brush, haltingly, unresisting. . . .

He did not wait to think but ran where the corpse of
the child rested on its frame. The frame was empty. The
overturned coffin lay on the ground. He turned it over with
his foot—it was empty. His body was cold and running
with sweat. He held his breath and listened. No sound.
Perhaps he had never heard it. Perhaps he had heard it
in his dreaming and, like his voice, it had persisted into
consciousness. There was no time to lose. Quickly, instinctively, he entered the woods. Creeping, listening, alert and
calm, he moved swiftly through the undergrowth, and yet
carefully he broke apart the brush and set his foot down
as though he stalked the unquiet ghost of the dead. The
night air was cool and heavy. He had gone a short distance
when, cooler, heavier, throat-stopping, the odor familiar
above all others drifted across his path. The trail was now
plain. He followed it.

The priest spread his hands over the oblation.

His foot came to sand and scattering palmettos. His nose
gave him warning and then his ears. Somewhere to the front
he heard a crunching and suddenly a low growl. He stiffened.
Near the ground, within casting distance, the darkness shifted.
It shifted in silence. As he waited, his eyes explored the distance, measuring, isolating. . . . The darkness moved again,
the crunching began again. Slowly he raised his arm: the dart
swished, the blood rushed to his ears. He heard no muffled
growl, no slipping away, but his hand was salty. He threw

again. The second dart went wide of its aim, and he realized the spot of darkness which had been his target had vanished into the general darkness the moment the first dart left his hand. Suddenly he was shaking, all his nerve gone; yet he forced himself, unarmed as he was, to stumble about the palmettos hunting what he feared to find and yet must find. Suppose he had not struck the beast? Suppose it was lying in wait, wounded and cornered? Had it done away with the corpse of the child? Had the corpse, even, been stolen while he slept and he now pursued some other beast?

Chilled and disheartened, empty of courage, he returned to the burial yard. He threw twigs and sticks on the fire, and it popped and blazed. He looked at the flames, leaping with cheer and warmth. They brought him no comfort. And then before the heat the scars on his back began to twinge and draw. With a start he drew away. Slowly, as a man turns upon his doom, he turned to the fire. His gaze was still fixed upon it long after the flames had fallen away when, hours later, the dawn came and time returned quietly to the forest. So was he standing when he heard the Indians file into the burial yard.

Take and eat ye of this, for this is My Body.

The bell rang three times and the priest, kneeling, adored the Sacred Host and, rising, elevated it before the altar.

He waited for the discovery, waited, waited . . . a woman cried out in a high shrill wail. . . .

Take and drink ye all of this, for this is the Chalice of My Blood of the new and eternal Testament. . . .

The bell rang, the priest knelt and, rising, elevated the Chalice.

In a moment they would see him standing apart . . .

Striking his breast and raising his voice, the priest:
To us sinners also . . .

They seized him and led him, bound, before Ucita. They did not tie him when they brought him to the slave post. His two guards, Big-Handsome-Child and Two-Fell-Together, motioned to him to sit down and they sat on either side of him. He took this to mean that at least he would not be condemned until the scouts who had been sent on the trail of the missing body returned. Ucita would want to deliver him up to the frame. Such had been his plan in giving him the bone yard watch. But the Indians would hold a council on him and even Ucita would not go against its expressed judgment. At least it was not customary, but then he was not sure whether a custom had been established in a case such as his. Big-Handsome-Child and Two-Fell-Together belonged to the White Deer hasomi. This was encouraging. If his death had been predetermined, they would have put guards of the Fish hasomi over him, since the mother of the child belonged to the Fish people.

Holding the Sacred Host, three times the priest made the sign of the Cross over the Chalice—three hours of agony—and twice away from it—the flesh and spirit are parted. The Host and the Chalice are slightly raised:
It is ended.

The Indians were gathering before the long council house. They entered according to rank. First Ucita with Him-Who-Leads-the-Cacique-by-the-Hand on one side and Mocoço-

Killer, the war leader, on the other. After them the beloved old men. Their flesh was like rotting wood, and the bracelets of fish teeth and pearls hung loose on their arms, but they held themselves erect and walked slowly up to the open piazza where gradually they faded into the cool shadows of the house. Then came the inihama, the second men. They passed through the town yard, haughtily, indifferently; then more quickly the ibitano and after them, the toponole. He saw them all out of the corner of his eye, for decorum ordered that he must show no interest in anything that bore upon his dangerous position.

Father . . . Thy will be done.
Over the Chalice hovered the body of Christ. The priest broke it and, holding the fragment in his hand, three times made the sign; then the fragment fell: the blood and the flesh were joined.
May this mixture and consecration of the body and blood of our Lord Jesus Christ be to us that receive it eternal life.

He must show no fear, either now or at the time of judging. Nor too much insolence. Insolence on the part of a prisoner is expectation of death. His guards would be watching to report his slightest movement. Even though they sat with averted heads, he was not fooled. He must show the same supposed indifference.

Lamb of God who taketh away the sins of the world, have mercy on us.

Outcries announced the return of the scouts. They filed across the yard towards the long house. What did they carry?

If only he could look. He could feel the tension of his guards and hear the low sounds of the Indians who were not allowed in council. And then he listened to the slow beat of his heart.

I will take the bread of Heaven and call upon the name of the Lord.

He was standing. The guards pressed his arms against their bodies. He walked between them. The bear grease on their bodies was hot and slick. On the piazza two beloved old women were brewing cassena. One fanned the fire with turkey feathers. The other stirred the drink with a gourd until the dark liquid frothed, and out of the handle he heard the talk of the brew. He passed with his guards into the house. *Lord, I am not worthy. . . .* Ucita's skull-like face confronted him from the royal bed, impassive under its perpetual grin. Arranged according to their castes the Indians sat in council. He felt their eyes upon him as he moved between the beds, but his own he kept at Ucita's feet. And then when they had reached a certain distance, Big-Handsome-Child and Two-Fell-Together raised their hands twice to their faces, saying, Hah, he, hah, hah, hah! From all the beds came the response, Hah, Hah! And then his guards went to the warriors' bed, and he was left alone. He did not move, or move his eyes. The silence grew.

To his lips the priest raised the Bread of Angels, laid it upon his tongue. And drank of the precious Blood. It was no longer the priest who lived. Jesus Christ lived in him.

Ucita pointed to the floor. Slowly he dropped his eyes. There at his feet lay a wolf and out of its breast, running along the gray sandy floor, was the handle of the dart. He took in his breath and held it.

At last Ucita spoke. "The little child is found and not far away the thief is found—dead." From all the beds came grunts of approval. He almost dared to hope. Behind him he heard a low humming, and a Waiter, bowing and singing in a low tone, went by him to Ucita, holding before him the conch shell of cassena. Ucita took it and drank and the Waiter sang, and when his breath was out, Ucita lowered the shell and handed it to the first councillor. The Waiter sang as before. As it passed from mouth to mouth, Ucita broke into a sweat and with great composure leaned over to vomit, spewing the liquid onto the floor at his feet. When all the first and second men had drunk, the Waiter came to him.

His hand shook as he reached for the shell. He drank deep of the bitter stuff.

May Thy Body, O Lord, which I have received, and Thy Blood which I have drunk, cleave to my bowels; and grant that no stain of sin may remain in me . . .

He began to sweat, a nausea seized him. He leaned over and the warm bitter liquid spewed out of his mouth.

Ite missa est.

There was the murmur of a great throng moving and a voice said, "You may rise now. It is over." And then he felt a jerk at his arm. He turned his head, his eyes focused. De Soto was smiling and his hand was on his sleeve. "You live again as a Christian, Señor. Among Christians."

A NOVELLA:

alchemy

WE LANDED IN PERU IN IGNORANCE. WE HAD ADVANCED IN uncertainty. Our ignorance was the hope of the gambler; our uncertainty the Indian's guile. We had advanced from our base, San Miguel, four days towards the mountains. Four days and we were still unsure of ourselves and the future. Nobody knew the state of Pizarro's mind, not even his brothers. It was common knowledge that he was never ready with a decision, and yet when forced he always managed to reach what proved to be a wise course of action. Generally he watched the brew of circumstance like a witch and let its smell tell him what to do. This was no longer possible. The progress of the little army's advance was such that all acts must be as quick and bold as the decision Pizarro, as Governor and General, had made at San Miguel, or all was lost.

I said four days. My statement may mislead you. We were four marches from San Miguel up the valley of the Piura, and it was always up that we marched. We were traveling in those low hills which from the coastal desert look as high as any mountain does in Spain but no more than broken ground before the bare and repulsive Cordillera supplanting the earth behind them. And so you must not think that it was that last bit of marching our army did—one hundred and seventy-seven men in all: sixty-seven cavalry, twenty crossbowmen, and three arquebusiers—which was responsible for our state of mind. We had been in Peru over five months.

We had been in that strange land over five months, and the golden empire of the Inca was as elusive as the day we landed in Tumbez. Tumbez . . . I cannot now speak that name without feeling quicksilver in my blood. It was the gateway to that fabulous, that unbelievable kingdom. Do I say fabulous? In the first marching, before de Soto arrived with his two boatloads of recruits, it was that word which bore up our spirits. The first stretch of coast was low and tropical. The Indians screamed like cats, they were filthy of habits and given over to the abominable crime. Nothing did we find in that province but misery and suffering. It was so poor, the Inca for jest levied upon it a tribute of lice. By day the sun and the hot planets drew the heat from the ground until it hung like vapor among the high places of the forest. Through this the soldiers marched as through steam, suffocating in their armor, often hungry, always weary and finding no more treasure after the first lucky raid on Coaque. In the night the moon and the cold planets took precedence, and on earth those who had cursed the heat huddled together in the chill of the long watches. "You will be free of this in Tumbez," Pizarro said.

A new and strange disease consumed us like rotten sheep. It fell suddenly, like the wrath of God. It knocked the lancer from the saddle, dropped the foot to the sands, or it fell quietly in the night while the army slept, so that by morning the sick were too weak to lift hand to mouth. It came as a swelling on the face and head, or like warts on the body, the color of ripe figs, about the bigness of figs, hanging from a string and flowing with quantities of blood. For seven months the army lay stricken. I speak now of the time before the actual landing. All the while Pizarro went from man to man, and even before the open grave he brought his hollow cheer. "These afflictions," he said, "will serve for jest at Tumbez."

To the island of Puna we moved and waited for de Soto's arrival. The Indians there held mortal feud with those of the mainland and were anxious to assist us. I will not recount our difficulties or our waning hope, or finally how the Indians rebelled, for at last de Soto arrived with the men of Nicaragua. Very quickly we got ready to cross over to Tumbez. The horses were put on the ships and the men who could not be embarked followed on the rafts of the country, ferried by the Indians. The Indians appeared friendly, but as the rafts neared the shore, where the waves break, they tore them apart and tumbled the Christians into the sea. Many were lost and all the baggage. Still others were taken to an island and murdered. But Tumbez was ours. It fell after a brisk fight. It fell—a pile of ruins. Not that we made the ruins. We found it so. The fortress, the temple, and several buildings stood, but they were empty and badly damaged. I found my charger and rode through the vacant streets asking the way to the Governor. Everywhere men were scattered, looking angrily for treasure among the fallen walls.

When it was learned what had happened to the rafts and

that the town was only a shell, there was such great sorrow it was a marvelous thing to see. Soldiers heaped maledictions on Pizarro for leading them, lost men, into remote lands with so sparse a population, and they cursed Coaque for its misleading riches. In the midst of this confusion I found Pizarro in the plaza, among a group of officers.

He sat his horse, his gaunt figure slouched in the saddle and on his head a wide-brimmed hat shading his eyes. The animal was throwing its head from side to side and whinnying at a small group of Indians being driven by in chains. I saluted silently.

Pizarro's oldest brother Hernando was speaking. "The city of gold," he said and his clumsy seat made his sarcasm the heavier, "a temple to the sun, rising in pyramids, painted in brilliant hues, housing treasure of uncounted worth. A convent for the Chosen Women near by. The Virgins of the Sun. A house full of virgins. Think of it, Señores. Think of it, for you will never see it." He threw his insolent head towards Pedro de Candia, the Greek knight, who as ambassador on the former expedition had described the splendors of Tumbez. The knight made no answer. He knew and we all knew the Pizarro pride, how it was matched only by the brothers' poverty. Whatever Hernando Pizarro thought, his pride would not allow him to abuse the Governor, but his poverty had been long.

"Not one," he continued, "but for all a virgin. Not the raddled meat of Panama, but fresh and tender cuts." He laughed shortly. "And behind those convent walls where we were to take our pleasure—correct me, Señor, if I misquote you—behind the walls, in the gardens as we lounged, these very virgins would come dancing to flutes twisting like silver snakes, their hair hanging to their shoulders, their faces, hands, and paps, to be sure the paps, exceeding smooth and of goodly proportions, as beautiful as the Dryads whereof the antiquities speak so much."

There was noise and movement everywhere about us, but we were silent and the air taut. I looked towards de Candia. His face was white and splotched. And then at Pizarro's brother. He had a lip which when it pleased him, and it pleased him often, could twist like a fat and vicious worm. Of the four brothers he alone was legitimate. "As they danced for us," he continued, "if we grew tired of so much alluring motion, we might feast our eyes upon the gardens. They were no common gardens but gardens whose fruits were fashioned of the precious metals. You saw the artisans make these pretty herbs, did you not, Señor?"

Pedro de Candia kicked his mount and rode away. The silence was now complete. Very softly, in the voice one uses to placate an angry woman, the Governor said, "Brother, your tongue will be your undoing."

"If we are not undone already."

"No, Brother,"—the voice, still smooth and placating, grew more distant—"we are not undone." As an afterthought he added, "But there is something amiss here."

I knew what he meant. In fighting among the barbarous nations the good soldier acquires a sense which warns of danger or whispers direction in moments of doubt. Men who lack this sense, I've noticed, perish in the Indies.

And then de Soto spoke. "I've gone over the fort. It is a fine piece of engineering."

All turned to him respectfully, as the captain of the men from Nicaragua. Pizarro grew attentive. "Yes?" he asked.

"It has three walls, or rather one wall which winds three times about its central keep. The foundation stones weigh tons." He paused to make sure this was understood. His small black eyes narrowed intelligently. He continued, "They are laid without mortar and fitted so nicely together that a woman's skewer may not enter the joints."

"Well, Captain?" Hernando asked impatiently.

De Soto smiled. "Do you see any quarries or beasts of burden?"

"There are the mountains."

"But many leagues away."

"Well, what of it?"

De Soto looked directly toward him. "How," he asked, "were these stones brought here without beasts and how put together with so much skill?"

"Perhaps the air of Peru makes them lecherous and they breed."

There was a moment of silence. The Governor turned his head and I saw the eyes from under the flopping hat seek de Soto's. "Yes, how did they come to be on this sandy shore?"

The Governor asked the question and then looked at each of his captains separately.

I can remember no feeling of surprise. It seems strange to me now that I had no feeling of surprise. Often enough I have known Indians to appear out of nothing. Many times I have looked up from the camp fire and found them squatting before it. How they came I never knew nor asked. Silence is of their very nature. Perhaps this was the reason I did not see the Indian cross the plaza and appear, unheralded, within our circle. Or perhaps it was our preoccupation with the Legitimate's bitter attack on Pedro de Candia and the mysterious implications of de Soto's comment. At any rate, unseen by us, the Indian had crossed the plaza and stood just out of reach of the horses. He wore a loose flowing robe of cotton stuff, dyed in alternating stripes of brown and gold, of the richest and brightest threads I had ever seen. He wore sandals of grass and in his ears two silver plugs, while about his head and fringed under the chin he had wound a silken scarf. The silk had a sheen not found in Christendom. Very simply the man said he had come in peace. He did not want to flee, for he knew what a thing war was. There had been war in Cuzco. And further it seemed to him that we were such fighters none could resist us. At the end he begged that his house be spared.

The Governor lowered his lance and made the sign of the Cross in the dirt of the plaza. "Tell him," he said to the interpreter, "to make this sign over his door." The Governor turned to Rodrigo Nuñez who gave out the rations. "Take nothing where you find the Cross," he said.

How shy and cunning is Fortune. Her waywardness is not the least of God's mysteries. Pizarro had seen in this Indian only the means of bringing the people back to Tumbez. The captains saw nothing but the soldiers' common business. I confess my sight was no better than theirs. And yet from this Indian's mouth had come all we wanted to know. He gave us the key to our fortune, the pattern of our action, the entire set of fatal happenings among the Incas which would allow us to fulfill our various destinies. And not one heart beat one beat faster. Not one of us, who all were Fortune's constant suitors, suspected the irony of her gesture.

So for the time being the name of Cuzco lapsed in our minds and we turned our efforts to rounding up the Indians of Tumbez. It soon became apparent that the valley could not be pacified until Chile Masa, the curaca of the town, had been found. De Soto was sent in pursuit. He tracked the curaca to the mountains, not too high nor difficult for horse, and there surrounded and took him. De Soto did not return at once but explored the country farther on. I mention this, a matter of no importance now, to show the morale at camp. The intimates of Pizarro accused de Soto and the men of Nicaragua of rebellious thoughts, and indeed I was disgusted with Pizarro's rule. His only virtue seemed a sullen and stubborn demand on Fortune, waiting, as he seemed to do, loutishly on her favor and showing above the straggly beard along the straight and lecherous mouth the appetite of an emperor. I was disgusted. Perhaps it was treason, but I thought how the land could be better pacified by . . . my captain.

When we came into camp with Chile Masa, my mind was so clouded with these thoughts that they did not allow me to see that a second time our way was being shown, and so plainly shown that an old sheep herder might see it. In the questioning of Chile Masa the Governor asked after Morillo and Bocanegra, the two men he had left behind him for spies on that voyage when he learned of the supposed riches of Tumbez. The curaca replied that Morillo died of the plague —I imagine the rope was his plague—and Bocanegra had been carried to Cuzco at the command of Huayna Capac, the Sapa Inca. There again that name of Cuzco. Instinctively Pizarro fixed upon it. What is Cuzco? he asked. Is it the place where the lord of the world dwelt. And was it rich? It had many people and vessels of gold and silver and things inlaid with the sacred metals. And where was it? The curaca turned his head towards the mountains. The size of little sand away, he said.

"And this Huayna Capac," Pizarro asked, "rules at Cuzco?"

The second Indian boy taken to Spain to learn the language, Filipillo by name and a scoundrel, undertook to translate the curaca's words. He stumbled over the sense, but it was clear that the great Huayna Capac was dead. His beautifully burning heart he had bequeathed to Quito, that conquered province which he loved so well and where he spent his later years, but his body sat in state at Cuzco with all his illustrious predecessors who keep the house of their father, the Sun. To his favorite and bastard son, Atahualpa, the child of the daughter of the last Scyri of Quito, he gave the province of Quito.

"Who rules then at Cuzco?" the Governor asked.

"His first born, Huascar," the Indian replied, "rules there over all the provinces of the old kingdom. After the death of their father the brothers lived for a while at peace, but they grew jealous of each other and now each fights to see who will take the place of the dead one."

This information Pizarro spread throughout the army, but his men said, "It is a stratagem of the Governor's." And so in disbelief and with low spirits the army received its orders to march.

To the south of Tumbez the desert begins. About twelve leagues wide it lies between the mountains and the sea. A waste of sand and rock, it is the domain of death and silence, a silence broken near its frayed shore by the scream of water birds and the bark of sea lions. Over this desert we began our march.

We had found a road. It ran in a perfect line to the south, marked out of the sand by stones. As the army set out, the men made an effort to sing their battle songs, but their voices made the silence more grim and after the first sweat they gave it up, ceasing even to jest or complain. Strict orders were given to spare the water. The road led somewhere, but we had no true knowledge of distances nor of what we would find. There was an all-too-common feeling that the Indians had tricked us to a dry death. The first night we camped beneath great drifts of sand curving like scimitars over the plain. In the distance we could hear the steady break of the sea. The waste of the sea, the waste of the sands, the mountains, the great waste of the unknown—into these we had gone.

The next day it was the same. Not once did that road bend or turn. I thought of the Holy Empire over which our Catholic sovereign is lord, with its borders lying uneasy against the lands of the infidels, how all its kingdoms and principalities for lack of good roads lie as remote from one another as though divided by water. And then hour by hour as I rode along, following this smooth and direct route, I asked myself what must these heathen be to outdo Christendom and bind their provinces so well together. I looked towards the mountains where we were told they dwelt, and suddenly they seemed more present, more threatening than the famished sands. By the third day I had ceased to reflect. We had put leagues behind us. We had pushed and were pushing our march steadily; yet to the left the mountains stood in the exact position as on our setting out; the same sea beat upon the same shoreline, the gray scimitars curved along the swallowing plain, the same road reached always before until, narrowing to a point, it lanced the horizon. Then I heard a voice saying, This is no road. It is a treadmill, and you are caught on its turning. I crossed myself. In that voice I recognized the enemy of man.

Without warning we walked into the green fields of Poechos. We held a mass of Thanksgiving and then took possession. From here we overran Parina, Tangarala, Piura, and the Chira valley. These valleys on the banks of mountain rivers were heavily peopled. There was food and water a-plenty, but little gold. Everywhere we sent foraging details we found the ground intelligently worked. At regular distances water from the streams was turned into the fields under laws regulating its distribution. Where it gave out or sank uselessly into the sand, areas of the desert had been excavated and sunken gardens built up in circular terraces. The Indians added fish heads and the droppings of the bird called guano, so that where nature had left all barren or poor, herbs blossomed and had their season.

Tribute of food and personal service was laid upon the inhabitants, a measure that worked for the glory of God and brought the heathen to a knowledge of the true faith. And were we Moriscos to make our own bread? Soon the Governor began building a town in Piura. He called it San Miguel in honor of that saint who had brought him such timely help in the fight with the islanders of Puna. This was all very well and it gave us a base for operations, but Pizarro seemed in no hurry to pursue the information gathered at Tumbez.

And then a thing happened to open up a little farther our way. A courier arrived from the outpost in the upper Piura, saying the Indians had revolted. De Soto was sent to restore order, which he did after a battle. Two curacas, Cango and Icotu, came in and yielded obedience. On our way to San Miguel with the prisoners, passing through maize fields in the lower Piura, we heard the sound of drums. We halted and presently women came dancing in a slow solemn step out of an alley between the rows of grain. The drums were low and had the sad beat which a loose skin makes. Others came after them, dancing and singing, turning and stamping with a man's garments in their arms. One held a headpiece adorned with feathers of gold so fine they trembled with every moment. One bore a bronze javelin and wooden buckler, another a sheaf of bronze-tipped arrows. Still others followed without anything in their hands but dressed in gay apparel and with silver plugs in their under lips. Last of all were the old women, bearing jars of chica on their backs—it is a drink these people brew from their maize. The old women turned slowly, lifting and setting down their feet in the dust, barely lifting them so that the dust ran like mud. They passed us by and made a circle at an open place near the summer house of the farm, and there all set in to wailing, stopping short altogether, like the running out of a piece. After this they sat down and drank from the jugs, and then one after the other they stood up and spoke. When each had finished, she drank again from the jug and her companions drank with her.

We had had our first sight of precious ornaments and de Soto turned and asked Cango, "What do they do?"

"They weep at the places where the dead one liked to walk."

When he said no more, de Soto asked again, "Who was this man?"

The curaca hesitated, then said, "A great warrior killed in the brothers' war."

We had had some such information of fighting, but here was visible evidence, evidence of the greatest possible importance. De Soto said casually, "Which of the brothers triumphed?"

"Huascar."

"Huascar is now sole Inca?"

De Soto had to repeat the question and then Cango told how Atahualpa was taken but escaped in the night, saying Inti, his father, had set him free. With them Inti means sun. Then he told how Atahualpa returned later with fresh troops

under his generals Quizquiz and Challicuchima, burned the
city of Tomebamba and put all to the sword, although the old
men of the city came out and prostrated themselves, begging
mercy. Tarrying near Caxas, he received the news that his
two generals had fought a battle on the plain near Cuzco,
routing Huascar's army and taking the Inca prisoner. The
Inca was now confined somewhere in the mountains and his
brother now wore the royal llautu.

"Where," de Soto asked quickly, "in the mountains?"

The curaca would say no more. "I'll put a little fire to his
feet," Juan Pizarro said.

"There is a better way," de Soto replied and turned upon
Icotu and asked if he, de Soto, looked to be such a fool as to
believe that the lone province of Quito could annihilate all
the forces of Tawa-ntin-suyo. That is what they call their
country, the four corners of the world. The ruse worked, for
Icotu, not to be outdone, began to speak. It was his opinion,
he said, that Huascar was undone because the people of
Collao, who are great warriors, did not assemble in time,
although he had heard that Huascar had fallen because he was
too grave and would never let himself be seen by his people,
nor did he ever come out to eat in the plaza, as was the
custom. And it was known that he had threatened to bury the
dead, since they had all that was best in the land.

"How is this," de Soto scoffed, "the dead more mighty than
the living? Can the dead throw a dart or give the whoop of
battle?"

The strange lord did not understand, Icotu replied. The
dead kept their palaces and all the service they had in life—
their plate, their golden ornaments, and all their trappings.
Nor could those who served them be relieved of attendance.
Provinces were set aside for their keep, so that it happened

when a new lord entered on his rule he had to get his own servants and eat from vessels of wood and clay until gold was mined and artisans fashioned articles of use and pleasure for his person, and for his dwelling. Each dead lord had a steward who understood the speech of the dead. If the dead wished to eat or drink or desired to divert himself in the house of the other dead or in the great plaza at Cuzco, he made his wish known and it was done as in life. Because the greater part of the people, the treasure and feasting was theirs, Huascar threatened to have them buried.

"And where did you say this Huascar was confined?" de Soto asked carelessly.

Before either Icotu or Cango could speak, a little man with the great chest of the mountains and ears split by golden discs larger than double ducats turned angrily upon the curacas. I noticed that he wore his hair as if on a comb and around his forehead he had a fillet, black and fringed to his eyes. "What do you, speaking of the affairs of your lord?" he asked. At this the curacas grew silent, nor could they be made to say more.

We had learned three things: first, of a town called Caxas which must be on the way to Cuzco; second, that Atahualpa had triumphed over his brother; and third, that the custom of maintaining the state of dead rulers, with all their possessions and attendants, made of Cuzco a respository of treasure never heard of even in the halls of the Turk. The words of the Indians rang true, and I was sure that they had spoken of things they would never have uttered save from the confusion they felt over the civil war. But there was one disturbing element. Would we have to face this Atahualpa, strong in victory? Where indeed was he? The Indians had been vague, as equally vague as to the whereabouts of the imprisoned Huascar.

Pizarro listened to de Soto's report, saw the gold ornaments taken from the little man and the two curacas, and said nothing. We all thought he would order the advance at once, but he settled into a state of apathy. It seemed almost that his courage left him, once the evidence of the thing he had pursued so many years grew plain. At least now we had more to go on than rumor. Of course the Indians had to be thoroughly reduced and all the lands divided, but he took no steps to hurry these matters to a conclusion. His indecision gave doubts as to his belief in our evidence.

In this state of uncertainty we lived for some weeks; then one day without warning he assembled the small army in the plaza of the town and caused all the trifles of gold and silver to be piled in a heap. He asked us to lend our shares to send back to Panama to speed up the arrival of supplies and reenforcements which had been left in the hands of his companion in the conquest, Almagro. He promised to pay us back, and perfumed to boot, for on the morrow the army would set out for Atahualpa's court.

And so it happened that in September 1532 we left San Miguel behind, crossed the Piura, and struck for the heart of the Inca kingdom, or what we took to be its heart. At Zarran, a town in the low mountains, the Governor divided the army, taking part with him to explore the Sechura desert to the south and sending the rest under de Soto to Caxas with orders for the whole body to reunite at Zarran within the week. I followed de Soto.

Caxas lay in a pocket of foothills. We reached it by a rough but man-made road which wound along the bare slopes. Just over the crest we saw the town. It was no mean place, built against a mountain wall for economy's sake, for the bottom of the valley was all in maize, potatoes, and other strange herbs. We hesitated in the sudden surprise of the place and then rode down upon it. As we drew near, we found the garrison drawn up to receive us. The Inca's army, if army there was, could be greatly exaggerated; but the Indians drawn up across our path showed too much order for comfort. They were very gay in their colored quilted armor, bright headpieces and bucklers painted in a lightning design of blues and reds. There must have been a hundred of them, formed in companies of a sort, which meant tactics of a sort. There were javelin throwers, men with slings, battle-axes, and squads of men with short bronze swords. On the flanks the bowmen stood proudly at ease. They looked much better disciplined than our own foot which, to speak the truth, were a sad lot, men desperate enough for any adventure, too desperate almost for use. It was not our policy to shed blood if we could help it. Our very lives might depend upon how we left things in our rear. With this in mind de Soto sent the interpreter forward with words of peace.

Not until that moment did I notice the gallows and the four Indians hanging by their heels. I had been too busy estimating the strength and temper of the garrison. At first the sight gave me no feeling of death, although the faces were stiff and swollen. Perhaps it was the dark skins and the quiet immobility of their swinging. I thought instead of mummies, and to think of mummies is never to think on death. The mummy has no estate, either being or non-being. It is outcast in time.

There was a movement in the Indian ranks. The ranks divided and I saw a man of authority come toward us. He was well attended, his tread slow and stately, and his carriage so perfect that the parrot feathers barely trembled in the socket of his head dress. He stopped a few paces from us—we had advanced as far as the gallows—and said without pause, "What do you want? Where are you going? Do you come in peace or war?"

"Peace," de Soto said, "food, and a way to the royal camp."

The Indian listened gravely while this was being translated and replied that our requests should be answered. At the end of his talk he thrust his staff toward the scaffold.

"Watch out!" a voice cried out.

The Indian looked angrily at the lancer. His attendants murmured excitedly.

"Who spoke?" de Soto asked sharply.

"I meant nothing, Captain. But if he jars the corpses, the eyes will pop out."

I looked more closely at the bodies. The eyes of the dead did bulge in their sockets, and they looked at the sky and their necks had frozen in the strain of looking. The balls clung to the bare edge of the rims, as though thrown into a spasm by the sight of some unendurable horror. They had bled a little at the noses, their mouths were shut against the disintegrating air, pariahs' mouths which found poisonous all that once had been sweet and familiar. But there was one whose mouth was open in full surrender and through its dark trough two rat-like teeth protruded, mocking the leer of depravity.

And then I turned away. The Indian lord was speaking of their crime, for de Soto had cleverly explained the soldier's shout as a request to know why the men hung. One, the Indian said, had stolen into the house of the Chosen Women. The other three had connived at the sacrilege. It was worse than sacrilege and could never have happened but for the brothers' war, since the virgins given to the Sun were also brides of the Inca and reserved for his couch alone. So heinous was the crime that the Indian dared speak of it only in low tones and with his eyes cast down. At the end he pointed his staff again at the bodies and regarded us in haughty disdain.

"To take what is forbidden is death," he said.

I did not attend him. A light breeze had risen. It moved the folds of the soft cotton breechclout covering the loins of the dead. As I looked at the cloth, so fresh and clean, washed that morning perhaps to bind the living flesh . . . as I looked, I thought how we all, heathen and Christian alike, stand forever in peril of our secret needs. Then, but not until then, did I feel in the presence of death . . . and the fear of death.

"Where does Atahualpa lie?" de Soto was asking.

The Indian looked straight before him. "The lord of the earth lies at Caxamalca," he said after a pause. "He delights in the baths of that place."

I didn't like the pause. It looked rather too much as if he was throwing us off the scent, for would a prince fighting for his life and throne take time to pleasure himself in the luxuries of the bath?

"And where is Caxamalca?" de Soto was quietly persistent.

The Indian turned and pointed to a gloomy peak rising above a mass of sterile dirt and stone which, though leagues away, stood up straight before us. Wherever we looked, it rolled, one vast terrestrial billow, topless and endless. I thought I saw a flash of triumph in the Indian's eye. It may have been imagination, for, as I turned back, he waited as before, without expression but silent and I knew watchful. De Soto gave him two hawk's bells and dismissed him. He showed no delight in the gifts, but the attendants rang them all the way into Caxas. They laughed as they rang them. It was not a pretty laugh to hear.

We still had nothing certain to go on. Always we heard of Atahualpa, but each time he was farther away. With this in mind de Soto determined to question the man further, especially after he learned that he was an officer of the Crown come to Caxas to collect tribute. Dressed in full armor, de Soto waited for his arrival, seated on a mattress which softened the stone shelf at the back of the room he occupied. It was late afternoon and tapers were lit, for the room was already in shadow. From outside there came the clank of harness and the gruff voices of the detail who had been sent to fetch the tax gatherer. And then the curtain hanging at the entrance was pushed aside by brown fingers. Slick and round, tapering to the long sharp nails, they looked like the claws of a bird . . . the Indian was inside, standing before the curtain.

De Soto motioned him to a stool. A servant brought two bowls of chica. With his right hand he offered the Indian drink. For de Soto he reserved the left hand. "Our guest is of greater rank than we thought," he said laconically. We drank in silence and after the proper interval de Soto put aside his bowl.

"Atahualpa is now undisputed lord of the realm?"

The Indian lowered his eyelids. The Sapa Inca ruled the four corners of the world. De Soto changed the question to that of gold. Was there much of it in the land? He pointed to the ring on his finger. When Inti the Sun and Mamaquilla the Moon made the earth, they worked hard and sweated much. This sweat sank into the ground, and that of Inti made gold and that of Mamaquilla hardened into silver, but it was not given to their servants to know how much. Only the child of the Sun might gather it for his use. How then did it happen, de Soto asked quickly, that the honorable tax gatherer had gold about his person, if only the Inca might use it? The **man** replied without pause that by blood he was of the House of the Sun and that when his illustrious kinsman deigned to show favor he made presents. Did the Inca ever make presents to the curacas of the towns? The Indian turned his head and spat upon the ground. Rarely were the eyes of these conquered chiefs blessed by sight of the Inca. It was the custom to take them to Cuzco, teach them the court language, but only so far were they favored. They were then sent back to their former seats to rule as vassals. Their sons and gods were kept in Cuzco as hostages. Only the clans of the blood were honored with the power of the realm. Descendants of former Incas, they were set above all and from their number the priests, the governors of the four provinces, the generals of the armies were taken.

As de Soto asked question after question, I could see he was convinced that we had to do with no set of scattered tribes. Plainly Pizarro was taking us into dangers never before encountered in the Indies. But there was honor and perhaps profit in carrying her Ladyship's banner so far into heathendom.

De Soto had the man plied with chica and while he drank I saw him look at our chests. De Soto saw his interest and turned a key in the locks. This seemed to please him and he took the key and locked and unlocked all the chests several times. We found amusement in such toys? he asked. De Soto explained it was a way we had of guarding our treasure. When the Indian understood the necessity for this, his manner suddenly changed. He grew reserved and haughty. I was puzzled for I thought the art of our smiths would amaze him. De Soto pressed him to say what he thought of their skill. He rolled his eyes, swelled his lungs with air, and let it out contemptously through his nostrils.

"Surely your people must be the wash of the sea," he said. "The weed of the sea clings to your chins. You not only steal from others but you steal from yourselves."

With that he rose to go. I took up my sword to beat him for his insolence but de Soto motioned me to my seat and very softly asked were there no thieves in Peru.

I don't think he would have answered, but he saw me take up my sword and remembered where he was. He was just drunk enough to show his pride and contempt for us. I was certain he was drunk when he spoke, for he assumed a mock judicial air. "To steal a man's woman is death. A judge who takes gifts steals truth. For him there is death."

"But if a man steals because he is hungry?" de Soto asked.

He was a long time silent, as if such a possibility was beyond his experience. At last he spoke. "A man who is hungry must eat. If he lack food and take it, the curaca of his village will be punished."

"But if the crops of the village failed?"

He shook his head. "In Tawa-ntin-suyo one may not go without. On the day set apart the Sapa Inca, in cloth of gold, attended by his court, goes out to the royal fields of Cuzco. There he takes a golden plow in his hands and sinks it, stirring the plentiful earth. Eight bloods of high degree pull it before him. And in the four corners of the world the earth is stirred by his people. First, the fields set aside for the Sun. Next, the fields of the sick and those away at the wars, and then each man turns his own. The farms of the Inca are kept to the last. On the day set aside, just as the great condor spreads his wings in the east and grasps the Sun in his claw, heralds all over the world stand in high places and sound their trumpets for the people to gather. Men, their wives, the unmarried, dress in their feasting clothes and go down to the fields. They are gay and sing of their lord's triumphs and of his virtues as they work, and at night they dance and leave the dance only to love. When the crops come to harvest they are stored. And all other things of use are stored. There can be no lack. If a province lose more than its share by war or famine, it is balanced by the plenty of other provinces. Already the Quipu strings have been tied for the damage you have done in the towns of the coast."

He ceased. Perhaps he thought he had said too much, for without asking leave he turned and walked out of the room. He moved so easily it was a moment before we could realize he had gone. We followed through the door—the cloth still swung from his touch, or was it the wind—but he was no-where to be seen. He had disappeared into the dark. Even as I looked, the sheer mountain walls soaked up their wash of color, the greens of the valley fields drank ink and all the valley pockets were in shadow, while upon the roofs of Caxas the night herons were silently dropping and gathering in their wings. I looked up to the high mountain plateaux where the great peaks sit. There, against the clouds, the sun was spending its last strength.

"The Paradise of Pleasure," whispered a voice.

The voice was so low I thought I had been deceived. There was no one near except the sentinel. "You spoke?" I asked.

"The great admiral. . . ."

"Yes?"

"When he saw these mountains from the other ocean, I heard him say—I was on watch and it was the turning of the tides—he said, Somewhere in those peaks must lie the Paradise of Pleasure."

We were on the right trail but we had not found the way. De Soto was not the man to turn back just as the chase got hot;

so the following morning we set out for Guancabamba at the risk of Pizarro's displeasure, as de Soto was exceeding his orders and so must delay the army's reunion. There was not the most sympathetic accord between de Soto and the Pizarro brothers. De Soto had been promised second place, and this place had been given to the Legitimate. De Soto kept his tongue, and for that very reason the Pizarros grew suspicious, as all those who break faith expect no better than they give. But, as I say, our captain did not let this stand in the way but pushed on to Guancabamba; and there, gentlemen, we found it: the great highway which ran between Quito and Cuzco. The moment I saw its flat stone surface, the shade trees which protected it, and the cool water running in troughs for the comfort of the traveler, I knew that we stood upon the borders of that which we desired, feared, and from which we could never be freed, whether it brought our most extravagant hopes or our ruin. The road seemed to have no end. As far as we scouted, it ran before us, the width of five bodies and with houses of shelter every two leagues. We halted at one of these huts for water, and just as we drew up, an Indian stepped into the road before us.

He looked at us calmly, nor did our strangeness frighten him. He might have been a monster bird who had dropped from the sky, for his neck turned in solemn ease and his gown of feathers was of so many colors I could not say how they had been matched. Two insolent drakes waited on him, but the big ears marked him for a man of station. He did not wait to be questioned. He addressed us. Instead of translating his greeting, Filipillo strutted to the front and asked him what he did there. I was amused. The boy had the manner of a burgher raised to a post of minor dignity. The Indian pretended not to hear him. Filipillo stamped his foot and spoke again. Slowly Big Ears turned his head and his eyes made vacant the place where Filipillo was. "What does he say?" de Soto asked. The boy gave no answer but stood trembling with anger. De Soto brought his lance across his back. "Speak, sirrah."

The spittle gathered around the boy's mouth, and then he answered. "He says are we the strangers with the beards his lord Atahualpa has sent him to find?"

We could not believe our good fortune. Not only had we got the direction; we had established actual contact with the Inca. At once we turned about, taking the envoy and his attendants, and made for Zarran. Not until later that day, not until two hours after dark in fact, did I grasp the real meaning of this encounter. Suddenly de Soto reined in his horse. There was a moment of confusion in the squadron by his abrupt action. It was soon righted and we resumed the march.

"Mother of God," I asked. "What is it?"

"I am a fool," de Soto replied.

"It is to be disputed."

"Here am I boasting to myself of our good fortune."

"You will be forgiven."

"You don't understand."

"No?"

"No. It is not we who have found the Inca. He has found us."

The full importance of what de Soto had grasped did not strike me until after Pizarro's meeting with the Apoo. So was he called in the Quechua tongue. Pizarro received him in a white velvet cloak, white shoes, and a broad white hat of felt. In such fashion did the great Gonzalvo use to dress in Italy and Pizarro liked to think himself a pupil of that soldier. The Indian servants set down the Inca's gifts; two stone fountains carved like fortresses, two shirts of vicuna wool embroidered in gold and silver, and a jar of dry and powdered goose flesh. The Apoo put his hand into the jar and threw some of the powder on Pizarro's shoulders and then he powdered his own. He sniffed the air and smiled. The smile vanished and he stood aloof and waiting. Pizarro examined each of his gifts. The shirts were finer than anything we had seen on the coast, good enough for the back of a king, but Pizarro did not let the Apoo see what he was thinking. Without hurrying, he handed the gifts to his page and, pausing, inquired of the Apoo if there was any message from his lord.

The Apoo wore the same black band I had seen several times before. The fringe hung low to the brows. It was no mere ornament—a mark of rank, I was sure, perhaps even more than that. As I watched, I saw that it made his face stand out like an idol's, open yet discreet, surprising the secrets of others, hiding its own. The fringe trembled and the envoy spoke:

"The Inca Atahualpa, lord of the world, asks what the strangers who have left their town such a great way off want in his land."

Too quickly and with too much deference Pizarro answered. "Tell your lord that his victories have made it my fondest wish to see him. I am now on my way to offer my poor services in his wars."

Filipillo finished interpreting Pizarro's answer. Pizarro waited with slightly inclined head. He waited beyond dignity. At last the Apoo spoke a sentence which seemed no more than a word—"Atahualpa waits for you in the mountains."

To end the pause which each moment grew more awkward Pizarro ordered his page to bring toys for the Indians and then had him shown through the camp. The Apoo was curious but unimpressed, and yet he asked shrewd questions. He stopped before a lancer and felt him all over, thumped the linked mail, and jerked his beard. This final impertinence was more than the Christian could bear. He took the Apoo by the scruff of the neck and soundly beat him with his sword. The Indian did not linger after this. He left us with a swinging stride. It was no time before he and the serving men had disappeared through the steep and turning pass. As long as he was in sight, I watched and did not think. But the moment he was hidden, I saw those long and even strides moving steadily, surely, softly away.

"So, he awaits us in the mountains."

The voice broke the silence. It was Alcantara, Pizarro's brother on his mother's side. There was no response. The men stood about in scattered groups. They shifted restlessly. In studied idleness Juan Pizarro drew his sword and very carefully, as though his fingers might dull its edge, took the point and bent it. It leaped and slapped the air, hummed like a single angry bee, then shuddered into stillness. He took his neckpiece and tossed it from him. The blade flashed and the cloth, in two parts, settled slowly to the ground. He leaned over and picked them up. "I would have cut his throat," he said.

Pizarro turned like a man shaking off a heavy sleep, and I saw that a profound change had come over him. It was apparent at once that what we, his officers, and what he, the Captain General, felt about the Apoo's visit had nothing in common. Obviously the Apoo was a spy. Obviously he was contemptuous of our small force, and it was plain that the Christians believed at last in the Inca's existence and in his power. It was plainer still that they did not like that waiting in the mountains. These were all practical and important considerations. But Pizarro had not only not sensed any of this information which military prudence, of necessity, should have made him consider; he had not considered it at all. Or so I felt. He said, briefly, "Break camp. I long to meet this Señor Atahualpa." Now that I remember, he spoke like a man who repeats another's command.

Within the hour we were under way, but the spurt of energy did not last. The army advanced at a slow pace, with the lack of will men show who look upon a beloved land they are forever leaving. At Motupe, for no reason, we delayed four days. I thought at first that Pizarro had reflected and decided to wait for Almagro who was long overdue. We could afford to wait now that we knew our objective. Indeed caution was perhaps our boldest strategy. But at the end of this time, without explanation, we took up our march.

We went southeast towards the gap we hoped to find in the mountain chain. The nearer we approached the more sober grew the faces of the men. There was no open expression of what they were thinking, yet there was a holding back and complaints, especially that the horses were curiously weak. De Soto's page came to him with the talk of pikemen who said that as soon as night fell, and it comes suddenly in that country, the dark congealed and took wing. Another reported that he had seen something as large as a dove flying low to the ground. It skimmed by his ears and yet there was no stirring of the air or whistling of wings. I was prepared to believe strange and unnatural things, but not that the dark could take wing and fly. I decided that I had over-estimated the army's courage. But when men whose hardihood I knew shook their heads and spoke of blood clots on their chargers, I began to listen. They did not lie. There were small, very small blotches on the neck and withers of the horses. I went with this to de Soto and he set me over the first watch.

That night I made hourly inspection and lingered at the corrals. As far as I could tell, all was well. The animals stood quietly in their halters, the mounted watch made its rounds. I found nothing amiss with the foot guard. They were at their posts in pairs, feeling the dark with their eyes, or listening with that puzzled expression an officer comes to know as a veteran watch. At the changing I went to my tent and lay down. At what hour I awoke I can't say, but it seemed the deepest part of the night. I woke up all over. The air felt taut. I began to imagine that while I slept some monstrous spider had shuffled its hairy legs along the dark and of the dark had spun out the invisible and treacherous glue of its web. And then I noticed the man next me turning restlessly in his sleep. Very carefully I shifted my eyes along his body.

His feet stuck out of his cloak. One of them turned and twisted like a thing apart from its leg. As I watched, it kicked free of what I had taken for a shadow until I saw the clumsy spread of the wings. They hovered a moment; then settled back down over the bare gray flesh. The foot no longer resisted. Without breathing, almost without moving, I reached for my cloak. And then, gathering myself together, I fell with the cloak upon it. The man swung up. His hand reached for his sword. I breathed, "Make a light."

The thing fought and scratched. The cloak was tightly woven, but the thing cut through the cloth and caught a finger. My dagger was ready. I stabbed well, for it screeched, and then slowly the little knives withdrew from my finger, smoothly and without pain. My companion held the torch as I lifted the cloak. There lay the creature, its ragged wings drawn tight to its body, with an undershot jaw, short cropped ears, and a broad leaf-shaped mouth. The mouth was open, and for teeth it had four little blades on opposite sides that worked together like scissors. "Let's cut him open," I said. My companion made no answer but breathed hard as I laid back the hide and flesh. It was very tough. Very carefully I went into the stomach. From its pocket fresh blood ran out, "Yours," I said. The man blasphemed and then turned to vomit. I touched the walls of the stomach. They were thin and weak, like a sponge.

"The blood-sucking bat."

At the bottom of its stomach I found three slimy, half-digested clots. I tumbled them onto the ground.

"The God-damned blood-sucking bat," he whispered.

Before puchero news of this adventure was known to every man in camp. It brought to a head the army's discontent and men used it to hide the true cause for their fears. After puchero Pizarro called us together. He did not line us up in military formation. We met like a village meeting at home, the men of station naturally withdrawn somewhat to themselves. Pizarro walked out of his tent alone. Usually his brothers were about him, and even now they lingered near, but he made the impression he wanted to make, of acting alone. He stood close to the men and began without preliminaries.

"I've called you together to say this." His voice was pleasant, even conversational. "Any man who is afraid to go on has my permission to turn back."

I looked at Pizarro and I looked at the men. They stood in groups, uncertain and surprised. The quality of the surprise was alarming. It looked too much like relief. The Indies are a gamble, but Pizarro was straining his luck. He strained it further. "To those who return," he continued, "I'll give the same amount of land and vassals apportioned at San Miguel.

The garrison is weak. I will be glad to have it strengthened."
He paused and looked straight before him. My respect grew.
"But," he added and his voice rang, "whoever wants his share
of the gold I believe is there—" his arm shot out to the finger,
the finger to the mountains—"step behind me."

The officers stepped over in a body and grouped themselves
near Pizarro. The scattered soldiers had not moved. Pizarro
waited. His manner was faultess: frank, fearless, and confident.
It must have been seconds, seconds upon which whole lives
turned, when a sergeant, a small strutting man, stepped
briskly across the divide and took his place to the right of
the Governor. He looked truculently at his fellows and stuck
his lance into the ground. It was a well turned piece. It
quivered in the light, flawless out of the tree's white heart,
flawless in workmanship. Its very beauty, I think, must have
stirred the army's professional pride. Very quickly the men
gathered around it, until only nine were left on the other side,
four from the foot and five lancers. A few returned the now
hostile stare of their former comrades, but the most of them
kept their eyes uneasily on the ground. One, standing apart,
could not suffer his isolation. He moved in. A rough and
contemptuous laugh greeted the poor show of spirit. Hard
upon the laugh came Pizarro's voice. "I keep my word," he
said. "Return to the—invalids." Then he gave them his back.

Those who returned to San Miguel were not alone in their
fears. Indeed all of us were certain a trap was being laid in
the mountains. At the foot of the narrow trail we must climb,
even Pizarro's unreasoning optimism seemed to leave him.
He waited for the Legitimate to question a curaca taken at the
last village, when it was perfectly plain that whatever the
curaca said could in no way be verified or change our plans.
Perhaps it was the sight of the narrow defile which each man

must climb alone—it was no more than a shelf worn in the abrupt rock wall—that made him pause. At any rate a halt was made for the Legitimate to go through with his useless business. The men had loosened their cinches and stood about in groups or lay quietly on the ground. They no longer had any opinions or, if they had, kept them to themselves. I watched a few go over their saddles and stirrups again and again, or try their swords, or feel the straps of their armor. The worst and the best soldiers are often restless when danger is certain but its direction unknown.

The curaca was stripped and tied to four lances. The executioner was squatting by the fire turning his irons. Leaning forward, with one hand before his face, he pulled out an iron and looked at it. "Not yet," he said, frowning slightly.

The Legitimate thrust forward his whiskered chin. "It will do, Señor. Put it to his feet."

"It is yet too hot," the executioner replied.

"Nonsense. Go ahead."

The executioner knelt by the curaca and waited. He said distantly, "I understand my trade, Captain Pizarro."

The Legitimate walked over and planted himself in front of the prisoner. The interpreter moved to his side. The executioner at last lifted the iron, looked carefully at the film of heat spreading and contracting; then, without speaking, he ran his hand down the Indian's leg, as gently as if he were about to shoe a two year old. "Hold the other foot, "he ordered as he grasped the ankle; then, barely disguising his contempt, "You may proceed, Captain."

The Legitimate put one hand on his dagger, one on his sword hilt and braced himself. He lowered his head and flung his words at the curaca's face. "The Inca thinks he will trap us in the mountains. No? He has troops in ambush on this very pass. No?" He nodded to the interpreter impatiently.

The curaca held a deliberate pause before he replied. When he spoke, the Christians turned their ears as if they understood the Quechua tongue.

"It is not the Lord Inca's habit to take a man of my station into his counsel."

The executioner did not wait for directions. He pulled gently at the ankle. "Come now," he said. "Lift your foot. There's no good in being stubborn." He spoke softly; then a few more pulls and suddenly he cracked the shin and caught the jerking foot between his legs. The hot iron dropped above the arch. The brown toes tightened and curled, and a hollow came into the instep.

"Here it is most tender, Captain. It is a waste of time to use the red hot iron. It will only burn up the foot. Pain must not be too sharp at first. It must have an artful progress. The best results are got when the prisoner feels it behind the eyes. Now, gently, like this." He rolled the black tool under the instep. A damp smoke puffed around the iron. The Indian stiffened. The executioner looked away and spat. "I never get used to the smell," he said.

The Legitimate shifted his stance. "There's no need to hurt," he said and his voice had the kindness of a wolf. "A few words and you go free. But the truth. The flesh is false, but the bone speaks true. Must we go to the bone?"

The interpreter put the threat into the low, plaintive Quechua tongue.

"Translation adds a refinement to my art," the executioner said.

I thought it delayed us unnecessarily. We waited for the curaca to speak, but he kept his silence. The Legitimate raised his hand and again the iron fell and rested upon the flesh. The damp smoke sizzled and licked about the darkening surface. The executioner lifted the tool and turned it over. A shred of skin clung to the iron. The Indian's eyes were bright, but his mouth kept shut.

"Again," the Legitimate said.

As the iron descended the curaca parted his lips, but first he lowered his eyes. At last he spoke. "The Inca is curious to see your sheep and you. Those with the moss on their chins whom he likes he will keep. The rest he will put to death."

"No element has such virtue as fire," the Legitimate said in triumph.

The executioner walked away and dropped his iron into water. It hissed, and a flash of pain passed over the Indian's eyes.

Pizarro had watched the trial with indifference. With indifference he heard the confession. Now that it was over he called his captains about him. "The path is rough and twisting. I won't waste time explaining the obvious dangers. De Soto will command the wayward. My brother Juan and thirty lancers will go with him. My brother Hernando for the rearward and I go with the battle. You are not to advance in one long file. Go in squads at broken distances. Now, let us be off."

I saw at once I had misjudged what I thought a loss of confidence. He had allowed the mockery of the trial from policy. Whatever the curaca gave out would be better for the morale than uncertainty. I watched the thin beard jab briskly and the mouth which it could not hide and the hard dullness of the eyes. Yes, he hurried into those mountains for more than gold, and he was a poor man, for more than the trappings and power of high estate, and he had the pride of the east.

We all paused a moment and said to ourselves, Now it has

come. For a moment all eyes were lifted towards the mountains.

"Bare, not a tree, and still. Jesu, they're still," Juan Pizarro said and his voice was low.

It was not so much the stillness. All mountains are still. It was the barrenness. De Soto went ahead. Juan and I rode close behind. No one of us spoke. There was only the occasional click as our horses struck their shoes and behind, among the thirty, the steady hollow ring of a loose shoe. Here and there a few dwarf trees clung to the rocky escarpment. As we mounted, the stream sank lower in its gorge. By this we judged the distance we had made. And by the horses. After some two hours they began to suffer. De Soto increased the halts. In the wayward he had changed Pizarro's marching order. The thirty rode head to tail where they could. Only he and I kept in advance. Juan made the point between.

But other bleak mountains were still above us, hiding the snowy range. And these were yet to climb. At one time the path ran at dizzy heights above the torrents which sliced the bulking earth; next it took the very streams for its way. Here the horses slipped on the loose rocks, but when the water rushed darkly through walls of stone almost closing over our heads, we dismounted and led them into the chill and sepulchral air. Through one of these half-caverns we passed, a cold and shuddering place. Out of the gorge the path rose to wind its way to the crest. The ascent now grew slow and more painful. After several hours the path turned sharply about a rocky bastion. I heard the wind, but I was unprepared.

Down the gorge it struck like a sheet of Greek fire. My horse reared and backed into Juan. There was a perilous moment. One hoof kicked the narrow ledge, and from under it a rock fell. I watched it drop and disappear into space. Below, on the floor of the gorge, the river lay like silver in a mold. I lowered my visor, for down the narrow way the wind blew a gale, driving sand and splinters of rock before it. My horse pressed the wall and trembled. I could not dismount because of my harness. I dug the spurs in, and half-creeping and half plunging we got to a resting place the Indians had made in the wall, a place some twenty feet square and lined by stone benches. Juan followed me there. I said a paternoster, for it was God's will my horse did not stumble. De Soto motioned to Juan to hold the lancers and then we dismounted. My face smarted and burned inside its prison, and I raised the visor. De Soto raised his and our glance met. His face was pinked in a hundred places.

It took some moments to calm the horses, but only a glance to estimate the gravity of our position. For several hundred paces the path ran with the gorge and then it turned abruptly, but whether abruptly up or down I could not tell. I could not tell for the wind and my blurred sight. I dropped on my belly, de Soto beside me, and slowly opened my eyes. Overhead the sand and particles flew by, but hugging the ground I could see through my scarf. I saw too well. Where the path turned, the opposite face of the chasm, a bulking slant-topped peak, almost closed the way; and there the wind sweeping down the canyon struck and multiplied its strength, forced by the narrow passage. Just at this point the Incas had built two round towers on either side of the trail. They had lookouts, windows for defense and in the righthand tower a door opening down to the very foundations.

The walls were sheer and inaccessible, and the one place where an attacking party might have got a foothold was faced with smooth-cut stones. I cannot say which was greater, my admiration for the engineer who had fortified this place or my despair. There is much loose talk among soldiers of impregnable works. The knights of Malta thought they had such walls, but the Turk breached them. In the passes of the Apennines there is Sforza, and yet it has been known to fall. Thus did I talk to stay my courage, for never had cunning turned nature to such perfect use. I looked through the windows and in through the door, but all was still. Too still, for the towers could not be empty. I didn't turn to de Soto. I delayed, and when finally I spoke I averted my gaze as men do who meet to assist at the rites of the dead.

"Ten men can stop an army here," I said at last.

"Well, we can't turn back. We can't leave the horses and we can't turn around, and besides we are halfway up."

"Or halfway down," I replied.

"We can't stay here." De Soto had a quizzical look, his face still set against the wind. The wind blew, whistling and skimming down between the walls.

"No," Juan said after a pause, "we can't stay here."

"We'll risk it," de Soto said with finality. "Juan, go back and hold the others. I'm going ahead and see what's up there. If I don't come back, push for the towers. If an animal gets out of hand, drive him into this place. Tell the lancers not to crowd the horses at the turn."

"Forgive me," I said.

"Yes."

We had to shout. We sounded as if we were quarreling.

"You gave me the forward post. I refuse to give it up."

De Soto looked hard at me and I saw his struggle with his pride and then he turned to Juan. "Hold his horse while I help him mount."

It was no easy matter, but we managed. The gelding lowered its head against the stinging air and pawed the ledge. Juan turned straight about. In time of peril I never saw a better man. Quick and skillful and with the courage to hold up his judgment, although his judgment was not always good.

I watched him in the windy pass, saw the sand strike his back plate. It splashed like rain on the bright steel. I gave a glance, then tightened the reins and kicked the horse's flanks. The gelding went forward with his battle spirit. He set his light hoofs down on the shaley path, and I began to breathe again. The thick air seemed for a moment sweet. We advanced half the distance, and it was all still in the towers. Any moment now, I thought. I know the Indian's cunning. The garrison should not have delayed so long. It expected to overwhelm a lone man and not waste its magazines. The windows grew larger. I strained my eyes yet in the deep wells behind nothing stirred. I did not understand until suddenly, looking up the steps carved in the rock to the tower's door, I saw just within a great stone balanced against the jamb. Move it a little and it would come hurtling down the steps. There was but one thing to do. Put the gelding into a gallop. Possibly we might pass the steps before the stone could roll and bounce us into space. We charged up the dizzy path which from the valley below did not make a line even on the face of the precipice. Above the abyss and level with me two condors dipped their wings idly into the air. Leaning inwards, my shoulder scraped the wall. I fixed my eye upon the stone. It grew larger. It moved, I thought I saw it move. Right up to the door I rode and struck it with my lance as I passed. The lance bent—there was no sound. The noisy wind had made a calm more constant than silence.

I knew at once the towers were empty, but I climbed the steps with care, paused and touched the stone, a foolish gesture, and entered. In the gray light I saw magazines of rock neatly piled and in a corner a broken arrow. I had the feeling of men leaving just before me. I could feel almost the lithe dark forms waiting, watching my approach out of their still slant eyes, their footsteps fleeing. I had the same feeling at the next fort, this time a larger work and one able to maintain a long siege, for besides the well-stocked magazines, there was water rising out of its covered parade ground; there were inner walls, fortified barracks, and granaries from which we fed. And behind the rocks for hurling, like sinister shadows in the failing light, the dry black llama dung lay in heaps. We reached this fort in the late afternoon, and by sundown the entire little army was encamped inside.

The air was dry and light and it gave me a swelling of the hands and lips. The horses were so blown I feared for some of them. I lay down by a fire of dung to sleep and in the privacy of the night tried to understand the Inca's mind. At either of these forts he could have stopped an army greater than ours. Had he no fear of us? Did he think to draw us further into his domain to use or destroy as it might please him? Or did we seem so mean he remained indifferent in his greatness? Certainly if he feared us, we had never advanced so far. Overhead the sky turned a silky black; the stars burned out the still and bitter air with instant luster, but no answer did they make to my question. But as I watched, they grew swollen and fell, burning the black fuel of the night until with horror I saw they were no stars but gold tipped arrows driving for our heads. I tried to rise, but my armor pinned me to the ground. . . .

I was sitting up stiff with cold. It was dawn. The fires had all burned out. My cloak and beard were icy and the scarf about my face. A faint stench of stale dung lay upon the ground. A few of the soldiers were stirring. Eight or ten old sergeants, the rejected of recruiting posts, lacking either an arm or an eye and quilted with scars, were moving about feeding their horses. They might be half fit for battle, but they would reach the field when others failed. I thawed a little and climbed the stairs to the rampart and there overlooked the brown and desolate ridges we had put behind us. They buttressed the high uneven plain. A thin white haze shut off the ocean, but the intervening desert, dull and monotonous, stretched as far as I could see. Could these be the gates of Paradise?

I turned away and saw de Soto rousing up the thirty. In no time he had them in the saddle. The crest was in sight but it took several hours to reach it, our animals stopping momently on the way. Their heaving flanks and distended nostrils told us what trouble they had in breathing the rare and frosty air. We had barely reached the top when one of the thirty fell from his saddle, bleeding at the ears, nose and mouth, and from the corners of his eyes. He began to vomit. I felt a slight dizziness and when I took off my gloves to help him, the blood was oozing from my hands. De Soto ordered a halt until the men could get more accustomed to the height. It was not until then I lifted my eyes upon the bleak and desolate scene around me. But it was not the bleakness that I noticed first. It was the awful silence. The men felt it too. They did not speak a word but sat gazing, like me, upon the Black Plain. And yet it was not a plain. It was an immense plateau holding up mountains and valleys, flatlands and dry stream beds. Only in front of us did the land run level, but here for many leagues it was plain. I call it land, though it resembled nothing we had ever seen anywhere before. We had climbed out of the world into a vast ash heap.

Without turning around—I suppose he hesitated to confront the reflection of this waste in the faces of the thirty—de Soto gave the command to go forward. After hours of riding we passed a troop of gliding llamas with their necks proudly curved. They stopped and turned upon us large, inquiring and timid eyes. Nor did they stir until we had all gone by, but stood with their suspicious ears thrust forward, ready on the instant to flee. Still deeper in we found near a marshy spot of ground ten or twelve vicunas grazing a belt of light green grass. I rode toward them to get a better look, for these were the sacred animals. The buck stamped his foot and made a sound, half neigh, half whistle, and they disappeared faster than deer. No other kind of life did we see. We were the sole inhabitants in this unpeopled world, and we were hurrying on our way.

Before the midday halt I picked up a speck in the road. I had been straining my eyes—it was dangerous to let your attention wander, the path was so faintly marked in stretches —so I thought at first the spot was a trick of fatigue. But I flicked my lids and it was still there, not only there but growing, not only growing but moving in our direction. For a moment I said, It is an animal, and then I realized that no animal would keep to the road in such a way. My interest quickened. Already we were advancing as fast as we dared push the horses; yet the pace increased almost of its own accord. And then at one certain moment the little ball exploded and I saw a toy man walking in our direction. Now I understand—indeed I understood it shortly afterwards—that it was the air, its rarity, marking out the figure so clearly at such a distance which gave me the illusion of magic. But to me then and there, wandering in that burnt-out strip of creation, that limbo of the bodied world, how else could the air seem but bewitched?

At last we met. I think the army had come to a halt. Certainly Pizarro had put himself in advance with the standard bearer and the interpreter and there received the Apoo who advanced with two mugs in his hands, drinking first from one and then from the other but always with a deliberate formality, the same he used before Pizarro at Zarran when he delivered the Inca's message. He stood erect and, pausing before he spoke, said, "The Sapa Inca invites you to drinking and I am come to drink in his name." Then he looked at the sky, quaffed the liquor in silence and afterwards kissed the air. Filling the mug afresh, he offered it to Pizarro with his right hand and to the captains with his left, saying "When will you reach Caxamalca? The Inca would know when to prepare for your reception."

In Christendom it would have been unseemly for an envoy to present his credentials in such a way, but I knew that the Indians in matters of state are more ceremonious than the Bishop of Rome; and so when he spoke of Atahualpa's power and his prowess in war, I listened carefully. The Legitimate said, "He's drunk." But he was not drunk. The long speech he made was designed to bring us trembling to the Inca's camp. Nor did the explicit form the invitation took deceive me. The elaborate presentation outdid the occasion.

Two days later a second envoy arrived. He asked the same question: "When will you sit down in Caxamalca?" Whatever doubts I might have had were now dispelled. We were in for serious trouble, but the credulous army, so wishfully did it look for grace, did not interpret the warning until Filipillo arrived with stories of bad treatment at the Inca's court. He was denied the mighty presence; he was beaten and almost killed. He escaped by saying that Pizarro held Atahualpa's men hostage for his safety. I think he spoke true, for when he saw the respect we showed the envoy, from very jealousy he fell upon him with a knife. The Legitimate knocked him down, and all the while the envoy kept his composure. Nor was Big-Ears ruffled when Pizarro asked how it was the Inca treated his man like a churl. Atahualpa, Big Ears replied, had withdrawn to fast. No man might view him at such times. And was it such a wonder that so scurvy a fellow was denied his presence? The wonder was that he only got a beating for his insolence. Who could believe that the strange Apoo had entrusted his embassy to a varlet? These answers seemed plausible—all too plausible. So I was prepared for desperate measures but not for what I saw when our little army, having put at last the Black Plain behind us, paused on the rim of the valley where Caxamalca raised its walls.

One by one we rode up to the crest of the mountain, and one by one fell silent. There below us spread the fairest and richest valley I had ever seen, with terraced fields along its sides, bottoms shimmering with green young maize, and, journeys away but seeming near by, a great mountain of snow, and about its top the frozen clouds made it taller than it was. So I remember this illusion. I must have seen it at a glance, one instant of sight, for there below the Inca had pitched his tents.

A man at arms may show no fear, but there were many there that day who but for their armor which laced their courage in would have slunk into Caxamalca and begged mercy of Atahualpa. The town lay to one side of the valley's bowl, like a town the plague has struck. No man nor woman nor child moved about its plaza or among the gay-thatched roofs. All life had fled to the farther and mottled slope. Wherever the eyes fell, whether upon the patches of yellow, the brighter reds, or the rusty llama browns, they failed to reach the limits of the Inca's camp. I had the feeling as I shifted my gaze from left to right and right to left that my head was a magic glass which spun the arrogant tents and pitched them where it willed. For could we believe what we saw, not thousands but tens of thousands of Indians, as great an army as ever our prince took down into Italy, and waiting for our . . . we scarcely numbered hundreds. Out of their midst there blew a lazy vapor. It blew out of the ground, out of a tiny house that sat alone, keeping at bay all this display of barbaric power. At once I knew I looked upon the Inca's baths. There Atahualpa took his ease and there, out of the indifferent vapors, the fate of Christians blew.

It seemed for a while that our eyes had murdered the will. My wits were as addled as the old hen who found her chicks tangled by tow and flax, for I thought not of what to do but of what the old writers tell of the two rivers which water the land, the Nilus which falls into the sea of Egypt and another of that name, but whether nature makes them to spring out of the mountains of the moon or of the sun or out of the tops of the rough mountains of Ethiopia the ancients do not say. Had we stumbled perchance on the land which hides the source of the other Nilus? There was a small stream running by Caxamalca and I knew that on the other side of these mountains there is a river whose gulf falls into the Ocean Sea fifty leagues wide and with so swift a course that by the violence and greatness of it the sea is driven back for leagues, although it is rough and enforced of a contrary wind. And they say the water is no way sour but sweet and fresh and able to be drunk far out to sea. Did I look upon its source? Did these Indians inhabit the mountains of the moon, or of the sun? Did any one hear me whisper, Is this Ethiopia? Its farthest province where Prester John, through the deep sea tunnels, led forth his might? Ata Hualpa? Prester John?

Pizarro gave a command. He had to repeat it. It was the command to descend into the valley. We formed in battle order and went down on Caxamalca in three ranks. To the right was the wayward. Here the best armed lancers rode and the men at arms, for several of us wore full armor. With these went de Soto and the Legitimate, dividing the command. To the left the battle formed, the pikes out in front, the sword and buckler behind them, ready to protect the flanks of the solid-moving pikemen or run around them and finish up their work. Juan took the rearward, the horsemen riding *à la gineta,* in their short stirrups from which they would rise and give an added length and a wider sweep to their swords. With these went the three arquebusiers and the crossbowmen guarding the single piece of ordnance. Out in front of all rode Pizarro and his household, the trumpeters sounding their shrill and brassy notes. We all took heart and went along singing Te Deum Laudamus. For one moment I caught Pizarro's eye. There was the haste in it that a lover has when he reaches the end of his journey.

Armed in form and point of war, we reached the floor of the valley. Without stopping we rode down upon the Indian host. Without haste or lagging we rode. Each horse's hoof struck the ground as though it might rise for the charge, and the trumpeter's lips half parted for the trumpet. Then within ten crossbow shots we paused, turned, and in full sight of the Inca's tents, moved towards Caxamalca. No shout greeted us, no hostile sally, but for the full league we went I could feel the thousands of Indians passing us from eye to eye. We drew up unmolested, unwelcomed, before the gates of Caxamalca. We looked over the low wall into the three-cornered plaza. It was empty. No one barred our way. Not even the meanest official stood up to greet or forbid us entry. We hesitated, listening for some sign of life, but no sound issued from the streets or the dwelling places. Desertion and silence was Atahualpa's reply to our challenge.

We continued to hesitate. It was not so much fear of ambush. I know that I dismissed the thought, for the Inca had turned his whole range of mountains into an ambush. And should one so great deal with his enemies like a forest chieftain? Why should he not, if it pleased him, empty this town of its ten thousand souls for our reception? And had he not, taking his ease with his wives, bathing in the perfumed waters, bade us climb mountains, struggle with all known hardships, and hurry over the Black Plain to put ourselves, without the slightest effort on his part, into the very fingers of his might? Were we not even then before his very eyes, performing the last steps in the progress he had willed for us? So, I reasoned, it must have seemed to Atahualpa. And so it must have seemed to many of us. No, we did not hesitate from caution, although scouts were sent into the town before us. We paused at those gates for one and only one reason: the air of Caxamalca had a fatal smell.

We made our entry with studied boldness, but as soon as the noise of it died away, the silence returned. There is a feeling of hunger about a deserted town, and this hunger breathed from the houses, hung over the roofs and narrow ways, usurped our places in the plaza and said,—You are already ghosts to inhabit this place. The scouts returned, all with the same report. Everywhere was emptiness, the people all gone and the trappings out of the houses, the large golpons on the western face of the plaza empty, the fort at its northern end undefended. Here and there a few old women sat in doorways or speechless on mats in the backs of rooms. We listened with no surprise.

"The Inca has strained his hospitality," de Soto said.

All the while Pizarro was riding restlessly along the third side of the plaza, a wall some two thousand paces long. Beyond it, in plain view, lay the Indian camp. I heard him call de Soto. "Take twenty horse," he said, "and go to the Inca. Say that I have come on behalf of God and King to preach to them and to have them for friends. Say whatever you will, but—" he turned quickly as though if he looked away the Indian host might vanish—"make this Atahualpa come to Caxamalca. That is your mission. Invite him to dine with me. This afternoon or tomorrow. Perhaps the day is too far spent. To-morrow. But the Inca must come to Caxamalca." The last words Pizarro said slowly and lovingly; then, breaking his mood, he looked sharply at his lieutenant to see that he understood. Before de Soto could bow his acknowledgment of the order, he had dismissed him.

I was stunned. I knew that Pizarro was not indifferent to the risk of placing a tenth of his army, more than a tenth in valor, at Atahualpa's mercy. Indifference was inconceivable; and yet Pizarro seemed to ignore all danger as one might who has full knowledge of the outcome, whose only eagerness is to cheat time and pronounce the end. I helped get the twenty together and we went at a trot until we neared the stream behind which the Inca had pitched his tents. There was an osier bridge between us, and on the other side a squadron of blackhaired soldiers. Obviously they expected to halt us at the stream.

De Soto saw the moment was upon us. Giving a signal to the twenty, he put his barb into a gallop and cleared the water. Through the host we rode and Indians gave before us, and we made a music as we went, a sweet grim music, with bells ringing against the horses' plates, the hilts of our swords clattering against steel, and at each saddle bow an extra cutlass clattering. Thus we swept on and thus we reached the baths.

I say reached the baths. It was rather the great open space around them, for the tents of the army did not intrude on the imperial presence. We crossed this yard at a walk, for de Soto thought it more seemly to approach in such a fashion. The interpreter rode at his side. We had scarcely arrived when we heard the sound of charging horse behind. It was as though the wind had blown back upon us the echo of our own hoofbeats. I turned to see the Legitimate arriving with a small body of horse. Evidently Pizarro had had a sudden qualm of fear when he actually saw how few he had sent among so many. The Legitimate rode up and spoke to de Soto. Together they rode forward, their lancers at a walk behind them. To the front and right, where the steam rose out of the earth in clouds, stood a great tank made of cut and fitted stone. "That is where the Lord Inca and his wives go to bathe," the interpreter whispered. "No other person dare enter on pain of death. It has two pipes, one hot, one cold, so that the water may be tempered for their worshipful skins."

I nodded, for I was looking at the small house adjoining the baths, the flurry—it was no more than that—of guards and courtiers standing before its entrance. I noticed other rooms evidently built for attendants and, at a respectful distance, azure tents set in strict array. "For his hereditary vassals," the interpreter said.

We halted before the entrance of the house. All was calm before it. The door was hidden by guards in azure mantles, their polished armor of bronze plates showing beneath, their legs bare to the blue and white sandals. Their helmets mounted like the pope's tiara, except that in place of three crowns the sun's rays, in formal pattern, circled, and out of their tops, stiff and fragile, parrot feathers curved arrogantly, reaching to the thatched roof. All had bucklers but certain squads were armed with darts, two to a man, and a peculiar sword hung at their sides. But dressed upon the shoulders of most lay battle clubs of bronze and stone with star-like heads, the radial points sharp and conical. Here and there the points alternated with axe blades.

"The Canari guard," whispered the interpreter.

In front of the guard the courtiers had arranged themselves, standing apart from a haughty figure. He was dressed all in spangled yellow, his sandals woven of silver thread with a dark blue tongue lapping his shins. Upon his head sat a dress shaped like an axe. It had a face carven on it. A sheaf of feathers leaned over his eyes and waved slowly as he moved. The dress sat so low upon his forehead the feathers seemed to sprout from his nose. About his neck ran a gorget of heavy gold beads and in his hand he held a staff as black as chocolate with loose feathers of the condor's tail in its knob. The staff was polished until it made the light run darkly over its surface.

"Are you the Lord Inca?" de Soto asked.

"No, no," the interpreter corrected him. "That is Rumenavi, old stone eyes."

I looked more closely at the Indian's face. In one pupil a cast had marred his sight until the eyes did seem hard and glaring stone.

"Where then is your Lord?" de Soto demanded. "Where is Atahualpa?"

Rumenavi did not answer but glared at horse and rider.

De Soto knew how to wait, what face it gives among these infidels; but Rumenavi strained his patience. He repeated, "Present me to your lord," and lowered his lance so that its point lay directly before the other's eyes. Perhaps this was indiscreet, but Rumenavi gave him an answer, a very brief answer. The Sapa Inca made his fast. He could not be disturbed. What did the strangers want?

"My business is with your master. Go tell him the envoy of the Sacred Caesarian Catholic Majesty, Charles, the fifth of that name, demands an audience."

He had scarcely done speaking when the guards withdrew from before the house. I had heard no command, but quietly and with precision they lined up on either side of the entrance. The courtiers prostrated themselves before a heavy curtain dyed a rich color, again azure, and hanging across the entire front of the house. As I watched, invisible hands took it and drew it slowly back. The first thing I saw was a frosty web hanging in vacant space, several feet above the floor and exactly in the center of the room. As the curtains drew farther away, the light entered and the web became a thin white gauze. Two hands appeared holding it; two arms appeared and then two light-skinned women. Between them, upon a low seat covered by a delicate mantle, sat a figure which they were shielding. The room was as bare as a cell.

No one moved. The Indians seemed to be holding their breath. And then Rumenavi took off his sandals, put a small burden of sticks on his back and, bowing and trembling, approached the hidden presence. Averting his gaze, he said a few words in a low voice. The silence grew unbearable. I felt the need to break it and spurred my horse a little closer. The guards moved towards me in a body, tightening their hands about their weapons. They grunted altogether and stopped.

At a command the women had dropped the veil. Atahualpa had revealed himself. At last we were in the presence of the son of the Sun.

De Soto waited for some sign from him to make known his business, but with his head lowered in contemplation Atahualpa kept the silence he had made. De Soto's horse reached forth its foot and pawed the ground. It shook itself. The furniture rattled and the bells on its plates tinkled. I knew the Inca must be as anxious to see us as we had been to see him, but he did not lift his eyes. Yet I thought I saw him glance at the animal's hoof. It was Rumenavi who finally asked de Soto to state his business. This he did. What he said I do not now remember. I remember only his anger.

His lord, Rumenavi replied, would decide what would be done with us after he had ended his fast. De Soto now raised his voice and said he would not leave until the Inca gave him a plain answer: would he, or would he not, come and dine with his, de Soto's, Captain General?

At last the Inca raised the head bound by the imperial llautu. Its fringe reached to his eyes. Each cord of the fringe bore at its middle a small golden tube, and when the head moved the tubes made a clear tinkling sound. Out of the llautu above white eagle feathers, two long red plumes taken from the tail of the pillcopichiu bird rose into the air. I was told that in all Peru there were only two of these birds, who bred in secret places that the diadem of each new Inca might be adorned. On the left side of this llautu was a plate of gold set in gems. Oval shells covered his ears. His eyes were shot with blood. He began to speak.

His voice was soft and like a bird's at candle light. It was true, he said, that he made his fast. By tomorrow it would be over. Then he would come to the place where we were. This we might announce to our lord. Tell him also to hold himself in readiness to account for the disrespect he had shown him, Atahualpa, by taking some matting from the room in Tumbez where his father, Huayna Capac, had been wont to sleep. Tell him, also, to be ready to repay all that he had taken between Tumbez and Caxamalca, the food as well as the other things. Such payment he was to hold in readiness against the morrow. Furthermore, take care none of his subjects moved out of the plaza, nor wandered over the town of Caxamalca. He specified which golpons we were to occupy. When he had finished, he lowered his eyes as a sign the audience was ended.

I was dismayed, for I knew de Soto would not leave thus chided. His barbary was wiry, intelligent, and trained. In the space before the baths he made him to prance, curvet, and charge, and at the end drove him straight upon Atahualpa. At a full gallop he brought him to a stop so close to the Inca the horse's breath blew in the Indian's face. Several of his subjects drew back in terror, but Atahualpa made no move nor did a wrinkle come in his grave, handsome face. Only this: as de Soto bowed, he turned his head and spat into the hands of one of his wives.

Pizarro gave out the order of the watch, and we waited for the night to come. It came suddenly, as we were finishing our rations of maize and a soup made from dried beans, which we drank out of our beavers. Quietly the outguards took their places. In the golpons horses might be uncinched but not unsaddled. The fires of the Inca had been lit long before dark. At first they made pale spots on the sky, but even as we watched the spots grew hard and bright. Pizarro walked down to the long wall. Gonzalo stayed behind, playing at dice. The bitter air crept down the mountains and settled about our feet. I thought I heard a noise and looked to the rear, but I saw only the shadows from the deserted buildings crowding the men bunched in the plaza and overhead the black fort swelling like carrion. Chaves took me by the arm. "I don't want you to think I've lost my wits," he said, "but I can no longer tell where the camp fires end and the stars begin."

I made him no answer. After a long silence, Pizarro asked de Soto with a certain wonder, "The Inca spat into the hands of his wife?"

"He will never spit upon the ground," the interpreter replied, "but for his majesty and state, when he has the occasion, uses the hand of the principal lady he loves."

"The pride of the heathen," Pizarro said angrily and walked away.

Later that night I lay down by the three arquebusiers. They had the only fire which was allowed to burn after dark. It was made in the mouth of the golpon and was screened by mantles and coats, but even so the men had orders to put it out as soon as they were done casting their bullets. They had used up their lead and were throwing copper trinkets into the open pot. One squatted by the fire watching the copper melt into slow and gluey bubbles. He had upon his face a look of puzzled concentration. At intervals he would reach forth his hands as though they had a purpose. They would falter and wave vaguely over the coals, catch the heat and rub it. His companions were cutting lengths of iron wire into thirds and fourths and bending each end into a hook. They spoke little, pausing long enough in their work to salute de Soto, who came in shortly afterwards and found me. The third man grabbed the long handle of the pot. "Ready?" he asked. The others nodded. One divided the mold with a leaf of iron as thin as paper, the other lay the two hooks on either side of it, the third poured in the liquid copper, picked up the mold and dashed it into water. Two bullets now clung to each end of the wire.

"These chain shot do great execution among pikes, Captain."

The oldest man addressed de Soto. "You put the two bullets together in the arquebus, so. They spread out when shot and will break three or four pikes at once. I don't know how well they work among Indians. If they come at us in mass. . . ."

I must have fallen asleep as they talked, for I was aroused by de Soto shaking me by the arm. "Are you awake?"

"Yes," I answered. "What o'clock?"

He did not answer me at once; then he said, "It is the turning of the tides."

We crossed the empty plaza. It was utterly dark; but as I glanced over the long wall, I saw in the plain that the night had thinned. Before the vase-like door of Pizarro's quarters a voice made a low challenge, and from either side of the entrance two heavy blurs moved out from the wall. I heard the halberds make a thud as they crossed. De Soto gave his name. The staffs fell sharply to the ground, ringing dully against their plates as the guards stiffened in salute. De Soto stooped over and entered the room. I followed.

The captains turned as though we had surprised them in some secret. Two torches had been stuck in opposite walls. Between these Pizarro stood. He was clad in full armor. Under the flickering light the shadow from his long gaunt figure lay flat against the painted wall, crawled and bent itself over the roof beams and blackened the thatch. In a group the officers faced him, the brothers, Francisco Chaves, Juan de Herrada, de Candia, and others. To one side stood Friar Valverde. They opened and gave us place. After the movement we had caused,

Pizarro said, "We are all gathered?" He waited a moment and I could hear the heavy breathing around the room. Then he began to speak. "Our scouts report that during the night a large force has passed to our rear. In the dark the scouts were able to get close enough to hear the enemy. It took the column well over an hour to pass. Filipillo reports that the Indians had ropes and spoke of tying us up as we fled." Pizarro paused. "This is Atahualpa's reply to my invitation. Great and small, these Indians are ever treacherous. We come to the backside of the world to bring them salvation, and they repay us with treachery. But we will know how to meet it." Again he paused, and I saw his eyes glint as he lifted his head, but they plunged almost at once into shadow.

"How?" de Soto asked.

Pizarro leaned slightly forward and an eagerness grew in his voice. "When Señor Atahualpa enters the plaza, there will be no one there to greet him."

The walls of the fort pressed against the darkness and then suddenly it was everywhere light. The plaza was empty. Not a Christian was in sight. Only bits of harness and scattered dung showed that ever the solitude of this heathen city had been broken. Over the fields beyond Caxamalca the air was clear and dry. From my stand in the large door of the golpon I looked across at the Inca camp. It was all quiet there.

Behind me a stallion neighed, hoofs pounded, metal struck metal. There were curses, harsh and brief. I turned about in time to see the unruly stallion brought in hand. In a few moments all was order again. Each lancer stood by his mount. The pikes were massed to the rear. To one side the sword and bucklers spoke together in low tones, and over against the

right wall the crossbowmen and arquebusiers leaned at ease.
One of them, with his head bent over, was testing the thongs
of his piece. I dismounted and gave the horse into the charge
of de Soto's page and walked to where Pizarro stood with his
captains. None spoke as I came up. Their eyes were all fixed
in the same direction, watching for some movement among
the tiny bright tents.

The sun swung high over the mountains and still we
waited. Not once had Pizarro taken his eyes from the door.
"The Inca must be washing with all his women today," Juan
said. A few leers responded to this jest but I was startled by
the roughness of his voice and realized that nobody had
spoken for a long while.

"Do you suppose the troops that passed in the night are
coming upon us from the rear?" the Legitimate asked in a
guarded tone.

Pizarro shook his head; then turned and glanced over his
shoulder at the companies of horse and foot gathered into the
large golpon. My gaze followed his. I noticed how thin and
galled the horses looked. The men were sitting, some of them
sprawling on the floor. Half our forces were in this hall and
did not crowd it. The soldiers' faces bore the marks of watch-
fulness which prisoners habitually show.

"Listen!" Pizarro commanded.

The blood rushed to my ears so that I did not hear; then
faintly beating under the blood's beat, like a thing that struggles not to expire, I heard a quickened throbbing.

"Drums!" Chaves said.

The cries and clatter of armor shut off all sound. Up from
the floor the sharp smell of sour clothes blew under my nose.
The golpon grew still again, and I was leaning forward to
meet the sound traveling under the air. It was sharp but like a

thing of moods it had changed. Out of the drums there came a thin high wailing of wind instruments and, thickening the beat, the slow-quick chant of voices. But no movement out of the camp. The sound might have been demons playing in a wood. I looked at the sun. It was near the hour of High Mass.

Thus it stood for a while. And then out of the camp into the fields on either side of the road the Indians began to pour. The two masses rolled forward like lava. For another while the road held clear; but suddenly as though it had just broken free, a bright tongue squirmed its way over the bridge. Upon its back a casket glinted in the sun, "Jesu, there are thousands of them."

On they came but so slowly it took them until near three hours of night to draw nigh the town. A haze of dust hovered above the Inca's array of forces and over the golpon. The horses were growing more and more restless. When their patience broke under the singing and the drums I cannot say, but at one certain moment they began to plunge and kick and bite. I ran to the gelding and took hold of the bridle. He had knocked the boy down and was pawing him. The boy rolled out of the way, crossing himself. This I saw without looking, for the confusion was growing. As it was about to break into panic, Pizarro's voice fell flat over the heads of man and beast. "Stand to arms! Lancers mount."

In no time at all, with the riders upon their backs, the horses stood as mild as carrier beasts.

The Indians were so close upon us we could make out their features. Dancing and singing chants of victory, bands of servitors swept the road before the lord's litter. On either side of it companies of warriors marched through the open fields. The Canari guard walked closest to the Inca, some two thousand of them surrounding him on either side. They carried themselves like peacocks and the shouts they gave on the downbeat of their tread was like the peacock's cry. Into the plaza filed the Inca's train until it crowded every part of it, and the noise stifled the air. I tried to count, gave it up, saw Pizarro reckon each company as it moved in through the gates. But he too gave it up and lifted his eyes to the sky. I followed his gaze. The sun was far down the western slope.

Suddenly the plaza grew still. In the silence a prince of the blood came forward. He was attired like the Sun's messenger with his garments girt about his loins, bearing a lance all studded over with golden nails. Out of the staffhead colored plumes fell to the ground. But the herald faded from our eyes, for Atahualpa had reached the gates. With even pace over the tops of heads the bearers whose life it was to stumble made the royal litter to glide like a lazy bird. But a giant and oriental bird, for the litter was lined with feathered robes and pillows of down, and out of the feathers jewels played with the failing light. Atahualpa's chair was of beaten gold, and the canopy raised over it, held in the hands of princes, was mounted with plates of silver overlapped by plates of gold.

The Inca lord sat like an idol in his robes, and about his feet the embroidery was as stiff as death. At his neck lay a collar of emeralds, fifty-two stones the size of a pigeon's egg, and from the stones hung carven topaz likened unto the sun and moon and the moon's fifty-two phases. Two fingers of hair fell at his ears and about his head circled the royal llautu. For scepter he bore a golden axe, and this he held immovable in his hand. Thus did he enter with the lord of Chincha at his feet, and thus did he come to a halt in the center of the plaza. Seconds passed. He moved slightly, turning his head. His voice at last broke the silence. "Where, then, are the strangers?" He asked.

The air about me turned sharp and acrid. I looked down.
A halberdier had made water in his hose.

The silence could not hold. An Indian captain was approaching the Inca. De Soto turned to Pizarro. "In God's
name. . . ."

Pizarro's voice, a little high but clear, cut him off. His hand
grasped Father Vincente de Valverde by the sleeve. "Go to that
Indian lord. . . ." His voice broke off. He gave the priest a
shove.

The priest slipped through the door, breviary in one hand
and upraised crucifix in the other. Following close behind
went the interpreter and Aldana, a good soldier. They advanced through the silent Indians until they came before the
litter. At once the priest began to harangue the Inca as
though the heathen understood the Christian tongue. Pizarro,
close in to the wall, peeped through the door. The Legitimate
said, "The priest is running the Pope's authority from Adam.
Give the signal, brother. He will speak us into night."

"Hold," Pizarro said.

The priest had just handed his breviary to the Inca, carefully holding his robes from touching the feathered litter.
Atahualpa took the book and turned it over in his hands. He
let it fall to the ground.

"Give him the sword for this sacrilege," Valverde shouted,
leaning over to pick the breviary from the dirt.

"He'll ruin us all," de Soto said under his breath.

Aldana drew his sword and flourished it, but he whispered
to the priest and they began hastily to retire.

The three arquebusiers and bowmen had quietly taken
their places behind the doors and cocked their weapons. Just
as the priest scuttled into the golpon, Pizarro waved his scarf.
Somebody shouted Santiago and at them! The arquebusiers

touched matches to their pieces. The room roared with re-
verberations of the explosions. The horses charged into the
open. From the fort sounded the heavy explosion of the
falconet. With the cries of chivalry on our lips and the bells
ringing on the horses' plates, we struck the Indians.

In the first instant of confusion the Indians stood as though
fastened to the ground; and then we were knocking them
down like ninepins. In as many seconds I lanced a dozen.
Then I lost count. I always aimed for the belly. There the
flesh gave as easily as butter, but once I grew careless—it was
so easy—and pushed through to the backbone. It took some
seconds to release the lance. I had to put my foot against the
Indian's middle; and, jerking back, I saw the priest running
in and out among the Christians giving absolution where he
went.

The Inca's retinue, almost at once, was reduced to complete
confusion. The surprise of our attack, its constant pressure,
drove his servants against the walls and buildings. In the
midst of the battle I saw the Inca's litter dip and roll like a
boat in a storm. Pizarro had reached within a lance of his
prize. The pikemen laid the lord's guards down in ranks,
the sword and bucklers ran through to finish up the boldest
who leaped at the pikes to drag them down. This close, but
no closer, did the Christians get. As one rank went down,
another took its place. The Indians had made a wall of death
about their lord and he, now still, now shaken, looked with
bewilderment upon what he saw.

Then into the cries and the trumpets, the explosions of the
falconet, there came a terrific crash, a gasping silence, and a
long wailing. The wall for some thousand paces had given
away and the Indians were spilling over into the plain. The
Legitimate, hanging upon the rear of this mass, drove them as

far as the baths. My horse was drawn into the tow of this flight and pursuit. With great difficulty I turned about and, with eight of my companions who had been swept aside, worked back towards the litter. Slowly we lunged through those remaining in the plaza until we reached again the wall of death. There we stopped. Grabbing mane and tail, at bridle and hoof, the Canari guard held us fast. For one we cut away four rose up to take his place. I fought until my mouth grew parched; hot wires burned along my arms; and still the Inca kept his chair. No word of encouragement did he give to the guard, nor did his vanishing fortunes seem to move him. Aloof, he watched the furious struggle for his person and his throne as if it were a show set forth for his pleasure.

The shadows began to creep up the mountain slopes. In spite of the success of our arms the approaching dark might lose us our prize, for unless Atahualpa fell into our hands, the scattering of his retinue was empty work. Not only empty work, but we were done for. This was painfully clear, and it was equally clear that we now faced something more invincible than steel and horse. Our adversary was death, and death served the unshaken majesty of this Indian lord.

With this thought in mind Pizarro made one last great effort and cleared the way to the litter where we fought until from very weariness a Christian drew his dagger to stab the Inca. Pizarro came between and turned the weapon. "Let no man kill him on pain of death," he shouted hoarsely. And then out of desperation some seven or eight of us rushed the litter, took hold of it and tumbled the Inca out of his chair.

At the sight the Canari guard gave up in despair. Some few fled, but the most of them stood helplessly about. They gave themselves up without further resistance. Later many of those who had fled returned and sat down around the house where their lord was imprisoned.

Atahualpa had scarcely been put away before night and a cold wind blew down from the peaks and settled over Caxamalca and the plain beyond. We, the victors, drew together in this strange place, thousands of leagues from Christendom, on the backside of the world, and in awe viewed what our hands had wrought. The dead and the hurt lay heaped in the plaza. The mighty host of the heathen lord was broken and scattered. A kingdom of riches such as we had never imagined lay to our hands and we, a few poor companies of horse and foot, had done this thing without the loss of a single life. Pizarro alone showed a wound, one in the hand, got in fending for his royal prisoner.

In the hiatus which follows every battle de Soto and Pizarro stood together in the sudden dark and looked over the wreckage, over the plain, to the sloping hill where, the night before, the Inca's host had lain around its thousands of fires. The two men looked on in silence. No longer would the stars be confused by the fires' glow. They were out—forever out. Perhaps it was of this the two captains were thinking. After a while de Soto's voice slipped through the darkness. "God's miracle," he whispered.

"Amen," I murmured or thought I spoke. Now I am unsure. Now that de Soto, Pizarro, all who took part in that conquest are dead, either dead or scattered, or like me fit only to speak of the things they did when their strength was in them, now the word sounds across the long past like the sign of an alchemical charm. That day a kind of alchemy was done. So it seems to me, now that I can see better the end. Most men are hastening to meet some disaster. Yet whatever it was which on that day of triumph filled the eyes of those two captains, it seemed to them a thing of radiance, in white robes and most beautiful. But beside them there was in attendance a companion clad in very different guise. As they reached out their hands to clasp their desires, that other—the dark thing—stepped forward to receive them.

A NOVEL :

a name for evil

To Edna

WHEN I SAW THE HOUSE I SAID, "THE LINES ARE GOOD. IT is in bad repair, but it will suit my purpose all the better." Its decay was not such that it was beyond restoration. Perhaps I should say regeneration, for I had bought more than a house. There was land attached and because land has history, is history rather, involving lives and fateful happenings, it is more exact to say regeneration. I ignored this fact, looking over the house with her that fall afternoon and talking excitedly over the problems which the abuse of indifferent tenants and croppers had caused, in their brutish way emphasizing the neglect of the owners. How sad, I reflected, and how evil a thing it is, to let a noble establishment be put into the hands of the depraved who care only for draining the land of its strength, always taking out, never putting back the food of life! But at the moment I must confess it was the house which occupied me. In spite of the decay it was beautiful on that day, a day bright and cool with the first dry breath of autumn. How much I would have spared us all, had I faced logically the entire meaning of the ruin we were about to enter and make our own!

I am convinced now there are certain places which the past holds, literally, absolutely, and with a tenure no present occupant can dispute. I do not pretend to understand the metaphysics of such a lien, but I have felt its power. I do not speak now of the grosser illusion of ghosts with chains and such tommyrot, and yet who can say that even they, in all their melodramatic clanking, do not exist? What forms of being, what substances, do we not today accept, which once the wisest opinion would have denied? Man's brain, whirling in the vacuum it creates, precipitates from nothing the once hidden secrets of the universe. I smile as I use the word. Even the laws of the universe in this dark crucible must find another definition.

At some remote time the farm had belonged to my family, not to my immediate forebears, but to a collateral branch of the Revolutionary major who "removed," as the saying went, to the current West of the time. There have been so many Wests in our national life it puzzles me no end why historians take so little account of the true meaning of this remarkable circumstance. Unhappily our scholarship took for model the nineteenth-century German method of objectivity with all its sterile accumulation of data for data's sake. So many sins, public and private, have been disguised by pseudo-scientific jargon. Like the mole underground the scholars dug and they dug, in their blindness through their dark tunnel.

And the historian most of all reflected this infatuation. To write straight English prose made him suspect among his fellows. To show imagination—that was professional suicide. The West, the progression of Wests: could he not see that there was more than accident to this repetition? The word, the faith rather of it, always in the American consciousness, the last resort of the desperate in fortune and body, what could it mean but one thing? To yearn for the West is simply to yearn for death. Why was it given to me, to me alone, to understand it like a prophet and to suffer it like a martyr?

I had just left Ellen somewhere in the house. The tenant's wife had given us permission to go through it, too obligingly I thought, or rather I didn't think. I only felt the woman's manner. But I paid her no mind, for I was enthralled with my wife's enthusiasm and her light gay movements about the dirty, scarred rooms. The wallpaper was torn from the walls, the plaster cracked and written upon, the edges of the floors painted the most horrid color of yellow; and where there wasn't the grime of years, the tenants' filthy disorder made even the grime look respectable. Through this Ellen sailed like an angel, exclaiming over the impressive woodwork, the winding stair, all the good points which she and I would revive for our own ends. I had never admired or loved her more than on that day. Her lovely little feet fairly seduced me all over again. There was something, as my father had said, about her gait. If he could have seen her then, he would have known it was the gait of a thoroughbred.

Disorder and ruin fascinate yet depress me. I felt the need for air and perspective and so went out into the yard. Soon I was busy at the problems before us. A small passageway between the kitchen and the main dwelling had been closed. This must be knocked out to restore the charm of covered ways meant to protect servants from the weather. The roof needed painting, window sills had rotted away, blinds were hanging askew or missing entirely; but I told myself that these were superficial things after all. The house, built of solid brick, was surely sound. How long it took me to finish these calculations I have no way of knowing. I merely wandered to the front of the house, thinking Ellen would be there. She was not there. This seemingly trivial fact contained for us the mystery of all fatality. It gave the slight jar to the door which even then was closing to shut us off from the natural world. The fateful moments of life are never discerned as they occur. Nor are they ever dramatic. At best they count as unimportant trifles to be brushed aside or forgotten. But later, when it is too late, we see them for what they are: signposts. It is for this reason they go unnoted. A sign points the way. It makes no comment on the end of the journey.

I called Ellen's name. The tenant's wife came to the door and said, "Ellen's in here."

I looked at her coldly. "Whom do you mean?" I asked. "Mrs. Brent?"

I felt both anger and pity for the woman. The unique triumph of universal education is the successful way it debases the mind. Besides making the ignorant arrogant, this spun sugar of our political carnival has corrupted manners. A little understanding of reading, writing, and ciphering caused this poor woman—I do not overlook her feeling of injustice, but alas, if one seeks justice . . . —to assert her feeling of inferiority by assuming a social familiarity which doesn't come by paying the poll tax. If she had been called on to justify herself, she would have said, "She ain't no better'n me." To this has come Jefferson's dream and to this the lifting of a political phrase out of the context of its time. In

God's sight we are all equal, but God's intentions are inscrutable. In the blindness of the world there is no alternative to good manners but brute force.

As we were driving away I said to Ellen, "I told the tenant he would have to find another place."

"But I thought you were going to let him stay on?"

I then explained to her my reasons. Her voice hastened, "But it is too late to trade for another year."

"I will find someone."

"But if you don't, we can't afford to let the farm lie idle and we are not ready to move."

"If the worst comes to the worst, we can take over," I said confidently.

"But the house—we can't live in it as it is."

"We won't be living. We'll camp at first and see it change under our hands. I think that would be rather fun."

"Fun?" She queried. "There's no waterworks . . . no . . . no bathroom."

"Mighty good people made out all their lives without a bathroom. We ought to for a while."

"I know, but, darling . . ."

"Now, don't you worry your pretty head about this. I'll fix it."

She was silent as we drove back to town.

2

As it turned out, Ellen's apprehensions were justified. I could not find a tenant who would take over responsibility for the farm. I did find a Negro family who had been associated with the place for many generations. This family moved in that winter, but we waited until early spring. To try to live in the house over the hard winter months would have exposed us to unnecessary hardship. After all *The Grove,* for so the place was called, was to serve us, not we it.

We arrived one day in early spring to take formal possession.

"Are you sure this is what you want?" Ellen was asking.

We had just stopped the car in front of the house and were looking at it. We had not alighted. We sat in silence, I at the wheel and she beside me. I replied irritably, or perhaps my voice carried a conviction that was rather forced. "Of course this is what I want," I said. And then as if to press her as an accomplice, "Don't you want to do it? We've talked and planned of a place all our own, a sort of base. Well, you've got to have a place to keep your books."

"I was only thinking," she said.

"Thinking of what?"

"It's going to take a lot of money and a lot of work. I thought . . ."

"Yes?" I was a little impatient.

"Only that we ought to be sure."

"Of course we are sure," I said and got out of the car.

I slammed the door harder than I meant to.

She came to me and slipped her arm through mine. I pressed her to me for an instant. I did not understand my mood. I felt as if I had been put on the defensive and that my defense was false. This made me irritable, for there was no apparent reason for it. Nothing had occurred to make me change my mind, but as I stood on the broad lawn and looked through the old ragged cedars at the dwelling, I involuntarily pressed Ellen's arm into my side. We had seen *The*

Grove many times, in fact and in the mind's eye, but we had never seen it empty before. The sloven Blacks—that was the name of the tenants I had ejected—gave it a certain if sorry kind of life. Well, life is scarcely the word. They had never lived there in the sense that you make a house reflect your being. Nor was it merely that they were slipshod tenants. I have seen croppers turn a shack into a livable and thriving scene of domestic well-being. The Blacks had done little better than camp at the place. Now gone, they could no longer divert me from seeing the truth. It was this truth which held my eyes and fixed me to the spot. *The Grove* did not look empty! Even in its forlorn condition it gave all the appearance of having a life of its own. What this might be I, in my ignorance, could not decide. But in a few short seconds this much of my feeling had clarified itself: whatever this life was, it was to become ours too.

With this thought in mind I turned to Ellen. I turned with the abruptness of the descent of this knowledge. "Come, darling," I said with spirit, "I must carry you over the threshold."

"No, you don't," she answered playfully but pushing me away all the same. "You've carried me over two thresholds already."

I tried to grab her but she raced across the lawn, under the great cedars and up to the entrance doorway. She pulled open the heavy walnut door and sidled in. "Wait for me," I cried and ran after her, but before I could reach the top step, the door slowly swung to between us.

I grasped the knob. It was old brass and well tarnished. I grabbed it, turned it, but the door remained fast. Nervously I shook it, shaking, and calling her name. She did not answer. I set my face against the long red glass, those happy inventions

of a day of much visiting, cast to give the host that moment
of advantage, after the knocker falls, when he may look out
but the guest may not look in. The redness of the glass blurred
the long entrance hall, and the winding stair wavered as objects do under water, but Ellen I did nowhere see. I had only
to run to the back of the house to enter, but I felt drawn to
that door. Through that door alone I would enter and find
my wife. It was ridiculous. The day was overcast and coldish,
as are so many early spring days, but it was ten o'clock in the
morning. Men were turning the land. In the field to the side
of the house two dogs were chasing a rabbit, and yet I felt that
to separate my hand from that tarnished brass knob would set
me adrift on a tow which would sweep me forever away from
the safe known into the swirling pools of strangeness. I made
a lurch at the knob—you can see how far gone I was in
hysteria—when at my ear a voice said, "Excuse me, sir, I'll
unlock d' door for you."

"But it isn't locked," I almost shouted.

The Negro bent down and slipped the old key into its
lock, making the necessary movement into a bow, with just the
proper inclination of his head in my direction. In that short
time I managed to compose myself so that I was fairly calm as
he stepped back.

"You can enter now," he said gravely, handing me the
key. "Them folks give it to me when they removed."

"Thank you, Johnny," I replied more easily. "Miss Ellen
went in before me. I could not understand how the door
locked itself."

He made no response to this but presented me the blank
mask of patience and reserve which with Negroes of a certain
generation seems to imply a secret commentary.

Once inside I hurried through empty rooms, each one

flashing its peculiar mark of decay and abuse . . . paper hanging from the walls, the stain of rain, old rags thrust through a window light. I hurried on, into the dining room, its grime and grease thick on the floor and splashed about the wainscoting near the mantel. The rusty flue mouth gaped obscenely. Charred holes gouged the floor where the Blacks and others like the Blacks had set the cookstove. It was the well-swept floors which set off these marks of debased living. Johnny had followed my directions. I noted this even in my distraction, for the landlord can tell by the way the new tenant reacts to his orders how well they will get on together.

But in none of these rooms did I find Ellen. I waited until I had got out of hearing of the hall and called. It was important not to be surprised again in Johnny's hearing. "Ellen!" My voice sounded no louder than an urgent whisper. "Ellen, Ellen" went before me up the back stairs and through the upper rooms of the L. But no reply did I get to an appeal become too desperate for the occasion. My alarm was absurd, yet for all its absurdity, how real!

The particular charm of the place lay in its L. The house itself was the usual multiple of the dog run, raised to imposing proportions, hall above and below, with four bedrooms of enormous size opening on the upper hall and attached to each room a small cabinet for dressing. Near the front of the upper hall a passage opened onto a long narrow gallery, with brick arches supporting the roof. This gallery repeated itself on the other side, so that one might walk entirely around the three small rooms, all in a row and opening to either view. Each room stood at a level lower than the one above, causing you to step down the arched way until you came to the bottom level. Here the gallery separated the end room from the other two. In this room I found Ellen.

The door stood open. A moment passed before she gave any sign of recognition. On seeing me, she started slightly. "Why, darling, you seem all in a fuss," she said, smiling sweetly and coming forward.

"Didn't you hear me call?"

"Call?" she returned with a winning innocence. How well and perfect was her surprise at the quality of alarm still in my voice! And truly now my alarm seemed foolish enough and I found I had nothing to say. As if sensing my embarrassment, she chattered in the thoroughly natural way of a good housekeeper. "Whoever cleaned up," she said, "gave out when they got here. Look. Nothing has been swept in this room. The dirt is inches deep."

"I'll speak to Johnny about this," I said and laughed heartily, too heartily, as it seemed to her, for the occasion. She looked at me with a queer expression. Naturally my sudden burst of laughter seemed strange to her, but I could not explain without alarming her or else seeming more foolish in her eyes. Neither did I want to do. And indeed my fears now seemed altogether fantastic, and having nothing to say, I grew silent once more. Ellen in her wonderfully tactful way began to speak.

"Look," she said enthusiastically. "We can make this entire upper L into our apartment. We will glass in the arches. One room shall be our bedroom. One an upstairs sitting room. That of course will really be mine, but we will call it ours. And this room—" she looked slowly about it—"dust and all, shall be your study."

"Fine," I responded with enthusiasm to match hers. "It is here we will begin the restoration."

Why, I do not know, but I said it like a challenge.

3

THE FEELING, PREMONITION, CALL IT WHATEVER YOU WILL— certainly it had no logical genesis—I had had before the door to the entrance hall stayed with me. Not that I brooded on it, nor even thought about it. It had entered my blood, changing its chemistry, diffused, unseen, awaiting the catalytic agent which would precipitate it, when it would appear in all the awful isolation of its elemental state.

I recall the busy weeks of this period, when I was both aware and unaware of the approaching connection of events so dire that now I wonder how, for a moment, I misread the signs. There was the small matter of the unswept room, trivial enough in itself and easily explained: the house was big and the sweeper or sweepers had merely overlooked the small room at the end of the L's second story. I should have forgotten it by payday, as indeed I forgot it during the interval; but as I made out the pay check it came to me to say, so casually there was not the slightest hint of what I sought, "By the way, Johnny, they didn't sweep the little room upstairs."

My statement was met by silence, so that I had to repeat myself. I did this deliberately, to take the proper strategic position to force from him the true reason for the neglect. Johnny's silence had told me what I had suspected: the room had not been ignored for any of the obvious reasons. I unbent somewhat and said in my most pleasant manner, "Come now, Johnny, what was the reason?" As I spoke, I looked directly at him, to let him know I would not laugh or assume an attitude by which he would lose dignity. He returned my look with the degree of confidence I had invited.

"That's old Major Brent's room," he answered.

There was no apology in the muddy white of his eyes. Nor in his voice. His speech was a statement, and he spoke it as if it were self-explanatory. But I did not let him off so easily.

"What do you mean, Major Brent's room? He's been dead seventy-five years."

"He a hard man. He don't like folks projecting wid his things."

"So you believe in ghosts?" I asked with reproving humor.

In a most polite way he followed the line of his evasion. "When he a old man, he stand on the porch there, in the dark, and ring the bell. And his boys better waste no time gitten up. He drove them hard as he drove he hands. He stand there and lay out the work for the day, work most folks take three days to do. He say, 'No triflen. If you kill a mule, I'll buy another. If you kill a Negro, I'll buy another.' And they say, 'Yessir, Pa.' Then he go upstairs to he room, and we all knowed he had eyes like a crow."

I waited before I spoke again. Then I leaned forward. "But, Johnny, you weren't living then."

"No, sir," he replied, with the proper deference for the amenities, and then resumed, "If us'ud stop at the end of the row to blow a spell, he tap the bell. We knowed what dat meant. The sun was sizzlen hot and the clods hot to our feets and our bref dried out our moufs, but didn't nobody tarry. Not here. No, sir, not here dey didn't."

"But, Johnny," I said with a slight edge to my words, "that was years ago, before you or anybody in this country was born."

"Yessir," he said respectfully.

"Ghosts can't hurt you."

"No, sir," he agreed.

"Then why were you afraid to sweep my room."

"Major Brent don't allow nobody in there."

I was baffled. Johnny was not senile. He was not crazy. He had all the guile and simplicity of a country Negro, and I was certain he was a man of character. In spite of myself he had put me on the defensive. It was he, not I, who determined the limits of our talk. I either had to lose my temper, a bad thing always for the boss, or accept the fiction that old Major Brent had a kind of immortality attributed only to demigods. Certainly he could not be numbered among ghosts of the common garden variety.

I shifted ground and tried to get at Johnny another way. I could not leave things as they were: that is, I could in no way accept the fiction his attitude would impose, the impossible position of allowing the spirit of a dead man to determine what would and would not be done at *The Grove*. At the same time I knew that I would fail if I had to come to grips with a superstition of such peculiar power. I had to recover control and I had to do it then and there. I thought fast. It did not take me a minute to reach a decision. I did what was left to do. I accepted the full measure of the challenge—a strange kind of engagement it was—between the living and the dead. I accepted it without hesitation and without reservations. My decision brought relief, as I raised my eyes and looked squarely at Johnny. "I am taking that little room for my study," I said and paused to let this information sink in. Then I added quietly, "Whoever occupied it in the past, be it man or spirit, can file no claim now. It is too late. Mine it is, and mine alone."

His expression did not change, but I saw that I had made my point and well made it. Seeing how my position had strengthened, I made it stronger still. "Of course, I can't occupy a dirty room. If your women are afraid of ghosts, I won't ask them to tend it." I could feel, oh with what joy I felt that I now held the reins! "If necessary," I said, "I'll sweep it myself." How well I had calculated I could see in the slight shift of the shoulders, a drooping and a straightening. Those few seconds told me much. He was not a servant who worked only for wages. That was the advantage I had over him. It was on that knowledge I gambled. He knew I could not be allowed to dust my own furniture. He said very simply, "I will tend the room."

I bowed slightly, to indicate that such would be agreeable to me; then to make the sure surer, to consolidate my already consolidated position, I spoke once more before he returned to the matter of farm business on which he had come. "You must know, Johnny, that if you look to a ghost for meat, your chin will get mighty dry." I was cool and reserved as I spoke, perhaps with a touch of humor, to soften the implied threat of my words. Then quickly I shifted the conversation.

I did this as much as anything to disguise my triumph, and it was no slight one. There would be no more of this business of referring to the dead as alive. Wryly I thought how nice it would be if old Major Brent would pay the taxes. A ghost was a perfectly recognizable myth. I could dispose of that. But a man who was immortal? That was not for me, not with all the other problems I had to confront. And so it came about that in my delight I allowed Johnny to choose what fields would be planted in tobacco, in grain, and in hay.

As he was turning away, he said, "I forgot to mention the corn ground. That field that lies next to the woods make mighty fine corn."

"Go ahead. Plant it," I said in the security of my triumph.

He put his hat on. "Major Brent likes his corn planted there," he said politely and, bowing slightly, walked away.

4

HOW WAS I TO TAKE THIS PARTING STATEMENT? AS INSOlence? I confess that was my first reaction. It took a while to quiet the anger in my heart, and killing anger it was. Only by great effort did I restrain myself as my blurred eyes watched him walk calmly away with my triumph. But reason prevailed, slowly as the pounding in my head eased its strokes. After all, I had to tell myself, I had given him permission to plant the corn where he chose. His comment was a small matter. This, at least, was the official view to take. For could not I have ordered the corn put elsewhere? If I was tricked into giving permission, it was I, the rightful owner and landlord, who had to be tricked. And so long as the duel kept to the rules, I was content. At least I would win or lose on my own merit and skill. But the more I turned Johnny's behavior over in my head the more I dismissed the idea of any intended insolence. He had been connected with *The Grove* longer than I. In his way he had shown respect for its tradition, certainly a virtue I should try to increase, not thwart. I was the interloper, the untried one. For almost the years of his life Johnny had seen owners and tenants abuse house and land. It was to his honor that he kept faith with the memory of Major Brent, the only man within his knowledge who had brought *The Grove* to its highest moment and then sustained it. In his tradition-respecting mind Johnny could find little help from

the dead. Countryman that he was, he was too familiar with
the natural order: the dead are dead. So dramatically, and
because of the drama to his mind believable, he went beyond
the laws of nature and endowed the Major with the mystery
of immortality and its limitless prerogatives.

So I worked it out at the moment. In those days I had skill
in such matters. I prided myself on knowing people better
than they knew themselves, and obviously the situation had to
be solved or I was faced with ruin. I could not actually farm
the land myself; I could not afford to lose a crop without
endangering all I had put into the venture, not to mention
my peace of mind, or Ellen's.

I am not a romantic. The true romantic has hidden pockets
into which his imagination secretes a drug to protect him
from the common evils of the hour. I am, I was, that most
unhappy of hybrids, the false romantic. With will and de-
liberation, and this is the essence of the difference, the false
romantic ignores the true nature of reality. For the time
being. And in the beginning he knows it is only for the time
being. With care and half-averted eye he hangs the veil of
illusion between himself and the world. Almost from habit
he believes the veil was hung by God, or in the most violent
falsification of his nature, he becomes God. I say almost, for
he never quite forgets what he is doing. There is this to be
said for him. More often the injury done is to himself alone.
The true romantic poisons the air all men breathe.

Later, in my study, where I threw myself on the couch,
exhausted from the ordeal, I began to review my situation.
How blithely I had gone into this business! And truly the
idea had seemed sound: establish my family in one location
as a safeguard against the hazards of my uncertain profession;
regenerate a family place and make up for the failure in

trusteeship of those who had gone before. Was this unduly romantic? There, on the couch in that little study, I seemed to myself no squatter but the proper kind of heir. And besides, how much more worth while, how much more manhood this undertaking demanded than to stay in town, spend our days in poker playing and entertaining casual drifters who came to us to fill their emptiness. What I had not foreseen was the magnitude of the undertaking. Both Ellen and I, she more than I, had had that moment of warning, standing there on the lawn when we had arrived to possess *The Grove*. This warning I refused to hear, and even now, when it sounded a second time and more clearly, for Johnny's obsession with the Founder was a line leading directly to the past—even now I might have withdrawn. Instead I rose to my feet and silently —for where was my adversary visible?—renewed the challenge. I would stay and fulfill my destiny.

And so the die was cast. It had been all along, but there is something final about deliberate choice, the act of will which saves or damns. In all good camaraderie Ellen and I set our double bed in one of the large rooms downstairs. How bare the bed made the room seem, and how impermanent our occupancy! The fact that it was a temporary arrangement did not help much. We had moved in below so that we could work freely on the apartment upstairs. Each night I had to look up at the cracks in the ceiling, at the strips of torn and faded paper. In spite of myself I began to feel unclean, spiritually at first and then more directly. I noticed if I were not careful, my body took on a poor-white smell.

During these days I wondered again and again at Ellen's good sportsmanship. If I felt so, how must she feel? Her acceptance of a situation whose demands grew daily more complex brought from me nothing but admiration. Ordinarily a man does not care how things look, so long as he knows they will improve. But a woman of beauty, and Ellen's beauty was renowned, requires time to maintain it. There is the ritual of the hair, the hands, the exacting, oh so exacting art of make-up. There are the thousand and one things which a man does not understand but which a woman practices with the skill and discipline of an artist. In ordinary conditions the husband has little occasion to be aware of this endless effort to remain young and beautiful. But here, at *The Grove,* this effort made itself painfully apparent.

As I watched her cope with the unending chores of housekeeping in her impossible surroundings and the renovation of our ruined grandeur, I felt the sweet pain of pathos bite into me, for her and for all creatures trapped by circumstance. She was one of those rare beings nature creates by accident. There was in her constitution almost a biological lack—an inability to suffer what we all must suffer, the plain facts of living. I said to myself that the power which creates made her as an image for all men to behold, an image of inviolability to change. This was her given function. This and this above all. She was never, oh never, to endure the common filth of living. But that same power had set her in the way of the world as it might hurl the ideal bird into the air and forget to give it wings to fly.

Or so it seemed to me in my partial knowledge as I watched her slim figure, the small well-shod feet, the tailored look—for so she always appeared no matter what she wore—pass through the halls and rooms still showing the corrosion of time. I began to tremble, thinking of the day when the scales would drop from her eyes, that divine web which hid from her the vast complexity of our situation. This thought sent me into renewed activity, the haste that is always waste, the desperate compromise to get a thing done, no matter how. And to find that after the moral defeat which all compromises entail things were still undone, or only started to be dropped at the capricious hands of carpenters and plumbers.

How near my fears approached the thing feared showed in an incident which happened at the lunch hour in early June. I was always coming or going on diplomatic missions to workmen. I came in, from what errand I do not now remember, and found Ellen standing by the table we had set up on the porch. The porch, I must add, had been repaired but, like everything else I had had done, was still unfinished. She was in tears. She stood back from the table, pointing at it, her face set in a strain of horror beyond any obvious cause.

"Look!" she cried. "Just look!"

The tone of hysteria in her voice frightened me. Quickly I looked where she pointed; saw the food set out and nothing more. I raised my eyes with a question. "But, darling, what?"

"Those flies," she replied, in loathing and disgust.

"Flies?" I repeated stupidly.

"All morning I've worked hard in the kitchen to prepare a good lunch. Now look at it. It's ruined."

"Flies are bad," I said. "But nothing's ruined. It's the time of year for them." I tried to soothe her as best I could. "Come, I'll shoo them away. As soon as I can get the wire, I'll screen in this part of the porch. In time I'll move the barn."

She turned on me a look more of incomprehension than anger. "That's all you ever say, Henry. In time."

"Why, honey."

"You do nothing to make it easy for me. All day you ride around and walk in the fields and woods. I do the drudgery." Her voice drew fine. "You don't know what I put up with. You don't care."

"I do care. You know I care. But there's a war on. It's hard to get things and get them done. I work at it every day, and I do care," I wound up. I thought I was magnificent in my restraint, but it brought me nowhere. She refused to eat with me or eat at all. She fled to our room in tears and shut herself in.

I had come in tired and hungry. Now my appetite was gone. I was also baffled and angry. My load was already as heavy as I could bear. To add to it in this way seemed unfair. The middle of a project is no time to judge it, nor judge me. So I felt, but I well knew that my feelings were beside the point. I turned away from the ruin of the meal, drew in my breath, and knocked at the door to our room.

She was sitting up in bed, her swollen eyes staring in utmost dejection.

"Darling, I'm sorry," I said. "I *will* make it better for you."

She seemed not to hear. In a pitiful, childlike way she lifted her hands and turned them over, as if she were seeing them for the first time.

"Look," she wailed, "how rough they are!"

I sat beside her and took her hands in mine and caressed them. But I could find no words for comfort. What was I to say? Your hands will grow smooth and white again? With no cook and no immediate prospect of help?

Suddenly, with fierce intention, she grasped my hands. "Let's go away from this place. While there's time. We are young now. It will take years to make the house livable, even decent. Then it will be too late." Almost as an afterthought she added, "We will be old then. Old—and ugly."

"Try to be patient," I said.

That was all I could say. I felt foolish but there was desperation in my voice, for I was really saying, "Don't shake my faith in myself." My next words showed the full measure of my desperation. "What I am doing, Ellen, is for you."

"Henry Brent, no other man would ask a woman to live like this," she said at last.

Her words struck like a blow; then I was lost in the blank swoon of the heart in which, moments later, the meaning of her accusation rushed. This was not the frailty I had feared. This was much worse: a rift to make two of one, a blasphemy against the union of marriage, where common ends diverge. I had not foreseen it nor prepared for it. Nor was I now prepared. I could only stammer, "But you agreed."

"I have tried," she said disconsolately and then raised her hand in a vague gesture toward the room.

My eyes followed. The hot midday sun was streaming through the curtainless windows, leaving not a shadow to soften or disguise the room's bleak and sordid appearance. In one upper corner long brown streaks, the color of tobacco spittle, stained the wall. And everywhere the endless plaster cracks. In one corner sat a trunk piled with clothes. A lone chair faced the cheerless hearth, a thing of pure utility with no promise of domestic comfort. But nothing pointed out the bleakness of our situation so dramatically as the bilious-colored paint that once had outlined the rug. I don't know why, but the bare middle of the floor contained for me at that moment the most violent threat to our venture: nay—to our life even.

At last I looked up, to face it out with Ellen. Erect, with her hands folded on the counterpane and tightly clasped, she sat withdrawn, immobile, straining into a stilled image, as if to move would open her body to the contagious air. What struck me most was her out-of-placeness in the room and also, in spite of her complaint about her hands, the certainty that the decay around us would never spread to her person or to her will. It might destroy, it would never claim her. I looked more closely and already saw marks of the struggle. Her old radiance had gone out of her, but she was still lovely to look at; and where all was sordid, she shone pure, trim, and immaculate. Shone was the word, but the light she gave off no longer came from an inner source. It was all surface reflection.

And there she was and there I was, in the full flood of high noon, mere flecks in the hot speed of the sun, its rush a bright stillness from window to window until the solid brick walls all seemed of glass. In self-pity and sorrow for creature kind I understood how along this burning way time fused with space, how there was neither motion nor surface but endless extension into which all was lost. I understood the feeble valiant effort of builders to raise walls against this burning force which in giving life made it ignominious. Instinctively I went to her and took her in my arms and lay between her and the bright glare. She misunderstood my intention and pushed me away. "Don't," she said harshly. "Can't you see we have no privacy here?"

5

I TRIED TO SHUT OUT THE MEMORY OF THIS INCIDENT BY RE-doubling my efforts. And during the following weeks I was up early and to bed late. Of course there was no time for my own proper work. Money was constantly going out and little coming in, but the house did show improvement. The back porch got screened in and painted, and our apartment upstairs was well under way, all except my office which I kept until last. That I would do alone. The wonder of it all was the way Ellen's spirits rose as the things got done. She seemed to have recovered entirely from her "breakdown," as she called it. She had even come to me and told me she would not let herself get out of hand again. My spirits rose too from this happy condition of our affairs, although there was a qualification to what I felt. Underneath this surface of good will and good heart I could feel from time to time the tremors of the earth we, so to speak, stood on. Well, the quake of which they were the forewarning was not long in coming.

My ear was to the ground, but I had allowed myself to drift into the state of hearing without translating the meaning of what I heard. I merely stored away the recordings without comment in that part of the mind where records are kept. Ellen's pleasure in what had been done blinded me to how little it was in relation to what we still had to do. There were as well growing doubts in my mind as to whether we would ever be able to complete the house's regeneration. The cost was mounting and fast mounting beyond my capacity to pay. If it was to be finished, we would have to do of necessity what once had seemed a labor of love; that is, do a great part of the work ourselves. This would take years out of our life and make of these years confusion and disorder, for a house must be so arranged that there is a place for everything. How could a well-ordered ménage function with everything topsy-turvy, with tools and lumber all over and debris scattered about? To set up the rooms as they were for living was out of the question. In the urgency of the daily crisis we would have to put off until the suitable time (which never comes) our intended restoration, until at last like the tenants who had gone before we would grow accustomed to our surroundings and carry a step farther, because of our corruption, the progress of ruin.

So Ellen's first gloomy prophecy in the light of the actual situation seemed truer than her more recent optimism. Even if by some miracle we brought the house to its former state, could we produce the conditions which had sustained it? Servants are as necessary to a large establishment as bread to the body. These might conceivably be obtained, but would the land sustain them? *The Grove* at its heyday was a going concern in every way. No money was brought in from the outside to run it. The land maintained the economy of the house, its hospitality and gracious living. But since those days the country has become an extension of the town. Let us be frank. It is servile. Its mores, the price it gets for its products, the clothes it wears, almost what it thinks, are determined by an absentee master. You may name this master what you please. It matters little whether its elusive all-powerful mechanism is controlled by management or by labor. On either horn the farmer is gored. So among the many difficulties to be solved and got out of the way was the insoluble one of history.

But sufficient unto the day is the evil thereof. On this old saw I lived and moved, dealing with whatever situation came up, putting it through or compromising it, and enjoying the respite it gave us both. Late at night we would talk of the progress made that day and of the things still to do, or more often we fell into bed too weary for words and stumbled out at light to take up whatever came to hand. And so our life went at *The Grove,* swiftly, pleasantly, as only it can go when two people who love each other, who have quarreled and made up, are doing things together. That it was slow, that it was little, that the means to prosecute it were fast diminishing, lay like shadows at high noon, which the eye wonders at but dismisses in the bright swelter of the hour.

The very brightness of this period, as I try to recall it, seems brief enough, scarcely more than a flash before the gloom which settled down. I remember no clear division between the night and the day of our ordeal. The change came suddenly, like the turning out of a light. What followed was the endless groping in the dark, when the familiar landmarks of the room turn strange, and the terror is greater for the knowledge that all you touch should be familiar. The darkness then seems no longer confined but the very core of night's wide spaces.

Often during this time I found myself thinking of my predecessor. I can call him that, for those who dwelt at *The Grove* between his time and mine might as well have never lived for any thought I gave them. I thought of him with envy and sometimes almost with hatred, for he had had all I was denied. I could almost see him beyond the grave willing me to make him immortal. *The Grove* was his conception. It bore the stamp of his mind and his will. And his mind and his will *I* was restoring and the better I did it the more I submerged my personality and the greener his kept. If into his habitation I could have established my family after the fashion of my hopes, I could have mocked him. The probability of my failure and his success haunted me. Was he really a better man than I? Could I in his place and in his time have done as well? Could he have coped with the situation, if our roles had been reversed? I could never make up my mind to these questions. At times I fell back on the frail comfort that I had undertaken an impossible job. But always the element of doubt crept in to plague me, for given any set of limitations one man will succeed where another fails.

The Grove had one feature which somehow had escaped the careless hands that had misguided so much else. It was the way the lawn sloped away from the house until it lost itself in a fine woods. Ellen and I had formed the habit, when the going got especially tough, of walking away from our troubles into the cool green spaces, where we strolled for hours on end. And always we returned refreshed to the battle. One evening about dusk, coming from the fields with the day's work behind, I passed through these woods on the way to the house. As I stepped out onto the lawn, I came instinctively to a dead stop. I say instinctively, but even now I do not know whether at first I felt or saw what confronted me. In one of the arches of the upper gallery stood the figure of a man. It stood in the arch which framed the door leading into the room we were doing over for Ellen. The house was a fair distance away, but through the cedars, as one must see it from my position, it appeared farther than it was. So it happened I could not quite make out the person's features. My first impression was that it was some guest looking over our improvements. I waved my hand and hurried across the lawn to greet him. When we first moved to the country, many of our acquaintances and friends made trips to see us. Their curiosity once satisfied they rarely braved the bad roads to make a second visit. But they were always welcome and so I went forward with pleasant anticipations. At that time of day objects are clear enough but the detail is blurred; so I had gone a little way before two things came to me, as it happened, almost instantaneously: one, that my greeting had not been returned; and two, that there was no car in the driveway by which a guest could have arrived.

The shock of this double surprise slowed my steps and I came again to a halt. As I try now to remember it, the shock I felt was not at first very great. It was more a feeling of things being not quite right. It never occurred to me at the moment to wonder how this man got on the upper gallery. I assumed that he had made himself known to Ellen and had given her a satisfactory explanation of his business there, or she would not have let him in. Our situation was remote enough, so that I felt little danger from the gentlemen of no location who wander the highways. We were definitely on a byway; still I had warned her to be circumspect about strangers. If they happened upon us all the more reason for caution, since their mere presence would demand a clear explanation. What changed almost in a breath my puzzlement to alarm came out of, or made, the chill in the air which tightened my skin and made it tingle with fear. I had stopped beneath one of the giant cedars and from this position I had a direct and unimpeded view of the house. I could see and what I saw intensified my feeling of things not being right to a positive knowledge of something being very wrong. What I got first on the rebound was the certainty that I had never before seen the figure who was making himself so free of my house. As this struck me, it also struck me that he had all the air of one whose right to be where he was could never be questioned. The synthesis of the eye makes the analysis of statement slow and cumbrous, so that what I now report in detail misconstrues by the limitations of print the exact intensity of the emotions which fixed me to the spot.

My first impulse was to call out; but, realizing that he had not yet seen me, I took advantage of this to spy on him. I suppose this was my intention. It may have been I needed time to collect my wits. I know I froze as animals do when they sense danger, swallowed up by the frightful quiet which seemed all the more sinister for being a grotesque mockery of the dying away, the closing up of sound, common to the day's end. But the quiet into which I had sunk, which made my breath seem gross and noisy, although I scarcely breathed, was the quiet of the wave's trough or that moment of breath-

lessness when a high wind shuts off suddenly to gather itself
for greater fury.

Across the space which joined us I tried to catch his gaze
moving slowly in my direction. But it passed above me as if
I were not there, pausing not even for an instant of recognition, all the while restlessly scanning the woods behind me.
How can I say how long this took? Time passed, but also my
recognition of it. This I know, time enough for me to see
him so clearly as to make friends of a lifetime seem shadowy
strangers passed in the street. I saw that he wore a hat—wide-
brimmed and black—but no tie or collar. One hand grasped
a staff, the other hung at his side. There was no movement of
neck or head, only the lustrous eyes, restless, searching, boring
the woods like gimlets.

My intolerable situation pressed on me. I opened my mouth
to call out, but even as I did so, he turned away and deliberately, as if he knew the way, walked in the direction of my
study. He passed behind an arch. I waited the seconds it would
take him to come out on the other side. I waited. I strained
my eyes. All to no purpose. He passed behind the arch. He did
not come out on the other side.

6

ONE DOES NOT RECKON TIME AT SUCH MOMENTS, BUT WHEN
I ran for the house I had the feeling that I had waited too
long. In one step I was on the porch. Another took me into
the hall. I bounded up the stairs and down the drops of the
gallery porch. Nothing did I see. Cautiously I put my hand

on the knob of the door to my study and flung it back. What I would have done had I surprised a vicious marauder I cannot say, for I had not stopped to pick up even a stick. Luckily, or unluckily—the edge of truth is finely drawn in such contingencies—I faced an empty room. I looked all through it, behind the door, into closets meant for bookcases, I looked under my desk, but in all this frenzied search I found just what I knew I would find—nothing.

I told myself I must be thorough. There was the upstairs apartment to go through. No opportunity for doubt must be left lurking in my consciousness to trouble me, now that the swell of what I had felt growing about us at *The Grove* had at last exploded in my face. I had lost that first charge of fear. Almost I felt a deep relief, a kind of courage I never knew I had. Here was something which would call up to the very last reserve my manhood. No more plumbers and carpenters, no more painters and paper hangers to try the patience of a dozen Jobs. Here was drama, with the first act started, and the protagonist on the stage.

I ran into Ellen outside my door. By now the world had reached the division between night and day, those few short minutes when the sky has just enough light to show up the dark, before it closes in. The moment we met I noticed she was a little out of breath, but what drove all else away was the look of her face. By reflection I saw how I must have appeared to her. "What in the world is the matter?" she asked.

"Do I look that bad?"

"Terrible, Henry."

"Terrible?" I was playing for time.

"You look like a ghost."

I looked at her sharply. "And how does a ghost look? Have you ever seen one?"

"Don't be silly. Come on down to supper before it ruins."

Her words made me certain that I alone at *The Grove* had seen the intruder. I had sensed this fact, if you will, even before she appeared on the gallery. But what occupied me at the moment, as I hung back, was whether to tell her or keep my counsel. I was not long in reaching a decision. It came to me in one of those flashes of intuition which predetermine strategy that Ellen must not know. At least not for the present, certainly not until I had had time to reflect, to sound the depths of whatever waters we were treading. This meant of course that I could not at that moment search the upstairs apartment. But, at once I reflected, there is the back stairs which opened an easy and quick escape. The visitor no doubt had already, had in fact before I arrived on the scene, disappeared into the anonymous regions from which he had come. So with alacrity I took Ellen's hand and led her down to supper. I went with the more willingness because I carried away one unshaken conviction. I would not be too late next time.

The strangest result of the whole encounter, among the numerous possibilities it opened up, was my part in it: that is, the change which came over me. It was the exact opposite to what one might have expected. My anxiety, my frustrations, all my gloomy preoccupations with my problem, every one of them left me. The business which had plagued me, had sent me endless miles on fruitless errands, still existed. The need to keep at it was no less urgent than it had been. The house still showed its state of limited repair, the farm work still moved on its original halting lines; the shift from a romantic preconception to actuality continued to rule our lives. Nothing had changed, and yet I had. All of this bothered me not at all. I was like a man aroused from the sleep of haunting dreams to a fair, brisk, and sunny day. And yet the reverse of all this came nearer the truth. I imitated Pilate. I did not examine the truth; I washed my hands of it.

How shall I describe the ensuing days? In this wonderful, almost miraculous, metamorphosis of feeling, of attitude, even of temperament which I had undergone, I let the problems which were arising daily more or less work themselves out. And work themselves out they did, after a fashion. This allowed me time for Ellen's society. It was only then, in the happy moments we spent together, that I understood how lonely she had been and how empty of the smaller pleasures my endless trips had made her life.

With Johnny's help we spent several weeks finishing the apartment. He could spare certain days from farm work as he had three stout boys to help him make his crop. Except for a local paper hanger and a cabinetmaker of some skill we did the entire job ourselves. I was particularly proud of the floors. These fell to me. I rented a sander, worked them down, filled them, steel-wooled them, shellacked them, steel-wooled them again, and finally waxed and polished them. I have been rapid in the telling of it, but it was the hardest work I have ever done in all my life, and it was worth it. The floors were of wide ash boards, and when I got through they shone like satin. We rather splurged on the rugs and draperies, taking the money laid aside for the whole upstairs. As I report it here, we seemed madly extravagant, but we had set ourselves high standards. The house deserved the best and with complete agreement we decided to do what we did well, even if it took years to whip the interior into shape.

I still think this was the only way, the bold way, to approach our problem. Could we be held to account if we fell into the error of judgment common to all doers-over of old

houses—underestimating the cost? I think not. With the
apartment in such shape that an honest decorator would find
little to criticize we had established a strong point inside the
enemy's lines. Within the walls of the three rooms we could
follow the small but so important habits of civilized living.
To this sanctuary we could retire, bind up our wounds, and
rest. And from here we could return refreshed to the battle.
With this surely gained, what was to keep us from extending
ourselves so that gradually we would set to rights the chaos
of ruin everywhere about? What indeed? This was the question I asked in the days to come and from every side approached for an answer.

7

BEFORE I GET ON, IT WOULD BE WELL TO PAUSE AND CATCH,
so to speak, my imaginative breath. I must be sure that what I
now relate has above all the correct emphasis. If I have forgotten the order, if I have misunderstood the least step, even,
in the progress of events so rapidly advancing toward their
fulfillment, I place myself in the way of fresh perils. Only this
time the perils are quite definitely of the soul. Never before
has the risk of judgment so involved the risk of damnation,
for if the truth I now disclose be not the truth but falsehood
disguised in the habiliments of innocence, what then am I?

Doing things together brought us, as I thought, so
close together that it made out of companionship a lovely
harmony which is often lacking in married couples well away
from the apprenticeship of the honeymoon. We felt as do peo-

ple who, thinking they have lost a fortune, prepare for the dark dread of poverty only to discover that the fortune risked, instead of being lost, has returned tenfold. The evidence of this would seem commonplace enough—no more than the comforts and petty luxuries of civilized needs which the apartment now allowed us, or rather gave back tremendously enhanced in value by the recent deprivation we had suffered. How shall I put it? The excitement and relief we shared will seem all out of proportion to the material value of our possessions. They were, indeed, little more than what a good salaried man in this preposterously wealthy country might command. There were soft rugs at our feet instead of dusty floors. There were curtains, beautiful to be sure, hanging at our windows. But who lacks curtains? We had a fine old bed, inherited but done over at our expense and with good springs, but still any traveling salesman might sleep as well.

We did have the advantage of Ellen's taste, and we did have something to work with which gave our quarters a distinction all the chromium plate in the world couldn't match. And at last we could keep the rooms clean. In the rest of the house this was a backbreaking job and one which got us nowhere. For all the sweeping, dust, that sign of abandonment, persisted. But now we passed from Ellen's room into her sitting room on clean beautiful floors, and from there across the corridor to my room. My room was less extravagantly done over; yet it *was* done over. But above all this our situation had a very special quality: on the one hand there was the apartment, on the other the rest of the house. In this sentence I have posited two worlds. The apartment allowed us to go on. It had blessed privacy. It was at times our refuge. It would come to have the grim tension of an embattled fortress.

One of the many disillusionments in which are contained

the successive small shocks of life is the habit of growing accustomed to what falls your way. So it was that before many days I grew somewhat accustomed to the apartment. I modify this rather unctuous pronouncement by "somewhat," for the tremendous difficulties of our undertaking never let me take our gains too complacently. This produced in me a curious reaction. There were moments when I was acutely sensitive to our predicament, but most of the time I wandered about in a state of lethargy. Ellen had plans for the kitchen and dining room, but she could not rouse me to tackle them. I always put her off. Looking back on it, I can best describe my state of mind as that of one anxious to enjoy the newness of accomplishment before it dulled. I felt, if I felt anything, that there was time for the rest—of course there is never time—or perhaps I felt I must allow nothing to disturb the exquisite pleasure of being with Ellen and having the leisure to satiate myself with her company in surroundings at last proper to her beauty and grace. I would sit in a comfortable chair, with my leg thrown over its arm and watch her at her toilet. I feasted my eyes not as an adolescent who eats until he cloys, gulping down the senses when they are keenest, but with a more deliberate taste. And yet for the moment I had restored my senses to an acute freshness, while practicing the melancholy ritual of enjoyment, knowing it would not last. At times it seemed enough merely to watch her pass across the room. She had a dressing gown, I remember, of some thin blue stuff over pink, which clung to her or fell away as she walked, confusing the eye with the delicate change of color. Out from under it moved her little feet. Usually I was aware only of their positive outward thrusts. But one day my eyes fastened on them to enjoy their singularity. I saw the slippers she wore, woven leather of gold and silver gilt, sink into the deep new nap of the rug. The slippers were old and tarnished. Suddenly, as if I might defend her against this warning of our predicament, I took her in my arms and held her fiercely.

"Darling," she cried. "Don't."

It took me several seconds for her appeal to register. I freed her slowly and sank back into my chair, listless and oppressed.

I do not want to leave the impression, certainly it would be a false one, that I did nothing but loll in luxurious fashion with my wife. I managed some work of my own, in my study, and I attended to the farm business. This last now took less time. I went to the fields only half as much, which was due in part to my better knowledge of the farm's routine and to what I might expect of the tenants. But most of this extra time came from Johnny's frequent appearance about the house. He seemed to take an interest in our venture and a genuine liking for Ellen. He had managed some way to get her a girl to help in the kitchen and without saying a word added the care of the apartment to that of the study. Seeing him more frequently allowed me to dispose of details of farm business which ordinarily would have taken me out.

One evening about milking time he came up to tell me the cows had got out. There were few fences on the place. I had not been able to get wire or posts; we had done the best we could with patching up, but good eaters, and they always make good milkers, will push through an old fence to greener stuff on the other side. The tale he had to tell was of an irate neighbor. The man, a Swede, and amiable enough himself but dominated by a wife who stood very much on her rights, had found the cows in his alfalfa. It was time to milk and the Swede had impounded the herd. Johnny suspected the Swede's wife had her eye on the extra milk, so nothing would do but I must go and free our stock.

In my haste I was well into the yard before I discovered I had forgotten my hat. Johnny glanced politely but significantly at my head. I at once turned around and, thinking fast, remembered I had left it on a chair in my office. It is a peculiarity of mine to dislike hats, an oddity which goes unnoticed in the opportunism of urban life. In the country, however, for a man of my station to go about the place uncovered, which I frequently did, made me seem odd enough to my neighbors, almost an outlander, at the least a man of eccentric habits and therefore of doubtful consequence. To go abroad in such a state of undress, on so formal and delicate a matter, would have put me in a highly disadvantageous position for the business which pressed for settlement.

So I hurried upstairs to the study. How little a man knows what he will find when he seeks. The moment I stepped into the room I felt a change come over it, a sudden drop, as if all the air had fled out of it. I was the only solid thing left, as heavy as marble and gross as lead, the center of a vacuum into which, on the instant, a stillness rushed, impalpable, impenetrable, and charged with the threat of an unnamable evil. The evil was not long in defining itself. How I knew it, or when it became clear, I cannot say, but I felt I was being watched by unseen eyes. I felt what all feel who suffer such exposure, the terrible compulsion to confront it. I knew exactly, with the sixth sense which warns, the direction of the intrusion: the north window above the outside stairway. I stood in a direct line of its view. Between me and it stood a desk. Casually I strolled forward and cunningly pretended to search among the papers which littered the desk's top; and then slowly, without moving my head, I raised my eyes. I brought them up until they reached the height at which I thought to find whatever I had to meet. I met nothing but an uninterrupted view of the encroaching dusk. At eye level the window lights were as transparent as glass can be.

But yet I was not freed. The same pull of that mysterious tension, fluid as water, strong as gut, drew my eyes yet upward. And there at the very top of the window, just out from the edge of one of the blinds which had blown to, I saw a face. It pressed against the pane in passionate anguish, its nose crushed white and its eyes, as limpid as a hawk's and dark as sin, leveled upon mine. I did not waver. I gave it back as straight a stare as it gave me. And then into my stare it vanished. It was there: it was not there, so sudden do these intruders complete their visitations. But it lasted the strokes my heart beat out the world's dark rhythm, an interval long enough for me to know all I had to know. Although the evening was rapidly falling, I saw as brightly as in a vision, with an unimpeachable certainty, that the face belonged to the visitor I had first met in the gallery's arch. But the horrible discovery, which attested to the rapid advance in our relationship, lay just in the stare he gave me and I gave back. Whatever he sought, whatever his business there, it was not with me. It comes back, as I recount it, with all the immediacy of the actual experience—it comes back in the intimacy I was made to feel with him. When his glance left mine to travel over the room, I was ignored as if I did not exist, or as if I were so deep in his purpose as to be his other self. It was this affront which banished the shock of this second encounter and sent me flying out of the room to overtake him before he could vanish—this and the knowledge that he had come there to do harm. I arrived on the back stairs in less than five seconds, but the stranger was nowhere to be seen.

The stairway made a curve which brought it under the shelter of the kitchen porch. Down the stairs I bounded, but he was gone. I felt no relief at this but anger that a second time he had escaped me. For form's sake I searched the back premises, I remounted the stairs and took a farther view. There were shrubs and outhouses and the old garden wall, behind which he could have hidden, but it came to me in that moment of search that he was not to be found in any such places. I drew out of the deep knowledge of the experience that I was the key to what he sought. I was the door through which he must pass to his loathsome desire. When I understood this, I was possessed of the calm, almost the comfort, which follows the dread of the unknown threat at last brought out and channelized.

Now that I knew my adversary, for it never occurred to me that he could be other than this, I decided to study him. This brought the impulse to see how he had so easily placed himself at the point of vantage to see into the room. The chimney narrowed at the level of the floor. I stepped upon it and with my hand on the blind peered around, just as I had seen him do. I found that my face fell a good foot below the face I had seen, but it evidently was high enough to frighten Johnny, who had at that moment come into the room, no doubt to see what had delayed me. I saw him stop in his tracks as I had stopped, and stare just as I had stared. His face could not pale, but it looked overlaid with a thin film of wood ashes. By that I could measure the degree of his fright. He turned on his heel and fled the room. I got down in time to meet him.

" 'Fore God, Mister Brent," he said, "what ails you?"

"What ails all men," I said, enjoying in my grim way the little scene about to be enacted.

"It ain't dat," he came back at me more vigorously than I had ever known him to.

"It's not, Johnny?" I returned with just a shade of irony.

"You ain't hongry, and you ain't daid."

"No, I 'ain't hongry' and I 'ain't dead,' but what would you say if I told you I had met, eye to eye, one foot above where you saw my face, pressing against the glass in pain and in desire, the one thing more drawing than hunger, the only thing as irrevocable as death?"

"Yes, sir," he said, his eyes opened to the yellow balls, and unfocused, like one aroused in the middle of the night.

"Why don't you ask me what it is? Don't you want to know?"

"What it?" he asked gruffly. His voice measured the strength of his emotion, strong enough, and that was strong indeed, to make him forget the amenities.

"Fate," I said.

I could see his relief as his body relaxed. But he was still not quite reassured. He did not know the word, but he thought it might disguise a more homely terror he would be able to recognize. His shoulders leaned slightly forward. "What do hit look like?" He asked.

"What does it look like?" I paused for the pure pleasure of it. "The terror of the deep."

"Yessir, but can you handle it?"

"I will know that perhaps too late."

He thought awhile and then with great dignity, restored to his manners and feeling the security of their limits, he said, "Mr. Brent, please sir, would you name it to me in your own words?"

"You mean, will I make you see it?"

"I don't rightly know as I wants to see hit. I wants to know what you seen."

"The shape of terror?"

"Yes, sir. Is hit big as you?"

"A head taller," I said. "A handsome face but ravished." I saw him nod. "With deep black eyes, a long rangy body, a black round-brimmed hat on his head."

"Yes, sir, yes, sir," he responded eagerly.

"Wearing a coat such as . . . such as preachers wear."

"Yes, sir."

"And in his hands a staff, not that he needs it to walk with . . ."

"Him need air thing to walk with!"

"Then you've seen him?" I cried.

"Seen him? Sho', I've seed him."

"Where? Where?" I could feel my eyes glow with triumph.

"Why, that's Major Brent," he said and then added quietly, "I sees him all the time."

8

I KNEW THAT SOONER OR LATER I WOULD HAVE TO HAVE IT out with Johnny. Now that the issue was joined I must secure my rear. I must discover just where Johnny's loyalty lay. I must know what he saw, but more than that, exactly what communication existed between him and the former master of *The Grove*. I come right out with it. I do not speak of ghosts or apparitions, I speak of Major Brent. To give a name to evil, if it does nothing else, limits its range and that is the beginning of accepting it. A week passed before an opportunity presented itself, the last week, as I remember, of July. Johnny had come up to tell me the corn and the tobacco had been worked over and to find what orders I had to give. We were in my study. I had him sit down in the chair opposite my desk. As I opened the conversation I was surprised at the calm, matter-of-fact tone I assumed. I might have been a doctor inquiring into the nature of a disease. "You must tell me, Johnny," I said, "just what you see—and how often."

He said rather too quickly, "I don't see nothen no more."

I could tell he had foreseen this conference and had come with his answers ready. Of course I could not let it rest there, although I had already learned by his manner to me, a greater deference, one thing I wanted to know; the company I now kept, so he thought, gave me a status which assured me I should fear no treachery from within the citadel. But this was not quite all I wanted to know, so I continued, "At what times has this visitor to *The Grove* appeared to you?"

He did not answer at once, but my eyes bored into him and held him locked in their vice. How shall I describe my feeling of power at this moment except to say I felt ageless? I held him until at last he spoke as one speaks out of sleep, his words bursting in a volley. "In de full of the moon."

"Always so?"

He nodded carefully. "Just befo'e d' moon change."

"Ah," I breathed, and then like a pistol shot, "but where?"

"Where ere he a mind to."

"But where in particular?" I insisted.

He thought awhile, then said, "Sometime he walk de fields, or sashay in and out'n the trees at the aidge of the woods."

I put my arms on the desk and leaned forward. "Did you ever see him inside the house?"

Cautiously he shook his head.

"But never to have seen him is no reason to believe he doesn't go there?"

"He know the way," he said.

"Does he ever speak?"

He shook his head again, then after a silence which seemed an emptiness rather than a break in time, he whispered, "He ain't need to."

"You mean?" I prompted.

"I knows what make him walk."

"Yes?"

"He doan rest easy."

"And why doesn't he rest easy?"

"All the meanness he done plague him."

"Johnny, were you ever scared?"

"No more'n to make me step light. I knowed I ain't done him no harm. I be layen in bed and tereckly I see he shadow flicker on the wall. 'Thar he,' I say. 'I must git up. He might need sumpum.' Sally Betts draw the quilts over her haid, but I gits up and pulls my clothes on. He'll go plunderen around and me followen."

Johnny stopped talking as if he had said all there was to say. But I had not heard all. So I asked, "What does he look like he's after?"

"He look powerful sad. He look lak he druv the world away and tryen to git it back with a lump of sugar."

"But what is it really, do you think, he is trying to get?"

"He know," Johnny said abruptly.

And that was all I could get out of him. When he left, I noted more particularly the niceness of his manner to me: it was the respect for and the deference to one who engages himself against impossible odds. This was of course easily explained by the superstitions of all simple people. He as well left me assured on another point. I had been fairly certain that Johnny saw no more than all those who believe in ghosts see, that is, the shadow of their imaginations, filled by old stories, myths which grow like moss about the ruin of the cornerstone.

But this was not what *I* saw. What I saw, I saw alone. I could in no way be complicated by my naïve attendant. And yet it was clear he would be of use to me, for I must have some relief from my unbearable knowledge, and he could serve in just this. To shut up my mind, never to talk, would drive me beyond my strength. Ellen I could not approach. So on this, for the time, we parted, I having got from him what I wanted and he—well, I must have seemed a proprietor of a very singular property, whose lines held matter for perilous argument.

9

MORE AND MORE I FELT THE NEED TO KNOW THE particulars of Major Brent's past. It was not straining credulity to assign to him more than an ordinary life. However, I needed some clue, and this I knew I could get from Johnny. He had hinted at things. I wanted to bring out to the light, or to the darkness, of my predicament what lay concealed in his mind. At the first opportunity I cornered him. "What," I asked, "did you mean when you told me you knew what made Major Brent walk?" He returned my stare, the only movement in his face the cloudy film which closed over his eyes, hiding his humanity behind the mask he presented me. And so he stood and so I let him stand, in the sure knowledge that he would speak in the end, despite the mask, despite the depths of his natural and supernatural caution. I had advanced very deeply in our relationship, for the magic of words had at last put him at my disposal.

"I done tole you all I knows," he said.

I knew this was the beginning of more, so I continued, to give him the momentum he needed. "Major Brent has singled me out, and I must find why. I have not turned aside, nor will I. This he suspects and it is for this he hates, perhaps fears, me. Whatever his power in the place he inhabits, in this world he is as helpless as my shadow, unless I make some blunder and through carelessness give him the substance he lacks. Now that you have spoken of him to me—" I said this slowly with great solemnity—"him you will never see again." I turned abruptly. "What does he lack that he disturbs my peace?"

Johnny remained as motionless as some black idol, with the thick hands bent to the curve of work lying blocked out in his lap, but at last he began to talk. The words passing his beefy lips came simply and with compassion and with the vast relief of one who disburdens himself of a secret too dangerous to keep or to tell, except to the muted ears of a culprit about to mount the scaffold, where all must be anonymous. In some such fashion, I felt, he considered me.

"The old folks say he always hongry. Hongry befo'e he eat and hongry after he wipe he mouf and belch. He wo'e six women out and made husks of his chillurn. The boys was windbroke before they knowed what he done to'm. When the

hands taken out the mules, they'd drap in the lot, too tared
to wallow. And the boys 'ud drap, too tared to eat. But they
never studied not minden him, and he kept tellen them, if
they wanted him to give 'em anything, to hold fast to the
plow." Johnny paused and looked beyond me, then: "Nair
one of 'm taken time out to marry except the youngest and
he pa drove him onto the big road. The boys wrinkled up,
but the Major clicked his heels in the air."

"Yes," I said. "What about the daughters?"

"Miss Euphemy. She war his onliest gal. He never give her
away. Couldn't find nobody good enough to suit him."

Johnny lifted one hand and lay it heavily over the other
and seemed to fall into a doze, but I brought him out of this
subterfuge. "There is something you are keeping back," I
said. "And Miss Euphemia?"

"They say she taken to locken him in his room." He indicated my study as the place.

"Why?" I was like an inquisitor.

"That ain't for me to say."

I received this rebuke in silence, which I tried to make as
ominous as possible, and then Johnny cast his eyes down and
said slowly, reverently, and no louder than a whisper, "One
day Miss Euphemy called the boys to the house and said
they pa was too feeble to walk. They must carry him to the
fields. They lifted him in his cheer, with two poles run
through it, and him setten up in the air dressed like a bridegroom. Them boys was already blowed from the day's work,
but he had'm tote him through ever' last field on the place.
It was sundown when they come to the barley field." He
hesitated, as if to recollect the exact details of the scene and
then resumed. "He made them boys put postes in the ground
and heist him on top of 'm. They swayed on their feets they

was so weary, but he didn't offer to let 'm set down. He never said nothen for a spell, but just set there and looked around. It was a turrible fine year for grain. Except for the tobacco the whole place from line to line was yallow with barley and wheat and oats. And him jest setten there looken at hit, until the boys and the hands circlen around got nervous, for the sun was nigh to drappen.

" 'Hit's purty and hit's mine,' he say. 'Hit's the purtiest crop I ever seen at *The Grove* and the biggest yield.' My pa heared him say them words. Then he stood up and taken one look around and dropped in his cheer. The postes rocked, but didn't nobody come nigh to sturdy 'm. It was gitten along towards dark before he roused hese'f again. 'Hit's taken me my life to do this,' he said. '*The Grove* has done the mostest hit can ever do. I knowed they was a perfect crop in it. Look around you and see it, for you'll never see air other one.' The boys looked about 'm foolishlike, not knowing what the old man had in mind. But he warn't long in naming hit. He reached in his big pocket and pulled out a sack. 'Lemuel,' he called. 'Sir,' his son answered like a boy and him in his fifties. He pitched him the sack and Lemuel caught it. 'Amos,' he said, and Amos stepped forward. He pitched him a sack. And then he called Josh and Abner and pitched them a sack. I'm given you each a thousand dollars in gold for your hire. It will start you in the world, for this place you will never till again. It has reached perfection. It can do no more.' He come to a stop and nobody didn't know what to say, but he spoke up once more and for the last time. 'I want ever' stalk of grain to fall where it grows and ever hill of tobacco to rot where it stands. My everlasting displeasure to him that tries to reap what I sowed. Now you may take your pay and go.' "

Johnny's voice stopped.

"And . . ." I said.

"My pa said the hands slipped away and nair one looked back. And the boys stood around like chillurn who'd lost their way, and then they left. And my pa said he never seen sich a bright light on no old man's face. He looked like a body busten out of the creek all wet with glory. Then it come to Pa he war the last one there. He had to pull his feets out of the ground to run. He said he shet his eyes and run, and when he opened 'm again the dark had growed out'n the fields and swallowed up the house. He shuck all night, afeared for day to break. He knowed them fields 'ud be bare as he hand."

"And were they?"

"Naw, sir. The fields was yellow as butter."

"And Major Brent?"

Johnny shook his head. "The cheer sot up 'ar in the air."

"Yes?"

I thought he would never get it out.

"It sot up 'ar, plumb empty. And one crow roosten on hit's back."

10

JOHNNY HAD GIVEN ME THE CLUE I WANTED, BUT ONLY THE clue. I knew I would have to untangle it. My imagination whirled on the periphery of my predicament. It was not ready to plunge to the depths of the center of truth. I deliberately refrained from making a premature decision. I drifted, if to circle slowly down the narrowing cone may be called drifting. There was time, but not too much time, to make decisions before the giddy swirl and the plunge and the suck.

The month of August went quietly enough on the surface. It was notable for one thing: the last opportunity for withdrawal. In the most cleverly conceived stratagems of doom, whether contrived by man or by supernatural powers, there comes a moment when escape is possible, a moment of clarity when the strain is released by its own tension. The way is always opened up by some incident in the daylight world, as plain, as restricted as a banker's books, and telling as little as do these books about the accounts they record. Though they tell little, without the understatement of such things as the double entry we would submerge ourselves hopelessly in the confusion of the multiple depths of our natures. The orderly life of individuals and society depends on the balance between light and darkness. We perish only when the sun gets jammed at high noon or the moon glides forever at the full. The chance to withdraw came to us in an offer for the farm. It was as plain and direct as that. A mild land boom brought a buyer to our remote location. He offered me a modest profit over and above all that I had put into *The Grove*. I took this offer to Ellen.

I found her in the kitchen. Tired of waiting for me to help, she had begun doing it over herself. Some way she had got together several girls of the neighborhood and they were painting the walls. She stepped down at my request from a stool, flushed from her work. A dash of paint spotted her cheek like a beauty spot. A strand of hair had got loose and lay fetchingly over her forehead. I saw her, as sometimes happens, with the freshness of our first meeting. This sight of her brought with it as well the state of mind of our courtship, when the world seemed as giving as the demands we would make of it. It was an unhappy vision, for it weakened my resolve to retreat.

We sat on the porch and lighted cigarettes.

"Isn't it going to be lovely?" she asked.

"The kitchen?"

"I've got it all planned. A double sink, shelves on the side, on the north end closets for brooms and things, and if you could only cut me a window . . ."

"Before we do all this, I've something to tell you."

"I know. We haven't the money. But, look, I can sell this ring. It's a rather nice one. I've got it all figured out. It will just, with careful planning, do what I want to do. I'd much rather my kitchen glittered than my hand. We don't go anywhere any more."

"Darling, I've had an offer for the farm."

"Oh." A pause. "How much?"

"A small profit."

"Oh." Another pause. "If it were a lot of money . . ."

"Of course if we really want to stay here. It's only a chance to get out without a loss."

"Do you want to leave?" she asked. "I had no idea such a thought had entered your mind."

I evaded her question. "I only thought I had got you into something tougher than I knew. I'm offering you a chance to get out with honor."

"Don't say me, darling. You got *us* into something, a something I'm rather beginning to like."

"I must point out," I went on, "the tremendous job still ahead."

She thought for a while. "Well, darling, whatever you think we ought to do."

"You know how I hate to turn loose, but you've been rather on my conscience."

"Why should I be on your conscience?" She looked at me frankly.

Hastily I said, "It's not that altogether. I've doubts about myself."

"Doubts?"

"Well, I'm not sure I can handle it, that I can, well, make you happy here."

She got up. We strolled out onto the lawn and sat under one of the large cedars. Elsewhere in the world which is August it was dry. The corn was twisting in the fields, the pastures were dusty, and even at night the cattle lowed with distress. Everywhere the sun beat down in the direct scorching way which only an August sun can do—everywhere except on our lawn. There is little shade to a cedar but there was plenty of walnut and oak to protect the grass. It was hot but there was still green for the eye to rest upon. Ellen leaned back against the trunk of the cedar. I lay on my back before her.

"This is a pleasant place," I said, beguiled by the clarity of the sun and the sanity of the physical world, when it pauses at recess and its real nature goes out of mind. "This *is* a pleasant place," I repeated.

"And it can be a fine place," she added. "I acted rather badly in the beginning," she went on, "but then I was overwhelmed. Now it seems simpler. I am happier. It is better for you than the town. There you always ran on the exhaustion of nerves. Perhaps in time we may have children."

I put my arms about her waist. "You are the only reality," I said. "I don't care if we can't have children. Our life is meaning. Everything else is illusion. Nothing must take you away from me."

Gently she released herself. "Darling, you make me a little afraid. Nothing is going to take me away from you."

And so it was decided to stay on. As we went back to the house, hand in hand, the intruder seemed no more threatening than a bad dream after breakfast and coffee.

At the door we were met by the mailman. He had a registered letter. I opened and read it.

"What is it?" Ellen asked.

"It's from my nephew Moss," I said. "He thinks he is going soon to be sent home from the South Pacific. It doesn't say why." I handed her the letter. She glanced through it.

"He is rather brief, isn't he?"

"I hope he is in no trouble," I said.

"You can never tell what the military will do. Probably battle fatigue." And then she said cheerfully, "He can help with the house. It will do him good to do a little honest work."

"Yes, yes," I said. "It will do him good. It will do us all good to see him."

But as I went into the house, I carried with me a strange feeling of foreboding.

11

AFTER THIS I FELT WE LIVED JUST AS OTHER PEOPLE DO. THE false romanticism which had landed me so blithely into the bramblebush of history tempted me with the prospect of success. The actual undertaking as opposed to the idea had impressed on me the heroic nature of the work and, as with all sagas, the involvements with the supernatural. My initial encounters with the shade of Major Brent, or whatever metamorphosis he had assumed, found me possessed of a courage I didn't know I had and an exquisite awareness of horror whose depths sank below and beyond mortal knowledge. The secret awareness that I was no hero I buried. In the same grave I put the fear that my courage was unequal to the perils of my situation. In the blind panic which was my state of mind but which seemed, because of its long duration, a clear, lofty objectivity, I banished Major Brent to his proper habitat and forbade him to trespass again. My first presentiment that all was not right with my nephew Moss faded into the picture of him as my heir, and I longed for his arrival. It seems rather complicated even now, but it all came from my talk with Ellen and her desire to live at *The Grove,* which meant of course that all would be well with us and my love for her. I don't think that I understood how my original interest in the place had shifted its emphasis. I still thought of myself in all sincerity as occupied with the difficult problems of regeneration. Our personal problems I took to be merely a variant on the central theme. But actually my interest now lay almost entirely and rather desperately in making *The Grove* seem attractive to Ellen. I was occupied with the usual American bourgeois habit, in spite of my ideas, in spite of my very principles, of giving my wife the comforts, the setting, the status equal to my love for her. In the beginning, when she went to pieces, the ruin of our love seemed imminent and my manhood threatened. Now that I see things so clearly I am certain that a loss of manhood was involved, for had I not caught from the infested air that disease of all latter-day Americans—to fail in a material way is to fail in manhood?

In such fashion I allowed myself to be taken off guard. There are no other words for it. What devious ways does not an imperfect apprehension take us? Had I been put on record before a jury of sensible men—I do not say peers, for where in the sweepings of this continent could the peer to such extravagant individualism have been found—and had I been asked in the presence of the twelve, Can you do it? I at least would have paused and assessed the odds for what they were worth, for I am a man of vision. But how we blot out in the gloom of mad endeavor the light which by exposing will thwart us!

And so it was, I say again in all honesty, I retired to my study where I worked every day and often far into the night at reviews and essays to get the material for our little campaign. I had had to borrow on the property to add to the sale of Ellen's ring, for it took a great deal to keep her in the frenzy of her work. She handled laborers better than I and, more quickly than I had dreamed, managed to finish the kitchen, the dining room, and get a start on the lower hallway. I worked confidently and scarcely felt the pressure of our economic situation. And yet of course it was money I had on my mind, so much so that I didn't dare think of it, lest I think to what ruin and disaster its lack would bring us.

And money did begin to come in, slowly at first in steady small sums, enough for the household expenses and a little laid by against the interest on the mortgage whose payment drew nearer with each ticking of the clock in the hall below. I raced my mind against the swinging of that round brass sun. It became an obsession with me. There endured such a synchronization between my mind and the clock's stroke that so long as I worked I could not hear it. But let me grow idle, or rest, it struck off with its impervious beat precious time forever lost. I now think I must have been a little mad. I dared not look the timepiece in the face but always hurried by with averted eye; yet I could never go fast enough. Once I thought by ignoring I had silenced it, but it stopped me in the doorway through which I fled. If only once it would miss a beat, but the unvarying regularity of the tick, the swing, and the tock drove me to desperate and inhuman work. Ellen appealed to me, saying I would be ill. Not even she could divert me. I could point to the need and the proofs in the form of the checks I showed her. What I could not point to were the terribly inhuman odds I strove against, and I do not speak of material things, but of those regions where time is unknown.

In no circumstances would I have broached the subject of those regions. The strangest comment on my state of mind was the way I was able to shut it out of my own thoughts. Its return came with the shock almost of a betrayal. I must have been asleep, how long I have no way of knowing, except that it was well after midnight—I had heard the stroke of that hour. My arms lay on the desk. They had disarranged the papers there and from the night sweat several pages of my novel still clung damply to my flesh. All I know is I found myself sitting erect and wide awake in the pressure of that alien and frigid atmosphere I had come to know and dread. My eyes were blurred from too much use of the tight sleep of the overtired, but they were clear enough to see through the open door the loathsome form of my guest. He hovered in the doorway to our apartment and I saw his left hand fumble as if he were trying to find the knob. So still was he, except for the purpose in that hand and arm, swollen to my view out of all proportion to the rest of his form, that I had the sickening illusion of the hypnotic sway of a snake practicing at the keyhole. My alarms and my disgust were equal. These overbore any thought of fear or courage. I was merely drawn to go forward and challenge him.

I arose from the chair and it made a long creaking sound of pain. With this sound in my head I strode onto the gallery and stopped within a few paces of the shadowy figure whose back was still turned to me. But let it not be understood that the figure was in any way vague. The frightful presence could have been no clearer had it been day at its brightest hour. Slowly the hand withdrew from the keyhole and the arm, so easily did it move, floated to his side. By this I knew he had become aware of me and, feeling an exalted elation at this recognition, I waited for his next move. I waited in the alarm of the tremendous advance he had made in the freedom of the house, for only now, at a range so close I could have touched him, did some part of the meaning of his persistence grow clear to me. But I had no leisure to examine it. He had turned.

He had turned to face me. I did not waver nor fall back but, all taut, met him. At once, for there was no mistaking it, I sensed the change in his bearing to me. I was no longer ignored as I had been in that encounter in our study, where his examination of the room in my presence gave me the queer feeling that he took me for an accomplice. There was none of this. It was clear now that he recognized in me the sole obstacle to his desire. I got it all from the hollow depths of his stare. I remember nothing of the features, only his look of hatred and malevolence which somehow included himself as well as me. These are hit-or-miss words. There is nothing in the human catalogue of feeling which I can draw on for analogy. I knew this: his appearance which I already felt too much to bear grew yet more intense. It enveloped the space we stood in, or what became space some moments afterward, for here again I stumble over words. The air, if air it was, made a chill and a silence in which nothing existed. Even I felt no true sense of being. We were isolated in some intermediate world. Not a sound penetrated from the night outside it, where the actual darkness disclosed its imperfections before the true image enveloping me. Though in the world I was shut off from it, or to draw a finer distinction, that part of the world where I was had been usurped by another. The chill was the dry chill of absolute aridity and the silence a silence of endless reaches where no sound was or ever would be.

Then my senses whirled under the impact of metamorphosis. I felt myself shift ground before a blast of heat. Perhaps I cried out, for the sudden contrast of what went before and what came after gave me a moment of pain. When I recovered myself, I saw that I was alone on the gallery, on a sultry August night, with not a breath of air stirring.

12

I HAD BARELY GOT MY EQUILIBRIUM BACK BEFORE I RECEIVED another shock, coming so hard on the first that the impact of the second seemed only a continuation of the first. It was the revelation of the purpose behind the apparition's return. The shock was the sickening effect this intelligence had on me. It surged through me with the clarity of euphoria—his position at the door to the apartment where Ellen slept, the intention in that ghastly hand. I know now that even at the time of his first appearance I nurtured some such fear, never daring, because of the insupportable implications it contained, to bring it up for candid inspection.

There was no doubt now about its being full blown. I knew, even though I cannot tell you why I knew, that I had prevented some terrific act of violence, some dreadful adventure in which space and matter were involved. I suspected Major Brent as the agent, perhaps out of a devouring need, the self-appointed agent of doom. The word I know has lost in the soilure of too many tongues its meaning. This meaning I now restore. Say the word aloud. Believe you speak it for the first time and you will understand the terror of my comprehension. You will understand my anxiety and reluctance to rush through the door and take Ellen in my arms, for, alas, I am earth-bound and subject to all the laws of matter. To defend what I loved against a force I could never reach—this was the excruciating nature of my torture. Had I even now lost her? Major Brent had vanished, but Ellen? I felt I had been in time, but could I—always this uncertainty—could I be sure? There was but one way to find out. Open the door and go forward into the room. This I did.

Noiselessly the door swung inward and, dark though it was, I could feel myself pale at what I saw: Ellen swaying just inside, in the nightgown she had worn on our wedding night, her eyes open but still asleep. The gown moved lazily against her body, blown by the sultry air which the door in its passage had stirred. She gave a little gasp and stepped back as my hands grasped her. And so we stood for an instant as I tried to speak. What came from my mouth sounded like the cry of an animal in pain. At last I said the useless words, "Darling, what are you doing here?"

She said rather wanly, "I thought I heard you call. I must have been asleep."

Gently, as one is careful of an invalid, I picked her up and laid her upon our bed. As I fumbled at the buttons of my shirt, she said, "Dear, I've had the most awful dream."

"Yes, I know," I said. With great care I tried to calm my voice.

"But how can you know?" she asked.

I did not answer. The buttons would not undo.

"Oh," she said and her voice was clearer. "What made you tear your shirt? You've none too many."

I mumbled something about the dark. I could not speak, I could not quiet the great perturbation in my heart until I lay beside her and had her body in my arms. Nothing but this old substantial truth could restore me.

At last I was beside her and she received me. Calmed, I lay on my back in the empty heaviness of release. Only our fingers now entwined. Out of a great distance she said, "I thought you had forgotten."

"Forgotten?" I repeated.

"That this is our anniversary."

I hedged. "How could you think that?"

"You've seemed so . . . well, so absorbed. At times I feel you don't know I'm here."

"You know what I've been doing. How I've had to."

"That's just it. Do you have to be alone all the time?"

I shifted ground. "Aren't you . . ." I hesitated.

"Happy?" she interposed and then her voice trailed off. When she spoke again, she seemed to speak out of some private truth. "Happiness. Oh, I don't know that that matters now."

I pretended to be calm, but what agonizing considerations laid waste my peace of a few moments ago! My voice must have sounded queer to her. It sounded queer enough to me as I said, "Happiness doesn't matter?"

"It's not that it doesn't matter. But there are other things."

"Other things?" My voice was casual, except for a slight tremor.

She turned and said with a kind of puzzled desperation, "I know you've got your writing to do, but, darling, you mustn't leave me alone so much."

"I shall never let you out of my sight again."

"I didn't mean all that, Henry."

"What did you mean then?"

She answered me in her own way, and I felt the pathos of her sad little gallantry, for what once had quieted all needs, answered all questions, had become itself the dark field of ultimate questioning. My head was still whirling with the various possibilities when at last her fingers fell loose from mine and I noticed the first misty smudge of day slide up the gap in the flowered curtains. In this faint light I looked at her pale lovely face, now closed to me in sleep. Had it closed to me forever? Had I, after all, been too late? Did the dissembling mask of sleep contain what I would find when the tale was all told? I probed into my consciousness, but it only gave back the wonder of my anguish and my desperate need. I longed for the future instant by instant, the flash of vision which would reveal my condemnation or my reprieve. I got the knowledge of a duller thing, the unhurried, unvarying lockstep which is time. If to this prison I resigned myself, it was not entirely without hope. Its restraining power restrained also another.

13

I MUST HAVE DROPPED OFF, LYING AT HER SIDE, FOR I FOUND myself sitting up in bed, my heart in a stifled pounding from the sudden wrench to consciousness and the sense that I had missed some terribly important engagement. I saw that I was alone. The curtains were still drawn, but the quality of light shining through the flowered figures told me how much of the morning was already spent. Hard on this came the awareness that while I slept another had had the chance to enjoy the freedom of *The Grove* with that insolent display of familiarity which made me so long to throttle him. My need to do him physical violence was great and my impotence so apparent that, for a moment, my imagination gave body to that density of air which he assumed at the demand of infamous longing.

I threw on my clothes and rushed from the room. The hours I had been sleeping Ellen had been unguarded. What disaster might not come of it, if once he got through to her, I dared not think. She had felt influences. Of this I was sure, but I was equally sure that I had so far saved her an actual encounter.

Once outside, in the gallery which lay between the study and the apartment, I paused an instant to decide which way to go. Never had I as now understood the full terror and meaning of time. To waste even a breath in a false start might be to lose all in the general waste of eternity. Short as it was, my hesitation allowed me to see through the open door to my study that someone was sitting at my desk. I advanced and found my nephew Moss, completely at ease in my chair, after the manner of young men profligate of that one gift they will spend the rest of their lives regretting. "Have you seen Ellen?" I asked. To this day I am unsure what I got as answer, but my ears caught the phrase, "In the flower garden." Intuitively I knew I had the right direction. With no further greeting or welcome, I rushed on.

The garden lay to the rear of my study. There was a stretch of lawn and then the wall. In other days one could have looked down into the garden, but it was so overgrown I did not pause but right off swung down the winding way. I had been inside it once, on my first visit when I came with the idea of buying *The Grove*. Intuitively I understood the temptations it would have for me and afterward stayed away. The degree to which a farm's economy can be brought is best judged by the flower garden. To have it at all is a luxury and evidence of discipline and sound management, for the garden needs attention always when the crops can least spare a hand from the fields. And of course it bespeaks that leisure which is the supreme attainment of civilized habits. I go as far, even, as to say that in the great ages the formal garden reflects the last refinements of the social pattern and, indeed, is the commentary that the age makes on itself. For what was Versailles laid out but to inter the feudality of France? Or what is any eighteenth-century garden but the very will of fashion, with its geometrical pattern, the clean little walks between the low, well-trimmed borders, that superior artifice where even the flowers seem denaturalized? But the house defines another truth. If it is old, it contains the whole tradition. One does not make a house. A house grows and as it grows binds together the continuous past. Because I understood this, until I had house and land well in hand, I knew it were best to stay away from the place I now approached.

The lock and chain had rusted together about the gate. But this was no hindrance. The wall had many gaps, where the brick had fallen into rubbish or had been robbed for various uses about the farm. Very quietly I pushed aside a straggly and overgrown box-bush, stepped over and was inside. For a moment I forgot why I was there. The garden was not large, yet it was not small, nor was it exactly as I had remembered it. I had had the image of an old-fashioned garden but not the perfect symmetry I now found. Flowers and shrubs and weeds were all overgrown in a common tangle, and luxuriantly overgrown from the extraordinary richness of the ground, but beneath this wilderness the plan was clear. It had been laid out in a circle, with a round springhouse upon a mound as its hub. A serpent's head, carved of stone, rose up out of the little brick house, with jaws widespread and dripping water. Once the water must have poured, for there was still evidence of the conduit circling the beds, each group of plots increasing in size as they approached the enclosing wall. And just here was the final touch of art. The wall, hexagonal in shape, softened but did not alter the meaning of the design. I stood enthralled and a little dizzy from the impact of the mind able to conceive this, the utter daring, the brilliant imagination, the Satanic pride of it. I saw afresh with what an adversary I had to do and again, when I looked to the resources I had, I very nearly gave in to despair. But no matter what the odds the soldier's response to danger is professional—he acts. I was a kind of soldier: I remembered why I was there. Swiftly I searched the undergrowth. I looked with a sharper eye and what I saw wrenched me for a moment from my obsession. The garden was a dump heap. Rotten tin cans, broken bottles, rags, half a fireback, all littered the place. There were piles of ashes, pocked with bits of charcoal beaten to the surface by countless rains, and a thousand other objects of refuse tossed anywhere about. In the midst of this I saw Ellen.

She was on the ground, in a cool white muslin frock, weeding one of the walkways. She did not see me as her head was bent to her work, and I was careful not to interrupt her. There was about her the air of innocence one thinks of as surrounding the sacrificial victim. Her hair had been brought up on her head, and I admired with the sweet sense of possession the purity of the lines of her neck, bent slightly around and down. Then my heart made that plunge of alarm, the infallible awareness of danger. It was all in the fierce rapidity of her hands and, in spite of the illusion of composure, a too rapt attention to what she did. All around her rose piles of weed and grass, neatly raked for the barrow. My gaze widened, startled at the amount of the garden she had cleaned, obviously more than one morning's work. I dared not reckon the number of hours, else I should have had to ask how she had done it at all. My wonderment grew into a question, Why had she made no mention of this to me?

So I was warned but my comprehension was slow to focus. I found myself, of necessity, returning to her hands. They were my clue. Then as I watched, I saw them quicken as though she felt behind her the shadow of the taskmaster. The tension in her frail body was painful to see, and it all drew to a point in the speed of her fingers. Exquisite, fragile, they drove at the dirt under some dreadful compulsion. I took all this in as I took in the certain knowledge that another watched as well as I. A sodden chill rolled out of the depths of the undergrowth, swirling in its circular track until it caught us up in the logic of its motion. All sounds of the bright morning fell away and, as they perished, so did my apprehension of the

alien air I breathed. I was no more conscious of the fearful
energy which underlay it than I would be aware, walking
down a country lane, of the world revolving in space. The
sick feeling I had had of violation, my helpless estrangement
before it, now entirely disappeared. It was as one equal to all
occasions that I slowly turned my head until, at last, it came
to rest facing the garden's center. I paused to sharpen my will.
I paused; then I lifted my eyes, brick by brick, up the slimy
springhouse wall.

14

I GOT TO THE STUDY AS SOON AS I COULD AND THAT MEANT, OF
course, as soon as I could get Ellen out of the garden and
safely into the house. I shut the door and leaned against it for
support. I had kept up my front in the garden. Only now did
I give in to the aftereffects of my trial of nerve.

"He has got through to her," I gasped to Moss.

There had always been great sympathy between my
nephew and me, but never did it show to better purpose than
in this, my tacit appeal for help. He confused me by no stupid
response, no tiresome questions. He merely leaned forward in
his chair and waited for more. The mere sight of him, the
wonderful feeling that I would no longer stand alone, this
knowledge and the privacy of my room, restored somewhat
my equilibrium. I had retired to my citadel and my faithful
seneschal was at my side; or to draw a sharper figure, my heir.

So it came about that what I had to divulge was given and
received as a matter of family concern. It was the ease and

grace of his reception that gave me the firm ground I needed, the familiar rapport which usually passes between father and son. Whatever the virtues of Moss Senior, and he was reputed to have many in certain circles, they did not thrive in his dealings with his son. My brother lived in the happily simple world where all things have a price, and the better the bargain the better the price, which is all very well, I suppose, if you don't drive bargains for the affection of your son. I never thought I would have sympathy for such limitations, but I fairly blessed them now as I quickly sketched for Moss the history of what had happened up to his appearance at *The Grove*. The boy's reception of my tale was so keen and ready it gave me the illusion of talking aloud to myself. "And so you see," I wound up, "I have failed, miserably failed."

"Failed?" I rather felt than heard the question, so softly did it drift my way.

"Yes, failed. To stand between Major Brent and his odious purpose."

"What is . . ."

"What is his purpose? It is also his desire." I fairly spat these out, so fresh was his fearsome image in my mind.

"And that?"

"I don't quite know. Oh, that I did!" I finished with a groan of perplexity. "I do know that it has to do with Ellen. Of this I am certain as I am certain of you, there, in my chair."

"How do you know?"

"How? How? I saw."

The shadow of a question crossed my nephew's eyes. It was plain I needed to be more circumstantial. "Not an hour ago, there in the garden, I beheld him with my eyes, like an evil smoke but also a solid, hovering above the springhouse. He filled my eyes and then went, like mist drying, down through the rotten floor."

"Did . . ."

"Did Ellen see? No, but she felt. She knew he was there."

"How?"

"I could tell by the look on his devilish face."

"But if she didn't see?"

"But I saw. The eager gleam, the contaminating look of his triumph." And I added in a low voice, at the marvel of it, "And it reached out like a solid thing and touched her. It was then I could stand no more. He disappeared." At the thought of this I fell silent, trembling before the memory of this hateful appearance. And as I looked across at Moss, I could see that it had welled up into my eyes by the reflection from his. More smoothly, for hatred is like hardening a stick by fire, I developed the line of my reasoning. "I had thought I stood between—he will not hold up to me, you see, he has his limitations too—but what I learned today is that some traffic has existed between them and for longer than I can know. What she did, what she was, in the garden showed me. And I have other cause to believe . . ."

"You mean?"

"We had a chance to sell the farm. She demurred, after having pleaded to get away. Now what could make her change her mind so suddenly?"

And then I heard, "But how can he get at her?"

"By making her want to come to him."

"But how? An apparition to a mortal being."

"It is one of the oldest stories. And who knows what promises he makes over the invisible lines of his communication—enough," I added grimly, "to make her want to know more."

"Then if she wants to know more . . ."

"His spell is not quite wound up? Good!" I almost shouted. "That may be our way out. We must hold to that. If we can prevent another meeting . . . We must watch, you and I, every hour of the day and night."

"I will watch at night," I heard.

"And I by day." This gleam of hope brought me up sharp to the practical way of carrying out our plan. I asked, "Does Ellen know you are here?"

He shook his head slowly and, for a moment, his eyes seemed to withdraw. With uncanny intuition I understood that he did not want her, or anyone, to know he was here. This brought me up to his own mysterious situation. His cryptic letter and then, without warning, his arrival. I looked more closely, berating myself for a too great preoccupation with my own affairs, and saw his travel-stained uniform, the dust and grime of the battlefield still on it, the pale look of strain and the jagged scar on his forehead running back into his head. I could not tell how far because of the blackness and the thickness of his hair.

I saw at once how painful any questions of mine would be. Matter-of-factly I took it up where he had left off. "I will put you in the old office out there in the yard. Johnny will bring your food. No one—" I emphasized this—"no one need know you are here. It is better that way."

On this we parted. I arose for my watch. It was understood that he would keep the study until night, when his would begin.

15

ALL BLESSINGS ARE MIXED. SO I FELT WHEN I HAD THE leisure to think how the tension would slacken now that Moss had come. But this very letting up gave me time to think, and for the first few days my thoughts were equally divided between my wife and nephew. I cannot tell what a wonderful comfort he was unless I also tell what marred this comfort. If I had let myself go, I should have gone as far as alarm at his ambiguous appearance, his noncommittal silence about why he was here and not with his outfit. I gave him every chance to explain himself. I hinted at battle fatigue, at a well-deserved leave. I even went so far as to open a discussion of psychiatry as practiced officially by the Army, saying what an advance it had made over the old brutal methods which reduced human performance to the extremes of cowardice and bravery. But no matter how subtly I threw out these different leads not one of them did he take. He would smile, he would listen politely, he would make some general observation—nothing more. I was forced to come back to my original impression: he was hiding at *The Grove,* but whether because of something he had done or something he feared might be done to him, I had to leave undecided.

This I was willing to do. After all he was here, I needed him, I felt surer somehow of withstanding what there was to withstand, in spite of the rapid and perilous advance of danger, which I never let out of my mind for a moment. It lay with me like a cold spring at the bottom of a pool. On the surface all was warm and even languid, but one had only to dive to know the shock of the chill beneath. I suppose I would have cracked up but for the respite I got from floating in the lukewarm upper surface. It seemed that everybody at *The Grove* conspired to keep me at ease, Ellen, Moss, and Johnny. I was touched at the way Johnny tried to rise to the occasion. When I told him the new duties I entrusted to him, he accepted them with understanding. He cleaned out the office and set up a bed, pretending he needed it for a storehouse. But the most remarkable instance of his tact showed itself in the way he met Moss. I had brought Johnny up to the study, first warning him that no one must know that my nephew was there. I told him that only he and I knew it, that even Miss Ellen did not know, and that if by any chance it got out, I would know who had been indiscreet. I made no open threat, of course, but my manner was as grave and ominous as I could make it. This, I knew, would leave its impression, for Johnny had conceived a tremendous respect for the possibilities of my nature. Moss was standing by the bookcase, reading the titles there. I said, "Lad, this is Johnny. He will look after your needs." Johnny gave a quick glance to the corner where Moss was, stiffened slightly—only I would have noticed it—and then stood there with respectful dignity, hat in hand, looking not at but just to the side of Moss's position. In any other situation I would have smiled at his cunning. Nobody could trap him into admission of seeing anything, and yet his stance told me he was aware of everything.

Moss turned, smiled in his charming way, and nodded; then he went back to the books. I never saw a more difficult situation handled by both parties with greater ease or discretion. My affection for them increased enormously and it became the seal to our common aim. It led me, without more ado, to probe farther into the last days of Major Brent on earth. Johnny had told me much, but there were gaps in the information and there was, as always, the confusing veil of legend. This I must strip away. "Monstrous on earth as in the void he inhabits," I began by way of soliloquy, for speaking the word often leads to truth which escapes the silent inquiry. Johnny heard but did not understand. Moss showed by his attention, a deeper stillness, that he listened. "For was it not monstrous in him to make such an end," I went on, "dispossessing his inheritors and bringing his daughter barren to her shroud, and for himself committing or permitting that last affront to tradition, the unmarked grave. Does anyone know where he lies?"

I put this to Johnny direct. I waited in the hiatus my question made and watched the bare shake of his head. "Ain't no grave."

"But he didn't just lie out like a heathen and let the crows pick his bones. Whatever his wish, whatever his need, he died in a Christian land."

"Yessir," Johnny solemnly said, "I knows of some Christians over towards Oak Grove."

"The authorities would not permit it. There must be the record. The record is the state's evidence of self-perpetuation, the link between the past and the future." I paused to change the tone of voice. "There was bound to be investigation."

I waited again. Johnny cast his eyes before him, covertly in the direction of Moss, showing his reluctance to talk about Major Brent in the presence of any witness, no matter how well recommended he came. But finally he said, "The High Sheriff knocked at Miss Euphemy's do'."

"Ah, hah. That's what I have been waiting to hear."

"And she come to de do'."

"Yes?"

"But hit taken right smart rappen on de do' to bring her.

The High Sheriff nigh wo'e out his hat fanning. She opened
de do' wide and shaded her eyes . . . so." Johnny lifted the
stiff black fingers to his forehead and squinted as one might
do who looks into smoke. "She looked over the High Sheriff's
lef' shoulder, she looked past his face, she looked over his
right shoulder, and then she shet the do'."

That, as far as I could gather, marked the extent to which
the law ever went in attempting to implicate Miss Euphemia.
The law must show cause and motive. The keepers of the
peace must have felt that there was in Major Brent's act a
threat to the general peace. But what had they to go on? An
old man, by his own will, drives his sons away and, again by
his own will, with witnesses to the fact, remains alone in the
middle of his fields. And is never seen more. His very act
was a symbol of social violence, but you can't bring a symbol
into court. And deeding the land to Miss Euphemia was further proof of his intention, but the deed had been on record a
year before his disappearance. All was regular. The proper
heirs had no recourse, no expectation of aid from the authorities. They inherited a title, the Dispossessed, and nothing
more but a hireling's pay. There would have been much
whispering, many dark allusions to the barren woman who
lived on at *The Grove,* who gave the name reality by letting
the sassafras sprouts take the fields, but the real terror before
which the keepers of the peace drew back lay in the meaning
of the act itself. And this they had no way of dealing with.

For what can the public guardians do but harden their
souls and dance mincingly on the sharp blades of power? And
at last fall and eunuch themselves, for the strongest heads
grow giddy at last? And clean up the blood of the victim to
make ready the altar for the next, for the victim they can
neither commit nor save, led all decked in garlands and

white, like innocence coming up for confirmation, but coming up to sacrifice and spilt blood to lay the oldest ghost of all, who will not lie but, like the absent lord, returns with the season to collect his dues? Pistol strapped to the bulging side, the ready grin on the florid face, the toothpick after meat, always they find themselves caught in the same dilemma. They hail the fornicator into court, but bastards drool on the doorsteps. They jail thieves, but the honor of the state is compromised by those who deal in its goods. Assaulters they fine, but broken heads mock them each Saturday night. If matters committed to their care, all actions plain to pragmatic eyes, go unresolved for all their resolutions and unchained for all their chains, what then could the High Sheriff do but cool his heels before the fact of a shut door which was not a fact at all but a threat and a symbol as old as night?

"And where will it bring me," I said aloud, "this cold scent, but where all false trails lead—back upon myself?"

"Ain't it the truf?" Johnny agreed and nodded wisely.

And it was the truth and on this I dismissed Johnny who, as so often before, had put it squarely up to me, without incriminating himself.

16

I DIDN'T LET OUT, EVEN TO MOSS, HOW HOPELESS I FELT about poor Ellen. So long as I didn't put it into words, I could keep my courage up. Words have a way of fixing a thing and, once spoken, may not be taken back. But the scene I had happened on in the garden was too depressing, even, for courage. As I turned to the springhouse to meet what I had to meet, I gave my back to Ellen. The moment of release I whirled about and met . . . well, I met her eyes. A faint flush brushed her features which had been so pale when I first came into the garden. The strain was all gone, her hands hung limp above the work she had been doing, but it was the eyes which confessed so clearly my fears. There was no avoiding the truth of their stare: they had seen all I had seen and more.

I went to her and lifted her to her feet. If then she had confessed openly and frankly, if she had told me even something of her peril, I might have been able to save her. It was the moment for confidences, and for a fraction of the moment I thought she would throw herself into my arms and ask for aid. But the moment passed. She said instead with an engaging smile—what a brave effort at subterfuge it was— "My, you startled me."

"I noticed," I replied, "your absorption."

She said with strange self-confidence, "This was a place I didn't expect to see you."

"And so you thought you were safe in slipping away."

"Yes."

"And now I've spoiled it all."

"Yes, you have spoiled it all."

The very boldness of this took my breath away. If only she had spoken with brutal intent instead of after the old usage of husband and wife which, because of its falseness, seemed to me all the more terrifying! As she saw my confusion, she went on, she even tried gaiety. "You see, I was not yet ready for the grand surprise."

I could only blurt out, "It was surprise enough."

"Don't you think I'm smart?"

"I have another word for it."

Something in my tone caught her up, for she said quickly, "I mean, haven't I done a lot? And without you suspecting a thing."

"I haven't been completely blind, you know."

"But you haven't known?"

"Known?"

"I mean about the garden. What's been going on here."

It was out between us now, in spite of the deliberate ambiguity of language. If I could only have torn away this last veil and heard the desperate truth, desperately spoken! It was on my tongue to say, "You think you have deceived me? But I know whom you meet and what he wants." But some feeling of caution held me back. I said instead, "Now, Ellen, this is too much." I waved my hand toward the walkways. "I'll send Johnny here to finish up. His crops are about laid by and the boys can help. I want you to stay closer to the house. I can watch you there."

"Watch me, darling?"

"Yes, see what you do." I thought I had carried the game a little far, so I added, "I need to have you near. Besides, this work is too hard for you." I picked up one of her hands. "It will ruin these. That would be a great loss to us both."

Carefully she withdrew her hand. "You should have thought of that when you asked me to come here," she said.

On the way back to the house she stopped once and said fiercely or so I was made to feel the passion in her utterance, "We have got to finish up. I have so little time."

"Time? Time for what?"

She did not answer me, but again I had that feeling of a confidence about to be made and looked my willingness to hear, to help, but she blushed and dropped her eyes and we went the rest of the way in silence.

In the following days I was with Ellen so constantly that what the garden had shown faded out of my consciousness, as the prints of a photographer's proofs fade in the sun. And there was a great deal of sun, which made us think of picnics. The work downstairs had gone so well that Ellen felt we could relax occasionally. She would fix us lunches and we would take to the woods and spread a cloth and eat and talk. It was great pretense and fun. Once we went several miles away, off our land, to a nice creek we knew, and here we spent the day swimming and lying about in the sun. My spirits soared, I even hoped, and if my conscience hurt me, it was on account of Moss to whom I owed such pleasant days and dreamless nights. Once in a mood of confidence I almost slipped up and told her what guest we had in the house. "I have something to tell you, Ellen," I said. "You must try to understand."

"What, darling, have you been keeping back? You've not got some horrible woman tucked away on the back side of the farm, with Johnny standing guard. Johnny has been very mysterious lately."

I caught myself up quickly enough. I took her hand. "No," I said. "It's just that I never really told you how much I love you."

"Will you love me when I'm old and a hag?"

"I'll love you always, no matter what."

"No matter what at all?"

"No matter what at all." I found I had grown suddenly grave.

"That's a large order, you know," she said slowly.

"As long as you want my love, and even when you don't."

"I shall always want it," she said, "and I am trying, you don't know how hard, to make you a good wife." Her eyes blurred and she dropped them, and her voice was low as she said, "But it is hard sometimes. There are things . . ."

"Things?" I prompted.

She leaned across the leavings of our lunch and kissed me. "If it could always be like this . . . if we could stay always this close together . . . if, if this were life and life not what it is . . ."

"Once we thought . . ."

"Yes, I know we thought that food and drink were a bore, something to fill out the interludes between love, that a house was a shelter, and that if we only followed the sun, we wouldn't need that." She turned to me a little sadly. "I remember, you see. It is you who have forgotten."

We were standing now. The sun flared with the false brilliance which dies into dusk and it fell on the littered cloth at our feet. For a moment the reflection from the white cloth, falling across her body, made glary stains on her tan, and then it dazzled my eyes and I closed them. And out of the darkness I said, "No, I haven't forgotten. I've tried to make it stick, forgetting that the honeyed moon passes into leaner quarters and, as a man must who would hold his love, turn the shelter into a house. But when the house is another man's house, and you no proper heir, in spite of title deeds and nine-tenths of the law, you are no better than a guest."

"I'm no guest," she said defiantly.

"No," I replied, and there was all the sadness of our predicament in my voice as I said it, "you are no guest at *The Grove*."

17

"F OR HER TO SAY," I REPEATED TO MOSS AS SOON AS I COULD get hold of him, "that she was no guest at *The Grove* brings us straight back to the garden. If she is at home here, and I am not . . . if she is mistress here . . ."

"Well, you are master."

"This is no time for levity," I said rather irritably.

"If not you, who then is?"

I paused at the directness of this. There is nothing like the question direct to clear away the vagaries of loose thinking. I rather blushed at what I had been thinking: unconsciously I had accepted Johnny's superstitious belief that Major Brent was master. How absurd this was Moss's plain speaking had made me see, for who can believe in a private resurrection? The dead might return in its own proper air, but no man in his right wits could say that this air could take on body. I had, in truth, come to accept Major Brent without being able to define him. This had confused me. Had he not abandoned *The Grove* to sterility, to a withering up of the traditional vine? Did he not will it to die with him? Then why should I have ever thought that he longed for resurrection? For if my problem was regeneration, his could only be a rising up to judgment.

"If not you, who then?" The question repeated itself.

I replied out of my bemusement. "Perhaps no one."

"No one?"

I was made to feel a distinctly youthful tone in this. It might have been my own youth accusing me of the failure of middle years. I was faced with what all face who try to explain the complexities of human experience to the young. I compromised as one does. I fell back on the logic of the situation. "Major Brent resents my presence here. You know his history. He returns out of a jealousy carried beyond the grave. Don't ask me yet why a shade can feel jealousy."

"But it is Ellen he haunts. Not you."

"And why not? Woman is the carrier of tradition. His own daughter he kept barren. If he could draw Ellen to him . . ."

"But how?"

"By luring her to her death," I said abruptly. "Why else do we keep such strict watch?"

"Is it for this we keep watch?"

"For what else?"

He said casually. "But death is such a common thing."

There comes a time in all strain when the recoil and the blow seem but parts of the same movement. At first I could think no farther than the utter irrelevance of his remark. I had received him back as the boy I had known, the dearly beloved nephew who had always looked to me for guidance. I had forgotten the scalding pot of war into which he had plunged. And indeed he had a scalded look, the lacquerlike cast to the features I have sometimes seen on the face of the young who suffer too quickly and violently the ills of the world. In peacetime it is bad enough, the mark of the sophisticate, but in war it is far more sinister, the rushing of experience over knowledge, a surface hardening and all soft confusion beneath. Sadly, as I regarded Moss, I understood that he was a casualty of war, one of those forbidden maturity, the process of curing which allows for the gradual mellowing of the sensibility. The truth was now plain. He had been cast out like spoiled meat.

And I had made him my main dependence. This unex-

pected complication compromised my whole strategy of defense, but for the moment I could only hedge. I said softly,
as one speaks to an invalid, "Don't you think that's beside the
point?"

But he looked at me out of his melancholy eyes and shook
his head in a slow puzzled way. "It's everywhere, all the
time," he said quietly.

"Yes, I know, but . . ."

"I had a friend. We were in the same hole. The water was
up to our armpits. I looked away and when I looked back, I
saw his head sinking into the water. I lifted him as well as I
could. He was there but he was not there. I got no relief for
sixteen hours. I just sat in the water with whatever it was
left I sat with. It took up as much room as he did, but it
wasn't him. I was life, but he wasn't even death. Death was
the air which cut across the top of the hole. I knew I had
only to lift my head a few inches to find it."

"That was a terrible shock," I said.

"I had another friend," he went on, ignoring me. "He was
in my platoon. The platoon was stretched out with good
intervals between the men. It had been quiet for some time.
It was a quiet sector. We were talking up and down the line.
He was some twenty yards away. He called down to me, 'Remember . . .' then a shell dropped. I was knocked out by the
concussion and when I came to, all covered with dirt and
the smell, I saw a big hole where he had been. I called out
his name before I could think. But he wasn't there. He wasn't
anywhere. Just that big hole where he had been. I felt a
little sick." He paused. "I didn't make any more friends."

"Look, lad, I know," I said, "but . . ."

"No," he replied in the same even voice, "you don't know.

But I know. There was so much of it. It was everywhere, all the time."

"That was war," I said. "This is a different thing."

"No," he persisted. "It's no different. What's different is crowding yourself in a hole. You are there and you wait for it, and it doesn't come. You just wait and you think of everything you can think of. You'd be surprised how little there is to think of. It's like a long-drawn-out life where nothing ever happens. The things that bite and crawl and suck keep you alive. Then it's over." He stopped, but added, "There's one other thing. To love very hard and don't ever do anything but love. As long as that lasts you are alive. Get away from anything that will interfere. Run if you have to."

"You mean I should run away from here?"

He nodded. "There's nothing else to do."

"I can do three things," I said. "I can tell Ellen what I know."

"But you haven't."

"I don't dare. Suppose she's deep in the business."

"So much the better. Before she goes deeper."

"It might drive her all the way."

"Go away."

"That's my second possibility."

"Then go, and now."

"It's not so simple. There is the money tied up here. It's not easy to cut such strings. Nor does any man like to give up."

"Giving up, winning, it's all the same."

"Where would we go now? Even if we could drop what we are doing. Isn't the pillar cut from the same tree as the post?"

"Go away," he said dreamily, "and take your bride away."

"Ellen," I said dryly, "is no longer a bride."

"My love would be always a bride."

"Lying in the slop of foreign holes has addled your wits, son. Listen. Do you think I don't know what a bride is? She is the one with the eyes in the back of her head, seeing both ways at once, the one miracle life is capable of, where innocence and knowledge meet before they fuse in the waste of the world. And you who fancy yourself the perennial bridegroom. Do you think I don't know what he is, at least in this country where there is only one season? He is the man with the strained neck, looking always back to Eden. He tries one way or another, and each time ends up in the blind alley of adultery. Or California."

I had tried to shock a little sense into him, and for a while I thought I had, but he only said, "And the third thing?"

"Stay and see it out."

As he made no comment on this, I filled the silence with my voice. "And that's what I mean to do. See it out."

But the silence remained.

18

As soon as I was alone, I got the full impact of the one-two of this blow. Moss could never feel, I now saw, the responsibility for *The Grove* that I had once hoped from him. He would never preserve and hand it on with care to *his* heir. To live for the moment, to burn life up in one great blaze, destroys the traditional thing. His attitude, really, approached much closer to Major Brent's than to mine. Each in his way would sacrifice *The Grove* to the private whim, the personal need of the individual. My disappointment was grave, but it was by no means, at this moment, my first concern. Moss's attitude toward death, which I had learned too late, meant that he would be of no further aid to me. How much of a hindrance I had still to learn. I felt, with some misgivings, that he would not intentionally betray me, but I could no longer put any confidence in him. Nor could I dismiss him easily. He knew too much. There was no way of getting around it. I had added to my burden— I had two now to watch instead of one.

But the first watch was in the hall below, where Ellen was busy taking off the old wallpaper with the help of one of Johnny's girls. I had bought her a small orchard spray and with this she shot a warm mist over the old paper, let it sink in, and then she and the girl took putty knives and worked the paper off. It went fairly fast and was less expensive than hiring a steamer and then finding somebody to run it. One of the most depressing things which was borne in on me, in the progress of my awakening to the real difficulties of regeneration, was my discovery that those following trades lacked professional integrity. It was not merely that any given craftsman—the word of course has lost all meaning—was unethical. Skill was gone, pride in the work; he was not even interested much in his pay, for the war and the government had diverted the workmen from a belief in that basic fear of want which stiffens the social morality in good times and makes all men of family remember the diversity of evil. This condition was not entirely the fault of those in public places; they were merely the representatives of this democracy of absolute corruption, for the evil had long been working in the yeast. Everywhere one felt a spiritual emasculation, for a man's final belief in himself comes from his attitude toward and his performance of his job. The soldier must be given ice cream to fight, all the rest of us must be bribed to live, for after all in spite of the conspiracy of silence and ignorance we, the impious, do know fear, the fear of those who sin against the Holy Ghost, the pretense that matter is all and that he who looks on the act of creation is himself creator.

As I came downstairs, I found Ellen in the great hall. She was alone, sitting on the floor, in the midst of the debris of strips of wallpaper and the tools she was using—putty knives, stepladders, pans of water and patching plaster. Doors back and front were open and a warm breeze had already dried the top layer of the dirty brown paper. She seemed small and fragile and not the occasion for the litter but some rare object, so still was she, which should have been moved before the work began but had been overlooked by careless eyes. Her own eyes looked toward the door but they had the bright gaze of preoccupation. She did not hear me as I came up.

I said softly, "A penny for your thoughts."

"Oh," she said. "It is you."

"You seem overwhelmed by your work."

"No, I was thinking about a long time ago, when I was sixteen."

"That's not so long, darling."

"It's centuries ago. My grandmother gave me a hat, I remember. It was my birthday. I thought it the most beautiful hat in the world. It had daisies underneath the brim and a soft blue ribbon which tied in a bow. How I walked and turned before the mirror! The world was very beautiful that day." And then she said sadly, "I never see daisies now that are half so pretty."

After a second I said, "Where is Maybelle? I thought she was helping."

"I had some things to wash. I'd rather do this than wash."

"You should have called me."

She rose with a little sigh. "It's rather a relief to get rid of you for a while." She said this pleasantly enough, but what is said in jest is often meant for earnest. "You've been sticking like a leech, you know. And I can't get any work out of you."

"I thought you liked me around."

"I do, but much better as a hand than watcher." She grew serious. "I don't know whatever possessed you to think you would like to do over this old place. You avoid the simplest job. It's lots of fun doing things together. Not much doing it alone." She smiled wryly. "I don't ask you any more. You groan so it takes all the pleasure away."

"You know that's not so," I said. "I want things to improve."

"You did once." She was facing me gravely, almost in accusation. "This is our home. We live here. We are putting our things here. Your things in a sense are you." And then she came out with it: "What is it that makes you loathe everything you do?"

This struck me like a bolt out of the blue. I felt that swollen clarity all blows give, and the incapacity to act. Mechanically I picked up the patching plaster and a putty knife and turned to the bare wall. It was my way of retreat.

"Now I've hurt its feelings," she said.

"I'm completely crushed," I replied.

This feeble effort at facetiousness failed, but it gave me time. And I needed time in which to recover from the surprise of this attack. It was so unlike Ellen. It was alien, hostile, the author of this exposure. But it was no stranger. I knew him well but not so well as he knew me, or I should have stopped this great forward stride of his. If I lacked proof before of comunication between them, I had it now. Ellen was too close to me to discover so revolutionary a change in feeling, a change which I myself, until the shock brought me the truth, was unaware of. It was true. I was beginning to loathe everything about *The Grove,* for the place had become the symbol of the waste of our lives, the subversion of my one idea.

As the putty knife flew down the cracks in the plaster, I could feel the look of defeat withdraw behind my eyes. The motion of my hands relieved me. My balance was restored, but I had to get out of the house. I had to move about. I turned and said, "Let's go into the garden and see what progress Johnny has made."

"But there's still so much to do here."

"We can't do it all in a day," I countered. "We are jugglers, you know. We have many balls in the air. To drop one is to lose the game." Strange words, and irrelevant, I thought, as I heard myself easily start a conversation so unrelated to my thoughts.

She took it up.

"It *is* rather like a circus, isn't it?"

"So it is. I will change the metaphor. I'm the tightrope walker."

"And I, the lady bareback rider?"

"No, darling, you are still the juggler."

"But are there lady jugglers?"

"Well, yes, and no. The juggler might—I say might—slip into a lady's skin."

"What fun for the lady!"

"And for the juggler."

"Oh," she said in mock withdrawal, "I shouldn't think it would be fun for him at all."

"No fun for the juggler?" I asked with lifted brow.

"No fun for the juggler. He has to keep the balls in the air."

She laughed gaily and I joined in, rather wryly, and then I said, "One reflects the company one keeps."

"You see then," she replied, "what an effect you are having on me these days."

"I, Mrs. Brent?"

She gave me a direct stare and, to be sure I did not miss her meaning, added, "Who else, Mr. Brent?"

19

THERE IS NO RUIN SO DEFINITIVE AS ONE THAT HAS BEEN cleared of debris. A dead city covered by silt or jungle takes on the anonymity of nature. Dig it out and you apprehend more than you would looking at a city crowded with the commerce of men. What you actually encounter is the ruin of life. All that man was and tried to be lies exposed in the bareness of the broken structure. The tremendous effort to exist and to persist finds there its ironic commentary. One dares not look too long.

As I came up to the garden, now cleaned of rubbish and undergrowth, an impression of personal and private ruin swept over me. The exposure was sudden and complete: the brick in the walks were uneven where roots had traveled; the borders of the flower beds showed a few scraggly box; here and there a rosebush grew out of shape. At the center the rotten floor of the springhouse looked crumbly and gray from the drying sun let in after so many years. All over, the garden was studded with the fresh-cut stems of bushes, like stobs driven in upside down. But the design, as a whole and in detail, was sharp and as importunate as a whispered message. And yet nothing had been restored. I could tell that Johnny had done, for him, a good job and one, as he probably thought, suitable for the occasion. He could not reach the bulging roots beneath the brick walks, and it was plain that what nature had marred would remain forever misshapen. It occurred to me that he had cleaned it as he would have cleaned a family burying ground for a reunion of the descendants, giving the place a general tidying up but leaving the sunken graves and broken headstones strictly alone.

"Why do you stop at the gate?" Ellen asked, interrupting my brown study. "It was you who would see it this time of day."

"Yes, I know," I said. "It was I."

"Well, then, won't you ask me to come into the garden?"

"Will you come with me into the garden, Miss Ellen, where it is always midsummer?"

"How poetic, Mr. Brent!"

"Not at all, Miss Ellen."

"But indeed, Mr. Brent."

"Midsummer," I mused. "Nature's deceiving pause. Come walk with me there."

"Haven't you mixed your seasons? Summer is past."

"In a flower garden there is only one season, Miss Ellen. The time of blooming."

"But flowers fade—" and she raised her arms melodramatically— "even here."

"Ah, yes. But one does not notice. That is the art of the garden, to have it always in bloom."

"A very pretty illusion."

"So that the progress of the seasons goes unnoted."

"I don't follow," she said, taking my arm.

"Consider the garden well, my dear. It has many uses, but first and always one thinks of love."

"Naturally."

"Don't you mean romantically?"

"Exactly. You are very quick today."

"And so . . ."

"Romantic love denies the seasonal return. It is a pretense, a love for love's sake, an aesthetic pretense, if you will. And for setting, the garden forever in bloom, forever withholding its seed."

"What a lovely illusion and how utterly barren! You were not so learned when you courted me." And then abruptly changing her tone, "How wonderful it would be if the garden were now in bloom, if it could have always remained what it was, and not its poor distraught self!"

"You see why I wanted to keep this for last."

"Oh, but I couldn't wait," she said in a strange tight voice. And then more calmly, "Thank you for having Johnny begin it."

"Well, there he is. Thank him yourself."

We went around to the far side of the springhouse where Johnny was. Ellen said, "You've done a wonderful job, Johnny."

He acknowledged this praise. "Hit taken right smart sprouten, Miss Ellen. We ain't made the show here we aimed to. Look lak we couldn't grub clost to the ground thout taring somethen up." He looked about him with measuring eye. "You can't rightly say that this war a hot-weather job noways. I reckon me and the boys done moved forty families' trash."

"It's a lovely spot," she said. "I shall spend a lot of time here."

"Hit war oncet a place for a body to take his ease in," he said, wiping his forehead and putting his hat back on. "But hit'll might nigh take one hand's time to keep the trash down now."

"Oh dear, do you think so?"

He reflected: "Hit'll last out this year, we being in the dog days."

"I think it's the loveliest plan for a garden."

Johnny responded as if the compliment were paid him personally.

"Major Brent war a man for sich as this. He a man to step around in sweet-smellen places. No matter how hard he drove heself, when he come to the house first thing right off he washed. He washed his har in scented ile and chewed spices."

"What a man!" Ellen said. I glanced her way. It was plain she delighted in hearing his name.

"Yes'm, in many ways. Excusen me, he was a great hand with the ladies. He used to promenade 'm here a sight."

Ellen did not reply to this. I said, "So he was a ladies' man?"

"In his sappy days, you might say he was a sporten man." Johnny indicated the walkways with a gesture. "He laid hit out like a race track. And promenaded 'm round and round. When he taken the notion, he'd stop and pick a bokay of sweet bubbies."

"I should think," Ellen said rather testily, "the ladies would have got dizzy, going around in circles."

"I've heared it made some of um faintified," Johnny reported gravely.

There was nothing forward in his manner or expression as

he said this, but Ellen did not like it. She took a step to end the conversation. Johnny reached out his hand. "Take care, Miss Ellen."

"What?" she said sharply.

"Hit's bad luck to step over a grave."

"Grave?" she asked and looked wonderingly at her feet.

"Grave?" I repeated.

"Yessir." Johnny pointed to the flat stone top of an outdoor tomb. "He didn't lay out no burying ground at *The Grove*," he continued simply. "He knowed he wouldn't need nairn for heseff. He just laid um all away in the garden here."

"All?" we asked in surprise.

"He wives," Johnny replied with just the proper degree of pride and respect. "Yes'm, he laid 'm out lak spokes in a wheel, all around the springhouse. All six of um."

"What a bluebeard!" Ellen said.

Johnny looked at Ellen for a moment. "Maybe a tech of blue. He beard war black as sin."

Ellen was down on her knees reading the inscription on the tomb.

"Six, Johnny?" I asked. "I'd forgotten there were so many."

"Yessir. I come acrost um under the bresh here." He gazed into the air. "I calls 'm his wives."

"You what?"

Silently Ellen passed from grave to grave, reading the inscriptions. Johnny followed her with his eyes for some moments, then said, "Miss Jane war the first un. Her chillurn all growed and scattered. He got Miss Sally in Montgomery County. She died. Miss Lizzie come from somewheres off. When she died, look lak he lost heart in visiting ladies in a proper kind of way. The rest of um jest kept house for him."

He threw this off in a matter-of-fact way, seemed to meditate, and then said, "Look lak, whether from fenced ground or off the commons, hit didn't agree with um none too well here."

By now Ellen had completed the circle. She was standing on the other side of the springhouse, rather straight, her face pale, her head up like a startled animal. But it was the eyes which alarmed me. For the first time I saw fright in them, but there was something besides fright. She was like one who, eating of a strange and rich dish, looks up suddenly with the knowledge that it is poisoned. "The poor dears," she whispered. "All but one died in childbed." And then without looking at either me or Johnny, she walked rapidly out of the garden.

Johnny and I remained a long time quiet. "No, sir," I heard him say at last, "hit jest didn't noways agree with um at *The Grove*. Some folks 'lowed they was too frail."

"What do you allow?" I asked.

"Nothen," Johnny replied.

Never did I hear so much put into one short word.

20

I KNEW THE MOMENT ELLEN LEFT THE GARDEN THAT WE ALL faced a fresh crisis. I even felt that I had the obvious chance to draw her back from the abyss where she tottered. But I could make the wrong move and send her plunging down beyond all reach, forever beyond hope of redemption. Still there was hope—I held to this—hope in the inkling she had gained of the sinister nature of the past. She had been dazzled by a mirage cast up for her in the arid reaches of the mind where she had lost the way. But there in the garden her eyes had been opened. She more than suspected the horrors she was drifting toward. She more than believed in their reality. I had seen it in her face withdrawing from the circle of the flat-topped graves. I heard the words "died in childbed." Those women had died; it suited the experience of that time to say of child. But Ellen asked, Six dead women—why?

The next move was mine, to seize upon this doubt, to show her the ghastly meaning of this warning from the grave. Was it an entirely unconscious slip that she had referred to Major Brent as a Bluebeard? I thought not. I must make the most of this before the colored mist of her bemusement again settled and she followed the way of its frightful promise. But how? I stayed awake into the small hours thinking of all possible ways to approach her. So far there had been only allusions to her ghostly intercourse. Her replies had been masterly in evasion. Upon them I hung alternately between hope and despair. But throughout this entanglement of half-formed decisions and uncertainties I held fast to one clear fact: so long as she was willing to play such a game she was unsure of herself. She had not quite tired of the world and me. This was one way of looking at it. There was another, much darker and altogether disheartening. Suppose she was already his creature and taunted me out of the slavery of her surrender? Perhaps it was weakness to deny this possibility, but deny it I did. What I had learned in the garden gave me fresh courage. But I must work fast. The time had come to take the risk of judgment, to call a spade a spade—and a ghost a ghost.

I slipped into my dressing gown, my dragon gown of eastern silk, and made my way to the little sitting room next to our sleeping quarters. Her door was shut. All was quiet beyond. Should I arouse her to disburden my mind? Would this frighten her and thwart my desire? I could not stand to see in my anxious state that mask she now wore so often. To succeed I must see her. As I hung there in indecision, it was solved for me on the instant. I knew as clearly as if I had heard the words spoken, that something awaited me outside.

I fairly floated into the corridor in the wonder of this knowledge. Even now, after all that has happened, and when the end is known, the miraculous quality of my sensation, the feeling of security and power it gave me, returns to haunt me. In that moment I experienced the irreducible essence of self, the mystery understood by all at death, that ecstasy of the spirit which a few religious glimpse in their contempt for matter but which I discovered as the absolute purity of self-hood. The gross weight of my body melted as jelly does in water, bone, muscle, and flesh no longer governed by but become that which is indestructible. You may call it illusion, but I say that for that particular pause in time I was the subject of a miracle. I stood for a moment at my threshold, but who can name the true name of the threshold I had reached? The night was dark and cloudy and a smell of distant rain freshened the air. The murky light of the moon streaked the edge of a cloud. Then like a young hound I struck the scent.

I can think of no better term. Some presence, hovering near, had passed. The trail it left was still sweet. That is the hunter's phrase and I was become a hunter. How shall I describe it? For one thing, it showed a definite direction but moved on a wavering line, such as air waves do. If anyone had seen me, he would have thought I was drunk and staggering to my room. There was of course no physical trail. There was nothing but the smell of moist air, and yet my nostrils flared, although I scarcely breathed, as they would have done at a scent blown past in a high gale. Curiously enough, what I remember best about it is the feeling of heaviness, almost of matter. I followed as one is drawn along the heavy footing of a dream. It swirled about my ankles in the slow heavy way of mist clinging to low places. Once I looked down, but saw nothing. I felt I could touch but could not touch it; could see but did not see it; could smell but did not smell it. I followed.

I neither rushed nor delayed. I walked with the sure, absolute balance of a somnambulant, and I walked unafraid. The darkness did not confuse. Nothing confused, nothing obstructed me. My earth-bound senses had all perished in the miraculous transformation they had undergone. I had now one sense, the sense of myself.

And all the while the night held dark, but my vision ate into it like acid. Along the back corridor I followed until I came to the small enclosed passage connecting the south end of the apartment to the upstairs hall. It was close, narrow, and rather poorly lighted even by day. At night one hurried through it with a childish feeling of unknown terror. And always at this hour the outside door was locked; yet I knew it would open to my hand. The door jumped at me; the scent, a thousandfold stronger, enveloped me.

I had no thought now but of Ellen's peril. I rushed to her door, but once there I noticed that the effluvium lay more heavily toward the opening into the hall. Why should it sweep to the very threshold of her room and then veer off? There was one plausible answer. She was even now being sucked along in its tow.

I hurried into the hall, but what I entered was a place deeper and broader than any hallway. Before me was the balcony. Its door was flung back and there I saw, with arms hanging limply, steps advancing in hypnotic tread toward the rotten balcony rail, not Ellen, but poor bemused Moss.

21

I WAS TOO FAR AWAY. I COULD ONLY WATCH THE MECHANICAL impulsion of his advance, the slight twist of the head as if he were straining toward something in the distance. I saw him fumble at the rotten banister, then put his hand lightly on the railing. Still like one who sees nothing close by, he raised his leg in even motion. This broke my spell. I called his name sharply. He hesitated, dipped his head as if to miss an obstacle; then proceeded to carry on the interrupted action. . . . I heard the wood give a long straining creak. It was not until this moment of peril that my voice got through to him. He shuddered, took a step back from the open space and slowly turned, as if still reluctant to give over whatever image it was that had drawn him so close to disaster.

I was carried forward on the upsurge of my relief. Relief . . . the sweetness of danger passed. Afterward there comes a lift to the simplest thing. The hall seemed its familiar self, its walls safe and comforting. I even forgot the threat to the peace of the house. The gruff thunder rumbling in the distance gave off a friendly sound. But I needed some physical reassurance. The residue of nerves had left in my body a dull swollen ache. Desperately I felt the need to hug Moss. I took a step toward him . . . and then the moon plunged into the clear. Under the slow spread of its light, the tops of trees grew sharply dark, the lawn appeared vaguely familiar, and there upon it an amorphous blotch of shadow, as though secretly slipping out of the picture, took on line and form, the head first, then the long body, and at last the insolent set of the legs I knew so well. There in all his evil stood Major Brent, his head thrown back into the light. The face, fixed on the balcony, still and glistening, showed in its hideous nakedness his purpose, a purpose the intent of which was already changing into triumph, as if he were sure of his victim. My eyes slowly dimmed and then went out. When I looked again, he had vanished. The moon had gone under a cloud, and the world was everywhere dark.

I felt myself step back against the wall for support. The five senses, somewhat flagging, had resumed their natural functions. "Well," I said wearily, "how did it happen? If I had been twenty seconds later, you would be lying on the bricks below." And then out of my exasperation, "How did he manage it?"

"How did who manage what?" I heard softly, almost mockingly.

I was in no mood for this. "For God's sake, boy, this is no time for evasions. How did he beguile you? What did he say? What do? You must try to remember."

"Beguile me?" Moss was all youth and confidence, with some bravado, as he returned me this question.

"Yes, Major Brent beguiled you," I said flatly.

"Major Brent?" he repeated as though the name came as an impossible surprise. "I've not seen your Major Brent." And then as if there were some need to emphasize his statement, "I have never seen your Major Brent."

I truly at this stage, pressed as I was with the increased pace of the drama we were enacting, felt that I had more than I could bear. It was possible that Moss's memory had been

wiped clean . . . unless—I must always face this uncertainty—
unless the enemy's insidious promises had some way made
the victim accessory to the crime.

"Perhaps you were dreaming and walked in your sleep," I
said to help him along.

"No," he replied blandly, "I am here because I want to be
here."

His tone irritated me beyond bearing. I did not stop to
reflect that this tone had been set by some prior command
left in the consciousness for just this effect. I could only blurt
out, and the harshness of my voice rebounded like an echo,
"Well, but for me, you would be lost in it."

"In your mind, Uncle, I am already lost," he replied.

"I have not said it."

I could think of no reply. I had again been taken by
surprise.

"No, but you think it."

"Of course I don't," I answered rather lamely, if truthfully,
for what I did think came close to the same thing. But how
could he know this unless he had been taught to read my
mind just as Ellen had been taught, when she accused me of
hating everything I did at *The Grove*.

There was nothing for me to do but to come right out
with it. "No, Moss," I said. "But you have been keeping something back. This is the hour for truth. Why do you hide
here?"

"What makes you think I am hiding?"

It was all so frankly outspoken, not only what he said but
his manner of speech, that I felt as if I were deliberately
creating a mysterious situation out of a natural circumstance.
I didn't carry much conviction, saying, "Well, by the way you
arrived here, for one thing."

"Didn't you expect me?"

"I did."

"Well, then."

How in the wrong I felt as I pushed it further, "I mean the way you appeared. You will admit it was unusual."

"But didn't you want me?"

"Of course." But I didn't let this clever flattery divert me. "You came here, a remote place. You didn't go to your father's house, where you would be known."

"I can't go home. I can come only to you," he said.

"But why?"

"You know why," he said.

I didn't know how to push this further. In his clever way he knew it, and he knew that I knew it. I changed my approach. "And the way you have kept hidden, coming out only at night. Sleeping by day."

"But that was your idea, Uncle."

This was a half-truth but it silenced me. My delicacy in the matter, from the sympathy between us which had led me to understand his predicament and not press him with it, now rendered me helpless. As I said no more, he drove me farther into my corner. "It was you, you know, who chose the day-time watch."

This wound me up and tied me off. What proof is there to a silent agreement, if one party refuses to honor it? What face I would have lost if I had given away to temper, before so much youth and candor and the innocent-seeming pleasure he took in catching me in his net. I could imagine the look of hurt and surprise in the soft dark eyes, the injured query and afterward the awkward drop of the head, for he liked to please and never had he been one to bear correction. This was the lesson I had learned and his father had not.

No, I had to accept the shift in our relations and act, when the need arose, within the new limits imposed. As we parted, I parted with the deeper knowledge of the enemy's skill and the fresh ground I had lost.

22

THERE ARE TIMES WHEN THE BEST OF US FALTER, WHEN WE feel sorry for ourselves. I had reached that hazardous state: I felt very sorry for myself. If I had been a man of deliberate evil, there would be some justice to the ordeal I was being put through. But what was I? Can any man answer this question? I tried to, in the chill of those before-dawn hours after I had left Moss. I left him with a good conscience. I was sure Major Brent would return no more that night, but indeed I was so low in mind that if he had, I would have said, Enter your domain and do your will. At least I think I would.

Where I wandered I do not know. My steps moved in reflex action to the real journey which went on in my head. And that took me down past the will, past the imagination, to the obscure area which the soul inhabits. Here there are limpid patches where lights play, but all else is opaque and of an endless depth no resources can plumb. But I probed as well as I could. Like two boys shouting threats across the circle of dust their fears are treading, I went round myself, and only when shame turned fear into pain did I suffer knowledge. Knowledge, the memory of where we go wrong but never quite why. There are two questions that may be put— What and How. The scientist asks What, the artist How, but in any case both burn in the same fire. The residue of one is ashes for the winds, the leavings of the other a thing of hard irreducible form, telling all and nothing, and its polish is the shine of agony. My agony was in the making, but who can leap clear of the fire, that leap which hurries time and rushes the end?

I had come to live at *The Grove,* for in my blood was the insistent need to abide. The wanderer wears smooth as a penny and tells fortunes, but never his own. The gypsy in the coonskin cap, making always his circle—this I fled and sought the place where the seasons make their orderly return, to the dwelling for the woman, to the earth for the seed, and I to my care. I came to a place with a western view. I was not the prodigal returning to the fatted calf, and yet there was one who saw me from afar, but he did not rush forth and fall on my neck. He waited and when I came I found a thing out of time haunting and mouldering bones. I found that the body has its seasons, too, and that they are brief and, diminutive of the great seasons, make one cycle.

And so it is that the great fear is not death but oblivion. And oblivion settles on an impotent man. It was this, I decided, which had kept Major Brent near the scene of his crime, for impotence has a larger meaning than the body's lack. In vanity and by will he had cut off his line; or so he had intended, but there he fell into radical error. Call it metaphysical if you will, but the progeny *The Grove* might rightfully claim as its due had gone to the grave with Major Brent. But it would not lie. A thing must live before it dies. And this progeny, forbidden life, drew back the shade of Major Brent and fastened him to the air of the place. Its mortal weight forbade him the felicitous reaches of infinity. To be neither of the world nor altogether out of it—that was his punishment. I had got this much, wandering through the tortured night, and I knew I had got it right. But it was not with this I had to do.

I will state it plainly. Every crime demands expiation, every expiation a victim. That he might go free, dispossess himself of the blur of mortality, Major Brent had chosen what I loved for victim. The nature of the sacrifice was not clear to me at this time, but my fears grew out of its vagueness, for I knew it was not vague to him. I had seen enough this night to know that his ghostly purpose had advanced almost to the moment of resolution. I must steady myself for the last onset he, even now, had withdrawn to loose. I probed no more. As I entered Ellen's room, our room, I had decided: we would flee *The Grove* before it was too late.

The night lamp by her bed was lighted.

"You are awake," I said.

The shadows from the lamp showed me only half her face, and the thin gown, falling over her frail shoulders and exposing the round breast, seemed already shadowy light withdrawing into deeper shade. "You are awake," I said again and crossed the room to turn up the lamp.

"What time is it?" she asked.

"Late or early. The roosters are crowing."

"They often crow at midnight. I think the deep stillness of sleep startles them, and they cry out that it is sleep, that it may be broken."

"It is after midnight," I said.

"Is it?" she said dreamily, looking all the while at my face, but I felt that her sight focused on some reverie of phantoms I was sure she now met with urgent, feverish need. Then suddenly her eyes became clearer and she said, "What are you doing up at this hour?"

"I might ask, Why are you awake?"

"I couldn't sleep. I've been thinking."

"About what?"

"About us and what we do here."

"For instance?"

"Well, for one thing, about you wandering at night, not coming to bed."

"Did I wake you?"

"Something did."

I sat on the bed and took her hand. I asked very slowly, "Do you know what it was?"

"Why, no," she said and yet this answer seemed to imply that I could tell her if I would.

I leaned slightly forward, as her attention was about to waver. "Do you know where it was?"

"Why, no. Why do you look so strange?"

I pinned her down. "Are you sure?"

"Well, no . . . yes." I felt her hand withdrawing from mine, but I held it fast. "I thought there was something out there. I couldn't be sure."

"Where?" I was calm, but oh, how insistent! "In the hall, perhaps?"

"Perhaps. You were in the hall, weren't you? Let go my hand. You are hurting me." She pulled away and said, "Have you seen anything?"

Go carefully, carefully, I warned myself. You cannot say you have seen a ghost and let her laugh the truth off, even though the laugh cry out in harsh falsity. I said, "The night is full of things, if you can see in the dark."

"Can you see in the dark, dear? I can't. I light a lamp."

We were now back at our old evasions, which skimmed the

surface of the things we feared to name but which by the very lightness of innuendo admitted its presence.

"Are you afraid of what you will see in the dark?" I asked.

"But I've just told you. I make a light. A light is a comfort to a lonely woman. Yet it makes her more lonely."

"Are you so much alone?" I said directly, dropping the banter.

"I have been. You see, you either work or wander around the place like a man with a bad conscience. You should have a bad conscience neglecting me as you do."

"But does it matter so much to you?" I asked leaning closer.

I had driven her into a corner. She looked away as if to escape and I pitied her with all my heart. If I could only have helped! But it was not for me to help. After a moment she collected herself. Her breath made a fast little gallop.

"Yes, it has mattered," she said. "But it may not any more."

Her voice and eyes were deliberately teasing; and then she came out with it so easily and with such self-confidence I almost felt in her the demand for my sympathy and approval. "There may be someone, you know, to take your place."

You may expect the worst and think you are prepared, but you are never prepared. The prisoner at the dock is never prepared, even though he reads his doom in the judge's face. The few simple words seem too slight for the finality of their intelligence. You cannot move. You sit motionless, with the sense of the stricken years between you like a glass and in the hall below the clock strikes the hour. You sit as though you would sit out time until the last stroke of the gong dies away and you rise and passionately take her in your arms and there is a gasp of pain in her breath and you say, "I will take you away from this haunted house."

She does not speak, though your desperate embrace bruises and you sense fear in her rapid breath, fear of what she does not understand in you, fear that she will be torn from the phantom who grows in her desire like a cancer. Then at last the strength goes from your grasp and you release her and she draws back against the headboard, with the fright now seen in her eyes and behind the wide iris resistance growing. You hear your dull words, dulled from the expense of passion, "How was I to know?"

After a while, when she sees your strength abate, she stirs slightly, but speaks clearly enough, "Where do you think you can take me?"

"Anywhere away from this."

"Do you think it will help to go away? There was a time for that, but that time is past."

"Time passes," I said vehemently, "but you make time too. I brought you here, but how was I to know what I would find?" And then I blurted out, for my words catching fire from themselves leaped trembling and out of control, "I'm afraid I'll lose you."

"That," she said quietly, "is a risk you must take."

I had expected denials, derision, some guilty mask behind which she might retreat, I don't know what I expected, anything but the surprise I got, the one thing that would silence me, this challenge to my manhood. And it was not only her words, but the manner she assumed, a quiet resignation, such open courageous frankness, such gleaming sorrow, how shall I describe the strength and weakness she seemed, except to say that she presented the devoted look of the victim, that fusion of innocence and desire which makes ecstatic the eye of the sinner as he ravishes and cleans himself upon what his glance devours.

But I was not that sinner. I was the one from whose arms she had been snatched by lot, and as I stood there, for a moment helpless, all my old longing for her love, the keener for the sense of the loss I would suffer, took hold of me. "No love shall supplant our love," I whispered, advancing.

"No, no," she said, drawing back. "Don't ruin everything."

But I did not hear. My hand pressed on the hot circle the lamp chimney made. The light flickered and then went out. For an instant the tongue of flame leaped at my flesh. My mouth swam in hot jets of pain and the silence swelled into one great swoon. She for a little resisted my arms, but at last I plunged into darkness.

23

MORNING SEEMED ETERNITIES AWAY. AS DID THE DAY OF OUR marriage when I waited for her at the chancel and she came forward as a beautiful woman toward a looking glass. There is no act of darkness so desperate that daylight may not compromise it. But how the dawn delayed! I could almost believe it conspired with the night, so dismally did it creep out of the east, behind a dew that was more fog than dew.

What folly made me think that violence could draw love back but the folly of desperation? Whoever finds again what he has lost? What wanderer returning home finds other than exile in the familiar landmark? Yet the loser seeks, the wanderer returns, and I must do what I had to do. I could smell the greasy stain of the lamp chimney as I sat on the bed's edge, waiting for enough resolution to get up and salvage what I could from the night's despair. I saw my scattered clothes on the floor and felt afresh that vast distance the quietness made between us, after the dry sobs, and the dead voice, "How could you do this?" And then in bitter wonderment, "How could you?" How could she not understand? I learned easily enough how one may maim what one loves. But that was the night. The light of day now seeped into the room. I reached for my clothes. They pricked like cold needles.

Outside the damp air brought me up to action. This day we would flee the place. First I would deal with Moss. He would get around me with no more equivocation. He must confront his secret and resolve it. I crossed to the old office where he stayed and entered without knocking. The smudge at the dirty window gave enough light to show me his bed had not been slept in. I drew closer to make sure. There was not a wrinkle on the counterpane. It had the cold, starched look of a bed made up for the casual guest. And then on the instant I discovered how far behind events were leaving me. The moldy, shut-up smell of disuse told me that Moss had never used his room.

There was not a moment to lose. I hurried toward Johnny's house and met him with a lantern on his way to the barn. The fog was so heavy he didn't see me until I was almost upon him, but he gave no sign of surprise. He stopped, hunched up with the chill, and waited. "Take me right now," I said, "to the spot where Major Brent looked over the fields for the last time."

He gave the lantern to one of the daughters. She moved off like a shadow and the fog enveloped her. One by one his boys passed, their bulks thinning until they, too, disappeared. I said, "We must hurry. We may even now be too late."

Johnny kept my pace, without seeming to increase the slow steady swing of the countryman. "I've just come from my nephew's room. He did not sleep there last night."

"Young folks runs at night," he said.

"I saw him last night. I saw whom he was with."

We went along and I said no more to let this sink in. There was no sound but the rub of my corduroys. "He was with our friend," I said significantly. I waited a few steps more, then: "I arrived in time to save him."

"What he want wid him?" he blurted out.

I half turned, but Johnny kept his glance before him, as if he were intent on not losing the way. "I thought *you* might tell *me*," I said. By slowing my words I gave them the empasis of an accusation. "You tend his room. You must know he hasn't used it."

Then Johnny did a surprising thing. He delayed his pace as if from indecision; then stopped and for an instant looked directly into my eyes. "Boss, you knows who him's after."

He turned away and resumed walking. His glance did not rest long enough on mine for me to make an issue of it, but I felt such a chill of revelation on the profundities of my situation that, of necessity, I sought for some superficial evasion. I dared not ask who. For days I was to be haunted by the depths within depths of his dark pupils swimming in those eyeballs the color of eggshell. They saw. What did they foresee?

The mist was lifting. It gave me my excuse. We came to a field where the fences had rotted down and upon the edges of gullies the washed field showed thin and red. A fury seized me at this evidence of Major Brent's will. I turned upon Johnny. "You haven't cleaned out these fence rows."

"Naw sir. Look like a body never do ketch up."

"They've grown at least forty feet into this field."

"They's still plenty ground."

What good now to tell him I had come to save and restore, now that I had thrown in the sponge and was leaving? But the evidence of my defeat was so flagrant I could not help saying, "This is what Major Brent wanted. To turn this place into a wilderness."

"He done it now," he replied in what I thought was a completely irrelevant tone.

"I came here," I said bitterly, "to make it so you and everybody at *The Grove* could have a more abundant life."

" 'Bundance?" I could almost hear his mind turning the word over. "You means meat aplenty in the smokehouse?"

"In a way, yes."

"I ain't never knowed the time." We went along for a while, I still mad and he . . . he said presently, his voice keeping time to his stride, "But looks lak time I burns my plant beds and sows 'm I ain't turned round good befo'e they needs setten. I works hit, suckers it, worms it, tops hit, cuts hit and hangs it in the barn. I ain't got my breaf good befo'e got to haul barn wood and fire hit. When the order's right got to git it down. Strip hit. Bulk hit. Then time comes to sell and you feels you done yo'ese'f a favor. You stands round waiten and the buyers and the pinhookers comes in jesten, and they strolls along, picks up a hand and flings hit down, and the man callen Hi, yi, yi . . . Sold. And nar, befo'e you kin spit, you been hiyied out'n a year's work." He paused. "No, sir. A body just ain't got no time for 'bundance."

No time for abundance. What has man time for? I should have asked, but what was the good now of struggling with his inertia? I did not even pause for bitterness. We walked on and under the sun the mist burned away and I saw we had reached a large woods. I said, "Which way?"

Johnny nodded before him. "That hit."

I did not understand. "That's what?"

"Whar you wanted me to bring you."

"That's no field," I cried in sudden panic.

"No, sir. Not no more hit ain't."

Even now I was slow to accept what I saw, so blinded was I by that image of golden fields abandoned to rot. There is the act, and there is the image of the act. But the slow turn of the seasons fills out the truth. I gazed at the buckbushes, the tangle of brush and briers and overhead the leaves of autumn shifting their masses of color, now showing, now hiding, the anonymous depths of the wilderness. "Let's hurry," I said.

Johnny drew back his foot. "This here is fur as I goes."

"What do you mean?"

"I ain't *never* been in them woods."

"But if I go . . ."

"That ain't me."

I said slowly, "Do you mean you are abandoning me, here and now?"

He looked up and down; said, "Hit make a body squinty-eyed to look at what you sees."

"Very well," I replied. "I'll go alone."

To this he gave no reply, nor did I look at him again. I started in, fearing but sure of what I would find there, not knowing whether I should be too late. The briers struck and bound me in their sharp festoons.

Johnny called out, "The cattle uses sometimes below."

"Why didn't you tell me?" I called back in exasperation.

I found the break the cattle had made and followed the

faint and winding path. Along this I hurried, dodging the slapping limbs until I found myself well in among the trees. Here I left the path, for it followed a simple instinctive route and, being cattle-made, would skirt the center where I was going. I took direction as well as my haste would allow and pushed on. It was not a large wood, that is not large enough to get lost in, but it was dense and had reached the season which is life-in-death. The black gums, the first to turn, appeared through the green depths, great bloody flowers already drying, and on the fresher leaves a faint brush of yellow cast everywhere its blight. This confused my eyes, but I plunged along, choosing the easiest ground until at last I found I had lost the way. If I had stopped calmly to take my bearings, it would have been a matter of minutes before I should have come close to the center. But the urgent need, the waste of time, and my bewilderment drove me on. Beneath my trousers I could feel the smart of brier and thorn; my shoes grew slick; I slipped and fell.

Weary and smarting, I paused half-blind with sweat and despair. I saw how deep a way in I had gone, for all about me the light grew even. There came an instant when I almost heard the woods catch its breath. It grew as still as quail in a brush pile. To the depths of this quiet my solitude abandoned me. I had suffered at *The Grove,* I would suffer yet again, but there was nothing to equal the terror of this solitude. Then out of it I heard a steady rhythm of breathing. I have no way of knowing when it began. I can only know that at some certain moment it must have begun. It was a sound such as one might hear in a dream, the surprise of its imminence when you first grow aware of it. But here in the woods I at once thought of some cornered beast. Yet a beast would have made no sound. It seemed to come from a clump of bushes close at hand. But it was not there. I heard it behind me. I turned, and it turned also. No matter where I looked, it was always somewhere else, yet always near. I began to run, now completely at hazard. What stopped me was the insolent, almost human complaint of crows startled on their perches. I looked up in time to see one swift black streak before it vanished, cawing, among the leaves. I looked down and saw my nephew Moss.

He was in a part of the woods more open than the rest, and his back was to me. I had only a moment, but I needed only a moment to feel the hard tight lump of pain in the throat and that terrible drop into emptiness which accompanied it. I had only to see the set of his back, his absorbing gaze, the force of which came to me as clearly as if I had seen it, to know that I had lost him. There was not much to go by, but the heart needs very little. He was erect through all the lean vigor of his person, but the tension in his shoulders told me volumes. They showed an extravagant longing for abandonment. All of this—what I felt and saw—fused in a flash of intuition, for I had no more than seen him before he began to move away. I cried out in my misery, "Stop! Wait!" but he was deaf to my appeal. I ran forward to seize him, to save him in spite of himself, but I was thrown back—the place was truly enchanted—by a barrier of thorn trees that struck deep into my flesh. When I had got around these, he was gone. I followed, running and stopping, in the direction I supposed he had taken. I called his name; but the deep hush, more hostile for my noisy progress through it, gave back no reply. He had literally vanished before my eyes. Or so I thought until, a few paces farther on, I parted the bushes and came out on the rim of a sinkhole.

It was a large sinkhole, great enough to have pulled small

trees down its rotten sides. For a moment I hesitated; then my eyes followed down the slope to the black gaping opening at the bottom. I shuddered and because action was the only thing that would save me, I made my way down the steep slick sides. For the last five yards there was neither purchase nor bush to hold to. There I stopped. There I faced the door to mystery. Fascinated and repelled, I looked into the black emptiness below me. One glance was enough: the hole was easily big enough for a man to fall through. In the silence which my long gaze made I heard the ominous sound of water running underground.

How long I remained staring I do not know, long enough to feel the dangerous pull of that subterranean sound, promising release, escape from the unbearable, the lull of utter rest and oblivion. What saved me, reminding me that I had another to protect, came from the blasting knowledge that there could be no rest, no lull of oblivion for me even there. Intelligence of this presented itself in the only way that could have returned me to action. I felt a break in the spell of my gaze. Raising my head, I looked directly across into the face of Major Brent.

Masked by cedar bushes, his eyes hung before me like rotten berries, reflecting the depths from which I had just turned away. I am not sure even now whether his gaze had been fixed there for my undoing, tricking me within the radius of its transfiguring power. I say I am not sure, and I am not; but I rather think it had to do with the completed act. Unless his cunning had achieved an enlargement of pattern so far unknown to my experience with him, I had surprised him considering not me but the ruin of his youthful victim. Triumph of a sort he showed, even though it was no more than the growl of the beast over his kill. Indeed, he had the look of one who has eaten the very vitals of his victim. But the fullness of my surprise was that I now saw in him a much younger apparition, as one who had truly eaten of life. The lips pouted in a sensuous curve; there was a glow on his features; but the face, the color of that brown which none resists, showed also the mark of his torment. And it was this— equal pull between the need and the suffering it made—which contained the secret of his appeal. But the horror which fixed me there evolved from the knowledge that he could both show and disguise damnation.

So I felt as I looked up and through the cedars confronted my enemy. Perhaps I should have called out, defied him. But would this have freed me from the festering curse which poisoned my life? It might have brought me temporary relief, but the need for it was stifled in what I can remember only as a heightening of the tension. My vision had sharpened. There was no satiety on those lips: they still hungered. I had scarcely taken this in when he turned his head in a restless start. Then he was gone, gone in the very act of turning, but not before I had caught the full force of his purpose, a purpose the intent of which, if he had spoken aloud, could have been no more plainly told.

24

Somehow I found my way out of the woods and back to the house. I remember half running into the yard, then a deliberate slowing to a walk. I thought: it is unseemly in me to be running: I shall bring forth questions which I cannot, or had better not, at this time answer.

I felt relief at touching base again, with what had happened in the woods behind me. Then it came to me why I had hurried: Ellen. What should I tell her? I had to decide, even as I wondered how she would receive me after the night's violence, so fresh to her, so remote now to me.

The house for the first time in months was a great comfort: its lines so sure, so firm. As I walked toward it, I almost sighed with relief and gratitude for its foursquareness. There it was. Ellen would be safe within. Tears suddenly blurred my vision, and now in the late morning light all my fears seemed groundless. But this elation was momentary because the facts were hard. I had first to make my peace with Ellen; and I would, of course, now have to tell her about Moss, even to the dark end he made. My story would bring the whole thing into the open. This were better so. So great a shock might break the enchantment. And besides there was no way to keep my knowledge secret. In the end the Army was sure to trace Moss. There would be questions. What ugly suspicions would not any silence of mine give rise to? Who would believe the truth? The state does not recognize ghosts. It will demand some reasonable explanation. If none is forthcoming . . .

Clammy sweat broke out on my forehead at the realization of the predicament my enemy had brought me to. I stepped quickly into the great hall and leaned my back against the shut door. For the first time I gave myself up to that low impulse, the instinctive fear only the trapped know.

Self-absorption stops all clocks, but after a while it came to me that the house did not seem the same as I had left it. At first it was no more than a vague disquietude, no more than the embarrassment one feels on discovering the change in old familiarity. And then I noticed—my consciousness was all alert now—the peculiar quality of silence the hall made.

I called Ellen's name and, not waiting for an answer, rushed upstairs. She was not there. I quickly thought of the kitchen.

Maybelle was at the sink, her brown hands idling in the dishwater. She did not look up as I came in, and I knew that things were very wrong. I asked, "Where is Miss Ellen?"

"She gone off."

"Where?"

"She gone off in the car," she replied after a pause, which I knew was a rebuke for my tone of voice.

"Did she say where she was going?" I tried to make my voice sound casual, but I knew it was useless. Maybelle knew that Miss Ellen never went off in the car by herself.

"She didn't say."

I had to get it out. "Was she alone?"

Some way, without turning her head, she managed to shift her eyes quickly toward mine; then drop them to her hands resting quietly in the greasy water. "I never seen nobody," she replied, looking through the little window at her head.

By now I was desperate. I blurted out, "Did she say when she would be back?"

"She never say."

Dreamily Maybelle picked up the dishrag and twisted it.

"Thank you," I said and turned to get out of the kitchen quickly.

At the door her voice stopped me. "She never give out no dinner. What you wants me to have?"

I stopped, at what tremendous effort of will only I will know. I collected myself to speak calmly, to give some illusion of order to this crumbling world. "Oh, bread, meat, whatever you have."

"Ain' no meat."

"Then anything you have in the house." Before I went out,

I had control enough to say, "Bring a cup of coffee to my study, please."

I did not go at once to the study. I wandered aimlessly, if wander describes what I did. To wander presupposes some degree of will. Shall I say, because I breathed, because my heart still sent the blood back and forth through my body, my feet moved, but with no purpose or direction? I must have passed through every room in the house, seeing without seeing, everywhere through surroundings once familiar, now merely nonexisting. I seem to remember saying, Ellen gone— saying it; pausing; saying it again, hoping to induce some sort of response. But it was no use. Nature's kind anesthesia had deadened my senses.

I became aware of a growing restlessness, and then I saw that I was in our bedroom. Here, if anywhere, I would feel her presence. This was her creation. There was not a thing in it that had not grown in the loveliness of her eye, or been touched by her hand. But I looked around at a strange place. The curtains hung stiff and cold. The chairs sat about on display. I looked hard at the bed, thinking memory would at least restore that to meaning. But I could see only the craftsman's design as he must have seen it in the moment of intuition. There was no history for me here. Quickly I turned toward my study. There the human presence would have left its mark. Only in such a place could I recover my identity.

The cup of coffee was on the desk. It was cold, but I drank it down. With it came release and realization of the desperate pass I had reached. Moss first, and now Ellen. She had seized the moment, oh how well planned, step by cunning step, and had gone to him. And I was helpless in this desertion, not knowing where or what even to do. Bound hand and foot and thrown into the ash heap.

Well, let her go to him. It's what she's wanted, to try the multiplicity of those dark practices his ghostly whisper set her longing for. How the old one must feel his triumph! For it was through me that she had gone to him, through me that he would at last and forever possess her. I had not been able to stand the strain. I had weakened and blundered, and he had known all along that I would! It was his way of showing his contempt for me. Oh, it was a nice, refined cruelty, this self-punishment he had devised, the black gloom of remorse of manhood's inadequacy!

I was a long time in this state. There was no pain. It was all pure suffering, a long suffocation like drowning, except that I was denied the sweet release into unconsciousness which drowning allows. And at last, when I thought I could stand no more, there began the slow dark pressure against the heart. The despondency this made is not for words to relate. Then suddenly the moment of ecstasy. When that passed, I felt as light as down, forever freed of my burden. I had done my best. I could do no more. I had nothing more to do. I could set out tomorrow, even now, on the big road and go until I dropped, with no thought but of what the day would bring and not much of that. And at night sink into sleep, sleep without dreams, and wake up with the sun as fresh as a child on the first day.

Naturally this sense of absolute freedom could not last. I knew there was more to come. Perhaps it was the shock of looking up and finding the day almost spent that brought me back to reality. Perhaps the door made a noise as it opened. The two things came so close together I cannot even now separate them in my mind, for before I could measure the consequences of the lost time, my eyes shifted and there, just inside the threshold, stood Ellen.

She stood with perfect calm, the door half open, and looked at me. I saw at once that she was no longer innocent. There was a surety of new power about her, a mysterious experience I could never share. I got all of this on the instant, and it was plain that she remembered the night's violence even as little as I. At the least she did not draw it between us like a curtain. She regarded me in a kind of puzzlement and her eyes were large with sympathy. What arrested me was the nature of this sympathy. It was not personal, but such as one, at moments of stress, might feel for all humankind. The pause during which we regarded each other lengthened. Perhaps she was waiting for me to question her. I was trembling too much to speak. Then she said with studied restraint, "I have bad news for you."

My heart lurched. I mumbled, "Yes?"

"I've been to town."

She waited, carefully examining my face to see if her statement held special meaning for me.

I said, "Yes?"

Carefully, as if she feared the words might not carry, she said, "Moss is dead."

I leaped up. "How did you know?"

My mouth was dry. The words at first did not come out. They sputtered, cracked and broke up.

She came forward calmly and sat me in my chair. "You are overwrought," she said.

I worked my mouth. A little moisture returned. I flung at her, "Of course, you know he is dead. You knew it even before I. It is now the most simple of the sorrows you will engage."

Nothing could shatter her calm. "Of course I knew it before you. The notification came while I was at your brother's. I am late because I stayed to help."

"My brother? How could he know?"

"The Army notified him."

"The Army," I leaped up, screaming.

"Yes, Henry," she replied. "The Army. Moss has been dead three months."

25

THERE COMES A MOMENT IN EXCESSIVE STRAIN WHEN THE body out of the economy of its mechanism, withdraws from the demands of the mind. My own had reached such a pass. It refused to send along the thin threads of the nerves any further shock. As I stood there, my flesh shut up in a self-protective paralysis, it must have seemed to Ellen that my grief was at the least extravagant.

She could have thought of it only as grief I now know. I tried to act as she thought I should act. It was in such a way I discovered the body's revolt. And the mind's endless energy. Released, it ran like an engine idling at high speed. But away from its proper vehicle.

A few simple words and a situation desperate beyond remedy had suddenly bettered itself. Indeed, would not the entire grounds for alarm have to be reassessed?

And I? What was I? How had I known Major Brent for what he was and been deluded as to Moss? Was it that the humors of matter still besmirched his spirit? While Major Brent had worn as thin as the air he inhabited? Or had I second sight? Did the veil at birth hide from me the intrusion of common things? Was I set apart to suffer the visions of phantoms sifting through this veil, warped of breath, woofed so fine the spider's glue, beside it, would twine as gross as hemp?

I was not so mad as to think I was done with Major Brent. A presence of such formidable proportions would not frequent the scene of its mortal life without some dreadful purpose. I held to this and to the feeling, irrational, unprovable, that somehow Moss had interfered, perhaps even to stay its execution. I felt hope, the bright gleam of it flashing in the whirl of my mind. But things were none too clear. Perhaps it was given me to understand this purpose but to remain tongue-tied. To savor the saving words but feel them dry up overnight like a cut flower. To fail.

To fail because we, the sensible inheritors, will not face the need for any such return. When we admit the possibility, and it is always with cowardly reservations, in our earth-bound blindness we see no farther than some sentimental explanation. This is our pitiful limitation. We cannot comprehend life out of time or without matter; yet we believe in it. We are attracted to and repelled by it. Witness the desperate need to come to grips with, to explain it, to take comfort from our fear of it, which is the fabric of all religious experience and the source of the great entelechies of philosophy and the ritual of churches.

But always the vocabulary fails. We have words: spirit, soul, life after death. We have myths: fallen angels, gardens of Paradise, the resurrection of the body . . . Yet what are these but material definitions made by the senses recoiling from timely limits and from the corruption of the body into which, at last, they must disappear? How can we, fastened to and made dizzy by the turning of the earth, see but as the drunkard sees or speak other than with a thick tongue?

Prolonging the period of shock, so that some way I might readjust myself to Ellen, I wondered . . . had I blundered upon the mystery of mysteries? And why was it I who must be drawn into the expanse of this passionate emptiness, fragmentary memories of which all men guard in the back closets of their minds, not knowing the meaning but only that there is meaning, as simple tribesmen perform acts of ritual about the shards of their past, with no memory of why or what they propitiate? I can only speak, like my brothers, with the tongue of matter. I therefore speak falsely even as I report the violent secret of the gods. Or if not that secret, then the shadow of the tension on the horizon.

Ellen came over to me. "You must take hold of yourself," she said gently, touching my arm.

"Yes, yes, of course," I said.

"Come on. A little food will do us good. Let's go down, have a drink, and get supper."

With a new assurance she took me in charge and I moved in the tow of her energy like a child. We went down the back way to the kitchen. Briskly she put on her apron. I shook up the fire in the stove and soon had it going. She must have been tired from a too-full day, but she went about getting the meal as if we were playing at house.

"You poor dear," she said, looking into the warmer. "You didn't eat your dinner. You must be starved."

"I was worried about you," I answered, looking at the potatoes lying in their shriveled skins, the fried onions limp and draining grease. But it was the odor of the thick bread, from which one triangular piece had been cut away, which made me withdraw; and for a moment it seemed to cast about Ellen's efforts a cheerless miasma, that smell of frostbite left-over potatoes have and the too-heavy soakings of warm grease.

She said, "Maybelle knows better than to make that kind of bread. I shall certainly speak to her in the morning."

I said, "What made you go to town?"

She seemed not to hear my question. I was aware in the click of her heels, the pause before the icebox that she had heard me. She said, "Fix me that drink, will you? And then separate these eggs."

I quickly had the drinks made. We touched glasses and fingers. "*Prosit*," she said and smiled. Her eyes became grave and she leaned forward and kissed me. "Darling, I know what a terrible shock it is. Moss was so fond of you. And you much more than an uncle to him." She added softly, "But you will be comforted."

"There are things I must ask you," I said. "Things I don't understand."

"I know, darling." And then, "You must go in to see your brother tomorrow. He is taking it hard, too hard. I think I felt sorrier for him than for Madge. After all, women can stand these things better."

Briskly changing her tone, "Now if you'll do the eggs and wash the lettuce. Oh, it's in the car. Will you bring my things in?"

I stepped out of the dark hall into the lesser darkness of the night. The stars were out, the sky was clear. I watched the flickering patches of light, so cold and bright, and for all the eyes that had sought them, terrifyingly remote, forever removed from human involvements. I shivered. There was a chill to the air, the first warning of winter. I took a deep breath and went to the car and picked up the bags of groceries. As I turned, I saw a dark shape waiting at the side of the drive.

"Who's that?" I asked sharply and leaned against the car to brace myself.

The figure moved forward, hesitantly but surely. "It's me, Boss."

"You, Johnny?" I had raised my voice out of the need to control it.

"You needs help?"

"No, no," I said. "I can manage."

He did not go away but remained where he was, and I where I was, with my back against the car. I let him wait, for I knew what he was here to find out. I let him wait, waiting myself, now that I had to phrase it, for an intuitive grasp at meaning. At last I said, and my own voice surprised me, remote, apart from me, as though it spoke out of the air and the air's distances had brought it from some far region of truth. "I went into the woods, and you would not follow. I went because I knew that I would find there some clearer meaning, and I thought that I had a part and that that part was to dispel the encroaching return of evil. Its rapid advance I had witnessed, but I could not define it. I knew the time was fast running out. And this was all I knew. The danger I sensed; I did not assess it. I lost my way and later found that the lost way was the right way. I saw my nephew Moss; I saw the pit into which he had gone; I saw the one who had drawn him there. And then I came to the house."

After a pause Johnny asked, "Mister Moss daid?"

"Yes," I replied, and my irony reached into the night. "But he did not die at *The Grove*."

A slight movement of the immobile figure told me the effect my words had had.

"No. No, he died three months ago, miles away, across the waters." I felt the pure clarity of the words as they slipped across the night.

"You say you seen him at the pit?"

Momentarily Johnny had lost his composure.

"Going toward it."

I waited, for what I was not quite sure, for some discovery he had withheld, an apology for his equivocal actions, but he quickly recovered himself. He said, "A mile don't mean nothen to a dead man."

"But he's been here. I saw him." Then I snapped, "Didn't you?"

I could hear my breath coming quick as I waited. He could not evade this question. Had I not brought him to the study where Moss was? Had I not given Moss into his care? My voice insisted, "Didn't you?"

The night seemed to grow darker, or did my eyes film, straining to see across the dividing space between us, leaning into it, to trap some expression, some disclosing movement of his body. But he receded. His powerful figure withdrew as into a murky fog. But his voice was not lost. It spoke in the formal courtesy I had come to learn as the barrier I could not breach. "No, sir," he said. "I never seen him."

"You never saw him?"

In my anger for the thing slipping away I stepped forward. I saw him plainly now, not a yard away, face me with his habitual dignity. And the smooth, silky tones, "Yes, sir. You brought me to yore room. You tole me he war there. It warn't my place to dispute you. No sir. But I never seen him myself."

"But the food you took him?"

"I throwed hit to the chickens."

"But the bed you made?"

"I never made hit but oncet."

I was close to him now, close enough to see the sweat bead on his forehead, and his eyes roll. Then I said right into his face, "Well, what was he doing here? Why did I think it was my nephew? And he all the time dead somewhere in the Pacific."

Johnny stepped back a step. He said very quietly, "Maybe he come here to tell you sump'm. Maybe he done tole you, kin you cipher hit."

My gaze must have wandered, for as I looked into the darkness to question him further, he was gone.

And then I heard Ellen's voice. "Where are you, dear?"

I saw that I had dropped the bundles. I picked them up and went slowly toward the back kitchen door.

26

I COULD SEE ALARM SPREAD FROM THE CORNER OF HER EYE, but she made the error of trying to cover it up. As I set the bundles down, she said, "You need a haircut. And a bath. You mustn't let yourself go because we live in the country. It makes you look, oh look so weird. I know now why the English colonials make such a ritual of the toilet."

"They are bored," I said.

"What made you so long? I was beginning to be worried."

"I ran into Johnny," I said casually. At least I had meant to be casual.

"At this time of night? What did he want? Anything wrong?"

"No. Just the usual thing."

She knew I was lying. Her manner became brisk again. "Well, supper is nearly ready. As soon as I put the meat on and make the bread. You can do the salad and I'll be ready to pull it together." She was kneeling at the flour bin. "I've poured you another drink. It's on the table."

"I hadn't finished the first one," I said.

"Oh," she replied. "Well, let's make it a loving cup."

"Let's," I said.

I took a long drink from mine and felt the hot sting at the bottom of my stomach. And then quickly I set to work. My hands broke the leaves from the lettuce head and I tossed them into a pan of cold water. I washed and picked the cress; threw in several leaves of the darker spinach; put some eggs on to boil. I took another drink. I began to feel better, much better, restored now as the spirits entered my blood and followed its intricate pattern into the veins. "It's wonderful what whisky can do for you," I said.

"You needed it, darling. You looked dreadfully undone."

"And you looked tired."

"Yes, I've had rather a day of it."

"What made you run into town? You must have made up your mind in a hurry."

"I did rather. Let's not go into it now."

"It's almost as if you knew . . ."

She turned to me. For the first time she seemed a little shaken.

"It is eerie," she said.

"You mean Moss?"

"Oh, the whole thing."

She broke off. Her voice resumed its light conversational tone. "I bought some tomatoes. They looked good for so late in the season."

"Maybe I'd better marinate them," I said. "Where are they?"

"In the top of that sack on the table. The small sack."

I reached down and brought them out, three large beautiful red tomatoes. I could tell they were solid meat through to the heart, with no hard green core, but perhaps a little ripe—so that they would leak around the seed.

"These ought to be drained first, shouldn't they?"

I held one up. It was almost ready to burst with ripeness.

"It's easy to see why they were called love apples," I said.

"The old people thought to eat them was to die, I've heard," she said.

"Do you suppose they made the connection?"

"Love sometimes kills," Ellen answered me gently.

I sensed that she had paused and that she had spoken out of some inner fear and that she was unaware that she had spoken. Not since her return, since the stroke of her news, had I felt so near to the rending of the veil which hid us from the truth. But how could I get her to tell me precisely what she feared?

I prompted: "There's an older truth about love and death."

"Well, I don't want to hear it. Not tonight anyway."

For a while after this the kitchen was silent, except for the light familiar sounds we made at our separate jobs. Into this silence gradually came, almost as if invoked, the feeling of communion as we went about the common meal together. I was ravenously hungry, I who had felt no appetite all day, and the smell of food, its promise of restoration, took on a tremendous significance. For a moment my exhausting vigil seemed as remote as some old fable lingering on in the mind from childhood. I went over to Ellen and put my arms around her and we kissed as we had not kissed for a long time. No words passed; there was no need for words, those props to faulty communication.

I released her and she began to make up the bread. It

seemed right that she should pass from my embrace to this, for her movements were a ritual as old as the world. A little frown shaded her eyes, her arms rose and fell in effortless rhythm, her hands seemed to punish and caress the flesh-colored dough. My eye followed the next step in observation: the dough was flesh-colored but it was not the color of life. My nerves were still inflamed. I stepped back a little from the biscuit block, for surely now I saw the meaning of Ellen's motion: she did the things with her hands one does to bring life back to the body of the drowned. Unaware that I had withdrawn, as though she still felt me there participating, she rolled the bread to the proper thickness and then took her biscuit cutter and with quick wrist motions cut the dough, lifting the small round pieces into the pan.

"Open the oven door, will you?" she said.

Her request had the sound of words, any words, which may be spoken but whose meaning only the initiate can understand.

The heat blew into our faces. As she leaned forward, her eyes glistened. Slowly she shoved the pan into the oven's mouth and I, as if the time had come to play my part, lifted the door until it clicked to with finality.

We stood by the stove a moment.

"I do hope they will rise," she said.

"Well, let's drink to the resurrection," I replied.

"Don't be sacrilegious, darling." She shuddered slightly. "It's bad luck."

I looked for our glasses. They were empty. "We're down to the loving cup," I said.

I held the tumbler toward her; her hands were dusty with flour.

She drank, and then I drank.

"You'd better hurry with your salad, dear. It won't be long now."

I rubbed the garlic until its strength hovered at the bowl's mouth, and then I picked up the lettuce, wonderfully fresh and crisp. I began to dry it.

"I'll declare, the water has done a lot for this."

"I know," she said. "It wasn't very good, but it was the best I could find. You don't get good lettuce out of stores. We must try to grow fall lettuce in the garden."

"The sun would burn it up."

"I wonder why," she sighed, "it will only grow well in the spring of the year?"

"I've told you. It's all greenness and water. It can't stand the sun. It's a plant that goes to seed quickly. There are people like that."

She caught my eyes, saw where the suggestion had led me, and said very softly, "Like . . ."

"I suppose. Like Moss."

We hung on the vast abyss his name made, when I deliberately broke the mood. I reached for the loving cup and handed it to her. "Let's drink to Moss," I said.

"All right, darling. Let's."

She raised the tumbler and held it before her for a moment with both hands. The light had struck the heavy glass and made a thin stream of fire in the amber liquid, so that it seemed to take on life from Ellen's hands. And then it came to me, looking at her with that clarity which can only be the focus of the true vision that I was in the presence of beauty which men of all time have been unable to resist, whose grace drives mad or leads to salvation—a grace impossible therefore miraculous, of incorruptible innocence and voluptuous play inexhaustible, the immortal heart spending and restoring at the same stroke.

"To our Moss!" she said. The shadow returned to her eyes. She sipped the drink and then passed the tumbler to me.

I grasped it.

"To Moss who will never die!"

And then I drained the glass. We faced each other and did not move.

"You are smiling?" she said.

"It's nothing. The most curious thing. Something completely irrelevant just popped into my head."

"But what?"

"I'm ashamed. I don't understand."

"I want to know."

"I was thinking of Jim. A colored boy on the home place."

"But?"

"What has it to do with Moss? Nothing. Absolutely nothing."

"Well," she said, "what about Jim?"

"Once at communion, when the chalice passed, he turned it up as I did just now and drank it down. He said, 'I love my Jesus so much, I'm goen drink him all up.'"

"Darling," Ellen said firmly, "what you need is food. And plenty of it. Get busy with that salad."

And I did, and she got busy. The light tap of her heels, the low clatter of dishes, her quick movements from kitchen to dining room, the ordered array of table gear, the last minute's seasoning—all of this, bending over the salad bowl, I half saw, half heard. From dish to dish, from table to oven, back and forth, she was now lost in that last act of pulling the meal together. I waited, expectant; and then squeezed from mouth to stomach, I took the blind spasm and the whirl, the after-faintness, the swallow, and knew that only food could save me from passing out. Concentrating, I walked a quick step to the dining room with the salad. The silver, the china, the bottle of wine, were in place, pure and shining, with the air of expectancy and the promise of fulfillment which the board takes on before one sits down to eat. Very carefully I walked back to the kitchen. In the bread boat Ellen was laying out the white napkin.

I waited. She opened the oven door. "The bread is done," she said.

"Good. I can't wait much longer."

"Here," she commanded. "Take these dishes in and be sure to put them on the pads."

I then brought the meat and put it before me. I stood, waiting for her; and she entered, bringing the bread boat, with the napkin folded three ways over the biscuit. She set it to her right and then took her seat.

"Now we can begin," she said and a sigh passed her lips.

I made a quick blessing and began to carve. The plates passed back and forth. In reverent tones of praise I said, "What wonderful food!"

'Thank you, love."

We did not speak again until the pangs of hunger had been appeased, sighing and sitting back in our chairs.

"I've got to catch my breath," I said.

"And I. My, but I was starved."

"I never saw you eat so," I said in a teasing way.

"I never had such need before."

At that moment, looking across the board now in such disarray, above the crumbs, the bits of food, the stains on the white cloth, above the dishes our apetites had emptied, Ellen and I at the same instant caught each other's eye and smiled.

It was a secret smile, perfect in its sympathy, almost perfect in its understanding. I knew at last that spiritual unity which is the end of marriage. And I knew that I might now speak and she would understand.

But she spoke first, a little sadly but with no false sentiment. She said, "One would think we had forgotten Moss. But we needed this. Particularly you, darling, to help you bear up in your sorrow and the greatness of your disappointment. You thought of him as your heir. Thoughts of him have made us feel justified in our struggle with this old place."

"Helen," I said abruptly, "his death is our salvation. I am going to take you away from *The Grove*. The place is haunted. We will be haunted if we stay."

"Darling, you called me Helen."

"My tongue must be a little thick."

"You almost drank too much."

"Yes," I said with awe which I hardly understood, "I almost did. But I am sober now. We are going to clear out of here. And tomorrow."

"Perhaps," she replied and the resonance of her voice made me tremble, "perhaps you will change your mind."

"It's made up," I replied, but the words died away.

"I have other news for you," she said, dropping her eyes to look up quickly and frankly.

"Yes," I whispered, sitting straight in the chair, sensing that from her lips would come the confession which would free or forever bind us to whatever fatal entanglements I had involved us in. Wild, mad thoughts raced through my mind as I endured the pause she made; but wild, mad, driving me beyond hope and despair, I sensed my inability to foresee.

"Yes," I said again, and my voice must have told her how

unbearable was my suspense, for she said quickly, but in a voice so low that I thought I had mistook it:

"I am going to have a baby."

I suppose I merely sat without expression, without sign of any intelligence on my face. She hurried on, "I know we'd thought this couldn't be. But I've suspected it for some time. And the doctor assures me it is so." And then, as I still sat motionless, without response, she added, "The child will come in the spring."

27

IT WAS NOTHING LESS THAN A MIRACLE: THAT A CHRONIC sterility should suddenly disappear without reason or possible explanation, and furthermore at *The Grove* which I had hoped to regenerate, thinking less of myself than of a larger pattern, although naturally I made a part of that pattern. After the surprise, the moment of unbelievable elation, the coincidence began to seem a little too pat. A miracle, of course, is a miracle. It is not to be explained. One explains the unexplainable by calling it a miracle. One does not really expect to witness it. And there was no other way to regard our prospect of an heir. If we had deliberately denied ourselves a child, later to reverse our decision . . . even then we might have expected a reluctant nature to deal with. But this—it was a bolt from the blue.

It came to me, not at first of course, but gradually and much later, that the changed status represented possibilities which I at first in no way even glimpsed. I could not have been expected to see beyond the fact, and a fact above all of such exciting vistas. At the moment it answered everything. It dispelled all my suspicions as to Ellen's communication with the sinister specter which haunted our lives, for obviously a pregnant woman is strange. Obviously she has had communication with the mysterious workings of life which a man cannot comprehend, and which certainly I, given my absorption with another mystery, equally insoluble, was in no way prepared to suspect.

But also it gave me a firm answer to what had come to seem an irresponsible, a romantic, act. Now I knew that my good daemon had deliberately led me to *The Grove*. Not to escape the accident of the world but to come into my own. I was now to be the head of a family, a true family, returned to my proper place, and that place physically and spiritually of a sound and explicable history.

I remained in this condition of elation for what was left of the fall season. We did not have that year a slow dying away into winter. The last of September was crisper than usual; it was even cold. And by early October we had had a light frost. Johnny had told me that the shucks were thick on the corn. I knew what that meant—a long hard winter. As time approached when the tobacco had to be cut, I had mighty little time for thinking. It rained a good deal, and when it didn't rain the days were cloudy. That worry which comes from the prospect of losing the year's work, of not paying taxes or the interest on the mortgage, began to creep through the farm. Every time we would meet we would tell ourselves that there was plenty of time. We would look at the tobacco, a fair enough crop, and say to each other there is plenty of time. And then we would look at the overcast sky. You've got to have sun when it's cut to make the leaves fall, or you can't put it on the sticks.

From the moment I took the lead I found the tension exhilarating. Formerly, emergencies and crises had filled me with the nameless fears that come from an inability to act. But this had passed. I found I had a real interest in what was going on. I found I could act. I had that sense of holding things in the palm of my hands; and it was due to my management that the tobacco was cut and hung in the barns three days before the killing frost. My neighbors were not, all of them, so successful. A few lost the great part of their crops, many too great a fraction. My reputation among these hard-headed people reached a height which certainly I and more certainly they had never expected. Even Johnny showed me greater deference. There was no marked change in his attitude, but he would ask my advice on little things, even on matters he understood better than I. Somehow I felt that the life of the place, for decades submerged deep within the ground, stirred again and slowly was groping through the hard-packed soil to air and light.

As Johnny and I parted one evening at dusk—we had been discussing the farm's luck—he turned to me and said, "Folks says you talks to the devil."

"Why, what on earth do they mean?"

The shadows of the night were rushing fast about us, so that I could not well see his eyes, but for an instant I was aware that they no longer regarded me from their habitual reticence. They fixed upon me an intimate, almost conspiratorial gleam. It quickly died. He said, "Hit puzzles them how you done it."

"It ought not to," I said, a little annoyed without knowing why. "They've cut and hauled enough tobacco to know how it is done."

"Yessir, that's the p'int," he replied softly.

I could get no more out of him. Nor was it necessary, for

the drift of his remark was clear. What was not clear was why he felt it necessary to inform me.

I repeated the conversation to Ellen. She looked at me very strangely, which also caused me to wonder. She was already beginning to show, as they say, and her face was changing somewhat; so it may have been nothing more than her condition. And certainly her reply was very sensible. "I wouldn't pay any attention to that," she said. "You know how envious country-people are."

I hadn't really paid any attention to it, not to take it seriously, that is, until Ellen advised me not to. I realized then that it had worried me a little, or rather that a grain of anxiety lay far back in my head and this incident had jolted it to the fore. Soon after we went in to supper and after supper sat down in our common living room and she and I began to talk about one thing and another, I remember hearing my brother's name mentioned and then sometime after Ellen saying, "You are not listening."

"But I am. You were talking about Moss Senior and Madge."

"I was saying," she answered with annoyance, "the stone they want for Moss's grave is too ornate. And it is rushing things so. It will be months before his body is brought back."

"I must have dozed off."

"Go to bed then."

I stood up to go. "I'll check the fires in the barns first," I said.

I heard her voice, waveringly, as from a distance, "Well, go ahead. Don't stand there in the middle of the floor."

"I'm going."

Once outside the night air braced me and I could think clearly again. I was absolutely sure I had got up to go to bed.

I had had no intention of going to the barns. Johnny would be there, or if not there, he would have checked the fires and left one of his sons in charge if he thought there was any need for it. I had stood up, opened my mouth to yawn—I was sure of this—and the words came out. They were not my words. No . . . they were not my words, but they were meant for me . . .

A light wind had come up and blew the wood smoke in the direction of the house. For some time the smell had sifted down the air like a clean, sharp spice. Now it came in heavier gusts, insistent, commanding. I began walking toward the first barn.

Even before I could see him, I knew Johnny was there. I called out, in no loud way but my voice went far, "Things all right?" And a little after I saw his shape against the large barn doors.

He did not answer until I came up. " 'Backer's still high. I picked up the fars a little."

"There's a ring around the moon," I said.

"Yessir, hit due to rain."

We were silent awhile. The night was soft. The smell from the barn, so clean and sharp, was somehow comforting. I wondered why I had felt uneasy, now that all things seemed clear at last, and right. I felt the sudden need to be confidential. We were both of us looking up at the sky. I dropped my eyes to a group of trees at the edge of the woods. The shadows there bred a stillness closer than the spaces of the sky. Looking into them, I said, *"The Grove* will have an heir sometime this spring."

I could see Johnny drop his gaze and fix it on the trees before us. Together we stared into the shadows and after an appropriate pause, he said, "You shore means to hold fast to the plow."

I don't know what I had expected, some conventional compliment, some acknowledgment which would show me he understood my fresh strength, my changed status. Perhaps I even hoped he would hint that now I deserved a son. Certainly I did not expect so ambiguous a remark and almost at once I felt a chill in the air, a desire to go, my confidence somehow betrayed. I could have kicked myself. What a fool to lay myself open in any such way! I said coolly, "I will take a look at the fires and go to bed."

Johnny did not stir. I looked at him expectantly. He said, "Hit's turrible smoky in there."

"I'll take a look anyway."

He undid the chain on the small side door with no other word, and I quickly stepped inside. I went head down into the stifling, flickering air. Almost at once my eyes began to water and the hot acrid smoke made me choke for breath. The little lips of fire, some slightly blazing, some mere red glows, lay in orderly fashion along the floor of the barn. I had never seen a barn going at night, and for one crazy moment I had the sense that the fires came out of swollen slits in the ground. I stood for a moment, breathing carefully through my nose and squinting, looking into the gloom. The four walls gave an unbearable sense of pressure, the solid tons of leaf above, the close ranks of greenish-brown blades thrusting downward their curling points, the bright points of the gleams below, driving the thin columns of smoke upward into the parting leaves, the darkness shifting, whirling in the reddish haze. My head began to whirl. Johnny wandered noiselessly through the smoke, reaching up, feeling, gently touching a leaf here, a leaf there. Once he turned my way. His eyes were open and set in a steady gaze. I reached up and fingered the crisp twist in the moist leaf.

And then I heard it, we both heard it at the same moment. We both turned at the same moment. There came a slight puff from the center of the barn, a few sparks, and a chunk breaking in two. My eyes were stinging, but they dried up at what they saw: the figure of a man stooping, bent over the fire. Gently his arms began to flap like a bird's, slowly, steadily, as if he were fanning the embers. I looked more sharply and he seemed to be pushing the sawdust against the burning chunks. I could almost swear the sawdust moved. As I stared, the motion of his hands changed to a pat and a scoop, and then to a slow squeeze, as if they were gathering up something that was about to escape.

Suddenly he became very still and I knew that he was aware that he was being watched. Almost imperceptibly his head bent to an upward twist, moving through the smoke. So still was the rest of his body, I thought of a jointed manikin whose neck was being moved by invisible strings. But it was no manikin. It was my enemy, Major Brent, and again his gaze was fixed to mine. Again I had the feeling that I had taken him by surprise. His face, as red as the coals he was hovering over, distinctly carried an appeal, but it was so loathsome in its naked directness he must have seen how it repelled me. In a flash he was threatening me, and the cold fury of it left me shivering in the heat of the barn.

And then my eyes watered. Furiously I wiped them, but when I saw again, Major Brent was nowhere. Where he had crouched, I saw only a thick column of smoke. It wavered as though something had disturbed it and then grew even, funneling steadily upward until it lost itself among the tips of the leaves.

Outside I waited for Johnny. He was leaning against the small portal. His hands with the swift, easy movement of long accustomed intimacy drew the chain through and noiselessly dropped a twig into a link. He remained for a moment pressed against the door, his head slightly bent and waiting.

I said hoarsely, "Did you see what I saw?"

It seemed a long while before he answered.

"I seen a chunk burn in two."

"And what else?"

Slowly, as one recollects the image before speaking, he said, "Hit flared, the sparks busted loose, but they ain't no harm to *them*." And then in a sudden change of tone, almost to a low rhythmic chant, "Firing a barn of tobaccer ain't the same by night. I knows what's there. I knows time I steps inside the do'. I can lay down in bed and know what's there. I knows what's in one fare and I knows what's in an'er." His voice trailed off. . . . "I don't have to see what I sees. I knows."

28

STRANGELY ENOUGH, AFTER I HAD SET OUT FOR THE HOUSE, my first reaction was a feeling of relief. The promise of an heir for *The Grove* had taken Major Brent by surprise. At the moment when he thought to draw near his chasm of victory, his entire campaign miscarried and he disappeared from view. Not that I felt for a moment he had gone for good, but as weeks passed into months, I confess I had hopes, even if doubt burned beneath like a pilot light. Now it was flaring, in the brilliancy of its flame I saw what had happened. Major

Brent had not fled: he had merely gone underground. This meant a change of tactics on his part. Failing in direct assault, if it is possible to refer to any of his methods as direct, he would now try us by surprise. Toward this end he lay in wait, and in a secret place which showed a public face. It was cunning of him but not cunning enough. I had found him out.

He had not expected me. Of this I was certain, for how else was I to interpret that appeal of his, so quickly changing into a threat? No, I was sure I had happened on a clue to his vulnerability. This gave me a feeling of self-confidence, in spite of the immense danger and everything now to lose, for who could believe other than that all his evil would turn upon the child? He must have known that I was come too late to *The Grove*. He must also have surmised that I would prepare it for our son.

In the acceptance of the changed situation I had no immediate fears for Ellen. She was not free of danger certainly; the danger was tremendously increased, but it was the kind I could face because she would face it with me. Indeed, I had now become her support, rather than she the object of my care. So it came about I did not go at once to the house but wandered over the place, questioning, trying to understand.

Gradually the truth showed itself through the confusion of half-truths, false conjectures, seemingly interminably mixed and obscure, like the shake of a puzzle when the disordered pieces fall each into its proper place and the whole is visible. The truth seemed simple enough, at least its paraphrase did. False romantic that I was when I first came with my idea, how was I to know when I bought a run-down farm to restore that I had bought nothing, that the fiction to own, in spite of deed and possession, describes the most ephemeral of all artifices? How was I to know that I had put myself in way of the past and the future, bemused by the mad fancy that I could reach into history and regenerate, a function proper only to a god? In greater humility and wisdom my idea gave way to a fuller vision of the rich complexities of circumstance and the unknowable mystery of the nature of *The Grove*. In this fuller knowledge it came to me with the suddenness of revelation: was not my idea the obverse of Major Brent's act, with the difference that he had died unrepentant and the vanity of his act bound him in torment to the shadowy air of the place, haunting it until that time he could work his release? And it was just in this that our danger lay. Unpurged, unregenerate spirit that he was, he would know only to seek his release through a repetition of the original error. But there is a blindness to phantoms. Beyond history, they think they may perpetuate it. I slapped my leg with glee as I thought of this. At least this was the conclusion I had reached that night and, once reached, the logic of warning Ellen without delay sent me toward the house.

I found her sitting up in bed, with the bedside lamp burning but with a dim flame. As I came up I saw at once the strain on her face.

"What is it?" I asked in alarm.

"Where have you been?" she demanded in a tight, injured tone. "You've been away for hours. I was about to dress and look for you."

"Is that all?" I asked with relief.

"Is that all? Is that all?" She repeated. "Leaving me to worry, not to know, lying here thinking of all the things that could happen. And in my condition."

"I'm sorry, darling, so sorry," I said softly, sitting beside her and taking her hand.

She withdrew it petulantly. "I can explain," I said hastily.

"Explain? Explain what?"

She looked up and her eyes were dark, swimming in dark pools.

It was not yet time.

I undressed and got into bed and before I could speak, she turned toward me, drawing her legs up, with her head close to mine and her hair outspread on the pillow. "Sometimes, dear, I get so afraid."

I ran my fingers carefully along her arm, barely touching the flesh and after a while I heard her sigh. And then she said, "It is only when I am tired or something makes me nervous, but I can't help thinking of those poor women. I know it is silly and that it was long ago . . ."

"Poor women?" I asked, not following.

"Yes. The women in the garden."

"Oh," I said. "Oh . . . Major Brent's wives."

"All of them died in childbed." What sorrow her voice carried as she said it, then, "I just can't get them out of my mind."

"You poor darling! They've nothing to do with you."

I drew her into my arms again. She snuggled close into my body and we lay together in the comfort of this embrace. When I felt her relax and grow quieter, I decided the time had come. I knew I must not be startling. I must in no way frighten her. And to me my voice sounded casual enough. It seemed in no way the bearer of what must have been to her strange tidings, a voice out of a dream perhaps, with the sharp impersonality of a dream. . . . "I saw Major Brent tonight," I whispered.

We had reached that hour of the night when the heart sleeps, but I felt in hers a skip in the gentle fluttering, then a great lunging stroke. She stirred, drew back her head, watching me, her eyes poised on the edge of shadow made by the lamp. "What did you say?" she asked.

"I saw Major Brent tonight."

Very carefully she withdrew from my arms. Her hand had scarcely pushed away the unruly hair when her bewildered voice said, "What on earth do you mean?"

"On the earth, yes." I was sitting opposite her. "But not from gravity."

She was shaking me now. "Wake up. You are dreaming."

Carefully I placed my hands on her shoulders and lifted her around so that the light might show my face.

"Do I look as if I were dreaming?"

Her hands fluttered before her, then drew back against her breast in instant spasm. In a deep voice, harsh, choked, not hers surely, she said, "Your eyes. Your eyes," and then in a loud scream, half-animal, half-human, she leaped to the floor, where she stood trembling.

I went toward her as carefully as I could, almost creeping across the rug, for I knew the slightest jerky movement would send her off again. In fact I was so shaken by this unexpected reaction to my carefully planned attempt not to frighten that I myself was unnerved.

The distance gradually narrowed between us until I was near enough to touch her. "You must calm yourself," I said. "You have behaved out of reason." And then more forcefully, "You must think of your child."

"I must think of my child," she repeated as a child would repeat a lesson. And all the while her teeth were chattering. I waited for what seemed a long time and she said again, "I must."

"Come now," I said and gently took her by the arm.

She was very docile as I led her back to bed.

29

IN THE FEW HOURS THAT WERE LEFT TO THE NIGHT I TRIED TO tell her of our danger. I went into the history of what I had seen. I tried to make clear the nature of the menace, how logically it came out of the past. At first she asked a few questions, but as I talked she gradually fell into silence, and once so still had she grown I thought she had fallen asleep. But she answered me quick enough when I questioned her. Fearing her fears, I showed her how much stronger our position had become since her pregnancy, but that in a way this was also our weakness. We must never be off guard. Nor must she ever be frightened into any rash act if Major Brent appeared to her. He was bound to await the right moment, when she would be on a stairway, or in some dangerous spot where sight of him could easily cause her to lose footing, with what disastrous consequences she could imagine. I wound up by saying, "It is your frailty or mine, some defect of ours, he will pounce upon to undo us."

I had done the best I knew to impress upon her the seriousness of the situation, but I must say I was disappointed at the way she took it. So much depended on close alliance between us, and it was just this that was somehow lacking. Her disbelief—I could call it nothing else—left me for many days in a quandary. Disbelief was the last thing I had expected, for obviously our ends were the same. Our sympathy and understanding had never been closer, and so much depended on giving the child a chance. Our sanity, our very lives might depend on it. One may imagine how at a loss I was when she accused me of being cruel, by telling ghost stories when she already had enough to worry her. These were more or less her words. It was useless to insist that my intention had been anything but that. To prove it I showed her how carefully I had gone about telling her. I had been matter-of-fact, in no way making it seem strange or unnatural. No, I had kept my head. I had been in a way a scientific reporter of the menace I had witnessed; I had even tried to define the nature of the evil. And for all my pain to be accused of indulging in a cruel jest!

I think at least I had made her see that it was no jesting matter. Early in December my brother Moss Senior surprised me by coming out to see us. He had once before made a perfunctory visit, to see, as he put it, just how big a fool I had been to bury myself away from civilization. His conclusion was that I was a bigger fool than even he had imagined—which, I remarked, was indeed a large order. So, when I saw him turning up the driveway, I knew he had not returned out of a sense of pleasure or for my society.

From his manner I sensed that Ellen had communicated with him in some way, and to save her embarrassment I took him walking over the place. I walked him hard with what grim delight one may imagine; showed him the crops in the barns, the stock in the lots, the plans for the coming year. I showed him the good land, the land that had to be rebuilt; I showed him the ravages of the past. At last, when he was on the verge of apoplexy I sat him down on a log to let him catch his breath. Then I said, "Now, Brother, what did you really come to see me about?"

He coughed, hummed and hawed, but at last came out with it. "What is this about you seeing ghosts?"

"Did Ellen write you?"

He hesitated, in his clumsy way trying to protect her. As if she needed protection from me! The idea was so preposterous I laughed out right in his face. Such a laugh would have made him angry at any other time, but I had fairly exhausted him, and much of his old contempt for me, which was only a part of his contempt for mankind, had softened since his son's death. The flesh, I noticed, hung loose on his jowls. His eyes, usually so sharp and cold, had begun to water. No, definitely he was not the man he had been. But something of his old self came out, as he stood up. "Ghost stories is damn poor entertainment for a pregnant woman."

I said coldly, "What did Ellen write you?"

He reached in his pocket and handed me the letter:

I have been thinking of you and Madge a great deal lately. Now that I am going to have a child your own sadness seems so much more real to me. I feel so close to you now. My thoughts of the child I am bearing, of the dangers he will encounter, of that first risk of air and light, seem all so tremendously grave. I try to get a better perspective by telling myself how narrow are my fears to your sorrow—the years of care and thought, the years of fear after fear for his safety. And then the sudden brutal news.

I suppose it is a kind of hysteria—but I often feel that we are so far away here, that so much could happen—it is hard to get a doctor. And then I wonder if this undertaking hasn't been too much for your brother. He feels so deeply—he is so highly nervous. At first I had thought coming here would do him good, but he told me not long ago that he saw the ghost of old Major Brent. He has got it into his head that it is some kind of a threat to us, particularly to the baby—not a very cheerful subject of conversation to me right now.

I was wondering if you could find us a place in town, where we could go at least until the baby is born.

I feel sometimes that a sort of doom hangs over *The Grove*. Perhaps I'll be seeing ghosts too if we spend the long winter months shut up in this house.

I tell myself that my foreboding is only a part of pregnancy and should not be indulged. . . . Don't give this letter too much thought. My love to Madge.

Ellen.

I stood there with the letter in my hand. My poor, poor Ellen! To what desperate plight had I brought her that she would turn to Moss Senior? To what desperate despair had I brought myself in so miserably failing to reach through to her? Never in my trade, where I succeeded modestly in making the illusions of life seem more real than life itself, never had I sweated as I had to present for her the true image of reality. Only to be caught, trapped behind the skill of my trade, so that she saw what only the world would see, a ghost story. I could not lay it to her condition: the failure lay elsewhere: in my style.

Major Brent—a ghost story! How that abominably monstrous spirit, hiding in air, breeding pestilence, must be chuckling at this turn of affairs! What desperate irony for me, perfecting the cry of wolf, wolf, now to be undone by perfection!

"You ought to get down on your knees to that little woman

for what you have done to her," I heard; and the arrogance of the tone crossed my nerves like a file. For the next few moments I was trembling beyond control. Blind murderous flashes disordered my senses. But I took myself in hand. At last, with tremendous effort I opened my eyes.

"Let's go back to the house," he said, turning abruptly. But I saw. He did not turn quickly enough to hide his fear—of me the brother he had always held in contempt.

We did not speak again until we reached the entrance way, when I said, "Obviously it will not be good for Ellen here now. Will you find us a place in town?"

"That's more sense than you've spoken in your whole life," he replied in a gruff surly way. And then his true nature came to the fore even in this situation. "Places are hard to get, but I think maybe I can put my hands on something. You leave it up to me."

"I always do," I said.

My brother had never been one to catch even the bluntest shadings of irony.

30

AND SO IT WAS SETTLED BEFORE HE LEFT FOR TOWN; IT WAS settled as the tea leaves grew cold in the bottom of the cups. We all made the best of an embarrassing situation. Even Moss Senior became civilized in a neolithic kind of way. And before he left for town, we actually set a date of departure, my brother offering us quarters with him in case he had not found us a place in the meantime. I protested this and, as it was growing late, invited him to spend the night. Ellen pressed him, but he refused. Soon thereafter, pleading bad roads and the approaching dark, he took his departure.

I could feel Ellen dreaded the moment when we would be alone and we both must face her going behind my back. I did not tell her that Moss Senior had abused her confidence and showed me the letter, for I was determined there was to be no further rift in our understanding. Whatever the failure it was mine, since it had been up to me to communicate. I told her quite frankly that I understood, that she must forgive me, that what I knew I knew, that I had acted for the best, and that for a long time now fleeing *The Grove* had not crossed my mind. I at last was beginning to feel at home here, at last the responsible head and equal to my responsibility. What I had not realized was her own fresh alarm, but I told her that I understood her difficulties of belief and thoroughly agreed that what she wanted was best, that above all we must think of her and the special meaning her pregnancy held for us both. She was very relieved and, I think, surprised. She kissed me and said, "Oh, I am so glad you understand."

"I do," I said. "But I must tell you I am not a pathological case."

She interrupted me quickly. "Of course not, Henry."

I went on. "There is more around us than the natural world."

"Of course," she said.

"I am more than your natural husband."

The sweet sincerity of her reply moves me now, as it did then, with all the fresh pity I felt for her and for myself as she put her hands lightly on my shoulders and said, "You are the father of my child."

I know I was close to tears, for I had to take her and hold

her tight, as much to gain control of myself as to comfort her. But I could not indulge in the weakness of feeling: I must be honest with her and with myself. So I said, "But, Ellen dear, you must believe me. I am not superstitious. I am not what you may have thought. I was never stronger. There is an evil influence here. That influence I have met and met again. It is a threat to us. It will not go until I make it go."

She thought a long while before she spoke again. Her words were quietly given, I could see she was struggling to understand. "How can you be sure?" she asked.

"How can you be sure of those tea-things there?"

"Why, they are there," she said.

"Exactly. And Major Brent is there"—I waved my hand toward the outside.

She lifted an empty cup. "This I can see, touch. Can you touch Major Brent?"

I put my hand on her stomach. She withdrew slightly; then became still, almost poised for flight. We both felt it, I the swelling movement roll within her. She looked at me. "He just kicked," she said.

"I felt him," I said.

Almost desperately she replied, "Don't you see? He is real. He is important."

"He is." I paused to give my words effect. "But can you see him?"

"Of course not. But he is no less real for that."

"Exactly. We do not need all our senses. One is enough sometimes. I have not touched, but I have seen Major Brent."

"But how can you know? You don't know what he looks like."

"But Johnny does."

"Johnny!" She threw his name at me in contempt.

"The descriptions match," I went on.

She turned away and began piling the tea-things on the tray. There was nothing but the soft clatter of dishes and tinkle of silver. Suddenly she looked up. "All right. But then I must go to town. It is not right to make this child suffer any risk, whatever it is."

"I've agreed."

This seemed to calm her. And I let it go at that and considered that it came off well. What use to tell her that nothing could be gained by moving to town? Was not the air everywhere familiar to Major Brent? For us to leave *The Grove* would only be to make us more vulnerable. To remove ourselves would in no way throw Major Brent off the scent. It would only place us in strange surroundings.

There was one thing sure in all of this: my brother. He acted true to form. With his usual lack of consideration for others, he transferred one of his key-men to another town so that we could have his house. Of course even Moss Senior could not throw the man into the streets without warning, the upshot being we could not get the house until the first of the year. In the meanwhile we were told in lordly fashion we could move in with our kinsman. But this I refused to do, and Ellen seemed content to stay on at *The Grove* until we could get the house. I made it clear that, if she wished, we would go to the local hotel in the interim. My thorough willingness to do anything she proposed, I think, made Ellen feel she was being somewhat of an alarmist and she hurriedly agreed the thing to do was to stay on at *The Grove* until the first of the year.

Even the weather seemed to conspire to keep us there. The days were mild and moist, with brisk chilly nights. It was perfect tobacco weather, and the crops were all got down and bulked and by Christmas a good part of it was stripped. We spent a quiet Christmas, thinking how different the next one would be. The rest of December went quickly, Ellen busy with the packing, and I in straightening out my accounts. We had set the following Monday to leave. On Friday the worst blizzard the country had known for twenty years blew out of the northwest. It began with a heavy downpouring rain, a regular gully-washer which lasted ten hours, when the wind changed and turned a slow drizzle into sleet. The temperature dropped twenty degrees in five hours. By the next morning the snow was deep on the ground and still falling. We stood together at our bedroom window and looked out on the wintry world. Hesitantly I said, "This will delay us. The roads are solid ice."

Ellen was so long making any kind of response I naturally turned her way. She was staring . . . well, she was staring into the frozen outdoors with such dismay, her shoulders drawn in and so pitifully thin and her eyes, all their luster gone, protruding in the set way of a doll's made for a melodramatic role. "This won't last long," I said heartily. "It never does in this country."

"I was afraid of this," she said. She repeated the words several times with desperate earnestness, as if she saw the proof of some truth she alone had been sure of. I touched her arm. "Come now. It's not all that bad."

"I won't be able to leave," she said.

"I promise you. Now make us some tea."

As it happened, I was a poor weather prophet.

Each day the thermometer dropped a degree or two. When the sun came out, and this was not every day, it would rise for a little and then sluggishly drop to its previous reading, or below it. The cattle stood hunched up in the barn lot, or picking at the frozen wisps of hay half sunk in the frozen mass about the barn door. When I would go out—there was much to see to—the cold struck me as exhilarating, but soon my face felt tight and dead, my nose sharp enough to break and always the bite at the tip. The warmth of my body drew in as a fire dies away into its coals.

The most amazing thing was Ellen's acceptance of the situation. After that first morning she showed me the quality of her courage. Her flurry of despondency had worried me. I expected her to grow difficult. But not at all. She had no thought of herself or of the child she was bearing. It was all for me. She could not do enough for my comfort. She made me tea whenever I came in from the outdoors. She made warm soups and especial dishes I loved. She would rush to get my slippers if my feet were wet and cold. She made me sit by the fire. She would look at me, when I went out, or when I came in, to see if I brought news of any bad luck. How intent was her regard before rushing off to do some errand that would make things more pleasant! She reminded me of those frontier women who molded bullets as they nursed their children. After several days of this I said, "See here, darling, you treat me as if I were an invalid. I don't deserve it. You are the one things must be done for."

"I'm all right," she said quickly.

"How do you feel?"

"Fine. Fine." And then she would be off as if she had just remembered something that had to be done.

In the evenings, sitting by the fire, she would pick up her sewing and sharpen her eyes on the needle, but I could see her watching to see if I had any wishes that might make the hours pass more pleasantly. There was an element of strain to all this, rather like that between bride and bridegroom when they find themselves, at long last, alone with the separateness of their personalities and the need desperately to wipe out the strangeness.

I look back on this as a time, a crucial time, in our lives. I was like the sentinel on a dangerous post who turns from his intense watch to relieve his eyes and rest his spirit at the bright blazing campfire. But what could I do? Ellen was making every effort to show me that the postponement of our departure did not matter. Could I have received this attention coldly and kept to my watch? Such would have been either brutal or heroic, and I was fitted to play neither role. Perhaps I needed this attention more than I thought: perhaps I was done in, exhausted by the continuous vigil. And certainly we had to fill the days and the longer nights, and we had only ourselves to fall back upon. Never had she loved me with so much frenzy, nor had she ever been so lovable. I felt that up to now we had only touched the borders of that dark and passionate grove.

But as the winter, so to speak, dug in I began to feel that something false had crept into our relationship. It was too intense; it could only properly belong to those who die young. It was not the thing to wear out a lifetime. And curiously enough with this awareness came an awareness of change in the aspect of the outside. For the first week the white world seemed beautiful—pure, absolute, bringing respite from the confusion and waste of living. Only in one place was there sign of life. Each day in the barn lot, where the stock was penned, the brown stains left by the cattle spread a little farther, grew a little darker. At first as I passed, I would look away. The lot was the one feature, no more than a speck in the vast whiteness, which marred the purity of what I saw. But it was not long before I found myself eagerly glancing toward it, as to some beacon, on my trips to and from the house.

When we were well on into the second week, the aspect of things had subtly but violently changed. The black poles of the trees stood up out of the white ground, as slick and brittle as on the first morning of the blizzard; the barns and the house stood apart, surrounded, isolated; each object, even the smoke from Johnny's chimney, a thin blue haze rising straight up, seemed caught in the air. But it was no longer the whiteness. It was the stillness now which made the disunity of this solitude.

In the room where I kept a great fire going, and it was a cheerful fire, the flames bending over the back stick, changing color as the heat became great or small, even here, just beyond the circle of the hearth the cold waited in the room, and the quiet there was the same quiet that had settled everywhere over our world. One would pass through it to the fire; the heat might even drive it from the room; but one had only to open the door and there it was, in the next room, filling the air, waiting. . . . Just as somewhere about, in some bleak corner, or in the wide open ways, there was one particular spot of air colder, more quiet, but also waiting. . . .

And then toward the last of the third week the white fog drifted in.

31

Mᴀ FIRST THOUGHT WAS: IT WILL THAW NOW. MY NEXT thought was of Ellen. I must tell her. After all, disguise it as she had, she desperately wanted to go away to have the child.

I made her dress and then wrap up in her warmest things, without telling her why. It seemed a foolish game to play, but I did not want her to discover the fog for herself. I wanted to show it to her. "But why so mysterious?" she asked. "Never mind," I said. "You will see."

Once outdoors I said, "Look. Isn't it beautiful?" And I waved my hand as if I had ordered it as a special gift for her.

She caught her breath. "It is beautiful. But why did you want to bring me out in it?"

We were walking toward the garden.

"I wanted to be the first to show you. The weather is changing. Soon I can take you away."

"Oh really, darling." Her voice choked ever so little.

We walked on. I opened the garden gate and we paused just inside.

"How lovely the garden is!" she said. "And how unreal!"

I saw what she meant. All the imperfections left by time had been covered. We seemed to be adrift in a white cloud, in some unknown ideal place, where we were the only inhabitants. The snow and ice had perfected the bordering hedges. The flowering bushes which, in summer, showed a few scraggly buds, now presented to our gaze the absolute proportions, the subdued glitter, of one blooming mass. Our feet crunched the walkways. The outlines of the paths were faintly visible; and along them we followed the circle within the circle, confining the fanlike beds. We wandered here and there. Once behind the white air the garden wall wavered like a shadow. Except for the soft crunching steps there was no sound. We moved in utter silence. The air was become silence at last made visible. Our solitude was complete.

"The glare no longer pinches my eyes," Ellen said.

"There's no glare here," I replied. "Wouldn't it be wonderful if, with a wave of the hand, we could make the summer garden as perfect as this? And once perfected, drench it in some such arresting atmosphere?"

"We can do it. Or almost," she said. "But not with a wave of the hand."

"No, not with a wave of the hand."

And then we found ourselves near the springhouse. It rose up into the fog like a monument, all its rotting structure transformed.

"Let's not go too near," she said softly. "Let them rest in peace."

"Always you think of those women," I said.

"I feel very close to them now," she answered. And then after a little, in some panic, "Which way is the gate?"

I put her arm in mine. "Don't fret. I know the way out."

She drew away. "But where is it? One could wander here for hours. I've heard of such things." She turned around and pointed, one way and then another, and I saw that her alarm was real.

"Don't get excited. I'll take you out."

I reached for her hand.

"No, no," she cried. "I'll wait here. I know where I am here. You find the gate and call me. I'll come."

I was torn between staying and going. To leave her in such a state seemed a kind of abandonment. I must calm her. But she would not hear of me staying. "Go! Go!" she said.

It was apparent I must end this condition of affairs as quickly as possible. To remain another instant might set forever the mark of terror in her eyes. In my haste I moved blindly into the fog. It was then, swallowed up by it, I found that in my solicitude for her I had lost direction. I stopped and looked every way into the white deep air, and every way it opened up but only to show itself. The solid whiteness had usurped the air. There was no center, no four points of the compass. Within the circle the circle had come to an end.

But I knew there was a gate and, feeling now myself some panic, I began to run, trusting to blind chance. I quickly enough came up against the wall, but it was the unbroken wall I touched. Time and again I retraced my steps, approached it by the next path, but always the gate eluded me. And everywhere the trodden snow and everywhere the motionless depth of the fog, the cold dull white cloud of it, and beyond it the hard substance of the wall, surrounding us, confining us, the little gap closed up. Then at one certain moment I discovered my center of being had become the nameless dread which lurks in dreams, is known but may not be named.

In this white blindness I reached to my forehead and brushed away the clammy sweat. Should I call out to Ellen and terrify her? Not yet certainly. Instead, slowly I trod the crystal floor, looking down, fearing now the effluvium which had replaced the air and which at first had seemed so beautiful.

So it happened that in this latter stage of my bewilderment the fog took from me the sense of time.

But remembering the woodsman's trick, I began myself to move in a circle, carefully widening it. This was a last resort. It might bring me back to Ellen. There was no other way now. Together again we could wait until Johnny came to feed the stock. If I shouted, he might hear me. But when would that be? Would the dark blot out this whiteness? Would Johnny feed early and slip back to his house before I could call? Once together again, I would explain to Ellen, and like a foghorn I would call out at intervals.

Treading the circle I had made, something, some intuition, made me lift my eyes from my tracks. There she was, barely visible in the opaque light, directly in front of me. She had not heard me come up. She stood with her head slightly bent, in the frozen tension of one who looks down into an abyss. Her hands were clasped over her bosom. I felt a boundless relief, but as I looked more sharply I saw that she was listening to no spoken words, but to some secret communication she was well practiced in deciphering. The whole appalling truth was before me.

"Ellen!" I screamed.

My anguish and the fixity of my purpose to save her gave to my cry its unearthly quality. She bounded forward, whirled around and, looking blindly at me, made the sound of a wounded beast. And then she saw me. For one instant she turned upon me a wild, transforming stare, when she began to back slowly away, moaning, "No, no, no," over and over again.

"Stop! It's me," I called out.

But she did not stop. It was then I saw toward what she was moving. A few steps away, on the platform of the spring-house stood my enemy, waiting. There was no need to look but in my instantaneous glance I saw that he was dressed as a bridegroom. And I saw his face, the hateful features I had come to know as well as my own, triumph and desire shining out of the hollow eyes. And then the two long arms reached forth.

"You shall not!" I shouted and dashed forward.

But I was a fraction of a moment too late. With a lightness she could not have managed alone Ellen leaped upon the platform where she was awaited. I heard a crackling of timbers, a long crash, and there before my eyes she and Major Brent disappeared into the depths below.

I tore open the old trap door, half ran, half slid down the rotten steps. I stood in the inner darkness of the pit, sinking up to my ankles in the oozing muck which for years had stopped up the spring's mouth. From above, where the floor had broken through, a dull light penetrated into the gloom—enough for me to make out the heap lying in front of me. With a cry of hope I knelt, I gathered her into my arms. Oh, with what passion I held her! Carefully now I whispered her name. She was slow to answer. Hoarsely I shouted it, but the round walls of the slimy pit, not she, gave back the lifeless word. Desperately my eyes reached for the light to make it show me her face. The light hovered, like a strain of breath, below the break in the floor. I saw it cast no reflection, but I saw this without surprise. Already I knew what it was I held in my arms, and I knew that at last Major Brent had triumphed and I was alone.

ABOUT THE AUTHOR

Andrew Lytle was born in Murfreesboro, Tennessee, in 1902; he attended the Sewanee Military Academy. Afterwards he studied for a year in France and then graduated from Vanderbilt in 1925. After managing a cotton farm for his father, he spent two years under George Pierce Baker in the Yale School of Drama; supported himself in New York acting, as he began the research on his first book, a Civil War biography, *Bedford Forrest and His Critter Company.*

Returning to Tennessee, he renewed his fellowship with the writers about Vanderbilt who at the moment were taking a fresh look as their common historic inheritance. He contributed to their agrarian symposium, *I'll Take My Stand.* He began writing fiction and found this, rather than the theater, to be his proper art form. His other novels are *The Long Night* (1936); *At the Moon's Inn* (1941); and *The Velvet Horn* (1957).

He has taught at Southwestern College, at the University of the South, where for a year he edited the oldest American literary quarterly, *The Sewanee Review,* and at the University of Iowa. Since 1948 he has been lecturer in Creative Writing at the University of Florida in Gainesville. He has received several literary awards, a Guggenheim Fellowship and the Kenyon Fellowship for fiction.

He is married and has three daughters.